For my parents, Paul and C_____ ___ _____ made it happen when I insisted on going to school halfway across the country for Creative Writing. Your support has made all the difference. I love you.

Pronunciation Guide

People

Cyra = SEE-ruh

Jaylan = JAY-lin

Brix = BRIKS

Eddin = ED-in

Pryn = PRIN

Samhail = SAM-heyl

Raina = RAY-nuh

Bressen = BREH-sen

Ursan = UR-sen

Jerram = JAIR-em

Glenora = Gle-NOR-ah

Lorkin = LOHR-kin

Jemma = JEM-uh

Phaedrus = FAY-druhs

Aramis = AIR-ah-mis

Sandrian = SAN-dree-an

Morland = MOHR-land

Places

Fernweh = FURN-way

Thasia = THAY-zhuh

Callanus = KAL-an-uhs

Hiraeth = HĬ-rayth

Solandis = Sōw-LAN-dus

Polaris = Puh-LAH-rus

Gendris = JEN-dris

Derridan = DAIR-i-den

Seatherny = SEE-thur-nee

Rowe = RŌ, Rown = RŌN

Other

Perimortal = PER-i-mohr-tl

Demoni =Deh-MAH-nee

Content Advisory: This book includes mature (18+) subjects and potentially upsetting situations that include graphic violence, death, threats and mentions of sexual assault, brief accountings of torture, abuse, and self-harm, drugging, and multiple explicit depictions of sex, including some non-traditional sexual practices and proclivities.*

* For details see https://karencpmcdermott.com/the-last-triumvirate

THE LAST TRIUMVIRATE

By Karen C.P. McDermott

Prologue

Jaylan braced himself for the piercing wail that was about to come from the infant bundled in the basket at the stranger's feet. He was an only child, but he'd heard the sound of babies crying enough times when he went into town with his father for supplies that he knew he didn't like it. Aside from the strain on his five-year-old ears, something about the sound of a baby's cry tore at him so he felt the child's misery as his own.

Jaylan looked to where his mother and father sat at the kitchen table having a hushed conversation with the stranger in the cloak as the baby made hiccup-like noises. The man had appeared on the path to their vineyard a quarter of an hour ago, the hood of his cloak pulled low over his head, and he'd strode directly to where Jaylan was helping his father fix their grape press. Jaylan knew the names of the tools and could pick them out of the box when his father asked for one of them.

The scuff of the man's feet on the stone path made them look up, and Jaylan's father stood as the man approached. His father's eyes never left the cloaked figure, but Jaylan's attention was fixed on the basket the man was carrying. He was disappointed when he saw it contained a sleeping infant tucked among some blankets and not a pile of sweets or toys.

That basket now sat near the stranger's feet, but none of the grownups noticed the baby's growing distress. They were speaking in such low voices that Jaylan knew they must be talking about things they didn't want him to hear.

"Papa?" Jaylan asked.

"Not right now, Jaylan," his father said, and Jaylan's skin prickled at the tone. It wasn't like his father to be short with him.

The infant waved its little arms in the air as its breath came in choking cries, and Jaylan tamped down his unease enough to sit on the floor and pull the basket toward him. At the table, Jaylan's father hissed

1

angrily at something the stranger in the cloak said, and his mother's voice answered in soothing tones.

Jaylan pulled the infant out of the basket as it began to cry in earnest. Its wails stopped for a moment as he jostled it, but they started again when Jaylan settled the infant awkwardly into the well of his crossed legs.

"Stop crying," Jaylan said to the baby. "Please?"

The infant didn't stop, and Jaylan tucked his arms under it to lift it off his lap. He rocked it back and forth, and the baby paused its lament. Desperate to keep it from starting up again, Jaylan sang softly to it, the song that his mother sang him every night before bed. The infant loosed a few more halting cries but then seemed to relax. Jaylan finished the song and began it again. When he finished the second time, he realized how quiet it had gotten.

He looked up and found his parents and the man in the cloak staring at him. He jolted when he saw the man's pale silvery eyes under the hood for the first time. The round middle parts were so light that they seemed to almost glow, but there was also a dark ring around each circle that gave Jaylan a strange feeling.

The man got up from the table, and Jaylan thought he was in trouble for taking the baby out of its basket, but the man just lowered himself to the floor and sat cross-legged next to him.

"You seem to have a way with her," the man said.

Jaylan looked down at the infant in his arms. He hadn't realized it was a girl.

"This is Cyra," the man said, and at the table, Jaylan's mother let out a soft, "Oh."

"What would you think about having Cyra for a sister?" he asked Jaylan. "She needs a family, and I've asked your parents to take her. Would that be alright with you?"

Jaylan looked up at his parents. His mother seemed as though she might cry at any moment, but his father watched him closely. There was a long pause before his father spoke to him. "We can take her if

2

you're okay with it."

Jaylan had never thought about having a brother or sister before. He liked that it was just him and his parents out here on the vineyard, but it was also a bit lonely. Some of his friends in town had brothers and sisters to play with, and while they sometimes fought with their siblings, they seemed to like having their company.

"I guess she can stay," Jaylan said.

His mother let out a sob, and Jaylan looked back to the man in the cloak. His odd-looking eyes were also wet with tears despite the smile he wore.

The stranger hefted himself up off the floor and went over to Jaylan's parents. The three grownups spoke softly again before his father nodded and shook hands with the man.

"I need to say goodbye to Cyra now," the man said, coming back, and Jaylan heard the crack in his voice. "Can I take her for a minute?"

Jaylan nodded and lifted the infant up so the man could take her into his arms. Then he got up off the floor himself.

The man held the infant close and bent his head low over her face. Jaylan saw his lips moving, although he couldn't hear what the man was saying. Finally, the man bent lower and touched his lips to Cyra's forehead for a long, lingering kiss. His shoulders heaved as he cried silent tears. He clutched Cyra tighter to him before he handed her to Jaylan's mother, who took the little girl into her own shaking arms.

"Take good care of her, young man," the stranger said to Jaylan as tears streaked his face.

Jaylan nodded. "I will. I promise."

The man smiled and nodded back. Without another word, he strode for the front door and left, closing it firmly behind him. Jaylan and his parents rushed for the door, but when they looked out, the man was no longer there.

"Who was he, Papa?" Jaylan asked.

His father shook his head. "I don't know. Just someone who needed our help." His father knelt so they were eye-to-eye. "You have

3

a sister now. We promised to take care of her and protect her. Can you help us keep that promise?"

"Yes, Papa."

"Good man," his father said, putting a hand on Jaylan's shoulder. "Your mother and I are counting on you. Cyra is counting on you."

Jaylan sat down, and his mother placed the baby in his arms. He looked into the face that just a little while ago was contorted in pain or rage or sadness. He didn't know which. Now, Cyra's face – his sister's face – was peaceful with sleep. He watched her little mouth move as if she was finally responding to whatever the man had whispered to her before he left.

The man had given Jaylan the job of protecting Cyra, and Jaylan felt the weight of that responsibility. He also felt pride in being chosen.

"I promise I'll take care of you," he whispered. "I'll do whatever you need me to do."

The baby's lips pursed into an odd smile, and Jaylan wrinkled his nose against the sudden stench as his new sister soiled her diaper.

Chapter 1

Twenty-two years later

My lantern hung low and heavy next to my thigh. Beside me, I could barely make out the faces of my brothers as we stood bundled in our heavy cloaks in the front yard just outside the house. We had three lanterns between us, but their light seemed loath to venture very far this early in the morning. It would be hours yet before the sun crested the horizon to reveal the rolling fields of grape vines stretched out like fingers over the land, but by then the first part of our work would be done.

I didn't mind the darkness or even the hours of labor that were to come. It was the cold that sapped my strength. That and the ridiculously early morning hour. I enjoyed my sleep, and I liked to be warm. Unfortunately, the task before us required me to forego both.

"Let's get going," my older brother Jaylan said as he pressed a large bucket and a pair of clippers into my free hand.

As usual, Jaylan looked rested and ready to work at this hour, which only made me curse him inwardly to the Nemesis.

I exhaled a misty breath that was quickly swallowed by the pre-dawn gloom as my younger brother Brix and I followed Jaylan to the edge of the fields where each of us broke off down a separate row of vines. The cold air stung my face, and I knew my gloves wouldn't protect my hands for long where they stuck out from the arm holes of the cloak.

Most of the harvest had been picked weeks ago, but we always reserved a few rows of grapes to make ice wine, an extra sweet wine that was a favorite of the people in the nearby village of Fernweh. It was made by letting the grapes sit on the vine longer to concentrate their sweetness and then picking them before dawn in the coldest hours of the morning to ensure that they didn't thaw before they could be crushed.

I set my bucket down at the end of one row and began picking. It was mindless work, and my thoughts strayed to the dream I'd had that morning just before I woke. I didn't know where I was at the time or what I was looking for in the dream, but I followed a moonbeam that slid along the floor of a house, and I eventually found myself gazing out a large window at the full moon over the ocean. I'd felt a presence behind me and turned to see...?

I couldn't remember now. I only knew those last moments had been full of such elation at having found what I was looking for. The remnants of the vision still left an aching void in my chest, and I felt the loss of wherever I'd been acutely, as if the place had been real, and I'd suddenly been cast out of it.

I could thank Brix for ripping me from the dream when he'd pushed open my creaky bedroom door and shoved an unlit lantern under my nose. I should already have been awake and dressed when he came in, but the dream had held my consciousness captive, refusing to allow me to wake until that last possible moment.

"At some point," I'd grumbled to Brix against my pillow, "you should probably learn how to start a fire."

"Why would I do that when I have you?" he'd asked, the grin apparent in his voice in the dark.

I'd growled my displeasure at him and tried to push the bitter chill of the room out of my mind as I pulled my hand from under the blankets. Gooseflesh rose on my skin in protest as I clenched my fist and concentrated on the feeling of warmth building between my fingers and palm. A small flame flickered in my hand when I opened it, and I lit the lantern so my brother's face was drawn from the darkness into its feeble glow.

Brix had turned wordlessly then to go downstairs while I called a sarcastic, "You're welcome," to his retreating back.

My brothers often took my magic for granted, meager as it was.

My powers had started to show when I was around three, and my

6

older brother Jaylan still bore the small burn mark on his forearm where I'd grabbed him with a flaming hand as a child when he wouldn't let me have the toy he was playing with.

I could draw water as well, which helped when we had dry spells and needed to irrigate the grape vines. My water magic was likely one of the reasons the vineyard I worked with my brothers was one of the more successful ones in the Polaris territory. Not that anyone in Fernweh would ever know. Magic was rare in the outer lands, and any show of it was usually met with hostility rather than awe, so only Jaylan and Brix knew what I really was.

Unfortunately, my magic couldn't help me right now. Almost two hours after I'd started picking, my gloves were soaked with sticky juice, and the tips of my fingers were frozen and numb. Half of the sky had turned purple as the sun threatened to peek over one of the fields, but I still had a row and a half more to pick.

I moved my bucket over to the next vine and picked three, four, five bunches of grapes before I stopped. I held up the lantern. There were still stems on the rest of the vine, but all the grapes were gone. Only frozen drying pulps remained on each stem.

I sighed and looked down the row. We'd only taken the netting off the vines last night before bed. Had the birds gotten to the fruit so quickly?

I moved to the next vine, but it too was barren of grapes. I grunted in disgust and moved to the next one. When I found the third vine completely empty, panic set in. Nemesis take me, just how many pounds of grapes had we lost? The ice wine was a specialty of our vineyard. It turned a large profit, and losing too much of the crop would cost us.

I walked down the row of grapes holding my lantern up to the vines, but each one I passed was bare. A weight settled in my stomach. This was too much damage for birds. Perhaps a herd of deer had come through last night.

I reached the end of the row and looked around in disbelief at the barren vines. Jaylan was going to be furious.

I turned to go find him when I heard a low growl from the next row over. I moved quietly and peered around the end post. I made out a large shape in the middle of the row, but I couldn't see it clearly in the dark. I walked around the post and held up my lantern, then gasped.

A huge black bear stuffed with winter fat sat on its haunches in the middle of the row. It leaned over every now and again to grab a bunch of grapes in its mouth and strip the fruit. Anger rose in my chest as I considered the damage it had done to our harvest.

"Shoo!" I said, taking a few steps closer. I held up my lantern to swing in the bear's face.

Its head followed the swing of the light, and a growl rumbled from its throat, but it didn't move. Instead, it went back to eating.

I looked around for a large stick, but I didn't see anything I could use. Then an idea occurred to me, and I removed one of my gloves. I held out a hand in front of me as I concentrated on drawing the cold moisture from the air and then pressed my hand out toward the bear. A jet of ice-cold water shot straight into its face, and the bear growled and pawed at it. It rolled forward so it stood on its four legs and shook its head, but it made no move to leave.

"Come on," I pleaded with it. "Just go."

I waved my lantern at it again, but the bear only followed the swinging light, so I threw out my hand once more. Another jet of water sprayed the bear in the face.

This time, the bear stood on its hind legs and roared into the sky. It shook its head furiously to throw off the water. I could see in the lantern light that the toes on one of its paws were white, and there was a white V, or perhaps a heart, in the middle of its chest.

I took a step back and the bear fell forward onto all fours, coming toward me now. I quickly set the lantern down, removed my second glove, and extended both my hands out, palms up. Flames flared up, and I held the fire out toward the bear. It reared back, roared again,

8

and then lunged toward me.

I realized I was standing in the route of quickest escape for the animal. The forest was at my back, and the bear wanted to run this way, but I was blocking its path.

I quenched the flames in my hands and reached down to retrieve my lantern so I could move, but the bear charged as soon as my flames were gone. I screamed and threw the lantern out, but the bear batted it away, and it flew under the vines to land in the next row. I backed away, but the huge beast was almost on me.

I tripped on the hem of my cloak and fell backwards just as the bear swiped out its paw. It was a blessing really, since the sharp claws would have opened my chest if I hadn't fallen out of the way. As it was, the claws raked across my shoulder, and I screamed again as both the cloak and my flesh tore open and white-hot pain shot through me.

Stars swam in my vision before being replaced by momentary blackness as my head hit something hard. I could still hear the roaring of the bear, constant and grating in my ears, and I reached back to grab my head as my vision cleared. My hand scraped against the wooden trellis post, and the wetness on my fingers told me I was bleeding.

The bear battered me from side to side and instinct took over. I kicked out, either to shove the bear away or else to push myself backward along the path. Neither worked. The ground was cold and hard at my back, and the bear swiped once more, opening a gash on my upper arm through the cloak. I cried out again and rolled to the side, crawling under the trellis wires into the next row, my arm and shoulder throbbing in pain.

No longer caring about escape, the bear tried to press after me, but its winter-rounded rump caught against the wire. I struggled to get to my feet, but the bear swiped out a paw and yanked my foot out from under me. I went crashing into the ground and coughed hard as the breath was knocked from me. I gasped air back into my lungs, and as if in answer to my need, a cold wind whipped through the vines making the drying leaves rustle.

Just as I recovered enough to move, the fastening holding the wire to the trellis post snapped free, and the animal surged through. I felt its presence over me and rolled onto my back to face it, my vision blurring with the effort. Drops of its spittle sprayed my face as I struggled to focus, and I shoved my hands up into the animal's chest, as if I could somehow throw off several hundred pounds of solid bear. My hands just sank into its soft body as sharp teeth aimed for my neck.

An image flashed in my mind of myself lying beneath the ground, what remained of my bear-torn body tucked in a coffin as Jaylan and Brix shoveled dirt over my grave.

The thought of my brothers putting me in the ground as we'd done with our parents ten years ago was unthinkable. Brix and I were still children then, but Jaylan had been seventeen, just barely a young man. I remembered his face as the weight of responsibility settled over him like a rain-drenched cloak as he realized he was now the guardian for two young children and the owner of a vineyard that provided the family's sole source of income. I wouldn't force Jaylan and Brix to bury another member of our family. Not if I could help it.

My back pressed against the earth, both the animal and the ground equally unyielding. I felt something rise in my chest, almost as if it was coming through the ground and flowing upward through me. Static electricity crackled through my veins, and my eyes widened as energy gathered in my chest before surging through my arms toward the bear. My head pressed back against the ground as my body jerked, and my hands prickled where they pressed against the bear's fur, which suddenly turned cold and gritty.

The bear froze above me, its face locked in mid-roar, and I became faintly aware the sky was beginning to pinken as I tried to bring my pounding heart and labored breathing under control. Everything was so quiet all of a sudden. This was the time of morning the birds were at their chattiest as they woke to greet the new day, but there was no sound now. No birds. No bear.

I looked at the bear again and realized it was no longer a bear, but something else. What hovered above me was not made of flesh. Ash? Perhaps I'd somehow incinerated the animal without realizing it, and there was now a bear-shaped pile of ashes above me.

I let my shaking hands brush along the bear's chest, and when I pulled my fingers back, I realized it was made of dirt.

I heard shouts in the distance, but I was incapable of moving or speaking as I stared up at the form I was sure had just been a giant snarling animal. I pushed against the shape but realized my mistake instantly.

I cried out and tried to scramble back as the dirt crumbled all around me and fell. I was only able to get halfway free before the damp earth collapsed on top of me. It pinned my waist, hips, and legs to the ground, and my breathing labored as the weight of it settled over me.

Jaylan and Brix called my name somewhere close by, but only a strangled yell escaped my lips in answer. I clawed at the dirt, trying to push it off me, but it was cold and heavy, and I didn't have the leverage to move it.

"Cyra!" Jaylan cried as steps pounded on the ground near my head.

Jaylan and Brix dropped to their knees near me.

"By the gods!" Jaylan swore. "How in the three hells did you end up under a pile of dirt?"

"Bear," was all I managed to say.

"Bear?" Brix asked, then looked around anxiously for anything that might be lurking nearby.

"Where?" Jaylan asked, looking around too.

I pointed to the pile of dirt. It was all I could do, but Jaylan and Brix looked at each other in confusion.

"Cyra, you're not making any sense," Brix said. "Did you hit your head?"

"Yes," I gasped. "Now get me out of here."

My brothers sprang into action and pulled at the dirt that lay on top of me. I took in deeper and deeper breaths as their efforts relieved the pressure on my stomach. Finally, when they'd moved enough to free me, they grabbed my hands and pulled me back out of the pile. My feet kicked out as soon as they could, helping them drag me to freedom. They tried to help me up, but I shook them off. My legs were shaking violently both from fear and the cold.

"Cyra, what happened?" Jaylan pressed me. "We heard roaring, and then you screamed. Were you attacked?"

I nodded.

"So where did the bear go?" Brix asked.

I pointed to the pile again. "The pile of dirt," I said, "is the bear."

They looked at me as if I were mad, and I didn't blame them. I knew how I sounded.

"Let's get you to the house to warm up," Jaylan said. He grabbed my upper arm, but I cried out in pain.

Jaylan let go immediately and yelled as his own hand came back covered in blood.

"You're bleeding!" Jaylan yelled. "We have to get her back to the house," he said to Brix. "We can figure out what happened later."

My hand shot up to grab Jaylan's shirt, and he grunted as I pulled his face down to mine.

"Listen to me," I said, trying to steady my voice. "There was a bear. I tried to drive it away, but it attacked me, and I...turned it to dirt. I don't know how."

Both Jaylan and Brix went perfectly still next to me.

"Alright," Jaylan said finally. "We understand."

They didn't. They still thought I was hallucinating, but I'd convince them later when my brain wasn't addled with pain and fear. Now that adrenaline was no longer thrumming through my veins, the pulsing pain of the wounds to my head, shoulder, and arm had returned with a vengeance, and I whimpered as the heat of my torn flesh burned through me.

Brix lifted me into his arms, and my head rolled forward to rest against his shoulder.

"Just hold on," he said softly as he carried me toward the house.

I looked down at my hands as they shook in my lap. Both were still dark with soil I was certain had once been a bear, and my entire body shivered.

"Hurry!" Jaylan called out somewhere next to me, but his voice sounded distant.

The sun was rising over the fields now, and I squinted against the brightness. My eyes fluttered as I struggled to keep them open, but the light faded again as I finally stopped fighting the darkness and let it pull me under.

Chapter 2

Five days later, my arm and shoulder were on the mend, but my mind wasn't. Fernweh's healer had stitched up the worst of my wounds and applied poultices to help the scarring, but she could do nothing for the nightmares that woke me several times each night. I'd bolt upright in bed, gasping and in a cold sweat, having dreamt I was buried alive under a pile of earth that was slowly crushing me.

I also dreamt of being attacked by a large black bear with a heart on its chest and white toes on one of its paws. When I tried to fight back, my powers didn't work, and I was obliged to make my exit pursued by the bear.

Once Jaylan and Brix were convinced I was no longer delirious, they listened more seriously to my account of what happened. While it was a new power for me, they eventually accepted that I'd turned the bear to earth, and after that, the phrase, "Well, that's a pile of bear," in fact became their new favorite way to describe something unfortunate. I did not find this nearly as amusing as they did.

As for the bear itself, or what remained of it, Jaylan and Brix took shovels and threw the dirt into the woods since we were reluctant to leave it sitting around.

Word spread quickly in town that I'd been attacked, but no one knew the details, and they never would. That I could wield magic was a closely guarded secret known only to my family. People in the outer lands didn't like magic or those who used it.

It wasn't hard to see I was different from my brothers. Jaylan and Brix had golden hair and bright blue eyes, and they tanned in the sun. I had long, rich brown hair that fell in waves down my back, and my pale skin burned quickly if I didn't protect it. People noticed my eyes the most, though. They were an exceptionally pale shade of silver-gray with dark gray rings around the irises, and they seemed to glow with an unnatural light, especially against my dark hair. I'd been told the effect was either entrancing or unnerving.

The townspeople knew I'd been adopted, but my parents were never forthcoming about where I'd come from, and that led to rumors I was a changeling they'd found in the woods. People believed my eyes were clear evidence I was not truly human.

I was human, of course, but no one besides Jaylan and Brix knew I wasn't mortal. Rather, I was perimortal, a race of humans known to have significantly longer lifespans and magical gifts. Perimortals weren't abundant in general, but they were especially scarce in the outer lands. Those that did exist congregated in cities because their powers naturally gave them influence and advantages over normal humans, so they lived in places where those benefits were most useful.

The stranger who gave me to my parents warned them I was perimortal when they took me in, but they hadn't known what to expect, and my powers frightened them at first. I didn't remember much of those early years, but Jaylan confessed one night after a few extra glasses of wine that there was a period our parents had all but locked me away, even keeping me from both him and Brix. According to Jaylan, he'd eventually been the one to convince them I wasn't a danger, even though he already bore the scar on his arm from when I'd burned him.

Unable to share the real story of the bear then, Jaylan told everyone he and Brix chased the animal off. The people of Fernweh arranged a hunting party that same day, afraid some rogue bear might attack them or their children, but unsurprisingly, they didn't find any trace of it.

On the vineyard, meanwhile, Jaylan and Brix had taken on the bulk of the crushing and fermenting work this week in order to allow me to rest and heal. This only made me feel guilty, so I decided to make myself useful by driving our wagon into town to get supplies today. I arrived in the main township of Fernweh around mid-morning and a few people called out greetings and well-wishes to me.

There were always some who wouldn't meet my gaze or who made it a point to duck into the nearest shop when I was around, though.

15

Fernweh was a relatively small town where most people knew each other, and those I saw regularly had long ago stopped being wary of me, but others still whispered behind my back. There were rumors that – if not a changeling – I must be either a perimortal or a witch. The popular opinion skewed toward witch.

I headed straight for the cooper at the far end of Fernweh when I arrived. Rodrick was working in his shop when I entered, but he stopped as soon as he saw me and rushed over.

"Cyra!" he said, pulling me into a strong hug.

I winced as he pressed against my still-healing wounds a little too hard, and he pulled back to look me over with concern.

"Thank the Trinity you're in one piece," he said. "How are you?"

"I'm fine. Just a few scratches."

He looked at the large bandage on my shoulder peeking from under the neck of my shirt and raised an eyebrow.

"Well, maybe a few deep ones," I conceded.

"They haven't caught the beast yet?" he asked.

"No. I doubt it's still around at this point. It's likely found a cave somewhere and started its winter sleep with a belly full of our grapes."

"Well, it's good to see you alive and well, in any case. What can I do for you? Is it time for new barrels?"

"It is," I said. "Really, it's past time to replace some of our older ones. We should've come to you sooner."

"Not a problem," Rodrick assured me with a wave of his hand. "I knew you'd be around eventually, so I saved some for you."

"Wonderful. I don't know what we'd do without you, Rodrick."

I followed Rodrick into his shop and waved to his daughter Maeve as we passed her where she was working on Rodrick's ledgers. We went into his storage room, and Rodrick showed me some barrels he'd stacked out of the way just for us. He had a gift when it came to barrel-making, but I knew he'd insist I examine them, so I bent down to take a closer look.

"Did you hear about the stranger that rode into town earlier this morning?" he asked casually after a few seconds.

I looked up from studying the staves on one barrel. Rodrick's expression told me he'd been dying to talk to someone about this.

"Since when are you such a gossip, Rodrick?" I teased him.

"Since this fellow arrived," Rodrick said seriously. "Never saw anything like him."

"Do tell," I said, only half listening.

Rodrick's response was all eagerness. "Well, to start, he's the tallest man I've ever seen. Taller than Brix by a few inches, I'd wager."

That surprised me. Both my brothers were tall, but Brix was about three or four inches over six feet. "That's very tall indeed," I said.

"Sessy thinks he's part giant," Rodrick said, referring to his wife.

I rolled my eyes. "So he's tall."

"Not just tall," Rodrick said. "Built like a stone wall as well. He rode into town on a massive black horse, and he's got long, stark-white hair."

"White hair? He's old?"

Rodrick shook his head. "Not much older than Jaylan, I'd guess." He lowered his voice conspiratorially. "Makes me wonder if he might be…you know, perimortal."

I pretended to be shocked. "Perimortal?"

Admittedly, this man had a fairly unique combination of features, so I understood why Rodrick was so intrigued. The cooper had long since accepted my own unusual appearance, and he might be the one person in town who wouldn't turn on me if he knew what I really was.

"He had two longswords on his back," Rodrick said, giving me a knowing look.

My gaze flicked up again. "A mercenary?"

"Most likely. He certainly looked the part."

It was rare that outsiders passed through Fernweh and rarer still that we got mercenaries, although it wasn't unheard of. We were the only town for miles, and a small one at that.

"I can't imagine there's much work for him out here," I said, "and

17

he probably isn't cheap to hire."

"I've heard villages will sometimes pool their money to hire a mercenary to take care of a problem for them, like if there's some kind of beast terrorizing the town," Rodrick said. He paused for a second. "Maybe we should talk to him about your bear."

I smiled. "I hardly think a bear would be worth his time."

"You never know until you ask."

I ignored the comment and stood up. "These barrels look perfect. I need to run a few more errands, but I'll leave the wagon here for your boys to load if you don't mind."

Rodrick sprang into action, the mercenary forgotten for the moment, as he went to find his sons to load the barrels. I left the shop to walk back toward the center of town.

I stopped at the apothecary first for more herbs and powders for my wounds. On my way in, I ran my hand over the garland of bay laurel leaves that hung over the door of the shop to ward off witches, perimortals, and other magical beings. It was my own private joke to touch the garlands around the doors of shops to prove – to myself at least – how ineffectual they were.

Inside the shop, I combed the shelves for the items on my list: chamomile, slippery elm bark, turmeric, bellim, and dandelion. As an afterthought I threw some cinnamon into my basket as well, although I wasn't sure what made me reach for it.

A few feet away from me, Pryn, the barmaid who worked at the town tavern, added turrow berries, stoneseed root, and wild carrot seed to her own basket. I raised an eyebrow to myself, as all three were used to prevent pregnancy.

Pryn looked up and our eyes met. I smiled politely at her, and she smiled back before turning away. I hesitated a moment, debating with myself, before I threw some stoneseed root into my own basket.

As I paid for my purchase, the shopkeeper chattered on excitedly about how the mercenary had been in earlier to pick up some things, and I heard similar stories at a number of other shops as well. The

18

mercenary had arrived early this morning, but he was probably halfway to the next village by now, and no one was likely to see him again.

I headed back toward Rodrick's about an hour and a half later, my arms laden with bags. As I passed the tavern, though, the door suddenly opened in front of me, and an arm shot out to grab my wrist and pull me inside. I shrieked in surprise, but a hand closed over my mouth to silence me as a man's body pressed me back against the door.

"Sshh. Do you want to bring the whole town running over here to see what's the matter?" a voice whispered in my ear.

When I didn't make any other noise, the hand lifted from my mouth.

"Nemesis take you, Eddin! You scared the three hells out of me," I said.

Eddin, the owner of the tavern, grinned at me and lowered his lips onto mine in a passionate kiss. My bags fell to the floor, and I reached up to wrap my arms around his neck but had to stop as my injured arm and shoulder objected.

Eddin ran a hand over the bandage on my shoulder. "Are you alright? I heard about the bear. I almost rode out that night to see how you were doing."

The "almost" pricked something inside me. "Why didn't you?"

Eddin looked at me uncomfortably. "I don't know. Our involvement isn't really out in the open. How would I have explained that to your brothers?"

I resisted the urge to point out that he was the only reason our involvement, as he called it, wasn't out in the open.

"And what if someone comes in now and sees us?" I asked.

Eddin reached over and locked the door. "We're closed," he said with a grin. He untucked my shirt and his hand snaked up under it to cup my breast.

I groaned as his hand kneaded it gently, but I pulled away a moment later. "I can't. We're shorthanded on the vineyard because of my injuries. I have to get back as soon as I can."

19

"When can I see you then?" Eddin asked, running his other hand down my leg.

When can I fuck you again? is what he really meant. Weeks ago, Eddin's busy hands would have had me begging him to take me in the back room of the tavern, but now his pawing just annoyed me.

I'd met Eddin for the first time here at the tavern months ago when I helped Brix bring over some wine. Eddin was relatively new to town, and he'd let me know his interest by making suggestive comments and brushing his hands over my body when Brix wasn't looking. He made his move a couple weeks later when I found myself alone with him in the tavern's storeroom. I'd been flattered by his attention and thoroughly aroused by weeks of his innuendo and increasingly bold touches, so I let him have me there in the storeroom on a stack of wooden crates.

The sex was good enough, and I assumed Eddin would begin courting me openly, but he seemed content to meet in secret for illicit trysts whenever I was willing, and I was willing more often than I cared to admit. The secrecy was exciting at first, and it made the sex more intense, but both seemed to lose their luster after a while.

It wasn't the first time I'd been used either. My unusual appearance was a novelty, and men were often attracted to me, if loath to admit it.

Eddin was the second man I'd been with. My first lover was a young merchant who'd come to Fernweh to explore business opportunities here. As it turned out, the only opportunity he'd seen fit to pursue was the one to get between my legs. A few weeks after taking my maidenhead, he'd left town and hadn't returned since.

Enough was enough, though. I wasn't going to continue letting men take what they wanted without giving something back.

"Don't you think it's time to…tell everyone about us?" I suggested to Eddin, pushing him back gently. I was tired of sneaking around, but more importantly, I wanted him to admit his attraction publicly. I didn't know why it was so important to me for him to do so, but it was. I didn't need a commitment from him, just…acknowledgment.

Eddin went still, and his face hardened in front of my eyes.

"I don't think that's a good idea," he said.

I frowned. "Why not?"

Eddin ran a hand through his light brown hair. "Cyra, where is this coming from all of a sudden?"

I blinked at him. All of a sudden? I'd been suggesting for weeks we let people know we were together, but Eddin always found a way to put me off.

I took a deep breath. I'd known for a while I needed to do this, but I'd found excuse after excuse to put it off. It was time now, though.

"Eddin," I said, "I think we need to take some time apart."

Eddin's hands were creeping over me again, but they stopped moving, and I felt his body go rigid. He pulled away to look at me.

"Are you breaking things off with me?" he asked. He sounded genuinely shocked, and that made me angry.

"I think that's best. We both know you have no intention of marrying me."

Eddin pulled away as if I'd slapped him. "Marrying you? Is that what you want from me?" He sounded almost offended.

"How did you imagine this ending?" I asked. "Did you think we were just going to go on fucking in secret until you found someone else you wanted more?"

He just looked at me, and I realized that's exactly what he'd thought. Unbidden, small flames ignited in my palms, but I quickly closed my fists to quench them.

"I should go," I said leaning down to grab my bags.

"Wait!" Eddin grabbed my shoulders and pushed me back against the door. I cried out in pain as his palm pressed against the claw wound on my shoulder. "Don't leave," he said. "Let's go in the back. We can talk about this later."

I shook my head. "No, I need to go."

I tried to push myself off the door, but he shoved me back and tried to kiss me again. I lifted my hands up to his face and shoved his

21

head backwards.

"Nemesis take you, Cyra! What are you doing?" Eddin yelled as he wiped at his face where one of my fingernails scratched him.

"I told you I'm leaving."

"Fine," he said, glaring at me. "I was getting tired of fucking you anyway."

I let out a sharp laugh and picked up my bags.

"You know," Eddin said, "some people say you're a witch."

I stopped but didn't look at him.

"I heard, in fact," he went on, "that you were in the vineyard fucking that bear the other night. I suppose it got rough with you, and that's how you got those cuts."

My head snapped to him. He was sneering at me.

I'd heard no such rumor in town today, and I definitely would have caught wind of it if it had been circulating.

"Is that what people are saying?" I asked Eddin. "Or is that what *you've* been saying?"

His sneer deepened. "It's what everyone will be saying by tomorrow."

I thrust my hands quickly behind my back as flames flared once again, and my bags fell down from my elbows to my wrists. I was trembling with fury, but I closed my eyes and fought the urge to burn two searing handprints into Eddin's chest. I quenched the flames again and fumbled behind me for the lock of the door. I managed to unlock it and pull it open.

"If I'm a witch," I said, returning Eddin's glare, "it would be foolish of you to say anything of the kind. You wouldn't want me to curse you, would you?" I opened my eyes wide, hoping the look I gave him would be sufficiently unnerving.

Indeed, Eddin stepped back, looking uncertain, and I took the opportunity to slip out the door. Once outside, I ran back toward Rodrick's where I found my wagon loaded with barrels. I forced a smile onto my face as I paid Rodrick for his work and started for home.

I reached the edge of town before I started shaking again. I'd need to tell Jaylan and Brix what happened to get ahead of any potential consequences if Eddin followed through on his threat to accuse me of being a witch, or worse, of fucking a bear. That would mean admitting to my involvement with Eddin, which I wasn't keen to do. I wasn't sure my brothers even knew I was no longer a virgin. They had to suspect, but it obviously wasn't a subject any of us were eager to talk to each other about, and the thought of the conversation made me a little queasy.

I swore and kicked myself mentally for not foreseeing how badly Eddin might take it when I ended things with him. I'd known he hadn't loved me, but I'd failed to see his potential for vindictiveness.

Part of me wished I'd shown Eddin my flames. I wanted to see the shock and terror on his face when he realized what I was. Maybe it would've been enough to keep his mouth shut, but I couldn't count on cowing him into silence. People could be too unpredictable, and my parents had drilled it into me at an early age that I couldn't let anyone besides them and my brothers know about my powers. It was a matter of life and death, they insisted.

I couldn't marry Eddin anyway, I reminded myself. I'd have to leave Fernweh altogether at some point. While mortals and perimortals aged about the same throughout childhood, the perimortal aging process slowed considerably between eighteen to twenty, as if nature was conspiring to give them as much time as possible to enjoy the strength and resiliency of their bodies.

Perimortals often lived hundreds of years, and it would soon become apparent that I wasn't aging at the same rate as Jaylan and Brix. They would eventually grow old, but I'd look much the same as I did now for long after they were gone. I needed to move to an area where perimortals were more abundant, and that meant my time as a winemaker would likely be over.

Nausea swelled again as I thought about losing my family and my livelihood all at once, and I cursed Eddin for making me confront these

23

painful truths.

⚜

Back at the vineyard, I pulled the wagon up in front of the barn. The door was open, and the tangy smell of fruit mixed with the aroma of baking bread from the fermentation yeast hit my nostrils.

Jaylan was usually in the barn this time of day, and I found him as soon as I walked in. He was balanced expertly on the rim of one of our large eight-foot-tall wooden vats where the grapes underwent their initial fermentation after crushing. As the grapes fermented, the skins and pulp rose to the top of the juice to form a cap that needed to be pressed back down into the liquid once or twice a day.

Jaylan had excellent balance, so he climbed up on the rim of the vats and used a metal rake to press the cap of grape skins and pulp back down into the juice. I'd suggested a couple times we build a railing for him to hold onto, but he was proud of his balance and stubbornly refused the offer. He'd only ever fallen into a vat once.

"You made good time," Jaylan said from the top of the vat as he pressed the rake down so that foamy, fermenting juice surged to the top. "Can Rodrick replace our barrels?"

"He had some ready for us," I said. "They're in the wagon."

"Really?" Jaylan asked, glancing up at me. He gave a small laugh. "I'm not sure why I'm surprised. Rodrick is always on top of things."

I gave him a weak smile and nodded.

"Is something wrong?" Jaylan asked, noticing my lack of enthusiasm for our new barrels.

"There's…something you need to know," I said.

Jaylan stopped pressing the grapes and met my eyes.

"Something happened a few months ago I've been hiding," I said.

Jaylan paused before he asked, "Are you finally planning to tell me about you and Eddin?"

"What? How did you know?" I asked in shock.

Jaylan shrugged and pressed the rake into the grapes again. "Brix said Eddin was pursuing you a few months ago. He pretended not to notice, but you weren't as subtle as you thought you were. More to the point, Eddin hasn't been quiet about what you've been up to. He was boasting to some of the men around town, and it got back to me."

I imagined my normally pale skin turned an almost unnatural shade of red, and my stomach sank to somewhere below my knees. Oh gods.

I could usually count on Brix not to be shy about speaking up on just about any topic, but the fact he'd never said a word to me about this showed just how uncomfortable the idea of confronting me about my love life had made him. He apparently had no issue talking to Jaylan about it, though.

"How long have you known about this?" I snapped at Jaylan.

He shrugged again. "I learned about it shortly after it started."

"And you never thought to say anything to me?"

Jaylan looked at me incredulously. "Do you think I wanted to insert myself into my sister's romantic life? You know that conversation wouldn't have gone well."

I crossed my arms over my chest. He had a point.

"So what happened?" Jaylan asked.

"I told Eddin we were done. He didn't take it well."

Jaylan stopped pressing again. "What does that mean?"

"He threatened to tell everyone I was a witch, and actually, that's the best part of what he threatened to do."

"What?" Jaylan asked, his own anger rising.

I pressed a hand to my forehead and closed my eyes. I was about to speak again when Jaylan's shout drew my attention. I looked up in time to see him lose his balance and fall forward into the vat of grape slurry. I groaned and started to rush forward to see if he was okay, but Jaylan surfaced again a second later sputtering.

"Cyra!" he gasped.

"By the gods, Jaylan. Are you okay?"

Jaylan wasn't looking at me, though. He grabbed the side of the vat and pointed over the rim. "Cyra, behind you!"

25

I whirled around and then gasped to find myself only feet away from the broad, leather-clad chest of a huge man. My gaze rose until my neck craned up and my eyes lit on a face framed by long, straight white hair. The handles of two swords peeked over broad shoulders, and I took a wary step backward.

It was the mercenary, and somehow I knew he was here for me.

Chapter 3

Fear twisted my stomach as I took in the massive stranger. The top of my head barely reached his chest, and he was every bit as solid as Rodrick said. His eyes were such a dark midnight blue that they looked almost black as they stared from under sharp brow ridges. His jawline seemed almost chiseled from stone, and I noted with surprise that he was incredibly…appealing. Somehow Rodrick had left that part out.

The giant wore all black, including the ornate leather armor that covered his shoulders and chest. Each hardened leather plate was outlined with a metal border that both reinforced and adorned it. His shoulders were wide, but his torso tapered down at his waist and hips, and long muscled arms ended in the largest hands I'd ever seen.

"Please don't hurt her," Jaylan said holding a hand toward the man.

"Why don't you step away from her altogether?"

Brix's voice came from behind the giant, and I looked around the man – not easy to do – to see my brother holding a pitchfork out like a weapon.

"Brix, no!" I shouted. "Stay back!" I knew if those swords on the man's back came out, Brix would be dead within seconds.

None of us moved for several heart-stopping moments as the stranger continued to take everything in. When he spoke, his voice was deep, but it held a smoothness that belied the rest of his hard exterior.

"Where's the elemental?" he asked.

We all just blinked and stared at him.

"What's an-" Jaylan started to ask, but the man cut him off.

"The perimortal who can control the elements," he clarified. "Which one of you is it?"

"That's me," I said quietly.

The man's eyes widened a fraction as our gazes locked, but if he was surprised by what he saw, he didn't otherwise show it.

"No, it's me! I'm the one you're looking for!" Jaylan said as he grabbed the edge of the vat and started to lift himself out.

"Lying to me will help no one," the man said to Jaylan. He hadn't raised his voice, but the threat was implicit nonetheless, and Jaylan fell back in silence.

The stranger frowned at Jaylan, taking in the deep purple juice dripping down his face and matting his hair. He lifted one long arm out toward Jaylan as if he might shake his hand, and my brother flinched. We all looked at him questioningly, but then Jaylan yelped as he was lifted out of the vat of grape slurry by some invisible force.

Jaylan rose slowly and hovered in mid-air as dark grape juice poured off him. It would likely stain his skin purple for a few days if he didn't wash it off soon.

The stranger moved his arm to the side and Jaylan floated along with it before he sank toward the ground. Jaylan touched down, still dripping juice so a puddle collected around him. I tried not to count the number of bottles of wine now seeping into the dirt.

"I'm Samhail," the man said to no one in particular. "I'm an emissary for the lords of the Triumvirate, and I was sent to find the elemental whose power they sensed a few days ago."

The three of us gasped.

"The lords of the Triumvirate?" Brix asked, lowering his pitchfork. "What do they want with Cyra?"

"Brix!" Jaylan said, gritting a warning under his breath.

Samhail exhaled with impatience. "I need to see the bear."

Jaylan, Brix, and I all blinked again and exchanged nervous glances.

"What bear?" Brix asked unconvincingly.

Samhail crossed his thickly muscled arms over his equally muscled chest. "If I need to ask again, we're going to have a problem," he said. He hadn't raised his voice, but his tone sent fear skittering up my spine like hundreds of spider legs.

"I'll show you," I said.

Jaylan and Brix both started to protest, but I held up a hand to silence them. "I'll be fine. Jaylan, go wash that juice off before you end

28

up purple for the rest of the week."

Jaylan looked at me uncertainly, but I just nodded to him. Finally, he nodded back, having realized, as I did, that if Samhail wanted to hurt us, he could easily have done it already. The man was clearly perimortal, and that was probably the least dangerous thing about him.

More importantly, if Samhail really had been sent by the Triumvirate, we needed to tread carefully. The Triumvirate rarely concerned itself with what happened in the outer lands, and it was to our benefit to keep it that way. If the lords chose to send forces here, there was nothing Fernweh could do to stop them.

Jaylan looked at Brix and inclined his head in the direction of the woods where they'd spread the bear. "Go with them. She doesn't leave your sight. I'll join you in a few minutes." Then he turned and ran toward the house.

Brix looked at me uncertainly, but he shifted his pitchfork to hold it like a staff and waited for me to lead the way. I gave him a look that I hoped told him not to do anything stupid, but he winked at me, which didn't give me confidence.

"This way," I said.

Samhail followed me out of the barn, and a few minutes later we were standing at the edge of the woods looking at the dirt that Jaylan and Brix had shoveled there. Brix and I huddled close to each other behind Samhail, Brix still holding his pitchfork.

"This is what's left of the bear?" Samhail asked, looking into the woods.

"Yes. We didn't know what else to do with it," I said.

Samhail turned halfway around to look at me. "And you did this?" he asked as he glanced at the bandage near my collarbone.

"Yes."

"And you're an elemental?" he pressed.

"I don't know what that means," I said, although I could guess.

"You can control one or more elements," Samhail said. "Fire, air, water...earth."

"Then yes," I said. "This is the first time I've controlled earth, but I've been able to use fire and water since I was a child."

While I knew perimortals had powers in general, I'd only met one or two that I knew of, so I didn't know much about the types of powers most perimortals had. I wondered if elementals were common.

Samhail turned around the rest of the way, and his eyes ran over me from head to toe. Brix shifted so his shoulder was now in front of me instead of next to me, and I put a hand on his arm to steady him. Brix was tall and strong himself, but he wouldn't win in a fight with Samhail. That much I knew.

Samhail turned again and walked into the woods. He bent down, scooped a small amount of bear-dirt into his hand, and dropped it into a small pouch he pulled from his pocket. Then he stood and walked back toward us.

"You'll need to come back to Callanus with me," he said.

"The three hells she will!" Brix yelled, and he stepped forward with the pitchfork.

Samhail's hand shot up, and one of his swords was out before we even realized he'd reached for it. He held it out straight toward Brix, who froze in place.

"It wasn't a request," Samhail said. There was no menace in his voice, but there was plenty in the sword.

I grabbed Brix's arm and pulled him back, murmuring calming words under my breath. Brix lowered the pitchfork, and Samhail re-sheathed his sword.

"Let's go," Samhail said, nodding to me. "You'll need to pack."

Brix and I looked at each other, but we followed Samhail back up the path toward the house. I wasn't planning to go anywhere with him, but we'd need Jaylan's help with that.

Jaylan was just coming down the stairs when we returned to the house. He'd hastily washed the grape slurry off himself and changed clothes, but his skin still carried a slight purple tinge to it.

"He wants to take her to Callanus," Brix said as soon as we entered.

"No," Jaylan said to Samhail. "Out of the question."

Samhail lifted a brow, either impressed or amused by Jaylan's conviction. I was rather impressed myself. I didn't think many men ever dared to tell Samhail no in his life.

"As I told your brother," Samhail said to Jaylan, "it's not a request. She's being summoned by the Triumvirate."

"Then we'll go too," Brix said.

"No! You can't. We're right in the middle of the season. You can't leave now."

It was a convenient excuse to make them stay home. I didn't want my brothers anywhere near the Triumvirate, or near one Triumvirate lord in particular. If even half the stories I'd heard about Lord Bressen of Hiraeth were true, I'd do anything to keep Jaylan and Brix here out of harm's way.

"We can't let you go alone," Jaylan said.

"Yes, you can," I said. "I'm not going to let you throw away all the work we've done this year just because some lords snap their fingers and want to see me. I'll be fine."

"She won't be alone," Samhail said. "She'll be with me."

We all looked at him as if he'd gone mad.

"And that's supposed to reassure us?" Jaylan asked. "How do we even know you're really from the Triumvirate? How can we trust you?"

We all looked at Samhail. He shrugged and reached into a pocket in his britches to pull out a piece of parchment. He handed it to me.

I opened the parchment and read it. It was indeed an official summons to appear before the Triumvirate in all haste.

"There are only two seals stamped at the bottom," I said, looking at the two wax crests, each next to a signature. One signature was that of Lord Ursan of Polaris, and the other was Lord Jerram of Derridan.

"Lord Bressen was away from the city on business when it was decided you should be summoned," Samhail explained, "but he's been informed of your imminent arrival and will be back to meet you."

Dread pooled in my stomach at the name. Lord Bressen was not the lord of our territory – Lord Ursan was – but there were few people in Thasia who hadn't heard of him. He ruled the northeast Hiraeth territory and was the overseer of Revenmyer, the prison where the worst criminals in Thasia were punished for their crimes. According to rumors, the inmates were forced to continually relive their worst fears and memories, and most eventually went mad. Stories of Lord Bressen's power and cruelty were told in hushed tones to children to make them behave, and the legends said he could bury himself deep in your mind and make you do anything he wanted. He could even make you drop dead with a single thought.

"Cyra," Jaylan said quietly, seeing the look of horror on my face. "We'll figure something out."

I looked pleadingly at Samhail. "Please, I can't leave now. My brothers will be shorthanded. Can I come later when the season is done?"

Samhail shook his head. "My orders are to bring you now."

"Is there really nothing you can do?" I asked, not bothering to hide my desperation.

Samhail studied me for a moment, then exhaled a long breath. "Let me send a message to the Triumvirate. Perhaps they'll have a suggestion."

Samhail left the house, and I assumed he'd gone to find something in the saddlebags of the huge night-black horse I'd seen tied up in front of the house. He came back a minute later with pieces of strange-looking paper and a pen. He wrote something on one of the papers, then held it up in the air between his index and middle fingers. A second later, the paper vanished in a puff of smoke.

"Message sent," Samhail said.

I whispered a silent prayer to the Trinity that the lords of the Triumvirate were feeling helpful, or perhaps merciful.

"You should pack now," Samhail said to me. "Barring a very unexpected response to that message, we leave after lunch. You have the next hour to pack and say your goodbyes."

32

Samhail turned and left the house as I stood there, unable to move. Jaylan and Brix closed in around me, and I breathed heavily as panic welled in my chest.

"Why do they want you?" Brix asked, but Jaylan and I just shook our heads.

"I better get some things together," I said, trying to keep my voice from shaking. If Jaylan and Brix thought I was afraid to go, they'd fight to help me stay, and I didn't want them getting hurt.

"I'll get lunch ready," Jaylan said as I climbed the stairs.

The finality of our surrender to the summons almost buckled my knees, but I managed to haul myself onto the landing and down the hall to my bedroom. I pulled out a small travel bag, but I soon realized I should've asked Samhail a lot more questions. I knew where I was going, but I had no idea where I'd be staying, how long I'd be there, or what kind of clothing I'd need. Would I be walking the whole way? Samhail had a horse, but I'd only seen the one.

I needed a bedroll at least, so I took a small pillow off my bed and rolled a warm blanket around it. Beyond that, I wasn't sure. I pulled out my good leather pants, plus a regular cotton pair, some shirts, a sweater, a few changes of undergarments, my toothbrush, my hairbrush, and a small pouch of money I'd been saving.

I had visions of meeting the lords of the Triumvirate in dusty pants and a well-worn sweater, so I went to my closet to pull out the nicest dress I had. It was far from courtly, but it was fine silk, and I'd bought it partially because the shade of emerald enhanced my eyes. My eyes were the one prominent feature I had, so if I could use them to my advantage, I'd try.

I came downstairs a few minutes later to see Jaylan and Brix already seated at the kitchen table. Lunch was laid out, but they hadn't started eating yet. I'd never once known my brothers to wait for me to start a meal, and the fact that they'd waited this time broke me. I let out a soft cry and grabbed the railing to steady myself.

Two chairs scraped across the floor as my brothers stood and rushed over. Brix took my bag and bedroll while Jaylan put a hand under my elbow and helped me to the table. I thumped heavily into a chair as my brothers sat down.

None of us moved to eat for almost a minute until Brix finally reached out and filled his plate. The certainty I'd had in the back of my mind that Brix would be the first to break our vigil and start eating made me smile, and I almost started crying again.

"Brix and I have a plan," Jaylan said quietly after we'd been eating for a minute or so.

"What do you mean you have a plan?" I asked.

Jaylan opened the cloth napkin next to him on the table to reveal a large kitchen knife.

My eyes widened. "Are you mad? What are you planning to do with that? Kill an emissary of the Triumvirate?"

"Hopefully it won't come to that," Jaylan said. "Maybe we can just scare him off."

I looked at him incredulously. "You think you're going to scare off the giant man with two swords who almost skewered Brix earlier?"

Jaylan looked at Brix, who obviously hadn't told him about his close encounter with Samhail's sword.

"Please," I begged Jaylan, "don't do this."

"Cyra, we're trying to protect you. I made a vow," Jaylan said.

I put my hand on his. Jaylan told me several times over the years how he'd promised he would protect me when I came to live with them as a baby, and I knew Jaylan didn't take that vow any less seriously because he'd only been five at the time he made it. Jaylan didn't remember much about the day the stranger brought me to the vineyard, but he was certain of the vow he'd made, and it was now driving him to consider a foolhardy course of action.

"Jaylan," I said, trying to reason with him, "if Samhail doesn't kill you outright for brandishing a knife at him, he'll only come back with reinforcements. Please, just let me go and see what the Triumvirate wants. We only risk making things worse if you and Brix attack."

Jaylan glanced at Brix, whose expression begged Jaylan not to let me talk him out of this.

"Fine," Jaylan said. "We won't do anything."

Brix groaned and slumped in his chair.

We ate the rest of our lunch in silence. I ate very little. I knew I should eat more to keep my strength up for the journey, but my stomach roiled every time I swallowed something down.

Before any of us realized how much time had passed, the front door swung open, and Samhail walked in without either a knock or an invitation. "Are you ready?" he asked me.

A sound that was half laugh, half sob escaped me. "No."

"Are your things packed?" he rephrased impatiently.

"I think so. I forgot to ask what I should bring or how long I'll be gone, so…" I held up my travel bag in answer.

"You just need enough to get us to Callanus," Samhail said. "You'll be provided with everything you need once you're there. I don't know how long you'll be staying. That will be up to the Triumvirate."

"How long does it take to get there?" I asked.

"We'll be on the road the rest of today, all day tomorrow, and most of the next day," Samhail answered.

I exhaled. That was farther away from Fernweh than I'd been in my life five times over.

"I received a message back from the Triumvirate," he went on.

We held our breaths.

"There's a vineyard about a day north of here. Lord Ursan is a patron of the vineyard," Samhail said, "and he asked them to send a few of their best apprentice winemakers to help out as long as you need them. You can expect the apprentices tomorrow afternoon."

The news was a mixed blessing. I'd still be leaving, but my brothers would at least have able-bodied and experienced help to get them through the season.

Samhail picked up my bag and bedroll, but he stopped to eye Brix, who was trying his best to look normal with a hand behind his back.

"I suggest you drop that knife," Samhail said to him, "or you'll end up losing that hand."

Brix went pale and slowly reached over to lay the large kitchen knife on the table. When it was safely out of his grasp, Samhail turned and carried my packs outside. I threw Brix an exasperated look as we marched after Samhail like prisoners to their execution.

"Do you have a horse?" Samhail asked.

"We have two," I said, "but they're needed to pull the wagon."

Samhail nodded and tied my things to his horse's saddle. "We'll stop at the stables in town and get you a horse. Until then, you'll ride with me."

My eyes widened a little as I thought about being so close to this giant of a man, even if it was only for a little while. Samhail just looked at me, and I knew it was time to say goodbye.

I turned to Brix, and he pulled me into his arms for a crushing hug. I was close to both my brothers, but Brix was nearer to me in age, and he'd been my partner in crime for two decades. The idea of being without him for the first time felt like giving up a part of my spirit.

"Take care of Jaylan," I whispered to him. "Don't let him drown in one of the wine vats."

Brix just hugged me harder, and it was several more seconds before I finally pulled myself away from him to turn to Jaylan.

Jaylan took his role as the responsible older brother seriously, but after the death of our parents, that role also became somewhat fatherly as well. If a sacrifice needed to be made, Jaylan made it, and I knew it was eating him up that there was no sacrifice he could make this time to help me. Part of me was glad there was nothing he could do. I didn't want to go to Callanus, but the idea of Jaylan taking my place or giving up more now than he already had, seemed wholly unacceptable.

I threw myself into Jaylan's arms, and he hugged me tightly.

"Take care of Brix," I whispered. "You know he's hopeless at making a fire without me."

Jaylan laughed softly and kissed the top of my head. "Be careful and come home soon."

I tried to let go of Jaylan, but my arms wouldn't move. Sensing I wasn't ready to part yet, he held me harder, and I started to cry.

His hand stroked the back of my head gently as he bent down to sing very softly into my ear.

"Though it waxes and wanes among the stars,
We feel its tug, a tether between our souls.
A beacon in the dark, a promise kept
To find each other and again be whole..."

I recognized the song as the one he sang to me when I was upset when we were children, one our mother had first sung to him. It was a strange song with lyrics I didn't fully understand, a love song perhaps, that referenced the moon, sun, and earth. Something about the song always calmed me, though. Jaylan had sung it to me every day for weeks after the deaths of our parents, and the song's supposed message of wholeness and healing had resonated with me in a new way in my grief. It had been eight or nine years since the last time I'd heard it, and my body shook all the harder as I buried my face in Jaylan's shoulder.

It was several minutes before I finally loosened my hold on Jaylan and pulled back to see that his eyes were red too. He ran his thumbs over my cheeks to wipe the tears from them and then kissed me on the forehead.

"You should go before the big guy becomes ill-tempered again," Jaylan whispered.

Samhail was, for once, waiting patiently for me to join him.

I let go of Jaylan and stepped back. I forced myself to smile and started to walk to where Samhail was standing, but I stopped halfway there and turned back to Jaylan.

"You should still talk to Eddin," I told him, my voice a bit shaky.

Jaylan nodded.

"Eddin?" Brix asked, looking at Jaylan. "Are they still together?"

Jaylan flashed Brix a warning look before turning his attention back to me. "I'll speak to him. He won't say a word when I'm done."

37

"Say a word about what?" Brix asked, and Jaylan once again shot him a look.

I was about to say something when I felt a looming presence behind me.

"Who's Eddin?" Samhail asked. "And will he be a problem?"

"He's no one you need to concern yourself with," I said. "He's a now-former lover who took it badly when I told him it was over this morning. He threatened to make trouble, but Jaylan will handle it."

"You finally got rid of that ass?" Brix exclaimed in relief. "Thank the gods!"

"Brix!" Jaylan snapped. He turned to Samhail. "I'll take care of it."

Samhail shook his head. "No, I will. Let's go."

He turned and strode back to his horse, and my heart beat faster as I realized it was time to go.

"I'll be back as soon as I can," I promised and fervently hoped it wasn't a lie.

I approached the horse and put my foot in the stirrup, but Samhail's huge hands came around my waist to hoist me into the saddle. My stomach flipped at the feeling of momentary weightlessness, and I glared down at him.

"I know how to mount a horse," I said.

He ignored my comment and mounted up behind me.

I wasn't used to riding with someone, let alone someone as large as Samhail, and I was very aware of his muscled thighs against the backs of mine. His arms came around either side of me to grab the reins, and I tried to lean forward so my back wasn't pressed against his hard chest. His body surrounded me, and I felt caged within his embrace. Yet something else fluttered inside my chest as well, something I refused to call attraction.

I had only a moment more to wave an unsteady hand at Jaylan and Brix before Samhail wheeled his horse around, and we cantered down the road away from the vineyard.

A cold emptiness settled inside me. I was leaving the only home

I'd ever known and the only people I'd ever loved to face the-gods-knew-what in a strange city.

I had no idea why the lords of the Triumvirate wanted to see me, but the odds it would be for something good were slim. I was, after all, headed to face a man people saw in their nightmares, a man people insisted was the human embodiment of the Nemesis. If the Nemesis oversaw punishment and retribution in the next world, it was Lord Bressen who oversaw it in this one.

And now he wanted to see *me*.

Chapter 4

As I expected, blatant staring and loud gasps accompanied me and Samhail as we rode into Fernweh a while later. I was used to a certain amount of attention when I visited, but this was beyond anything I'd experienced. Samhail was already a sight unto himself, but seeing me on the giant black stallion in front of him seemed to be making people lose their minds. Samhail himself was oblivious to the commotion we were causing, and I imagined he must be even more used to the attention than I was.

We entered the town at a canter, and people parted to let Samhail through well before we got to them. We headed straight to the stables at the other end of town where Jax, the stable owner, approached us cautiously as we dismounted in front of his barn.

"Can I help you with something, sir?" Jax asked, keeping a healthy cushion of space between himself and Samhail.

Samhail pulled a leather pouch from his saddlebag and tossed it to Jax. The man caught it against his chest and looked up wide-eyed at the heavy clink of coin that sounded inside.

"The woman needs a fast horse with good stamina to get us to Callanus," Samhail said.

Jax nodded, still looking a little bewildered, and hurried into the stable. He returned fifteen minutes later with a beautiful dappled gray mare that was saddled and ready to go. The horse was one of the finest I'd ever seen, and minutes later we were off again, this time with me on the mare.

"Now where do I find Eddin?" Samhail asked as we rode back toward the center of town.

"There's no need for you to get involved. Jaylan can handle Eddin," I said.

He just looked at me, and I sighed. "He's usually at his tavern."

Samhail made for the tavern, and I spurred my horse after him. I caught up just as he was tying his horse to the railing in front.

"I'm going in for a drink," Samhail said as he strode inside without waiting for me.

I blinked. Did he seriously think I was going to let him confront Eddin on his own? I slipped off my mare, tied her to the railing, and hurried after him.

There were three other people inside who'd all begun gaping at Samhail the moment he entered. I didn't want this to be a public affair, but the chances of keeping it private were quickly slipping away. Samhail inevitably drew people's notice.

I caught up with him and grabbed his arm. He looked down at me, and I shook my head as emphatically as I could without making it obvious. "Please, not in front of everyone."

He glanced at the other people in the tavern and nodded. I let go of his arm, and he sat on one of the bar stools, which groaned ominously under his powerful frame. It was a testament to the stool's craftmanship that it didn't surrender itself into a pile of sticks.

Eddin was behind the bar, and Samhail already had his full attention, although he spared a quick glance for me. I was pleased to see the angry red mark on Eddin's cheek from when I'd scratched him earlier.

"A shot of whatever you recommend," Samhail said to Eddin.

Eddin eyed him warily but grabbed a bottle off one of the shelves and poured the drink.

"I also need a private word with the barkeep here," Samhail said to the room at large without turning.

Chairs immediately scraped across the floor as the three patrons rushed to leave, and I closed my eyes in defeat. I'd hoped to avoid attention, but this was easily the most excitement the town had ever seen. Everyone would know everything by tomorrow.

Back at the bar, Eddin pushed a glass of amber liquid toward Samhail, who sniffed the contents, then downed them.

"Mmm, good choice," Samhail said setting the glass back on the bar. "Now let's talk about the lady here for a second."

"What about her?" Eddin asked, glancing at me again, and I couldn't help my pleasure at the slight quaver in his voice.

"I heard there was some unpleasantness between you this morning," Samhail said.

Eddin's eyes widened, and I could see he was weighing whether it was better for him to lie to Samhail or just admit to the 'unpleasantness.'

"She and I might have had some words," Eddin admitted finally.

I strangled a laugh, and the words were out of my mouth before I could stop them. "You accused me of being a witch and fucking a bear."

Eddin turned a shade paler, and Samhail glanced back at me, brow raised. I returned his look, daring him to comment.

"Is that true?" Samhail asked, turning back to Eddin.

"It's what I've heard," Eddin said defensively.

"It's what you said you'd tell people," I corrected him.

"Okay, fine!" Eddin barked at me. He turned back to Samhail. "But she is a witch. Everyone knows it. I can only imagine what she was really doing with that bear."

Eddin had apparently decided that if he was going to go down, he was going down in a ball of fire. He looked pleadingly at Samhail, who'd gone perfectly still.

"She's just a little whore-" Eddin tried to continue, but the words were choked off by one of Samhail's blades against his throat. I gasped at how fast Samhail had moved and then wrinkled my nose as the smell of urine floated through the air.

"The lady," Samhail said calmly, "will be a guest of the Triumvirate at the Citadel in Callanus for a while. I doubt their lordships would be pleased to hear unpleasant rumors about their guest are being spread back at home, so you'll assure me that won't happen."

"Y-yes," Eddin stuttered as he shook violently.

Samhail looked at Eddin another moment before leaning back on his stool and re-sheathing his sword almost as quickly as he'd drawn it.

"Good. Then we have an understanding, and as long as I don't hear rumors are being spread, I don't have to come back. And rest assured," he added, "I will hear."

Samhail stood and tossed a coin on the bar. Eddin still hadn't dared to move.

"It's time to go," Samhail said walking past me. "We shouldn't keep the Triumvirate waiting."

I resisted the urge to look back at Eddin and instead followed Samhail. The town would inevitably know something had happened between me and Eddin, but I was at least confident that rumors of witchcraft and bestiality wouldn't await me when I came home.

Outside, Samhail and I mounted our horses and rode for the edge of town without another word. I only pulled my horse up next to Samhail's when we passed the limits of Fernweh and were on the road going north.

"Thank you," I said to him. "I'm not sure if you made things better or worse in the long run, but it was worth it to see Eddin wet himself." I paused. "Maybe you should have cut one of his balls off for good measure, though."

He chuckled. "Remind me sooner next time. I'd hate to go back now."

"Missed opportunity," I said, feigning disappointment. I paused again before asking, "Is there any chance we'll find an inn tonight?"

"The towns are few and far between out here," Samhail said. "We won't find lodging until tomorrow night at the earliest." He urged his mount into a trot, and I followed, letting my mare fall back so I wouldn't feel the awkard pull of trying to make conversation. Samhail didn't strike me as someone who engaged in casual chatting for the sake of it.

We stopped a few times to rest and water the horses, but otherwise Samhail and I rode for several hours until it started to get dark. We found a clearing a little ways off the road, and I set to work gathering wood for a fire while Samhail went to see if there was anything to hunt. By the time he returned with a rabbit dangling from his hand, I had a decent cookfire going.

"I forgot how handy it is to have an elemental around," Samhail said, nodding at the fire. He took a dagger out of his boot I hadn't realized was there and began skinning the rabbit.

"Are you planning to share, or do I need to go hunt my own?" I asked, not sure how I'd gotten comfortable enough already to tease him. I'd met him only this morning, and he'd shown me at least twice how dangerous he could be, yet I no longer feared him.

Samhail pointed to the fire. "You've earned your share for the night."

I nodded and watched him prepare the rabbit. It was dawning on me that I'd left Fernweh and had no idea when I'd be returning. Last week, being attacked by a bear and turning it to dirt was the strangest thing that had ever happened to me, but today's events reset that bar.

Minutes later, the rabbit was sizzling over the fire, and Samhail cut pieces to lay on two metal plates as I lifted my eyes to the double blades behind his shoulders. I'd hurt my right hand once and tried to do everything with my left hand for a week, but it just didn't work as well as my right. I tried to remember back to the two times I'd seen Samhail pull his swords. I thought he'd pulled a different one each time, but I wasn't sure.

"Why do you have two swords?" I asked, unable to keep quiet any longer.

"So I can fight with both hands," he said without looking up.

I huffed a laugh. "I assumed that much. But do you fight equally well with both?"

"Yes. When I first started training, I tried fighting with both hands to see which one was stronger. As it turned out, I used both equally well, so I learned to fight with both."

Samhail handed me a plate of rabbit and sat down to eat. Even though I was about half his size, he'd divided the meat almost evenly between the two plates.

"Do your swords have names?" I asked before taking a bite of the rabbit.

Samhail paused mid-chew and raised a brow at me. "Do they need names?"

I shrugged. "No. It's just that a mercenary came to Fernweh a while back, and his sword had a name. I think he called it Bone Breaker."

Samhail just took another bite of his rabbit.

"So…then your swords don't have names?" I pressed when he remained silent.

Samhail heaved a deep sigh and put down his plate. He wiped his hands on a cloth that lay over his thigh and reached behind him to pull one of the blades from its sheath. My eyes ran up the blade as the flames from the fire flashed across its polished surface.

"Sure," he said. "This one is called Righteous Hand."

He reached behind him again and pulled the second sword, holding it up so it too reflected the fire. "And this one," he said turning the blade from side to side so the fire flashed in its length, "is called Lefteous Hand."

I let out the breath I'd been holding, and my eyes flew back to his. There was laughter dancing in their dark depths.

My chin rose a notch. "You're making fun of me."

Samhail smiled and re-sheathed both swords together in one swift, practiced motion.

"Only men who need to feel important name their swords," he said as he picked up his rabbit leg again. "They're the same men who name their pricks, and neither tend to be very impressive."

My eyes dipped to his groin. I looked away again quickly, but it was too late.

"I assure you I've never had any complaints," he said with a grin.

I opened my mouth to stammer a reply, but Samhail held up a hand to stop me.

"There have been some blades over the centuries wielded by truly legendary warriors that bore well-earned names, but not every hunk of sharpened metal some would-be-warrior calls a sword deserves its own name. The practice of naming one's sword has become an epidemic of idiocy lately. The name is more a reflection of the warrior him or herself than the actual sword, and most warriors I know are just not good enough to deserve a sword with a name."

I blinked. That was the most words I'd ever heard him speak all at once, and it was an honest-to-goodness rant. I didn't even try to hide my smile, and Samhail glared at me.

"I'm sorry," I said, amused. "I just didn't realize you felt so strongly about this."

He grunted.

"But if you don't mind me saying so, you yourself seem like a great warrior. Not that I've seen many warriors," I qualified, "but you're certainly the most impressive warrior to ever come through Fernweh."

"You've never seen me fight," he pointed out.

"True, but you work for the Triumvirate, and I don't imagine they'd employ anyone but a great warrior. It makes me wonder what you did to get stuck escorting a no one like me."

Samhail stared at me a moment. "Is that a question?" he asked.

"Would you answer if it was one?"

"You're a maddening woman," Samhail said, then added under his breath, "Which makes we wonder if maybe I *am* being punished."

It was my turn to glare at him.

Samhail finished his rabbit and set his plate aside. I was full already, so I offered him my half-eaten plate, and he accepted it.

"For the record," Samhail said, "I don't work for the Triumvirate. Not in the way you're thinking. I work for myself, and when the Triumvirate needs something, they ask me if I'll do it. Usually I accept the job. Occasionally I don't."

"And why did you accept this job?" I asked. "To be honest, it seems beneath you."

He looked at me for a long time, and I started to think he wouldn't

46

answer.

"The Triumvirate doesn't send for me unless they have a matter of vital importance that needs to be handled," Samhail said finally. "I don't know exactly why they want to see you, but if they sent me, it's because it's critical you arrive at the Citadel safely, and they weren't willing to take any chances."

"And that's all you know?"

"That's all I know. They wanted to see you, and they're willing to pay me a lot of money to make it happen."

I didn't understand. Why so much fuss over me? Had killing the bear been that heinous an act that I needed to be called in front of the Triumvirate to answer for it? Would I be punished? Would I be sent to Revenmyer?

My stomach lurched at the thought, and I willed the rabbit I'd just eaten to stay down.

"Lord Bressen…is he really as horrible as they say he is?"

Samhail shrugged. "What's your idea of horrible?"

"Is it true he can kill people with a single thought?"

"Yes."

My breath hitched in my throat. He hadn't hesitated a second. I'd half-expected him to tell me that was just an overblown rumor, but he'd confirmed my worst fear with one word.

"Have you seen him do it?" I asked, my voice going rather squeaky.

"Yes."

I shivered and wrapped my cloak around me tighter.

"They say," I said, not sure why I continued to ask questions I didn't want to know the answers to, "that Lord Bressen is the Nemesis Incarnate. Is that true?"

Samhail sat back and regarded me as I tried to recall everything I knew about the Trinity, the triarchy of gods worshipped by most people of Thasia and around the Arystrian continent. The Creator, the Protector, and the Nemesis.

The Creator was the god who'd made the world and all that was now in it. You prayed to the Creator if you wanted to do anything from grow a garden to have a child. Artists prayed to the Creator for inspiration, and women prayed to the Creator to make them fertile.

The Protector was the god who watched over all the world and defended and sheltered everyone in it. Parents prayed to the Protector to keep their children safe, and merchants prayed to the Protector to ensure their ships made it safely to port.

The Nemesis was both an enforcer and a punisher, the god who ensured order in the world by setting the laws of nature and administering justice to those who broke them. The Nemesis was the god that victims prayed to for retribution against those who'd wronged them, and the god you prayed would never find you if you were guilty of a crime or sin. The Nemesis came for you when it was time to face your final judgement, and the terrifying Lord Bressen was said to be the Nemesis's right hand in the human realm.

"Lord Bressen punishes people all the time," Samhail said, apparently understanding what I really wanted to know. "He is, after all, the overseer of Revenmyer, and punishment is part of his duties. He's also by far the most powerful of the three Triumvirate lords. He's able to control the minds of just about anyone, and yes, he can and has killed people with just a thought."

My breathing shallowed as Samhail spoke. I wanted to run as far from here as I could, but Samhail would catch me and bring me back. The Triumvirate chose him for a reason, after all, and I realized it wasn't to protect me as I'd assumed, but to ensure I didn't escape.

"But," Samhail continued, and I found I was holding my breath, "Lord Bressen doesn't punish women for killing bears in self-defense."

I pushed a long breath out through my mouth and put a hand on my stomach to steady the churning there. It did sound ridiculous to be worried when he put it that way, but I had to ask. "You're sure?"

"He may punish you for annoying me," Samhail said wryly, "but not for the bear."

I glared and picked up a stick to throw at him petulantly. Samhail caught it and tossed it onto the fire.

"Get some sleep," he said. "We'll start early and ride as long as we can tomorrow. And just some advice, I'd avoid calling Lord Bressen the Nemesis Incarnate to his face."

I nodded before getting up to retrieve my blanket and pillow from my saddle. I laid them as close to the fire as I dared and watched the flames curl and sway for a long time until my eyelids started to flutter. My head was still full of questions and fears. I wondered if Jaylan and Brix had managed to get their own cookfire going, and the thought of them sent a sharp pang of despair through me.

I could still go back, I thought. I could wait until Samhail was asleep, then ride as hard as possible and hide until he stopped looking for me.

Even as my mind plotted the details of my escape, my body surrendered to the inexorable pull of sleep. The sound of crackling wood fused with the din of woodsy night noises to finally pull me under, and the last thing I saw as I closed my eyes were two burning embers that looked back at me like glowing red eyes.

Chapter 5

The hand pressed over my mouth seized me with instant panic before I was fully awake. I tried to bolt upright, but an arm flew around me and anchored me against something hard.

"Stay still," Samhail whispered in my ear, the urgency in his voice making me freeze. "And put out those damn flames!" he hissed.

The warm glow on either side of my body told me flames had ignited in my hands, and I quickly balled my fists to quench them.

"I'm going to take my hand off your mouth," Samhail said softly. "Stay quiet."

I nodded against what I realized was Samhail's chest, and his hand lifted from my mouth.

"What's happening?" I asked.

"A large group traveling on the road."

It was pitch-black all around us, but I could see twenty or so lanterns about a hundred yards away. Whoever was there probably couldn't hear us at this distance, but we didn't raise our voices above a whisper.

"Highwaymen?" I asked.

"Probably. Traveling at this hour of night is suspicious, but I'd prefer not to find out either way."

I waited for Samhail to release me, but he didn't seem inclined to do so as he knelt perfectly still behind me. It was just as unnerving as sitting in front of him on his horse. I could feel his warm breath close to my ear, and I trembled for reasons that had nothing to do with the cold air or fear.

My tremble must have made Samhail realize he was still holding me because he let go, although he didn't move away yet. Neither of us said anything else until the procession moved further down the road and we could no longer see the glow of their lanterns bobbing in the distance. Only then did Samhail move back to his place on the other side of our camp.

"I probably would have slept through that if you'd just let me be," I said. "My brothers insist I can sleep through a stampede of horses."

"Good to know, but I wasn't going to take any chances they'd hear your snoring."

My mouth fell open in outrage. "I do not snore!"

Samhail just chuckled. The man had a sense of humor I never would've expected from a warrior like him.

I laid back down and pulled my blanket tightly around me again. It was colder now that our fire was out, and I shivered.

"We can't relight the fire," Samhail said from somewhere in the darkness. "They'll see it if they circle back."

"I know. I'll be fine," I lied. It was going to be hard to get back to sleep now.

"There's another option," Samhail said.

I didn't move. I had a feeling I knew where he was going with this.

"Do you trust me?" he asked.

That was a loaded question. Did I trust him to get me safely to Callanus? Absolutely. Did I trust he wasn't going to hurt me? At this point, yes. Did I trust him not to take advantage of our bodies pressed together for warmth? Well, that was another thing entirely.

For that matter, I wasn't sure I could trust myself. Samhail was a striking man and being pressed up against him on his horse had given me ideas.

I heard Samhail move, and a heavy blanket thumped down on top of me before he got down and climbed in close behind me, his front pressed tightly up against my back. One large arm came around to drape across me, and any thoughts I'd had of protesting died unvoiced. Gods above, he was so warm.

Once settled, Samhail didn't move again, and I laid awake for several minutes until his even breathing told me he was asleep. Only then did I let the heat of his body draw me back to slumber.

My eyes fluttered open the next morning to find the broad expanse of Samhail's chest only inches from my face. Sometime in the night I'd turned over to face him, and his scent – leather and earth – filled my nostrils. His arm was still draped over me while his hand rested against my back. I realized one of my knees was also thrown over his thigh.

Nemesis damn me. I needed to move, but I wasn't sure how to do it without waking him.

"It's about time." Samhail's voice rumbled in his chest near my head. "I didn't want to disturb you, but we need to be on our way."

So much for not waking him. I wondered how long he'd been holding me like this.

Samhail threw off the blanket to get up, and I squealed as the cold air hit me. I pulled the blanket back around me quickly as my body objected to the loss of his warmth.

Samhail piled wood and leaves into the fire pit we'd used last night, and I got up to light the fire, the blanket still around me. He thanked me, and I nodded before going off to relieve myself. When I returned, Samhail already had a breakfast of dried meat and biscuits ready. I shook my blanket and pillow out and stowed them back on my saddle before coming over to eat.

There was a pot of water on the fire I thought was for tea, but I soon found it was for washing. After breakfast, Samhail stood and pulled off his shirt. He dipped a rag into the water and ran it over his torso for a rough cleaning.

I tried not to gape at him, but I'd never seen a more magnificent body on a man. Granted I'd only been with two men before, but I'd seen plenty of others shirtless, and none of them had ever looked like this. My eyes roved over the lean muscles that flexed and bunched as Samhail ran the cloth over them. Gods above. His perfect chest and shoulders were broad, but they tapered enticingly into a V of muscles that disappeared into his pants. I could count the ripples on his stomach, and his biceps and triceps rolled down into strong forearms that eventually ended in large hands. I wondered what it would feel like to have those hands wander over my body even as I watched them travel over his.

Dark markings on Samhail's forearms drew my eye, and I examined the design on his skin that ran halfway up to his elbows like vambraces of ink. Black bands encircled each wrist before giving way to a geometric pattern of diamonds and herringboned rectangles that faded away a few inches below his elbows.

"Are those tattoos?" I asked.

He looked down at his forearms. "They're sacred markings that identify my kind when we're in human form."

My mouth dropped open, and I blinked at him. "When you're in human form? So then you're not..."

"Not human." Samhail finished for me. "No, I'm demi-human. My human form is one of two I can take."

"Like a shapeshifter?"

"Not exactly. The form shapeshifters take is determined by their magic. I'm essentially a different race of being. My other form is part of me."

I waited for him to offer more, but when he didn't, I couldn't help asking, "And what is your other form?"

Samhail looked at me for a moment. "Something I hope you never need to see."

My eyes moved over him anew as if looking for a hint of what lay beneath his skin. He made it sound like he was some sort of monster.

A clean cloth landed in my lap, and my mind snapped back to awareness. Samhail was smiling at me, and I knew he'd caught me staring.

"If you want to wash up," he said, indicating the cloth.

I stood and dipped the rag in the pot of hot water. I was deciding the best way to wash under my clothes when I noticed Samhail watching me. "I'm not undressing," I said.

He just grinned and put his shirt and armor on again while I used the rag to wash my face and whatever I could reach without removing anything. We'd arrive in Callanus tomorrow, and I could get a real bath then. For now, washing would be subject to triage, both because of the cold and the company.

Ten minutes later, we'd packed up camp, doused the fire, and were on our way again.

We'd been fortunate so far. The group we'd seen last night was the only hint of trouble. In reality, Samhail himself was probably the most dangerous thing on the road. I hadn't really seen him in action, but I doubted we'd encounter anyone or anything he couldn't handle.

We passed only a few other travelers, mostly merchants moving their goods between towns. Pleasantries were exchanged, but little else. Samhail was an imposing figure with his white hair, black armor, and two swords, and people eyed us warily as we approached. He rarely said anything to anyone we passed, but I greeted everyone we met warmly, if only to assure them we meant no harm.

According to Samhail, the city of Gendris, where Lord Ursan lived, was only a few hours northwest of us. Lord Ursan wasn't there now, though. Rather, he was waiting in Callanus with the other two Triumvirate lords for me to arrive with Samhail.

Thasia was made up of three territories, each overseen by a lord. Most of the time, the lords lived in the capitals of their respective territories, but at various times of the year they converged on Callanus, which sat almost in the middle of Thasia, to deal with business that was pertinent to the country as a whole. Apparently, I was part of that business now.

I shifted in my saddle, trying to coax some feeling into my backside. I wasn't used to traveling, and the long hours of riding were starting to get uncomfortable. I had no desire to draw out the journey any longer than necessary, so I'd let Samhail set the pace without complaint. He kept us moving with only minimal breaks for the sake of the horses, so I was surprised when he reined up suddenly. The sun was sinking low in the sky, but there was still at least an hour of daylight left before we'd need to stop.

"What is it?" I asked, reining up next to him. Samhail stared intently at a section of the road that bent around to the left where the forest was denser.

"Turn around," he said quietly.

"What?"

"Turn your horse around and ride back the way we came. I'll find you when I can."

I wanted to protest, but it was clear he'd sensed danger. I pulled my horse around, but it was already too late.

"Samhail!" I said in alarm, and he looked behind us.

Several men emerged onto the road with weapons drawn. Most had shorts swords or daggers, but one had a crossbow, and it was pointed straight at Samhail. When we looked back, the road ahead was full of armed men as well, four of whom were on horseback.

I looked at Samhail. His face was grim, but I didn't see any sign of true worry. Could he actually fight this many men? There appeared to be around twenty, and it occurred to me this must be the band that passed by us in the dead of night.

"What do we do?" I asked.

"You won't do anything but ride fast."

Armed men surrounded us on all sides, but I assumed if it came down to fighting, Samhail could kill a lot of them. What I didn't know was how willing he was to spill their blood. While I recognized the grave danger we were in – that I especially might be in – I didn't know how many of these men I wanted to see turned into corpses. If there was any chance of talking our way out of this, I had to take it.

"Gentlemen," I said loudly, cutting the silence, "my apologies, but you appear to be blocking our path. Can I impose on you to move, please?"

The men around us chuckled and looked at each other. Even Samhail quirked a brow at me, but I only shrugged at him.

"Well, aren't you an interesting one, girl," one of the men on horseback said. He looked perhaps like their leader. "Never seen eyes like that before. You some kind of witch or something?"

I ground my teeth. "So I've been accused recently. Would you mind moving, please?"

"Beggin' your pardon, miss," the man said, his tone mocking, "but there's a toll to get through this road that you'll be needin' to pay first before we can let you pass."

"And how much is this toll?" I asked.

Samhail seemed to be surveying the men, and I hoped he was working on a plan.

"Let's start with your horses and any coin you're carrying," the man said, "and then we'll take *you* for the night as well." He leered at me, and my stomach knotted as I glanced around to see more than one ogling look.

"Hmm," I said, pretending to contemplate the offer. "My counteroffer is that you let us pass, and my companion lets you live."

Samhail turned to look at me again, but his expression was unreadable. I hoped he wasn't angry at me for making threats he'd have to make good on. I didn't think the men would take me up on my 'counteroffer,' but I hoped Samhail looked menacing enough to give them pause.

"Did you hear that?" the man on the horse said as the others laughed. "Her companion will let all of us live." He turned back to me, and his voice turned ominous. "How about we take turns fucking you on his corpse after we kill him instead?"

I narrowed my eyes. I was done being nice. If they wanted me, they were going to have to drag me down fighting. I held out a hand in front of me, and fire burst into my palm. I was pleased to see the flame was large, and I moved my hand slowly so they could all see it.

The men took a step back at the sight of the fire burning in my palm, and that's when Samhail moved.

He spurred his horse and the animal surged forward as Samhail pulled his swords from their sheaths. He held the blades out on either side of him as the giant stallion thundered down the road, its hooves kicking chunks of dirt into the air. Samhail's reach was long, and any man who'd been standing on either side was sliced across the mid-section. I'd been as surprised as the men to see him move, and I gasped as one man was completely cut in two by the razor-sharp blades.

The man behind us with the crossbow loosed his bolt at Samhail's back, but the bolt bounced off the armor and fell harmlessly to the ground. I didn't know why the crossbow proved so useless, but my next thought was that I had to stop the man from reloading.

I wheeled my horse around and spurred her toward the men behind us. Two of them had already turned to flee when they saw what Samhail's blades did to their companions, but the man with the crossbow was indeed reloading. I charged right at him and knocked him to the ground before he could wind his next bolt. I considered chasing down the two deserters, but I didn't want to leave Samhail alone. He'd taken out half the band in one charge, but there were still plenty more of them.

I turned my horse again and spurred her back to where Samhail was off his horse and cutting down men left and right, his blades flashing even in the dimming light. One of the men saw me coming and broke away from the melee to run at me with his sword drawn. He got only a few steps before he pitched forward onto the ground with a dagger in his back. I recognized the handle of the dagger as Samhail's, and I looked toward him. Samhail pulled one of his swords out of a body on the ground where he'd apparently stuck it long enough to draw the dagger out of his boot to throw it.

I looked at the blade in the man's back. I needed a weapon, but the thought of pulling the dagger out of a body was disturbing. I couldn't let Samhail do it all on his own, though.

I slid off my mare and ran toward the fallen man. I grabbed the handle of the dagger with both hands and pulled. It slid free of his body, but it took more effort than I anticipated, and I fought down a wave of queasiness at the wet sound it made coming out.

I turned toward Samhail, ready to help, but I needn't have

bothered. The fight was over.

A few men were fleeing into the woods as Samhail stood in the middle of a pile of bodies, but anyone still near the road was dead or dying. Spots of blood flecked Samhail's face and hair, and his armor looked wet with it, although it was hard to tell on the black leather.

I took a step toward Samhail, his dagger still in my hand, but I registered the alarm in his eyes half a second too late.

"Cyra!" he yelled at the exact moment I was jerked backward by a rough hand on my upper arm, and I felt the cold steel of a knife at my throat. I gasped as the blade bit into my skin, and a drip of blood trickled down my neck.

"Stay back or I'll slit her open from ear to ear," said a harsh voice at my shoulder. I recognized it as the man on the horse that I'd taken to be the gang's leader. Samhail had been advancing toward us with both swords out, but he pulled up short at the threat.

"You have two choices," Samhail said to the man. His voice was calm, but his body was still tense and ready to move. "If you take that knife down and let her go, I'll leave you with one hand left to wipe your ass. The hand currently holding the knife is already forfeit. If you make me take it away from you, you'll die screaming."

"If you move, I'll kill her," the man countered.

Samhail's dagger was still in my hand at my side, and I held it up a couple inches to show him. The man behind me didn't seem to know I had it. Samhail's eyes narrowed when he saw the blade, and he shook his head the barest amount in warning.

"You let me leave now, and when I'm far enough away, I'll let her go," the man said.

"She's a ward of the Triumvirate. I can't let you leave here with her, and the longer you hold that knife to her neck, the less chance you have of leaving here at all."

The man's attention was fully on Samhail, and before I could reconsider, I reached up and sliced the dagger down across his forearm. At the same time, I threw my head back into his nose. My intention was just to get my neck as far from the blade as possible in case the man jerked it toward my throat instead of away from it, but I heard his nose crunch against my skull, and dull pain throbbed through my head. The man cried out as his arm fell away from my neck, and I threw myself forward onto the ground.

Samhail moved as soon as I did. By the time I hit the ground, he was already in front of the man with his swords raised. I looked up in time to see the blades slash downward on either side of the man. They hit his shoulders, and his arms fell cleanly away as Samhail severed them. I blinked as warm blood splattered my face and the man's body crumbled sideways until it hit the ground like a slab of meat.

Either there was no sound, or my mind blocked out whatever noise the blades made when they cleaved through bone and flesh. I heard the man's piercing scream well enough a second later, though. It rent the silence of the woods, and I clamped my hands to my ears to block out the agony infused in every long second of that high-pitched wail.

Samhail was standing over the man, who writhed on the ground while blood spurted from what was left of his shoulders. "Give the Nemesis my regards," Samhail said before he ran a sword through the man's chest and the wailing mercifully stopped.

My mind recoiled at the sight of the limp form on the ground gushing blood that pooled in a large, crimson puddle. I remembered there were more heaps of dead bodies lying in yet more pools of blood at the other end of the road, and I rolled over to face the ground in case I needed to vomit. I inhaled big gulps of air as Samhail knelt down beside me and put a hand on my back.

"Are you hurt?" he asked.

I touched my throat, and a tiny amount of blood came back on my shaking fingertips from the nick where the blade had rested. I shook my head. "It's just a scratch."

I still clutched Samhail's dagger, red with the blood of two men now, and I shoved it back toward him, eager to get it out of my hand.

"That needs a name now too," I managed to say when he took it from me.

"This is Fred," Samhail said before re-sheathing it in his boot, and a strangled laugh escaped my throat. "Can you stand?" he asked.

I shook my head again. "I just need a minute."

"We don't really have a minute. It's starting to get dark," he said as he lifted me into his arms. "Don't look down."

Samhail carried me to his horse and lifted me into the saddle in one fluid motion before walking away. I made the mistake of trying to follow him with my eyes, and I caught sight of some of the mangled bodies. Severed limbs littered the ground as numerous faces stared up with vacant eyes. I forced my gaze back to focus on the stallion's neck.

Samhail returned with my mare and tied her reins to the back of his horse's saddle. He mounted behind me and nudged the stallion forward. My mare knickered nervously as we rode past the bodies, but Samhail's horse stepped deftly over dead limbs and pools of blood as if he did it every other day of the week.

"Are we just going to leave them there?" I asked quietly when we were a few yards beyond the last body.

"I'll send a message to Lord Ursan to let him know what happened," Samhail said. "He can order guards from Gendris to retrieve the bodies."

"And where are we going?"

"There's an inn about half an hour from here. It's a little out of our way, but we'll stay there tonight."

I sighed in relief that we wouldn't have to sleep out in the cold woods tonight. I was covered in blood, most of which had come from Samhail when he picked me up. It was smeared on my back from riding in front of him, but I knew my face was also flecked with the blood of the man who'd lost his arms.

I'd wanted to see Samhail the warrior in action. The thought of what he might be capable of had seemed exciting, but the reality of it was sobering, and I didn't speak again as we rode toward the inn.

I was sure I'd made things worse when I spoke to the highwaymen.

Maybe Samhail had a plan that would've gotten us out of there alive without anyone needing to die. I'd tried to help, but I felt instead like I was the catalyst that had sent everything spiraling out of control.

A voice in the back of my head reminded me they'd planned to hurt me. They likely would have raped me repeatedly and then killed me if Samhail hadn't acted when he did, but none of that mattered to my guilty conscience. All I saw were bodies scattered on the road because of me.

We arrived at the inn after dark, and Samhail dismounted before helping me off his horse.

"I'm sorry," I said quietly as I stood in front of him. I couldn't look him in the eyes.

"For what?"

"That you had to kill all those men because of me."

Samhail put a finger under my chin to lift my face so my eyes met his. "Those men were dead the moment they stopped us. You didn't do anything wrong."

"I taunted them."

"You kept them distracted while I analyzed the best way to attack. You bought me time."

"There's nothing I could have done or said…or not said, that might have kept things from ending the way they did?"

Samhail shook his head, then seemed to reconsider. "Actually, yes. Next time stay on your horse and flee when I tell you to."

"I thought you might need me," I said weakly. Out loud, I realized how ridiculous the idea was, so I added, "But if you want to be stubborn about it, you're on your own in the future."

Samhail chuckled. "Duly noted. I'll let you fight the next horde, but for now let's check in and get some rest. Tomorrow we arrive in Callanus."

Chapter 6

Samhail and I were awake and ready to leave the inn shortly after sunrise the next morning. I'd gone to bed early after taking a long bath where I scrubbed myself as hard as possible, but I kept thinking I saw spots of blood. Most turned out to be stray freckles, but I winced every time I saw one.

I was surprised the innkeeper even agreed to give us rooms last night, covered in blood as we were. When Samhail pulled out his orders from the Triumvirate, along with a hefty bag of coin, though, we were welcomed with open arms. Hot baths and dinner awaited us shortly after.

Mercifully, there'd been enough rooms that Samhail and I each had our own. I'd needed time to process everything I'd seen over the last two days, and that was easier to do without Samhail nearby. As it was, my mind had wandered while I sat in my bath, thinking about what he might be doing in his own room. He'd been covered in blood, so surely he'd been taking a bath as well. I hadn't been able to get the image of Samhail wiping his bare chest with that cloth out of my mind, and my imagination had taken things to an entirely new level.

When had I turned into such a shameless wanton?

When you met the most incredible-looking man that's ever come through Fernweh? a voice in my head answered helpfully.

Samhail and I set off right after breakfast and rode faster than normal for the first hour or so. We'd detoured off-course to get to the inn, and Samhail was determined to make up the time.

His clothes and leather armor were clean again, as was the rest of him, and I tried not to blush as my wicked thoughts from last night resurfaced. His white hair showed no signs of having been splattered with blood, and both our horses had been bathed overnight as well. Any evidence Samhail had slaughtered almost twenty men in the woods yesterday was now gone.

Samhail and I rarely spoke when we rode. He liked to keep his attention focused on our surroundings to look for danger, which had proven necessary yesterday, so I wasn't inclined to distract him.

We stopped for lunch in the middle of a field, and Samhail pulled a large bowl from his saddlebags that I filled with water for the horses.

"How much farther is it?" I asked.

"We should get to Callanus before evening. You can see it from here."

"What?" I said snapping my head to him.

Samhail pointed north. Sure enough, far in the distance I could see the light gray towers and walls of a large city.

My stomach dropped. For two days I'd just wanted to get to Callanus so I could stop sitting on a horse, but now that the city was in sight, my dread at what awaited me rose. Despite how far we'd come, I was more than willing to turn around and ride all the way back to Fernweh if it meant not having to face the Triumvirate.

"This last part of the journey is the most dangerous," Samhail said, drawing my head from its fog of terror.

"What? Why?"

"The quickest way to Callanus is through the Soundless Woods, so that's the way we'll go, but there are some forces in there I'm not sure I can fight."

I blinked. I had trouble picturing anything Samhail couldn't fight, and I didn't want to try. More importantly, if there were things in there he couldn't handle, why were we going into the woods to begin with?

"Can't we go around?" I asked.

"It would be an extra two days to go around, and the terrain would be dangerous for the horses. Plus the Triumvirate is eager to see you."

I grimaced. "Have you been through the woods before?" I asked.

"Several times. I went through on my way to come get you."

It relieved me that Samhail had entered the woods more than once before and come out unscathed, and I hoped his luck wasn't due to run out now.

We packed our saddlebags and were back on our way shortly after. It was another two hours before we reached the edge of the Soundless Woods. It didn't look any different than other woods I'd seen, nor did it sound any different. Birds chirped in the trees, the wind rustled the leaves, and the sounds of small animals skittering around in the brush added to the overall din of forest noises.

"Why do they call this the Soundless Woods?" I asked as we rode in. "It sounds noisy enough to me."

Samhail shrugged. "Supposedly there's something in here that can make it so silent it drives travelers mad, but I've never encountered it myself."

I tried to imagine a silence so dense it would make me lose my mind, but I couldn't wrap my head around the idea. Growing up in a house with three children, there'd always been lots of noise. I'd often sought quiet time to myself as I got older, so silence was a boon to me. It was something I craved occasionally, not something to be feared.

My more immediate issue was that we were slowly getting closer to Callanus, and the closer we got, the more I began to panic. There was now a permanent knot in my stomach that tightened with every step my horse took.

I'd never seen any of the Triumvirate lords, but my mind built them up into cruel, monstrous men who would glower down at me from their thrones, pronounce me guilty – of what, I wasn't sure – and throw me into the nearest dungeon to be tortured. I was particularly terrified of Lord Bressen, who I imagined had cold eyes set into deep sockets, a weathered old face with no capacity to display compassion, and gnarled hands that ended in claw-like nails. I had no idea how old Lord Bressen was, but I couldn't imagine that anyone rumored to have his mercilessness had aged well.

My hands were shaking by the time Samhail called for us to stop near a stream. I dismounted my mare and led her to the stream for a drink, then barely managed to tie her reins to a tree. I sat on a rock several feet away from where Samhail sat closer to the stream. He offered me some fruit and cheese to eat, but I shook my head. My stomach was twisted with anxiety.

Samhail frowned at me. "What's wrong?"

I considered telling him I was fine, but my shaking hands belied that.

"I can't go any further," I said.

Samhail cocked his head at me in question. "Are you tired? This isn't really a good place to sit for long. We need to get through the woods as soon as possible."

"No, I mean, I can't go to Callanus. I need to go home. I need to turn around right now and go back to Fernweh."

Samhail's face grew serious. "That's not possible. You've been summo-"

"I don't care!" I said, rising to my feet. "I can't go to Callanus. I won't go."

Samhail popped a final piece of cheese into his mouth and regarded me as he chewed.

"I'm not going any further," I repeated softly.

He exhaled heavily. "I don't want to drag you under duress, Cyra, but I will if I have to."

I held out my palms and fire flared in them. I was relieved to see the flames were large, like the ones I'd conjured for the highwaymen. "Then you'll have to," I said.

Samhail arched an eyebrow at me but didn't move.

I must've lost my mind to think I could fight him, but I was beyond caring. Dread coursed through my veins at the thought of what might await me at Callanus, and that dread was making me bold. The only way I was going was if Samhail dragged me kicking and screaming.

"I understand you're afraid," Samhail said, "but you know this isn't a fight you can win."

"Try me," I said, but the words were more of a sob than a threat.

Samhail stood up and brushed his hands against each other to wipe off any crumbs, and I remembered belatedly just how much bigger than me he was. Bigger and much faster. He didn't make any move toward me yet, though, and I tensed, ready to run or fight as needed.

"Cyra," Samhail said as if reasoning with a small child, "your only options here are to ride into Callanus on your own horse, or to ride in thrown over the saddle of mine. I don't have a choice here. The Triumvirate summoned you, and they're paying me very well to make sure you arrive safely. I'd prefer to have you ride in under your own power, but if you force my hand, I'll bring you in as my prisoner."

My heart dropped, but the flames in my hands only flared brighter as his words fanned my panic.

"Please," I whispered. "I'll give you whatever you want."

Samhail's eyes narrowed. "And exactly what do you have that you could offer me?"

"Whatever you want," I reiterated, and my eyes locked with his.

"You don't have anything of value to give me," Samhail said reasonably, but I saw his eyes rake down my body.

I swallowed. "If that's what you want," I said, acknowledging what I assumed he'd been thinking. I'd offer him anything if he agreed to let me go home, even my body if that's what it took. He was attractive after all, so I supposed it was a price I could pay easily enough. There was a chance I might even enjoy it.

Samhail looked at me with interest. "You'd really offer yourself to me if I let you leave?" His tone was more curious than anything, but whatever I'd seen in his eyes a moment ago was gone now.

"Yes," I said, but I was no longer hopeful we might have a deal. "Promise me you'll let me go back to Fernweh, and I'll do whatever you want."

"And if I don't?" Samhail asked.

I let the flames in my hands flare. "Then we fight."

Samhail smiled at me and crossed his arms over his chest. "You're not nearly as afraid of me as you should be," he said, clearly amused.

His tone was light enough, but there was something ominous in his words that made the knot in my stomach clench even tighter. I recalled what Samhail had done to the highwaymen yesterday. Part of me was afraid of him then, of his power and his utter lack of mercy, but I knew that wasn't what he meant.

"You won't hurt me," I said. "You may be dangerous, but you're not dangerous to me."

I was playing a risky game here, and I sounded more confident than I was.

Samhail cocked his head. "Is that so?" He uncrossed his arms and walked toward me. "There are different kinds of danger."

There was something in his eyes I couldn't read, but for the first time since we'd left Fernweh, I was suddenly wary of him.

I held out my palms toward him and the flames flared again. "Stay back," I ordered, but he kept coming.

I wondered if I could throw my flames, but I knew the question was moot. I wouldn't hurt Samhail, even if I had the power to. He was calling my bluff, and I was out of options.

Samhail continued to advance on me, and I didn't realize I was retreating until I bumped up against a tree. I glanced back quickly to see what I'd run into, but when I turned back, he was there. I cried out as he grabbed my wrists and pinned them to the tree above my head.

"Extinguish the flames," he growled at me.

I tried to move my hands, but they didn't budge. I knew they wouldn't. Samhail was far too strong, so I clenched my hands and the flames died.

"Good," he said. "Now, are you riding your own horse into Callanus, or are you riding there thrown over my lap?"

My eyes snapped up to meet his. He'd left the 'over his lap' part out last time, and my mind was now going in an entirely different direction. Apparently his was too, because he leaned forward to let his body press me gently against the tree.

"Fine," I whispered. "I'll go quietly. You made your point."

"Have I?" he asked, his voice husky.

I opened my mouth to answer, but his lips descended on mine

then, quickly and brutally. I jolted against him, not from surprise or fear, but from the wave of heat that shot straight to my toes. I was suddenly grateful to be pressed against the tree as my mind reeled and my knees went weak with a desire beyond anything I'd ever felt.

Samhail let go of one of my wrists, and his hand gripped the back of my neck, making me a willing prisoner to his kiss. His lips ground into mine as his tongue invaded my mouth, pressing mine out of the way in its unrelenting onslaught. He devoured me, branded me, and for a moment I couldn't breathe as I tried to make sense of the maelstrom of sensations coursing through my body.

Samhail's kiss was meant to be rough and punishing, a warning to remind me I was utterly at his mercy, but I had no will to resist or escape. My free hand gripped his armor, and I held him to me as my tongue now met his with equal zeal. My hips arched into him of their own accord, and a moan issued from somewhere deep in my throat.

Samhail groaned and released my other hand so he could grip my waist and pull me against him. My newly freed hand wrapped around his upper arm and dug into the massive muscle there, both to hold him to me as well as to keep myself standing. I would crumple at his feet if he let go now.

Samhail pulled his mouth away from mine, and I took in a gasping breath. He was breathing hard as well. I held his gaze without blinking, and in my mind, I was daring him to kiss me again.

Something blazed in Samhail's eyes as he seemed to wrestle with himself. A moment later, his mouth descended again, but slowly this time. His lips brushed mine in a sensual caress, and I melted into him. The hand holding my neck slipped down to my backside, and he pulled me against him. I could feel the hardness of his arousal against my stomach, and the tightness growing between my legs intensified.

One of the horses nickered loudly behind us, and Samhail pulled back instantly. I might have ignored the sound, but Samhail was too accustomed to recognizing the signs of danger to ignore the panic in the animal's cry. He was suddenly alert and listening intently.

"What is it?" I whispered, trying to listen.

Both horses nickered this time as they stomped the ground and pulled at their bridles. My mare whinnied in terror and reared back. Her head snapped forward as it met with the resistance of the bridle. Samhail's horse jerked its head and pawed the ground as well, trying to back away from the tree.

Samhail let go of me and ran for the horses as I fell back against the tree. "Untie the reins before they break their necks!" he yelled.

The horses were bucking and jerking in real fright now, and I launched myself off the tree toward my mare. I tried to get close enough to pull the slip knot loose, but she was frantic, and I thought she might trample me. Samhail had already pulled the knot to release his horse, and the animal immediately fled into the woods.

"Pull it!" Samhail yelled as he positioned himself between me and the bucking mare.

I darted forward and yanked on the strap that released the knot. The reins sprang free, and my mare reeled around to follow Samhail's horse into the woods.

"What spooked them?" I asked as the woods went still again.

Samhail didn't answer. He was slowly scanning the trees, so I did the same.

"There," Samhail said, and there was an edge to his voice.

I looked where he was facing, but I didn't see anything. There were no men, no monsters, and nothing moving through the trees. For that matter, I couldn't see that far into the woods because of the...

I went cold.

A thick blue-gray fog was rolling slowly through the trees, and I realized then how quiet it had gotten. There were no birds singing and no small animals skittering around in the undergrowth. It was as if my ears were blocked, and it made sense to me all of a sudden how a silence could be so profound that it was almost maddening. I tried to pop my ears the way I would have if they'd been clogged with water, but the muffle remained.

"What is that?" I asked Samhail, and my voice sounded muted in my ears.

Samhail hadn't moved yet. He raised a hand out in front of him and some kind of percussive force reverberated from it through the woods. I saw a blur of energy radiate out of his palm, and the trees in its path shuddered and swayed from its impact, but the fog didn't so much as twitch.

Samhail held out both hands and another forcefield rocked the woods. Trees in its path split their trunks and branches crashed to the ground as the wave spread out like rings of water on a pond, and this time, the fog did react. It came on faster.

The blue-gray mist poured through the woods like a stream off a mountain, flowing over rocks and around trees as it headed straight for us. Small plants on the ground shriveled into dry, brown stems, and the woods behind the fog disappeared as the trees were quickly swallowed into its nebulous form.

"What do we do?" I asked Samhail, my voice rising.

"Run!" he said as he grabbed my arm and spun me around.

My feet were moving before the word had left his mouth. I ran as fast as I could in the only direction the fog wasn't coming from. I could feel rather than hear Samhail's heavy steps thudding behind me as the effects of the fog continued to press on my ears. I knew Samhail could outrun me – his legs were much longer – so he was purposely staying behind me to keep himself between me and the fog.

Something dense and heavy grew in my ears, and it seemed, paradoxically, as though I could hear the silence whining in my head. The lack of sound was almost palpable, and I could feel my mind coming undone as I tried to make sense of it. I felt something wet in my ear, and the fingers I lifted to it came back with blood on them.

Samhail's voice seemed to come from far away. "Left!" he ordered, and his hand pressed on my waist to reinforce the direction. I could barely hear him as the clogging in my ears grew more intense, but I veered left without question. I wasn't sure if the pounding in my chest was just the vibration of Samhail's heavy footfalls drumming on the ground behind me or the hammering of my own heart as I ran, but it rattled my insides.

I kept my eyes focused on the ground to avoid falling into any holes or tripping on rocks or tree branches. I looked up only long enough to see if there was anything big in my path as I serpentined through the trees and ducked under low-hanging branches. I knew without looking that Samhail was only a step or two behind me even though I could no longer hear or feel him.

As I plunged through the brush, brightness grew ahead of me. The woods were thinning. As the path cleared, though, our ground began to run out as we headed toward a cliff. Several yards in front of us, the ground fell off into nothingness as another cliff face rose on the other side of a canyon far beyond our reach.

I started to pull up, but Samhail's hand on the small of my back pushed me forward insistently. His voice vibrated in my ears, but I couldn't hear what he was saying anymore.

There must be water below. He intended to jump.

I just hoped the water was deep. I didn't relish the idea of a cold bath, but my bigger concern was making sure I jumped far enough out so I didn't hit anything on the way down or break my neck when I hit the water.

As we approached the edge of the cliff, I tried to pull up again so I could look below first, but Samhail's hand was unyielding. He yelled something else, but his voice was so stifled it sounded as though he was yelling to me from a mile away.

"But —" I started to protest before I realized I could no longer hear my own voice. Something wet trickled down my neck, and I knew my ears must be bleeding in earnest now. I sped up again and eyed the fast-approaching drop.

Any resolve I might have had about jumping evaporated as the space widened before us. My body rebelled again only a step or two from the ledge, and I pulled up short.

I opened my mouth to object again, but Samhail's body slammed into mine, knocking the breath from me. His arms wrapped around me like iron bands, one circling my waist and the other anchoring my shoulders to his chest as he launched us out over the chasm. I looked down and could see there was indeed water beneath us…The small, lazy trickle of a meandering brook far below.

Then we were falling.

Chapter 7

I tried to scream, but despite the abundance of air rushing past us, my lungs refused to inhale as I watched the ground rise up to meet us. Unable to move my arms under Samhail's iron grip, I clenched and unclenched my hands as if I could will the air to keep us aloft.

We rocked sideways, and Samhail grunted and tightened his already strong hold around me. It was several seconds before I realized the ground wasn't approaching as fast as it should be, that we weren't falling straight down but looping in wide circles.

Gliding. We were gliding toward what I could now see was in fact a small river, not wide or deep, but a river nonetheless. It would still have killed us to plunge into it from the top of the cliff, but we were apparently destined for a softer landing than I'd anticipated.

We leveled out, and I watched the water rush by below us as we soared a few yards above it toward a grassy patch of open field on the other side. We slowed, and my legs dangled down before Samhail hit the ground in a smooth run and held me upright long enough to get my footing.

He finally eased his vice-like grip on my chest and waist as we came to a stop, but he didn't let go yet, letting me catch my balance. I remembered how to breathe, and I took in big gulps of air as I let Samhail keep me upright. When I trusted my feet to move, I turned in the circle of his arms to face him.

Behind him, giant membranous, bat-like wings hovered partially closed above his shoulders. I had no idea where they'd come from, but they were the most welcome sight I'd seen since we began this journey.

"Are you alright?" Samhail asked me.

In answer, I slipped through his arms and fell in a heap at his feet before turning to vomit into the grass. He squatted behind me as I heaved up the contents of my lunch. One of his heavy hands rested on my back while the other gently gathered stray locks of my hair away from my face. I retched again, and his hand rubbed gentle circles around my shoulders.

"Feel better now?" Samhail asked when I finally stopped.

"You have," I said between gasps, "something...on your back."

He pretended to seem shocked and looked behind him. "Where?"

I choked out a laugh, and Samhail caught my elbows to lift me off the ground.

"Apologies for the rough ride," he said. "Flying for the first time can be harrowing, especially if you're not expecting it. You handled it better than others I've flown, though."

"Do you fly people around often?" I asked.

"Not often, but if I need to be somewhere quickly, and I don't feel like waiting for my companion to walk or ride a horse, then yes. I've been known to fly people short distances."

"Have those always been there?" I asked, pointing to the two giant wings on his back. "Did I somehow not notice them until now?"

In answer, Samhail shrugged his shoulders and the wings folded back into nothingness behind him with a whooshing flap.

"It's a metamorphosis," he explained. "I have a...beast form that lays dormant until called upon. I can manifest various parts of it, like the wings, at will."

He'd said he had another form, but I hadn't pictured something with giant taloned wings. Now I imagined something monstrous roiling beneath his skin.

He chuckled, as if reading my thoughts. "Don't worry. I keep the beast well-contained until he's needed."

I wanted to ask him more, but I could still taste the tang of vomit in my mouth. I walked past him toward the river and knelt on the bank to swish my mouth and drink some of the water from my cupped hand. My stomach objected to the ice-cold river water, but I breathed deeply and waited for the feeling to pass. When it did, I cupped more water into my hands to wash the dried blood from my neck and ears. Thankfully, my hearing seemed back to normal.

"After we jumped, an updraft hit us, and I had to adjust to keep from being blown into the cliff face. Was that you?" Samhail asked.

I hoisted myself up unsteadily to my feet, remembering the sudden rocking I'd felt when I thought we were falling. Until recently, I'd only been able to call fire and water, but the bear proved I could control earth. Maybe I could manipulate air as well. I frowned as I remembered the times at home when I'd been scared or angry, and a strong wind had seemed to come from nowhere. Had I been able to control air all this time and just not realized it?

"I don't know," I answered honestly. "It's possible. I remember trying to make the air hold us up, but I've never purposely summoned wind before."

I looked around, but I could no longer see Callanus from down here. Our horses were gone as well, possibly dead, and I felt a pang of sadness for the gray mare I'd grown fond of. Still, I held out hope she'd fled to safety before the fog rolled in.

"What do we do now?" I asked.

"That depends on you," he said.

"Me?"

"We're not far from Callanus. I'll fly us the rest of the way if you can handle it."

My face must've turned green because he gestured up the river. "Or we can walk."

My legs were still wobbly, so the thought of walking wasn't much better, but for now it was preferable to flying.

"Let me walk a bit," I said. "At least until I'm sure I won't vomit again, then we can revisit flying."

He nodded and motioned for me to lead the way. I started moving along the stony bank, and he fell into step beside me.

We walked a few minutes in silence before I spoke again. "You were trying to scare me before, when you kissed me." It was a statement, not a question, and I wasn't sure what made me bring it up.

Samhail was quiet a moment. "Truthfully, I don't know what I was

75

trying to do. It might have just been an excuse to kiss you. I've been wanting to since you woke up in my arms the other morning."

My stomach flipflopped at his words, but I didn't respond.

"I assumed you'd be horrified and try to get away, but…"

"But I didn't," I finished for him.

"But you didn't," he said. "I shouldn't have done it, in any case."

I wasn't sure if that was an apology, but I didn't press him.

"I offered myself to you," I went on instead.

I felt his gaze but wouldn't meet his eyes.

"You did," he confirmed.

"You declined the offer."

He sighed. "I couldn't accept it. I agreed to bring you to Callanus on behalf of the Triumvirate. That's an obligation I take seriously. My reputation would be at stake if I failed to bring you back, more-so if I failed because I betrayed the Triumvirate's trust in me."

I'd never had a chance, I realized. For a warrior like him, reputation was everything, and what I'd offered him was nothing by comparison.

"Besides," Samhail went on, "if I ever do have you, it won't be as payment for anything. You'll let me take you willingly with no other expectations between us."

Lightening shot through my core, seizing my entire body, and I pulled up short. He stopped walking and looked at me.

"Problem?" he asked, grinning.

"That's quite a promise."

He winked at me. "I only make promises I can keep."

My stomach trembled, and I willed myself not to imagine what it would be like to be with him, to have his hands on my body or to have him moving inside me.

I blinked the images away before they could take shape and then looked around. We hadn't gone very far yet.

"How long will it take us to get to Callanus this way?" I asked.

"We'd have to camp out again overnight," he said.

I closed my eyes. That wasn't going to work. I didn't mind delaying my arrival at the Citadel, but we didn't have any of our supplies, and I could only imagine what the night would bring after what Samhail had just confessed. No, this wasn't going to work at all.

"And how long if we fly?" I asked in resignation.

"Maybe half an hour," Samhail said.

I knew I was going to regret this. The thought of being pressed up against Samhail's chest for the next thirty minutes while he flew us was almost as alarming as our other options, but it was ultimately the lesser of all the evils.

"Very well," I said. "We can fly."

"Are you sure?"

"As long as you fly carefully. I can't promise my stomach is going to hold out."

"No diving or barrel rolls. Got it."

I glared at him, and he held up his hands in submission.

"I promise to be careful," he said.

I raised a brow. "And you only make promises you can keep?"

Samhail grinned, and his huge black wings flared out behind him again. I was in awe for a moment as I took them in. They were strangely beautiful, and they fanned out impressively on either side of him.

"Let's find out, shall we?" Samhail said as he scooped me into his arms. "Ready?"

"As I'll ever be."

I had the sense of being pressed downward as Samhail's wings beat hard and sent us shooting into the sky. The ground fell off as the cold air whipped around us, and I pressed myself tighter up against him. His body was hard against mine, but he was also strangely warm, and I let myself savor the feel of his arms anchored around me. Flying this way wasn't so bad, especially if I didn't look down, and I soon settled in as best I could for the rest of our journey.

Half an hour later, Samhail landed on the flagstones of the Citadel's courtyard. Several guards glanced at us as he set me down, but it was clear they knew him and weren't surprised by his sudden arrival.

I locked my knees to keep them from buckling and vowed I'd never fly with him again. The second time was better with me cradled in Samhail's arms rather than clenched against his chest, but my stomach still lurched threateningly a few times despite his valiant efforts to keep us steady. Birds looked so graceful when they flew, but Samhail was no bird.

He stowed his wings again as a guard who looked older than the others rushed over.

"You're early," the guard said to Samhail. "We didn't expect you until later today."

"We would've arrived later if we kept our horses," Samhail said, "but there was a change of plans and we had to fly."

"We were worried actually," the guard said. "A patrol found your horse with a gray mare in one of the outer pastures, but there was no sign of you. The patrol is heading in with the horses now."

"The horses are okay?" I asked in relief, wondering how they'd gotten around the fog.

The guard looked a little surprised to be addressed but nodded. "Yes, my lady."

"Gilbert," Samhail said addressing the guard, "this is Cyra of Fernweh. Cyra, this is Gilbert, Captain of the Citadel Guard."

"A pleasure, my lady," Gilbert said, but his tone was unconvincing.

"I'll show Cyra to her quarters," Samhail said to Gilbert. "If her bags are still on the saddle when the horses arrive, make sure they get up to her room."

"Of course," Gilbert said. "Will you bring her down to the Great Chamber as well, or should I come get her?"

"I'll bring her," Samhail said. He turned to leave, but Gilbert's voice called him back.

"The lords want to see her right away," he said.

Samhail frowned. "Is Lord Bressen back?"

"Not yet."

"They're not to question her until he returns," Samhail told Gilbert in a tone that brooked no argument.

My heart had leapt at the news that Lord Bressen wasn't here, but Samhail's words dashed any hopes I had of facing the Triumvirate without him. I gave Samhail a wounded look, but he ignored me.

Gilbert looked a bit nervous. "If...if Lord Jerram and Lord Ursan hear she's arrived, they'll want to see her immediately," he said.

"Then make sure they don't hear she's arrived until Lord Bressen returns," Samhail said.

Gilbert stiffened a bit, and I could almost see him trying to decide if he was more wary of the two Triumvirate lords or of Samhail.

"I'll do what I can to delay the news," Gilbert said finally.

Samhail nodded and put a hand at my back to steer me up a set of wide stone steps toward the entrance to the Citadel. It was a massive structure with a central building of light-colored granite and three wings that branched off the main building. We'd landed in a front courtyard within the high stone battlements that encircled the whole thing, and I wished I'd thought to catch a glimpse of it from the sky before we landed.

Guards opened two massive carved wooden doors for us to pass, and Samhail strode through them without pausing. I had to hustle to keep up with his long strides as we passed through an airy foyer decorated with tapestries, a soft round rug, and a giant crystal chandelier hanging from the high domed ceiling. The foyer led to a short corridor before the building once again opened into a sparsely decorated rotunda with four ornate doors at regular spaces.

"Where am I staying?" I asked, praying Samhail wasn't leading me to a dungeon cell.

"You have a room here in the central building," he said. "Each of the lords has their own wing when they're in residence. You can go anywhere you want in the central building, but don't go into any of the wings, and don't leave the Citadel itself for any reason."

"Am I a prisoner?" I asked him.

"No. For now, you're a guest…with restrictions."

That sounded like a euphemism for prisoner to me, and Samhail's "for now" seemed rather ominous, but I was relieved to hear I wouldn't be a captive in the usual sense.

"This is the door into the central building," Samhail said, heading to one of the doors across the rotunda carved with the word "Central" on it. "The other three doors lead to the lords' wings."

I looked around and saw doors carved with the names Hiraeth, Derridan, and Polaris, the names of the three territories.

We entered the central building, and a couple minutes later, Samhail stopped in front of a door a few floors up.

"I believe this is the room they've assigned you," he said as he pushed the door open and ushered me inside.

The room I entered was as far from a prison cell as I'd ever seen. It was easily the most lavish room I'd set foot in, and I had trouble believing it was where I'd be staying.

The room was open and airy, with tall windows framed by gauzy curtains that swayed in the breeze coming in from the balcony. Two silk-covered chairs and a table were set off to one side of the balcony next to a fireplace, and across from that, a huge bed made up with bright white linens, midnight blue covers, and mounds of fluffy pillows stood against the wall. The gray pelt of a large animal was draped on a cushioned bench at its foot.

A writing desk stood against the wall near the door, and another table with four chairs sat nearby ready for use. Ornamental vases and statues topped plinths in the corners, and large paintings of various subject matter hung on some of the walls. Finally, a door at the far end of the room led to a private bathing chamber tiled in white marble that boasted a huge soaking tub.

I gaped at the opulence around me as I walked around the room. This must be a mistake.

Someone cleared their throat from the door, and I turned to see a young woman around my age peering in. She had bright green eyes and golden-brown hair with streaks of blonde tied up at the back of her head in a loose bun. She was dressed in a plain white shirt and skirt of brown cotton.

"My apologies for the intrusion," she squeaked as she took in Samhail, "but I've been assigned as the lady's handmaid while she's here. My name is Raina." She bobbed a quick curtsey.

I smiled at her. "Pleased to meet you, Raina. I'm Cyra."

"My lady," Raina said with a nod of her head.

"I'm not a lady," I said. "I'm not sure why everyone keeps calling me that."

"You're not a lady in title," Samhail said, "but you're a guest of the Triumvirate, so it's a sign of respect for that status. It's how the Citadel staff will address you for now."

There was that "for now" again.

"Shall I draw a bath for you, my lady?" Raina asked, eyeing my traveling clothes and the dust on my face.

Before I could answer, there was another knock, and Gilbert stood in the doorway.

"The lords know she's here," he told Samhail. "Lord Jerram saw you land. I can't stall them any longer. They want to see her now."

"Lord Bressen?" Samhail asked.

Gilbert shook his head, and Samhail swore.

I didn't understand why Samhail wanted Lord Bressen here so badly. Two lords was less intimidating than three, and I'd be fine with never having to come face-to-face with the terrifying Lord Bressen at all, despite Samhail's assurances he wouldn't punish me.

"She needs to come now," Gilbert said apologetically.

"Like this?" I asked. "I'm filthy."

Raina stepped forward and grabbed my hand. "At least let me wash your face and brush your hair, my lady." She turned to Gilbert. "The lords can wait for that at least, can't they?"

Gilbert frowned but nodded his head. "Five minutes, and then I need to bring her."

Raina pulled on my hand to lead me toward the bathing room, and I gratefully hurried after her. Almost exactly five minutes later, she'd scrubbed any skin that wasn't covered by my clothes and worked a brush through my windswept hair so it no longer looked like a complete wreck. I barely had time to thank her as Gilbert hurried me out of the room with Samhail on our heels.

I followed Gilbert back down the stairs and through several corridors until we came to large, ornately carved double doors. The doors opened of their own accord to reveal a spacious room with three large seats at one end on a raised dais. Figures sat in two of the seats, and I swallowed hard as I got my first glimpse of two lords of the Triumvirate.

"My lords," Gilbert announced, "Cyra of Fernweh to see you as requested."

Gilbert stepped aside and waved an arm for me to enter the room. Samhail followed as I stepped inside, and I found his presence comforting.

"Come forward," one of the lords called, and I walked cautiously into the room.

The chamber was completely round with no windows, and the walls were covered with heavy tapestries that did nothing to soften the feel of the space. The three chairs on the dais weren't quite thrones, but they also weren't normal chairs either. They were large and cushioned with tall backs and wide arms, and they seemed to be made for people who were slightly larger than the men who now occupied two of them.

At the risk of taking a liberty I wasn't allowed, I looked at the two lords as I approached. The man in the chair directly before me looked a little older, somewhere in his forties by human standards. He was a bit stocky and was likely the shorter of the two men, although it was hard to tell while he was sitting down. His golden-brown hair and beard were just starting to go gray, and his brown eyes looked kindly enough on me that I relaxed just a little.

The other man appeared to be in his late twenties or early thirties, although that again meant little regarding his actual age. He had light blonde hair with hints of copper, and his eyes were a clear, pale blue. His face was smooth in an almost boyish way, while his strong cheekbones gave the only indication he might be older than he looked.

In short, both lords were far from the ogres I'd pictured so far.

"Samhail," the older man said, and Samhail stepped forward to offer a little bow. "Thank you for getting our guest here in one piece. I trust you didn't have any other issues after the incident with the brigands?"

"We ran into a little trouble in the Soundless Woods," Samhail said, "but nothing we couldn't work around."

"Very good," the man said and extended a hand to his side.

Samhail moved forward to take a place against the wall between the man and the other empty chair as if he was now on guard duty, and I suddenly felt exposed standing in the middle of the room by myself.

"Come closer, my dear," the older man said, and I took a few more steps toward the two lords until I almost reached the foot of the dais.

"I'm Lord Ursan of Polaris," the older man said, "and this is Lord Jerram of Derridan. Unfortunately, Lord Bressen of Hiraeth can't be here at this time, so we'll proceed without him."

I looked at Samhail to see what he thought of this, but his gaze was focused somewhere behind me, and the hint of a smile curled his lips.

"Am I late to the party again?" a smooth voice drawled from the doorway.

Ursan and Jerram both stiffened as their attention shifted behind me, and a shiver walked its way up my spine. I knew before I turned around who'd spoken.

Lord Bressen had arrived in time after all.

Chapter 8

The power that suddenly permeated the room settled on my skin like an oppressive humidity as I turned to face the monster behind me. My jaw fell open, however, as I realized the face of the man who stood in the doorway was not one that would haunt my nightmares, but one that would consume my dreams.

Lord Bressen was easily the most stunning man I'd ever seen. He looked about Jaylan's age, if not slightly older, but he had a warrior's physique like Samhail. His short hair was night-black, and he had the faintest shadow of black stubble covering his sharp jaw in a way that only enhanced what was already an unbelievably beautiful face.

His presence was more than his beauty, though. Both the way he stood, confident and graceful, and the deceptively disarming expression on his face spoke of a dominance beyond the prodigious mind powers he possessed. His allure nearly pulled me toward him, even from across the chamber, and I swallowed down my disquiet at how easily I might have succumbed to that tug if it had come from anyone else but the Nemesis Incarnate.

Something churned around the lord, and I narrowed my gaze to bring it into focus. A dark aura or halo encircled his body, but whenever I tried to concentrate on it, the halo dissipated, burning off like fog in the sun. It was as if the halo could only be seen in my periphery, and I soon gave up trying to capture it.

Bressen raised a hand to casually fix the cuff of his impeccably tailored black jacket, and I watched his muscles flex enticingly beneath the fitted fabric. Every move was unhurried, and when he finally lifted his eyes lazily to look across the room, I saw they were a brilliant shade of deep turquoise. They sparked momentarily as he took in the scene, undoubtedly assessing everything he saw, although his expression remained disinterested.

The chamber was perfectly quiet, and I glanced back at Samhail, who was no longer trying to hide his smile. I made a mental note to yell at him later. He could've warned me that the 'monster' I'd so feared was actually the most incredible-looking man in all of Thasia, a title, I realized, I'd given to Samhail himself only a day ago. While Samhail was striking, though, Lord Bressen set a new bar for desirability altogether.

Ursan recovered first from the interruption, drawing my attention back to him. "Bressen," he said, his voice suddenly over-cheerful. "So glad you could join us. We weren't sure when to expect you, so we got started. I'm sure you understand."

Soft footsteps echoed in the chamber, telling me Bressen was approaching.

"On the contrary," Bressen said from somewhere close behind me, "your haste confuses me, Ursan. Our guest looks like she just got off her horse. Surely, we could have given her at least a couple of hours to bathe and rest before calling her down to interrogate her."

I looked down at my clothes. Raina had tried her best to clean me up and brush my hair, but I still bore the signs of traveling. I probably looked better than I smelled, and my face flushed with embarrassment.

"This is hardly an interrogation," Jerram said. "We just brought the girl here to have a little conversation."

"In my experience," Bressen said, "conversations are better had over dinner than in a throne room."

He was next to me now, but I kept my eyes down, not daring to look at him. I noticed he had an accent, though. There was a smoothness in the way he said his 'A's, and he didn't seem to pronounce the 'R's at the ends of his words. The effect was rather pleasing to the ear.

"We'll bear that in mind for next time," Jerram snapped. "For now, if you're done chasing down escaped prisoners from Revenmyer, perhaps you'd like to join us for this conversation. Your objection to the venue is noted."

"In a minute," Bressen said, waving a dismissive hand. "I'd like to

85

take a closer look at this 'scourge of the land' you brought here."

Scourge of the land? What in the three hells was he talking about?

"Hmmm, not quite what I was picturing," Bressen said, and I could feel his eyes moving over me.

That makes two of us, I thought.

"Based on what the seer told you," Bressen said to the lords, "I was expecting more..." he paused to look me over again, "more horns."

My head snapped to him, but he was walking around me now.

"Or at least a tail," he added from behind me. "So disappointing."

My face flushed even redder as I realized he was looking at my ass.

"My apologies for not being the monster you expected, my lord," I said through my teeth.

The words, full of sarcasm, were out before I could stop them, and I closed my eyes as I prayed to the Protector I wouldn't end up in a dungeon after all. There was silence as I held my breath.

"You're forgiven, my dear," Bressen said, amusement in his voice. "We can't always live up to the expectations of others."

I felt his presence behind me as he stepped closer and leaned in so only I could hear his next words. "I suspect, after all, I'm not quite the monster you were expecting either."

I stiffened and felt the color drain from my face. If he'd been reading my mind, I hoped he didn't know that my first thought had been how stunning he was, and I flushed with embarrassment again.

Bressen pulled back, and I caught a whiff of musk and...hot cinnamon. I closed my eyes as the scent jarred something in me I couldn't quite wrap my mind around.

"If you're done now, Bressen," Jerram said in irritation, "we'd like to get on with this."

Bressen finished his circuit and stood before me.

"Is this necessary?" he asked in a bored voice. "She doesn't look like she's here to eradicate us."

My head snapped up again, and Bressen's turquoise eyes locked onto mine. He started in surprise for a second before his eyes narrowed, and he stepped toward me. I tried to lower my head, but he caught my chin and forced my face up to his. His eyes were even more beautiful up close, and I swallowed as I froze under his gaze.

I hadn't realized how tall he was. Not as tall as Samhail, of course, but he surely topped Jerram and Ursan. I also couldn't help noticing the small dimple in the center of his chin, and I had to tamp down the inexplicable desire to run my finger over it.

"Bressen?" Ursan asked.

"Yes, she has unusual eyes," Jerram snapped. "Let's get on with this already."

"So unusual," Bressen murmured, more to himself than anyone. "So...uncommon."

"Bressen!" Jerram yelled, his patience clearly gone.

Bressen released my face and whirled to head toward his seat on the dais. He sat down, crossed his legs, and leaned back looking bored.

I glanced up at Samhail. He looked serious and was watching me intently. I shot him a look I hoped told him he had some explaining to do, but he just raised an eyebrow.

"Well, now that we're all here," Ursan said, "let's get started with this, uh, conversation." His smile didn't reach his eyes as he turned to me. "Do you know why you were invited here?"

"No," I said, then added despite myself, "and with all due respect, my lord, it feels as though I was ordered here today, not invited."

I had no idea where I pulled the temerity to say that to him, and I regretted the words as soon as they were out of my mouth. Indeed, Jerram and Ursan looked taken aback, although Bressen was smirking.

I looked away from Bressen quickly. I was so confused. I'd been expecting a cold, cruel monster, a man aged before his time by malice. Instead, I'd gotten a beautiful, young lord – arrogant and mocking for sure – but seemingly not without some empathy.

Ursan shook off his shock first. "My apologies if you were given the wrong impression about this visit. Samhail can have that effect on people."

I wondered how Samhail felt about being blamed for my supposedly mistaken belief that I'd been forced here today, but his expression was neutral.

"In any case," Ursan went on, "you came to our attention about a week ago when you used some rather powerful magic. One of our seers in the Priory sensed your power and had a vision about you. That vision was…concerning, to say the least."

I blinked. "Concerning, my lord? In what way?"

"We were hoping you might be able to shed some light on that," Jerram said. "The seer wasn't able to get a clear picture of what was happening toward the end. She only sensed great power and great destruction."

I gaped at him. "Destruction?" I asked incredulously. "From me?"

"Yes," Jerram confirmed.

"The seer's vision showed two empty Triumvirate seats, but she couldn't tell which two," Ursan said.

I let his words sink in before my eyes widened. I stepped back unconsciously, and Jerram and Ursan both sat up straighter as if ready to chase me. Bressen watched me closely, but he hadn't so much as shifted in his chair thus far.

"So you think…" I said as I tried to wrap my mind around this revelation, "You think I'm here to…destroy the Triumvirate?"

Jerram nodded, but Ursan cut in quickly, "Perhaps not on purpose, but yes. The vision suggested as much."

I couldn't seem to close my mouth as I glanced over to see if Bressen agreed, but his face gave away nothing. Of the three Triumvirate lords, he had the least reason to fear me. If he had any suspicions that I was a threat to him, I'd be dead before I could blink.

My blood chilled in my veins. I had to clear my mind of any thoughts that might seem at all threatening, or I wouldn't leave this chamber alive. I tried to make my mind a blank, to fill it with nothing but blackness, but panic made my thoughts race instead.

I felt a prickle at the back of my neck and redoubled my efforts to block out my thoughts. Something hard and impenetrable like a wall slid up in my mind, and I exhaled in relief. Movement from Bressen caught my eye as he sat forward and frowned at me.

I tried to think back to what I'd heard about the Triumvirate lords and their powers. Ursan was a shapeshifter. He could take the form of any animal, and it was rumored he could control animals as well, but I only knew this because Ursan was our lord in Fernweh.

Likewise, I only knew about Bressen's powers because they were so infamous. He was one of the most powerful Triumvirate lords to ever exist, and many wondered secretly why he hadn't yet killed Ursan and Jerram to take control of Thasia for himself.

Jerram was the biggest unknown. He had to have powers because Triumvirate lords were always perimortal, but I couldn't recall if I'd ever heard what they were.

All of this flitted through my mind as I realized these three powerful men thought I was a threat to destroy them, whether purposely or accidentally. It was beyond ludicrous, and I needed to make them understand that.

"My lords," I said, "I can assure you I'm absolutely no threat to any of you whatsoever."

Jerram smiled wryly. "We'd like to believe you, but we can't just take your word."

"Then tell me what I need to do to convince you," I said, turning to him. "I'll do anything I can to prove I'm no one of concern."

The fear in my voice seemed to make Ursan and Jerram more comfortable, but Bressen still frowned at me. He remained leaning forward in his seat with his chin propped up on one hand, and I wished he would stop looking at me like that. There was something unnerving in his stare, and the irony that this was how others felt under my own gaze wasn't lost on me.

"Tell us what happened a week ago," Jerram suggested.

"A week ago?" I asked, my mind suddenly blank. "With the bear!" I said, remembering.

Both Jerram and Bressen glanced at Ursan at my mention of the bear, and I recalled again that Ursan had a special affinity for animals. I paused to look at him, but his face betrayed no anger. "Go on," he urged me instead.

I launched into my tale. When I was done, I looked at the three lords, but none of them gave anything away. "It was a fluke occurrence," I said when they'd all been quiet for almost a full minute. "I've never done anything like that before, and I'm unlikely to do it again. You have nothing to worry about from me."

"Unfortunately, my dear girl," Ursan said, "that's not really true."

My heart fell.

"To conjure fire and water is a fairly common power, at least among elementals," Ursan continued. "The elements can be wielded as weapons easily enough to kill, but to kill another living thing by changing it into the element itself...well, that's something I don't think I've ever seen."

I looked at each of the lords again, but none of them offered anything else.

"What does that mean?" I asked.

"It means we'll need to look into this some more," Jerram said, "and while we do that, you'll need to stay here."

I swayed on my feet, wishing I had something to grab onto. I didn't want to stay here. I couldn't spend every day wondering if the lords would find some evidence to determine I was a threat to them and decide to imprison or kill me.

"Please," I said in a hoarse whisper, "just let me go home, and I promise I'll never trouble you again."

Jerram shook his head. "That's not possible."

My knees buckled then, and I sank to the floor, breathing hard. Tears threatened in my eyes, but I wouldn't give the lords the satisfaction of seeing me cry.

Jerram and Ursan rose to their feet when I fell but didn't attempt to approach me. Bressen watched me as usual but didn't leave his seat.

I looked to Samhail with a silent plea for help. He'd uncrossed his arms and looked as though he wanted to come to me, but I assumed he wouldn't do anything without permission from the lords.

"Perhaps that's enough for now," Ursan said. "My girl, I promise you'll be taken care of while you're here. There's no need to go to pieces just yet."

Another "just yet," I thought as my head sagged. My body felt so heavy right now.

"Samhail," Ursan said, "would you take Cyra back to her chambers so she can rest and freshen up after her long journey?" His tone was kind, and I glared up at him from the floor.

"We can all talk more at dinner tonight," Jerram offered. "Cyra, you'll join us tonight as our honored guest."

I gave Jerram the same glare I'd given Ursan. Was he serious? Honored guest at a dinner when I was essentially a prisoner here?

Samhail arrived at my side a moment later and lifted me into his arms. "You'll be fine," he murmured to me. "Just breathe."

I put an arm around his neck and laid my head on his shoulder. I didn't trust myself to speak, but I was grateful for his help as he carried me to my room.

Raina was there when Samhail opened the door and brought me inside. She cried out at seeing me unable to stand under my own power and rushed over to check on me despite her wariness of Samhail.

"Draw a bath," Samhail told her. "Cyra should clean up and take a nap. The lords will expect her at dinner tonight at seven o'clock."

I shook my head against his shoulder. "No. No dinner."

Samhail set me down on my feet but held onto me to be sure I could stand. My legs felt steadier, but I was in no mood to indulge the lords that were holding me against my will.

Samhail grabbed my shoulders and shook me gently. I winced a little as his hand pressed the place the bear scratched me, and he loosened his grip.

"Look at me," he ordered. "I know you want to go home, but you need to stop letting the lords think you're afraid of them."

"I *am* afraid of them."

Samhail shook his head and smiled. "No, you're not. I saw the looks you gave Jerram and Ursan. You're angry at them, but you're away from home and unsure of yourself."

He hadn't mentioned Bressen, and that reminded me I had a bone to pick with him. I threw off his hands and narrowed my eyes. "Why didn't you tell me Lord Bressen was-"

I stopped, not sure how to finish that thought as Samhail raised a brow at me and smirked.

"Why didn't I tell you he was young and attractive?" he finished for me with amusement.

I hit my fist on his chest. "You let me believe he was a heinous old monster."

"How was I supposed to know that's what you thought?" Samhail asked innocently.

I had the urge to slap the grin off his face, but he was the only person I almost trusted right now, and I couldn't afford to alienate potential allies.

"You're an ass," I said, but there was no anger in my voice.

"Would you have believed me if I'd told you he wasn't a monster?"

"Probably not," I admitted, "but you could have at least tried to convince me."

"Duly noted."

I shook my head. "I just can't believe that's the man I've heard all those tales about. Jaylan and Brix will never believe it when I tell them."

If I ever got to tell them, I thought.

"Make no mistake," Samhail said, "Bressen is a very powerful lord, and everything I told you about his abilities and the things he's done is true. He's still extremely dangerous. He's just not the demon the rumors make him out to be." He glanced over my shoulder. "It looks like your bath is ready."

I turned to see Raina waiting for me at the threshold of the bathing chamber.

"I'll be back before seven o'clock to bring you to dinner," Samhail said. "Get some rest and come down prepared to show the lords you're not so easily cowed."

"Thank you," I said, infusing the words with my deepest gratitude.

He smiled and gave me a quick nod before leaving.

I turned to Raina. "I need a look for dinner that makes the lords of the Triumvirate tremble before me. Any ideas?"

Raina grinned roguishly at me. "I think I can make that happen, my lady."

Chapter 9

By the time Raina helped me bathe and wash my hair, I could only nap for an hour before it was time to get ready for dinner. My saddlebags arrived earlier, and I was able to retrieve the one gown I'd brought with me. It was a little wrinkled, but Raina brought it somewhere to be ironed, and she returned with it just in time.

She also had several emerald-encrusted hair combs and an emerald pendant in hand. I gaped at her when she presented them to me, but Raina assured me the Citadel had a vault full of jewelry available for guests to borrow. She said the Citadel clothiers had been given my size and would be creating an entire wardrobe of clothes I could use while I was here.

I wasn't sure how they'd gotten my size, since no one took my measurements, but I'd already noticed things worked differently here. There was a subtle magic that pervaded the fortress and lubricated its inner workings. For one, my balcony doors were open, yet there seemed to be an invisible barrier that kept the chilly outdoor air from coming inside.

It was foreign for me to sit in a chair and let Raina fix my hair and put on a bit of makeup – which I'd never used before – but I couldn't argue with the results. I hardly recognized myself when she finished. Whatever she'd done around my eyes made them blaze in a way that was even more prominent than usual. She'd pulled my hair up elegantly and held it there with the jeweled combs, but a few dark tendrils fell around my face to make the coiffeur less austere.

I slipped into my gown a few minutes before Samhail was due to arrive. The dress was a deep emerald silk with a slightly flared skirt that fell to the floor. It had long sleeves, but it was cut across the top so my shoulders and neck were bare. I'd seen it in a shop window one day and hadn't been able to take my eyes off it. I spent an outrageous amount of money on it and quickly hid it in the back of my closet so

Jaylan didn't see it. He would've been annoyed to know how much I paid for it, but I rarely bought anything frivolous and decided to treat myself with the coin I'd saved up. I imagined using it as my wedding dress someday, but the gown had sat unworn thus far. That I was wearing it to have dinner with the lords of the Triumvirate at the Citadel was something I never could've foreseen.

I looked at myself in the mirror when Raina finished fastening the buttons at my back but frowned as I saw the pink slashes across my shoulder. I'd forgotten about the claw marks from the bear. The marks on my arm were hidden under the sleeve of the dress, but the ones on my shoulder were still very noticeable.

"I can't wear this," I said to Raina.

"Why not?" she asked. "You look beautiful in this color, my lady."

"My scars." I ran a hand over them. "I forgot they'd show."

Raina looked at the marks but shook her head. "This is why you're here, no? You killed the bear that did this?"

I was surprised she knew that, but I'd heard the most well-informed people in any great household were always the servants, as they tended to hear everything.

"Yes, but it was an accident," I answered.

Raina shook her head. "You were attacked, and those scars are evidence that you survived. Don't hide them. Wear them proudly, especially in front of the lords."

"They already think I'm a threat. Maybe I shouldn't reinforce that."

"As you said, they already think you're a threat," she argued. "Now make them believe it. You asked me to give you a look that would make them tremble." Raina pointed to the marks. "This is it."

I looked at myself in the mirror again. In a strange way, the scars were almost ornamental, like a tattoo across my shoulder and down one collar bone. Maybe Raina was right and I needed to stop trying to convince the lords I wasn't a threat and start trying to convince them I was. In my experience, having no power rarely made a person safe from someone with power. It only made them an easier target.

Convincing these lords I was powerless would only make it easier for them to control me. I needed to do the opposite.

"Alright," I said. "You're right."

Raina smiled as a knock sounded at the door. She answered it and quickly stepped out of the way as Samhail strode in.

He looked me up and down appreciatively, and I saw his eyes linger on the claw marks. He inclined his head in approval. "Are you ready?"

"Lead the way," I said.

He extended an arm, and I hooked my own through his. He was wearing a black jacket and black pants as usual, but the clothes were much finer than the ones he'd worn for traveling. The shirt under his fitted jacket was a deep royal blue that made his white hair show all the brighter, and his swords and armor were absent for once.

According to Raina, each of the lords had their own private dining room in their wing, but when they were all in residence, they ate in the main dining room of the central building to facilitate discussions and cooperation. All the lords were there when Samhail and I arrived, although no one was seated yet.

The room was larger than I pictured, as everything here seemed to be. A long table that seated twelve stood in the center of the room, while another table sat empty against one wall. The opposite wall held a row of windows that would let in the morning sun, but the table was lit now by several candelabras on top of it and three huge crystal chandeliers above it. The room seemed brighter than it should've been, though, more evidence of the magic that kept the Citadel running.

Ursan stood with a woman who was about his height and had amber eyes with hair to match. I recalled now that he was married, but I couldn't remember the lady's name. I should've known something like that, but news from Gendris rarely reached us in the outer lands, so if I ever knew her name, it had long since slipped my mind.

All heads turned when Samhail and I entered, and what little conversation there had been stopped. Jerram gaped at me while Ursan and the woman looked surprised. Bressen glanced at me with seeming indifference but then did a doubletake and looked back. His eyes ran boldly up my body and lingered on the claw marks at my shoulder. His eyes met mine briefly before he turned away again, and something fluttered in my stomach at what I thought I saw there.

"Ah, my lady," Ursan said coming over to meet me and Samhail. I noted I was now 'my lady' and not 'my dear' or 'my girl' as I'd been earlier that day.

Ursan grabbed my hand before I realized what he intended and patted it as if he was consoling me after some great loss. I resisted the urge to pull it back.

"I hope you're feeling better," he said, releasing me. "You gave us a fright earlier."

I straightened my shoulders. "Much better, my lord. Thank you."

He glanced at the claw marks, seeming a bit taken aback that I displayed them so openly, but he recovered quickly. "Let me introduce you to my wife. This is Lady Glenora."

The woman stepped forward and extended a hand to me. I had no idea what the protocol was, and I suddenly wished I'd asked Raina more questions about what was expected of me. I took a chance and curtsied to the woman, then took her hand. I wasn't sure if I was supposed to kiss it, but she clasped the hand I offered and gave it a quick shake.

"It's so nice to meet you...Cyra, is it?" Glenora said.

"Yes, my lady."

"Now that everyone is here, shall we take our seats?" Ursan said to the room at large.

Samhail led me to a seat midway down the table and took a place opposite me while everyone else filled in closer to the end. As soon as everyone was in place, a side door to the kitchen opened, and servants came in with trays of food. They made their way around the table adding items to everyone's plates, and I watched in awe as mine was filled with roasted duck in a citrus rosemary sauce, seasoned potatoes, green beans with herbed butter, a tender cut of beef, wild rice, and salad garnished with nuts and fruits and dressed with some kind of vinaigrette.

I'd never seen this much food in my life, and I hoped they didn't expect me to finish everything. Another servant poured wine, and my eyes widened when he got to Jerram.

"That's my wine," I blurted out, recognizing the bottle.

Everyone looked at me, and I flushed with embarrassment yet again.

"There'll be enough wine to go around, Cyra," Jerram said, "but if you need some right now..." He held out his glass for me to take.

"No, my lord," I said quickly. "My apologies. I just recognized the bottle. That wine was made at my vineyard, the one I share with my brothers."

Everyone looked at the bottle, and the servant helpfully held it out to the room.

"You made this wine?" Jerram said, holding up his glass.

"Yes, my lord. Again, my apologies for causing a stir. I just didn't expect to see a bottle of it here."

"We've been serving it for a while now at the Citadel," Ursan said. "It's one of my favorites, but I had no idea this was your vineyard."

The servant came around with the bottle, and I held up my glass for him to fill. I took a sip of the wine and was relieved to find it tasted as good as I'd hoped. At least our vineyard was well-represented.

"Cyra," Ursan said drawing my attention, and I noticed he had no meat on his plate. "You'll visit the Priory tomorrow morning to meet with the seer who had the vision about you. We hope she'll be able to tell us something else if she can meet you in person."

I paused mid-chew. I wasn't sure if that sounded like a good idea or not.

"Samhail will go in my place," Bressen said before I could respond. "Something came up in Hiraeth, and I need to go back again."

"Another escape from Revenmyer?" Jerram asked with gleeful condemnation. "You really have lost your grip on that place, haven't you." He seemed to take satisfaction in the idea.

"I do need to look into something at Revenmyer," Bressen said, "but I'm not at liberty to share that business with you, Jerram. Just rest assured I have everything in hand."

Jerram scoffed. "If you say so. In any case, there's no need for Samhail to go to the Priory. Ursan and I can fill you in when you return."

"I'd prefer to have Samhail go," Bressen said. "He's not connected to the seer's vision, so he'll provide me with an unbiased perspective on what she says."

Jerram waved a dismissive hand. "Suit yourself."

Bressen grinned. "I always do."

"Cyra," Glenora cut in before Jerram could say anything else. "Will you join me for tea in our solarium tomorrow after your visit to the Priory? It's rare that I get any female company here at the Citadel."

"I'd be honored, my lady," I said, a little surprised.

"Excellent," Glenora said. "I'll send someone to escort you when you return."

"You're not going to the Priory?" I asked her. The idea of having this genial woman there had momentarily soothed my anxiety, but apparently that wasn't the plan.

Glenora pulled a tight smile onto her lips. "There's no need for me to be involved in Triumvirate business," she said, and I got the sense she was repeating something she'd been told. Indeed, Ursan was focused on his plate all of a sudden.

"We've also decided to host a ball in your honor in a couple weeks," Jerram said cheerfully.

I paused with my fork halfway to my mouth and looked around the table, but only Jerram and Ursan seemed excited about this. Glenora held the same tight smile on her face, and Bressen and Samhail both looked annoyed by the news.

"A ball, my lord?" I asked.

"Word has gotten around Callanus about the vision the seer had, and there's been some…unease in the city about it," Ursan explained. "No one knows any of the details, of course, just that it contained potentially dire news. Likewise, the gossip mills learned of your arrival, so the city has been speculating wildly about who you are and why you're here."

"The ball will introduce you and demonstrate to everyone that there's nothing to worry about," Jerram said.

I had the urge to remind them that they themselves hadn't yet determined there was nothing to worry about, but I kept silent.

"It's an opportunity to show the city you're cooperating with us, and that you're just a simple woman and not some harbinger of destruction," Ursan said, his tone lighthearted.

"It's an opportunity," Bressen cut in dryly, "to put the power and authority of the Triumvirate on display and cow the populace."

"That's cynical, and not at all true," Ursan admonished him.

"Then you won't mind if I don't attend," Bressen drawled.

Ursan looked alarmed, and Jerram looked angry.

"You'll come," Jerram spat out, "because we need to present a united front, and unfortunately that includes you."

Bressen leaned forward to look Jerram in the eye.

"You need me to come," he said, his voice harsh, "because my presence will stoke fear in the guests, and you want them to be afraid."

"Not true," Ursan insisted, shaking his head, but his words lacked conviction.

Bressen clearly knew people feared him, and I wasn't sure whether it was arrogance or brutal honesty on his part to state it so baldly. Perhaps both.

"Gentlemen," Glenora cut in, her annoyance apparent, "if I'm going to spend the next couple weeks planning a lavish ball to entertain Thasia's elite, then everyone is coming."

Glenora leveled her gaze on Bressen as if daring him to contradict her. He didn't, but instead sat back in his chair as he and Jerram continued to glare at each other.

"My apologies for these two," Ursan said, trying to laugh off the obvious animosity between the lords. "It's to be expected when you put two headstrong men together, I suppose."

Bressen rolled his eyes while Jerram continued to stare daggers at him. I glanced over at Samhail, but he was calmly eating and had barely looked up from his plate the entire time.

"I have two brothers," I told Ursan with a weak smile. "This isn't entirely new to me."

That was an exaggeration. Jaylan and Brix fought occasionally, but not with the rancor Jerram and Bressen clearly had for each other. Bressen's eyes flicked briefly to me, but Jerram ignored my comment and went back to eating.

"Then it's settled," Glenora said. "Everyone will be there and on their best behavior."

I suspected she was one of a small handful of people who could get away with talking to the lords like that.

In any case, it appeared that Bressen didn't regularly leave a path of dead bodies in his wake, as some people in Fernweh claimed. Despite myself, I was fascinated by him. I hadn't understood why Samhail was intent on making sure Bressen was at my first meeting with the Triumvirate, but I did now. Jerram and Ursan seemed to side together often, and Bressen was the counterbalance to their alliance. Samhail had likely been afraid they might coerce me into doing what they wanted, and he knew Bressen's presence would make that harder.

Whether that was because Bressen was genuinely a good person under all his arrogance and intimidation, or whether it was simply because he enjoyed frustrating Jerram for the hell of it, I wasn't entirely sure. Again, perhaps both.

An hour later, Samhail escorted me back to my room as I tried not to think about how full I was. I wasn't used to so much choice, so I'd overdone it a little. I'd also probably drank a little more wine than I should've, and I felt a lightness in my limbs as we walked.

"Are those dinners always so tense?" I asked Samhail when we were out of earshot.

"Jerram and Bressen have never gotten along, but they usually pretend to tolerate each other better than that," he said. "I suspect everyone is a little more on-edge than normal."

"You were quiet at dinner."

Samhail grunted. "Jerram objects to my presence at meals, so I don't generally say anything unless it's necessary."

I frowned. "Why does he object?"

"I'm not one of the lords, for one. It also doesn't help that Bressen and I have known each other a long time and are friends."

I looked at him in surprise. Samhail clearly had a lot of respect for Bressen and knew him well, but hearing him describe them as friends caught me off-guard.

We arrived at my door, and I faced Samhail. "What should I expect tomorrow?"

"Expect to be tested in some way. Beyond that, I'm not sure."

I exhaled deeply. "Thank you for all your help today. I'm not sure I would've made it through everything without you."

"You would've been fine. You're stronger than you give yourself credit for."

Samhail reached up to run his fingers gently over the claw marks on my shoulder. He trailed them down along my collarbone, and gooseflesh rose on my arms under the sleeves of my dress. My breasts peaked, and I wondered if he was thinking about our kiss in the Soundless Woods, as I now was. Part of me wanted to grab his hand and pull him into my room, but another part held back.

Samhail leaned in and reached down near my waist. My body tipped forward of its own accord, and I tensed in anticipation as I waited for him to pull me against him. Instead, I heard the handle click, and my door swung open behind me.

"Get some sleep. You've had a long day," he said, his voice husky.

I swallowed and backed into the room. "Goodnight," I said.

I watched him go as he headed down the hall and wondered where his room was. I decided it was better if I didn't know.

He was right about one thing. I'd already been through more in the last week than I had in the rest of my life, and I'd survived it all so far. Hopefully tomorrow would bring more answers, and I'd be on my way home soon.

Chapter 10

I met Jerram, Ursan, and Samhail the next morning in the rotunda for our trip to the Priory, which was the main house of worship in Callanus where the priests and priestesses who served the Trinity lived and worked. At least, that's what Raina told me.

We had no equivalent to the Priory in the outer lands. Worship in Fernweh happened informally and on an as-needed basis, mostly in the privacy of one's own home. There were no designated temples or areas where people gathered as a group to worship the Trinity the way people in larger cities did, and we didn't use priests or priestesses to guide our devotions.

The Priory wasn't far from the Citadel, and I rode in the Triumvirate's covered carriage with Jerram and Ursan while Samhail followed on his horse. Some people gathered in the streets to watch us pass. Most waved, and I got the impression the Triumvirate was either well-liked or well-feared in Callanus.

I was glad Samhail was with us. I knew his allegiance was to the Triumvirate, but I still trusted him to watch out for me. He was wearing his swords again today, although I wasn't sure whether to feel worried or reassured by that.

The Priory loomed large over the city as we approached. It was an impressive building of white marble, even larger than the Citadel, with a domed roof and three tall minarets that rose up around it. Stone gargoyles sat vigil every twenty feet or so along the parapets of the building at the roofline and also at the tops of the minarets. Gardens surrounded the Priory, and those were separated from the city proper by a fifteen-foot wall of the same white marble.

The gardens and the Priory itself were usually open to anyone, but I learned they'd be closed to the public in another couple weeks for the Harmilan, a sacred holiday throughout most of Thasia. At that time, only a select number of people would be allowed in.

I'd heard of the Harmilan before but didn't know much about it. Its celebration was another practice that hadn't survived in the outer lands, and I wondered if I would even still be here by then.

We exited the carriage and climbed the wide stairs up to the temple with Samhail right behind us. A priest in light green robes waited for us at the top. He appeared to be in his thirties, and his light brown hair was pulled back into a short ponytail at his nape. He gave the lords each a low bow before he turned and led us into the building.

We passed straight through the foyer, and the priest led us into the main worship hall. The perfectly round room was made of the same white marble, and oil lamps flickered all around the space. There was a dais toward the center of the room, and a large marble altar stood at the back. Stone tiers of seating rose up the sides about two-thirds of the way around the hall, and three giant stone statues nearly reached the vaulted ceiling around the main dais.

The statues were roughly carved and appeared neither male nor female. One statue cupped its hands and extended them outward, as if offering a gift. Fire burned in the outstretched hands as if there was a basin of oil there, and I wondered how the priests or priestesses got up to refill it. Another statue stood with a shield in one hand and sword in the other. The last wore a hood and held a set of scales. I was fairly sure the statues represented the Creator, the Protector, and the Nemesis respectively.

The priest led us straight to the dais where a young woman in light blue robes waited for us. She was short and slight with shining red hair that fell all the way down her back, and her wide blue eyes held a perpetual look of mild surprise.

When we'd all gathered on the dais, the priest spoke to Ursan and Jerram. "Welcome back, my lords. You may remember me from our first meeting. I'm Lorkin, and I'm sure you remember Jemma." He motioned to the woman.

"Yes, of course," Ursan said, nodding to Lorkin and Jemma. He turned to me and Samhail. "This is Samhail. He serves the Citadel for important business, and this is Cyra of Fernweh. We believe she's the perimortal Jemma saw in her vision."

I glanced at Ursan and frowned. It sounded like they weren't sure I was the woman in the vision, and I wondered for the first time how they'd figured out who I was. Samhail had asked for 'the elemental' when I first met him, I realized, so he'd only had a vague sense of who he was sent to find.

"Is Lord Bressen not here?" Jemma asked timidly.

"No," Jerram snapped. "Lord Bressen has once again decided he has more important things to attend to than the future of the Triumvirate and the welfare of this city."

Jemma shrank even further into herself, and I couldn't help feeling sorry for her, even if she was the reason I'd been dragged here from my home.

"Well then, let's proceed," Lorkin said. "Jemma, please see if you can learn anything else about the vision."

Jemma nodded and walked toward me. She reached out a hand, but I pulled back from her, and she stopped, looking startled.

"What's she doing?" I asked warily.

"My apologies," Lorkin said. "I should've explained. Jemma is one of our more accomplished seers, but even the best seers sometimes have trouble understanding the images in their visions."

Lorkin gave Jemma an encouraging look, as if he knew she needed the extra assurance.

"When a vision is too vague," he went on, "a seer can sometimes clarify details if they come in contact with the person or object from their vision. Jemma was going to touch you to see if anything becomes clearer for her. Will you allow that?"

Ursan and Jerram looked at me eagerly. Samhail's face was passive, but he gave me the barest nod.

"Fine," I said and stepped carefully back toward Jemma.

Jemma moved forward again to place her hand on my cheek, and I flinched at how cold her fingers were. For a moment, nothing happened. Then I sucked in a breath as the chill from Jemma's hand pervaded my entire body and my vision went dark. The bright white marble of the Priory disappeared, and I was back in our vineyard on the morning of the bear attack, the sun still too far below the horizon to provide any light.

I watched from outside myself as the bear roared at me while I hit it with water and waved my flames at it. I couldn't hear anything, but I could just barely see myself fighting with the bear in the darkness. I knew it was me, but I could see how the darkness and the slight fuzziness of the vision made it hard for Jemma to give the lords a good description of me.

The attack seemed to pass in a blur until power swelled in my chest and the bear froze in mid-roar. I felt the exact moment the animal's life ended – pinched out like the flame of a candle – and my chest clenched painfully. I hadn't felt the bear's death at the time, but I felt it now, and the sudden emptiness of something that was there one second and then gone the next nearly brought me to my knees.

As my vision focused again and I looked at myself through the distance of Jemma's eyes, I realized just how close the bear's jaws had come to my neck. Had my power not surged when it did, it would've only been a second or two more before my brothers found me with my throat ripped out.

Other images flashed past me then, but most were too quick to see. The blood was apparent enough, though, and I saw pools of it on the ground along with…arms. I saw Samhail slash off the arms of the highwayman before the images rushed by again giving me only hints of what they were. Tigers…two glowing red embers in the dark …splashing water…someone's lips grazing my neck…me wielding a sword against Samhail…my own eyes gazing back at me…and something huge and gray.

Finally, three large thrones emerged in the vision, two empty and one occupied by a shadowy figure. Nothing about the vision was very clear, and this part was even less so. The thrones swirled around, making it impossible to determine who the figure was, although they didn't look much like the Triumvirate seats I'd seen in the Great Chamber anyway.

Cold tendrils wrapped around my legs as I tried to take in the vision, and I jerked back in alarm. I felt Jemma's own shock, then, as if she'd just realized I was there with her. A face materialized through the darkness, but it disappeared an instant later as my connection to Jemma was suddenly severed. I blinked, trying to reshape the contours of the face in my memory, but it was gone. I looked at Jemma as the Priory came back into focus, and she stared back at me in terror. I had the sense she'd broken off the vision prematurely before the face we'd seen could be fully revealed.

"What?" Ursan asked urgently, looking between the two of us. "What did you see?"

Jemma and I continued to stare at each other until she finally shook her head and stepped away from me. "There's nothing new," she said. "I saw the same thing as before."

I'd been holding my breath, and I exhaled. Jemma hadn't seen anything that might confirm I was a threat to the Triumvirate. Unfortunately, she also hadn't seen anything that would convince them to let me go back home.

"Go through it again now that the vision is fresh in your mind," Ursan said.

Jemma looked panicked, but she dutifully recounted everything we'd seen. Or almost everything. She left out any mention of the face at the end.

Other than the beginning, very little of the vision made sense to me, particularly the part where I saw myself fighting Samhail with a sword. I didn't ever picture something like that happening, so I was inclined to take the whole thing with a grain of salt.

"There's still only one lord left?" Ursan urged her.

Jemma nodded. "Two of the three thrones stand empty at the end, but I still can't tell which ones. The person seated there is in shadow."

"Look harder," Jerram said with annoyance.

Jemma shook her head. "I can't. The last thing I saw is the woman, but the light is too bright. I can't see her face."

Jerram and Ursan exchanged glances, and from the look that passed between them, the information about the woman wasn't something Jemma shared the first time around. Indeed, I hadn't seen any woman when the vision cut off, so I wondered if Jemma must have seen her the first time.

"What woman?" Jerram asked, confirming my suspicion. "You didn't mention a woman the first time around."

Jemma's eyes widened, and she looked between the two lords as her mouth opened and closed without words. "I'm sure I must have mentioned a woman," she said, her voice quavering.

"You didn't," Ursan said, and even he sounded angry for once.

"I…I'm sorry, my lords," Jemma stammered. "The images rush by quickly sometimes. It's hard to catch everything. She's just a faceless form bathed in light."

All eyes turned to me, and my gaze darted to each of them in turn.

"You can't possibly think it's me," I said incredulously.

"Why not?" Jerram asked. "It's you that Jemma sees at the beginning of the vision. Why couldn't it be you at the end?"

My mouth opened and closed as Jemma's had while I searched for an answer. I could come up with nothing, so I closed my mouth again.

"Is there anything else?" Ursan asked Jemma.

"No, that's everything."

"Are you sure this time?" Jerram snapped, and Jemma flinched.

"Yes, my lord," she said, lowering her eyes.

"We should talk in private for a moment," Ursan said to Lorkin.

"Of course, my lord," Lorkin said.

"Cyra, will you excuse us a moment please?" Ursan said.

I nodded, and Ursan, Jerram, and Lorkin turned to go.

"Come, Jemma," Lorkin said to her, and she followed as well.

"Samhail, you might as well come too so you can keep Bressen in the loop," Ursan said.

Samhail looked reluctant to leave me alone, but he turned to follow the others out, and I was left in the giant chamber by myself. Clearly, I was the only person not meant to hear their conversation, and I wondered why they hadn't just asked me to step out for a moment rather than leaving themselves.

I sat on one of the bottom tiers of the amphitheater. The Nemesis statue stood across from me, and I looked at its oddly passive face and then to the scales in its hands. The Nemesis was usually seen as a dark force in the Trinity, an avenger and a punisher. People prayed to the Nemesis for vengeance when they'd been wronged, but something about that never seemed right to me. The Nemesis's scales suggested balance, and vengeance hardly seemed a way to maintain balance. Punishment was different than vengeance, and the Nemesis's purpose was to maintain order, not exact retribution. Or so I felt.

For that matter, the Nemesis always seemed like the most equitable god of the Trinity. The gifts of the Creator were often distributed unequally if not outright arbitrarily. Two women might pray to the Creator for a child, but only one might become pregnant. Two humans could be born, both given the gift of life, but one might be born mortal or sickly and live only a relatively short time. The other might be born a perimortal and enjoy a significantly longer life, made easier by the gift of magical powers.

So too did the Protector's blessings seem fickle. Everyone prayed to the Protector to watch over them and theirs, but the Protector seemed to pick and choose whose prayers to answer.

During the Great Flu, Jaylan, Brix, and I had prayed daily to the Protector to spare our parents when they'd become sick, but the Protector ignored our pleas and surrendered our parents to the Nemesis nonetheless. Meanwhile, plenty of others in Fernweh, who — gods forgive me – were less worthy, lived through the blight.

Likewise, Samhail and I had been ambushed in the forest by a band of highwaymen ten times our number and come out unscathed. Yet how many other travelers had those men managed to rob, rape, and kill before Samhail's blades cut them down? How many others had the Protector failed to shepherd safely through those woods?

Only the Nemesis's gift was certain. The Nemesis took everyone to their final rest eventually, and those who didn't pay for their sins in this world paid for them in the next.

I heard a door open somewhere in the hall, but the size of the space made the noise echo, and I couldn't tell where the sound came from. I stood up and looked around.

"Hello?" I called. "Is someone there?"

My answer was a low growl from beside the dais somewhere, and I went still. Then I saw them, and my mouth went dry as I remembered an image from Jemma's vision.

Three giant white tigers padded slowly toward the dais, having come in from a side door at the end of the seats. Their white fur and stripes blended with the white marble and its veins of dark gray so I might have overlooked them if they hadn't been moving.

I gasped and backed away, but drawn by my movement, the tigers looked at me in unison. I froze again, but it was too late. They'd seen me and began to stalk toward me.

"Help," I said, softly at first. I was caught between wanting to scream for help and hoping the tigers would leave me alone if I stayed quiet and still.

"Help!" I yelled louder as they continued to prowl closer, and my voice echoed hauntingly around the room. "Someone help me!"

I knew no one was coming to help, though. Samhail warned me I'd be tested, and that's what this was, perhaps only the first of many.

"Samhail!" I called, my voice rising in panic.

If anyone would come for me, Samhail would, but seconds passed, and not even he came. The tigers circled me, and I looked around, weighing my options. I could run, but they were faster, and I had a feeling the doors to the hall were now locked anyway. Ursan and Jerram wanted me to fight. They wanted to see what I'd do when my life was again on the line. I had a hard time believing Ursan, who didn't even seem to eat meat, would sacrifice these animals if he thought I might be able to kill them, to turn them to earth as I had the bear, but it seemed as though he would. For that matter, Ursan and Jerram were far more confident I could save myself from the tigers than I was, and the chance they were taking with my life made me angry.

Flames flared in my hands, and I willed my magic to make them as big as possible. My heart ached at the idea of hurting these creatures, and the fire sputtered because of it. I had no real hope the flames would ward off the tigers anyway, particularly if Ursan was controlling them, which he must be. When I'd transformed the bear to earth, I'd been pressed up against the ground, bleeding into the dirt. I remembered feeling a oneness with the earth at the time, and I'd just about surrendered myself to the Nemesis when I managed to summon that hitherto untapped power.

Circumstances were very different today, though.

"I can't do it again!" I yelled. I knew they must be watching somewhere.

My yell incensed one of the tigers, and it swiped out at me. I stepped back out of the way just in time and ran through my arsenal in my head. I didn't have much. My fire and water wouldn't get me far, nor would wind. I was also certain I couldn't do the earth trick again, not just physically, but mentally as well.

Running might not get me far, but it was all I could do, all I'd let myself do. I flared my flames to scare the tigers back, and when I saw an opening between them, I dashed through it. Giant claws swiped at me as I ran between two of the tigers and headed for a part of the wall where oil lamps burned in sconces. I pulled one lamp off the wall and splashed the oil across the floor in front of me as the tigers approached. Already burning, the oil blazed into a pool of fire as it spread out along the floor and the flames rolled across its surface.

The tigers pulled back, growling and snarling at the flames, but they didn't fully withdraw, and I saw them trying to find a way around the fire. Normal tigers might have retreated, but, if I was correct and Ursan was in fact controlling them, these wouldn't give up so easily.

I ran to the next sconce and spilled the oil from its basin along the floor as well, trying to keep the wall of fire between me and the tigers. Unfortunately, while the increased surface area of the oil spread the flames out more, the fire burned the fuel much quicker, and the flames were already starting to die down. The tigers inched closer, and I called a soft breeze to fan the flames. They blazed up higher, making the tigers rethink their advance, but only for a moment.

I could make my way around the room like this, dumping oil lamps to keep the tigers at bay, but I'd eventually run out of lamps. Still, there was a door close by, so I ran for the next lamp and dumped its oil on the floor as the tigers stalked me on the outskirts of the flames. I grasped the handle of the door, but as I suspected, it was locked.

A growl sounded behind me, and I whirled to see the fire dying out in one area. The tigers saw their way around the barrier and began to pad toward it.

As the animals came around one side, I fled over the other. I jumped the flames and then sent a small wind back toward them so they flared around the tigers. The animals growled in fear, and I ran for the next door. I yanked the handle, but it too was locked, and I looked back to see I'd only given the tigers an idea when I jumped. All three leapt over the fire and ran for me.

I tried to flee but pulled up short as one of the tigers cut me off, lunging in front of me and swiping out a paw. I pivoted out of the way, but I hadn't been tracking the other tigers, and I spun directly toward a second tiger. I tried to stop my momentum, but it was too late. The second tiger lashed out with its claws, and I felt that familiar white-hot pain as the flesh on my thigh tore open.

I screamed in agony as blood quickly soaked the side of the blue gown I'd just gotten from the Citadel clothier, turning it dark purple. I screamed and crumpled to the floor as my leg gave out. I clamped one hand against my thigh as blood continued to gush through my fingers.

In my other hand, a weak flame flared up. I willed it to flare stronger, but it died out altogether instead.

"I can't do it!" I yelled into the empty hall.

The tigers were closing in now, stirred by the blood pooling on the floor under my leg. One of the tigers moved toward me, and I turned to look it straight in the eye.

"Stop," I said softly. "Please stop."

The tiger paused and regarded me curiously. It cocked its head as if suddenly unsure about what it wanted to do, but the other two tigers were still closing in. I closed my eyes and waited for the next blow, or for those huge teeth to sink into me, but the final stroke never came. I opened my eyes and found all three tigers sitting on their haunches. They'd stopped a few feet away and were staring at me.

The door at the far end of the hall flew open, and several people rushed in. I was light-headed, but I instantly recognized Samhail in the lead. He had Lorkin by the collar of his robes and was dragging the priest alongside him. Next to him, Ursan hurried to keep up.

Ursan waved a hand to the side, and the three tigers stood and retreated back toward the door from where they'd come. Samhail reached me and threw Lorkin down into the space vacated by one of the tigers.

"Heal her now!" he roared at the priest. He pulled one of his swords from its sheath and held it out at Lorkin, who scurried back away from it. "Help her, or I start cutting off limbs."

"Samhail!" Ursan admonished him. "Sheathe that sword immediately!"

Samhail ignored him, continuing to hold the sword out, and Lorkin sprang into action.

"Let me see," Lorkin coaxed, gently pulling my hand from the gushing wound on my leg.

My hand was covered in blood, and I was shaking all over. I laid back across the floor as my body could no longer hold itself upright.

"Cyra!" Samhail hissed from behind Lorkin.

"She'll be fine," Lorkin assured him quickly. "Just stay back and let me work."

Lorkin lifted the hem of my skirt to bare my leg and laid his hands down over the torn flesh. I jolted as I felt some kind of power flow into the wound, something warm that was halfway between pain and relief. I could feel my skin knitting back together, but I stayed down, not wanting to see what was happening.

Samhail's expression was darker than I'd ever seen it, and I knew he was beyond furious. His sword still hung in his hand at his side. He'd lowered it, but in defiance of Ursan, he hadn't yet sheathed it.

Ursan watched Lorkin work with concern, and I wondered if he hadn't meant for the tiger to wound me as badly as it did. Jerram had come in as well, and he looked annoyed, as he often did. He leveled a dark scowl at the back of Samhail's head.

"That should do it," Lorkin said finally, and I sat up.

Lorkin hovered his hands over me, and the blood on the floor, my dress, and my hands disappeared. The slashes from the tiger's claws still marred my dress, though.

"Are you ready to stand?" Lorkin asked me.

I looked down at my leg. There were no marks there at all, and I nodded.

Lorkin stood and grabbed me under one arm to help pull me off the floor, and my dress fell back down to my feet.

"How do you feel?" he asked me, glancing quickly at Samhail.

I put pressure on my leg, but it seemed to be good as new. A spiteful part of me thought about pretending it still hurt, just to scare Lorkin, but I knew the tigers were Ursan and Jerram's idea, and the priest probably hadn't had much choice.

"I'm fine," I said. "It feels normal."

Lorkin looked visibly relieved, and only then did Samhail re-sheath his blade. Behind everyone, Jemma stood by herself. She watched me carefully, and I caught her gaze. A look I didn't recognize flashed in her face, as if she was trying to tell me something, but I didn't understand what.

"We should head back to the Citadel," Ursan said. He motioned to me. "Come, my dear."

The endearment sent rage pounding through my blood, but I didn't say anything.

Samhail's face darkened again as well. "You can ride with me if you don't want to be in the carriage with them," he said softly as we left.

The offer warmed my heart, but I didn't want to risk angering Ursan and Jerram.

"I'll be fine, but thank you."

Samhail nodded in understanding.

I looked again at Jemma as we passed her. She was still trying to tell me something, but I just shook my head slightly, telling her I didn't understand. Jemma looked stricken, and I wished I had Bressen's mind-reading powers.

None of us spoke on the short ride back to the Citadel. I'd come to Callanus harboring a healthy fear of Bressen, but it was apparent he wasn't the lord I needed to watch out for. Bressen may exude danger outwardly, but the real serpents had hidden their fangs well. Until now.

Chapter 11

There was a knock at my door minutes after I returned to the Citadel. I opened it expecting Raina or perhaps Samhail, but it was a Citadel guard.

"Yes?" I asked.

"I'm here to escort you to tea with Lady Glenora," he said.

I swore inwardly. I'd forgotten all about tea with Glenora, and it was the last thing I wanted to do right now. I was exhausted and still shaking from my encounter with the tigers, although admittedly my threshold for facing deadly threats seemed to be increasing.

Excuses flashed through my mind, but none seemed a good enough reason to cancel on the wife of a Triumvirate lord. I also liked Glenora and didn't want to alienate her, so I exhaled deeply and opened my eyes.

"I need to change clothes," I told the guard.

"I'm sure what you're wearing is fine."

I turned to the side and showed him the slash marks across the thigh of my dress. "I need to change clothes," I repeated.

The guard flinched when he saw the slashes and nodded. I closed the door in his face and went to find something to wear. Ten minutes later, I'd washed my face, changed into a dress without claw marks in it, and now followed the guard into Ursan's wing of the Citadel.

I was surprised – although I shouldn't have been – to find all manner of animals wandering the halls as the guard led me toward the solarium. Cats abounded, curled up in the arms of statues or on windowsills, while both dogs and wolves chased each other around or fought over bones left over from last night's dinner. Some sort of monkey scurried past my feet, and an eagle perched atop the rim of a large vase on a pedestal in the corner of one hall. I saw as we entered the solarium that peacocks wandered freely in and out of the open door that led to the garden, and I almost jumped out of my skin when what I thought was an empty tree turned out to have a large green lizard in it.

Glenora was already seated at a table in the center of the room laid out with numerous plates of sandwiches, cakes, cookies, bread, chocolates, and two steaming teapots.

"Cyra," Glenora said, "I'm so glad to see you. Come sit down."

I took the chair across from her, and Glenora dismissed the guard with her thanks.

"Help yourself," she said with a sweep of her hand. "I grow all the plants for my own blends." She pointed to four ceramic jars of dried tea leaves.

"This is a ginger cinnamon blend," she said, pointing to the first jar, "then lavender and lemon, hibiscus and rosehip, and finally black tea with oil of bergamot." She pointed one by one to each of the other three remaining jars.

I'd never had anything more than simple black tea with breakfast back home, and all four of the teas sounded wonderful.

"I'll try the ginger cinnamon one, please," I said, realizing only after I'd said it that Bressen had smelled of hot cinnamon yesterday. I flushed, but Glenora didn't seem to notice as she handed me the tea jar and selected the black tea with bergamot for herself.

"How was your visit to the Priory?" Glenora asked me as she poured hot water over her tea strainer.

I stopped mid-pour as I held the other pot of hot water over my own strainer.

"It could have been better," I said carefully.

"Oh? Why is that?"

I sighed as I realized she probably didn't know about the tigers. By her own admission, Ursan didn't discuss Triumvirate business with her. She was probably trying to get information out of me.

"For one, I don't think anything was resolved," I said.

"Why do you say that?" Glenora asked as she passed me a small plate of sandwiches.

"The seer didn't see anything new," I explained. "She touched me to see if it might give her more details, but it didn't."

"She still wasn't able to see which two lords will…?" Glenora trailed off, and I realized her next word was likely going to be "die."

I shook my head, wishing I had a more promising answer for her.

"That's not ideal, but it's not bad news per se," she said. "Did anything else happen?"

There was a casualness to her inquiry, but I wondered then if maybe she already did know exactly what had happened. I opted for brutal honesty.

"I was also attacked by three tigers," I replied back just as casually.

Glenora stopped stirring her tea and looked at me. "Excuse me?"

She looked genuinely shocked, and I felt bad for assuming she knew about the tigers.

"I'm sorry," I said, "I didn't mean to blurt it out like that."

"Well, now that you have, you need to tell me what happened."

"I…I'm not sure how to do that without offending you."

Glenora raised a brow. "And why would you offend me?"

"Because I believe Lord Ursan sent the tigers after me as a test."

She smiled. "Oh, I'm certain he did, but why would you think that might offend me?"

I had no idea what to say to that, so I just sat silently.

Glenora set down her tea. "My dear, can I be direct?"

I nodded. "Please."

"I realize you've been pulled into an awkward situation here, one that is – to you, I'm sure – also rather frightening, but consider this from our perspective. We received news that the Triumvirate, an institution that's ruled Thasia for thousands of years, may be in danger of collapsing. A seer predicted that events in the near future that seem to connect to you would result in only one lord remaining in his Triumvirate seat. We assume that lord will be one of the current ones, but we don't know for sure. Nor do we know what happens to the other two lords. Presumably, if they no longer occupy their seats, they're dead."

I blanched as Glenora laid it all out like that.

"For all your seeming innocence," Glenora went on, "an accomplished seer thinks you may present a danger to either my husband, or to the other two Triumvirate lords. If you can't see how that might worry Ursan, at least consider how the possibility of losing my husband might affect me."

I flushed with embarrassment as Glenora looked at me pointedly. In my haste to feel sorry for myself, I hadn't considered how the other people involved in the vision felt. Glenora might well find herself a widow. I had no idea how I could personally bring that about, but I understood that feeling bad for me wasn't her main concern at the moment.

"I'm sorry," I said to her. "You're right. I didn't fully consider what the vision meant for you and the three lords."

Glenora nodded and picked up her tea again.

"I still don't think sending three tigers after me was the most effective way to handle the situation, though," I couldn't help adding. I quickly took a sip of my own tea but coughed when it burned my throat.

Glenora raised a brow but then smiled. "Fair enough. I give you my word you won't be attacked by any more animals while you're here."

"Thank you. I appreciate that."

"In the interest of our mutual benefit, then," Glenora said, "do you have any idea how you might be connected to this seer's vision?"

I shook my head. "Unfortunately, none whatsoever. I just make wine. I didn't even know until recently there was a name for the powers I had."

Glenora looked at me questioningly.

"Samhail said I'm an elemental," I clarified.

"Ah, yes. Samhail. I don't get much chance to speak with him. How was your journey here together?"

I took another sip of tea to avoid having to answer her right away. The journey was complicated to say the least, and I wasn't about to share the more personal details of it.

"We encountered a problem or two," I said. "We were attacked by highwaymen on the way here."

I figured it was safe enough to tell Glenora about that.

"Oh my!" she exclaimed. She'd just taken a bite of cake and pressed a hand over her mouth as she chewed. "Were you alright?"

"Yes, thanks to Samhail. He killed most of them."

Glenora just stared at me wide-eyed, and I realized Ursan may not have told her about the type of services Samhail provided to the Citadel.

"I'm sorry. I didn't mean to shock you," I said. "Samhail is…very good with his swords. Neither of us was hurt in any case."

Glenora looked pale, but she recovered and waved a hand. "It's fine. Ursan doesn't tell me these things, and now I understand why."

I nodded sympathetically.

"I've heard Samhail and Lord Bressen are close," Glenora observed. It was a statement, but I understood the inherent question.

"I'm not sure," I said. "Samhail mentioned they were friends, but I don't know how they met or how long they've known each other."

I was certain now that Glenora had only asked me to tea to get information out of me, but I had some questions of my own.

"How did you and Lord Ursan meet?" I asked her before she could question me about anything else.

Glenora looked a little surprised, as if she hadn't expected me to be forward enough to ask her any questions, but she recovered quickly.

"It was an arranged marriage of sorts," she said. "You're from Polaris, are you not?"

"Yes, from Fernweh, in the outer lands."

"Are you familiar with the Durian rebellion?"

"A little," I said. I remembered my parents mentioning it once, but I didn't know a lot about it. "That was a couple hundred years ago,

121

wasn't it? The old lord of Polaris died without an heir, so a distant cousin ascended to his Triumvirate seat. There was a struggle for control when a nobleman from another part of Polaris challenged his claim."

"Yes," Glenora said. "The distant cousin who ascended to the Triumvirate seat was Ursan, and that nobleman was my father."

"Oh! I'm sorry! We're rather isolated in the outer lands," I offered sheepishly. "The details of politics don't always reach us." I was embarrassed I hadn't known this, and I felt the need to explain to Glenora why I was ignorant of what seemed to be an important piece of Thasian history.

Glenora waved a hand. "My father managed to keep the conflict going for almost a year. He amassed a small army in Duria and created enough problems for Ursan that Ursan was having trouble fully securing his claim to the Triumvirate seat. The lords of the other two territories, Jerram and Bressen's fathers, stayed out of the fray for a time, but the struggle in Polaris started to affect their own territories. My father was better at playing the political game than Ursan was, and it looked as though the other two lords might back him over Ursan at one point."

I was enthralled by her story. I'd never heard any of this, and I was fascinated to think I now knew some of the people involved in the conflict. Clearly Ursan had won eventually, but I couldn't see how.

"What happened?" I prompted Glenora.

"Ursan knew his support was fading, so he made an offer for peace," she said. "He promised to take me as his wife and make my father his chief advisor if my father withdrew his challenge and backed Ursan."

"And your father accepted?"

Glenora chuckled. "No, of course not. The tide was shifting in my father's favor. He would've been a fool to accept such an offer."

She was right. If the other two Triumvirate lords were willing to back her father, the smart move would have been to push his

122

advantage, not settle for a lesser deal.

"So then how did Lord Ursan end up maintaining his seat and marrying you?" I asked.

"Ursan finally learned how to play politics and found some leverage," she said, smiling sadly. "He threatened to cut off certain resources to the Derridan territory that Jerram's father relied on. Jerram's father didn't want to take the chance he might lose if the whole country went to war, so he backed Ursan and convinced Bressen's father to do the same. In an unfortunate twist of fate, my father also became ill shortly thereafter and couldn't continue to press his challenge. He'd lost his potential allies, and his health was failing, so he went to Ursan and asked if Ursan would honor his offer to marry me. Ursan had no reason to honor the offer, but he did anyway. My father survived long enough to see us married."

Part of me was sorry I'd asked her to tell me the story. It broke my heart, but I was glad I now knew this history.

Outside, the screaming cry of an animal that sounded like something between a yowling cat and crying baby broke the silence, making me jump.

Glenora shook her head in disgust. "Damned peacocks. They may be beautiful, but they're annoyingly noisy bastards. Don't tell Ursan, but I'm secretly happy whenever one of the wolves goes rogue and eats one of them."

I wasn't sure whether to be shocked or to laugh. Instead I asked, "Can I ask why you think Lord Ursan agreed to marry you? Did he…?" I trailed off, suddenly uncertain about asking the question.

"Did he love me?" she finished. "No, not at the time. He thought it was a good political move, a way to make people who'd supported my father happy."

"And how did you feel about marrying him?" I knew it was a very personal question, but I couldn't help it.

"I was unsure at first," Glenora admitted. "I met Ursan once before, and he seemed like a decent man, but he was my father's enemy. Before my father's health failed, I probably would have refused to marry him, but after, I was faced with the prospect of being alone in a world where my father was branded a traitor. Ursan's agreement to honor his marriage proposal was a blessing because it ensured I wouldn't be held accountable for any of my father's actions against Ursan or Polaris."

"It seems like you and Lord Ursan have made things work."

Glenora smiled and put a hand over mine. "Ursan hasn't always been the perfect partner, but I've grown to love him in my own way. We built a life together despite our contentious beginnings, and I have no regrets."

Glenora seemed to blush as she said this, although it was an odd blush. The rosiness appeared to glow on the surface of her skin rather than from within it.

"That's a lovely way to look at it," I said.

Glenora took her hand off mine and drained her teacup.

"Well, I hadn't expected to tell that story today," she said, seeming a little flustered.

"Thank you for sharing it with me. I know I had no right to ask any of that of you, but it helps put my own situation in perspective."

Glenora nodded. "I should let you get back to your room. You've had a long morning."

"Yes, thank you for tea." I said. "It was nice getting to know you."

Glenora inclined her head, and we both stood. "Take care of yourself, my dear," she said as she walked me to the door. "I'm sure it will all be sorted out soon."

Outside the solarium, the guard who'd brought me was still waiting, and I followed him back to the rotunda.

"I trust you can find your way from here," he said.

I nodded, and he disappeared back behind the door to Ursan's wing of the Citadel. I started up to my room, but I was startled to meet Jerram in one of the corridors halfway there. For once he looked genial and not as annoyed as he usually did.

"Ah, Cyra," Jerram said as he stopped in front of me. "I was just looking for you. Would you favor me with a walk in my gardens?"

My heart sank into my stomach. No, not today. I couldn't handle any more of this today.

"My lord," I said carefully, "I'd love to accompany you on a walk, but I humbly ask that we do it another day. I just met with Glenora, and I'm exhausted after such an…exhilarating morning. I'm afraid I won't be good company to you right now."

Jerram's face was blank for a moment, and I held my breath. I'd gone to see Glenora because I was afraid to cancel on her, but now I was declining the offer of a Triumvirate lord. I was about to take back what I said and agree to the walk when Jerram's face eased into a smile.

"Of course," he said. "I'm happy to postpone a walk until you're feeling up to it."

I sighed with relief. "Thank you, my lord. I appreciate your understanding and look forward to you calling on me again."

He surprised me by leaning down to kiss my hand. He gave a little bow, then turned and left without another word. I watched him go before hurrying on toward my room. I half-expected to run into Bressen as I rounded the corner, but the hallway was mercifully empty. I darted inside my room and shut the door to lean against it.

Even aside from the attempted interrogations, I wasn't used to seeing this many people in such a short period of time. On most days, Jaylan and Brix were the only two I interacted with. I needed to figure out how to survive here at the Citadel or I'd go mad long before they figured out whether or not they wanted to execute me.

Chapter 12

I considered feigning illness the next morning and asking for my breakfast to be sent up, but in the end, I just went down to the dining room. I'd skipped dinner last night, but I resolved that I wasn't going to hide while the Triumvirate decided what to do with me.

Raina seemed to know when I was awake each morning because she knocked and entered with a tray of steaming-hot tea only minutes after I stretched and threw off my covers. I wasn't used to having someone bring me tea or help me get ready in the morning, but I didn't mind it. I liked Raina. I didn't need to guard myself around her, and I realized quickly she was both an expert in Citadel protocols and a fountain of information when it came to everything I wanted to know about both the fortress and its lords.

Ursan had been in the Triumvirate the longest, about two hundred years, which confirmed what Glenora had said yesterday. Jerram came next, having held his seat for seventy-three years following the death of his father, while Bressen's father had died only about twenty years ago, making Bressen the newest member of the group.

The Triumvirate had been all-male for a while now, but there was no law that it had to be. The last several Triumvirate lords had all just either had sons to pass the seat on to, or else – as in Ursan's case – the closest living relative was male. In fact, had her father succeeded in wresting a seat from Ursan, Glenora herself would have been the first woman in the Triumvirate in close to three hundred years after her father died.

When I arrived in the dining room after Raina helped me dress, I was relieved to find only Samhail was there. I'd waited as long as possible before coming down to breakfast in the hope of avoiding everyone. For his own part, Samhail appeared to be waiting for me. He had no plate before him, and he was sitting back in his chair with his boots up on another seat.

We greeted each other with polite good mornings, and I went to fill a plate with food.

"How are you doing after yesterday?" Samhail asked when I sat down. "I wasn't sure if I should've checked on you after you missed dinner."

I was glad he hadn't come up. I needed some time alone, and I was uncertain how I felt about him at the moment. Something still bothered me about the Priory yesterday.

"Did you know what they were planning to do?" I asked Samhail, ignoring his question. "At the Priory, with the tigers?"

He exhaled deeply. "No, they didn't tell me. I didn't know until they let the tigers in."

"And you didn't try to stop them?" I asked incredulously. That he could have watched me being attacked and not done anything to stop it hurt a surprising amount. I'd called out for him specifically, and he hadn't come.

Samhail took his feet off the chair and leaned toward me over the table, although he wouldn't meet my eyes.

"I couldn't," he said, and his voice was pained. "If Bressen had been there, he would've stopped Ursan and Jerram, but I don't have the power to tell two Triumvirate lords what they can and can't do. You have no idea how much I wanted to stop it. The urge to help you was...agonizing."

His eyes went a bit vacant as he seemed to remember, and I frowned at him. Regardless of how badly he'd wanted to help, he hadn't done anything until I'd been injured.

"For the record," I said unsympathetically, "being clawed by a tiger was also agonizing."

His eyes snapped up to meet mine, and I saw the regret in them. I knew his hands had been tied, but I still couldn't help feeling a sense of betrayal. Even worse, I'd been relieved to hear Lord Bressen wouldn't be joining us at the Priory, but if Samhail could be believed, Bressen's presence might have prevented me from having to face the tigers. I'd seen firsthand the other day how Bressen challenged and checked the other two lords. In my defense, though, I'd never imagined Ursan and Jerram would attack me that way.

"I stopped them as soon as you were hurt," he said. "It's the best I could do. I'm sorry."

I looked at him in surprise. Samhail didn't seem like the type to apologize to anyone.

"I sent a message to Bressen to let him know what happened," he went on. "He should be back soon."

"You seem to trust him," I said, furrowing my brows. "I don't understand why you're so determined to believe he wants to help me."

"I've known him a long time. He's a good man."

"How do you know him?" I asked, Glenora's questions from yesterday suddenly burning in my mind.

"Bressen and I met during our military training, probably a little over a hundred years ago now. I served in his father's army for a time before striking out on my own, but I returned to his father's service twenty-five years ago during the war with Rowe. Bressen and I fought together."

As perimortals, Bressen and Samhail looked much younger than they actually were if you judged them by mortal standards, but I didn't have the courage to ask Samhail how old he was. I was twenty-two myself, which meant Bressen and Samhail met each other and trained to fight together long before I'd even been born.

I hadn't been alive during the war with Rowe either, but I at least knew a little bit about why Rowe had invaded Thasia. Rowe sat on the far western edge of the Arystrian continent, and Thasia was the only country that bordered it, mostly along the Derridan territory. Rowe could reach other parts of the continent via the Prosperon Sea, but going anywhere by land meant crossing through Thasia. Rowe had several profitable exports, but the Triumvirate had been imposing high tolls on Rown merchants entering Thasia to move their goods.

A year or two before the war, King Sandrian of Rowe negotiated an easing of the tolls, and that had helped, but it wasn't long before Sandrian decided that taking control of Thasia and eliminating the need for tolls altogether was an even better deal. He resented the need to negotiate at all, and he also wanted control of the caronium mines in Derridan, so he'd invaded, intent on overthrowing the Triumvirate and adding their three territories to Rowe. Luckily, he failed.

"Cyra?" Samhail said, bringing me back from my reverie.

"To answer your earlier question," I said, spearing some eggs on my fork, "I'm fine. I just need to stay out of everyone's way until this is over. Glenora already interrogated me over tea yesterday, and now Jerram wants to take me for a walk in his gardens. I just want to be left alone." I shoved the eggs angrily into my mouth.

"Has anyone shown you the library?" Samhail asked.

I swallowed the eggs and perked up a bit. "Library?"

"Finish your breakfast and I'll take you."

I dug into my food, and fifteen minutes later Samhail led me to the library at the back of the central building. It wasn't a huge library by some standards, but it was far bigger than anything we had in Fernweh, and it was big enough for what I needed.

"Take anything you want to your room," Samhail said.

"Thank you. And thank you for making sure they healed me yesterday," I added.

Samhail shrugged. "Bressen would've had my head if I let you bleed to death on the floor of the Priory. It was self-preservation."

"Well, thank the gods you enjoy having your head attached to your body then," I said.

Samhail smiled and left the library as I began to look around. There was a fireplace at one end, and a large window at the opposite side. The two walls in between were nothing but bookshelves that ran from the floor all the way up the thirty-foot walls to the ceiling.

I took in the familiar smell of old paper and ink that suffused the air as I wandered. My parents took us to the city of Bourne once when we were children, and we'd gone to the library there. I'd been awed by the sheer number of books, and the smell was one of the most distinct things I remembered about the place.

I reached out and ran my hand along the spines of the books, savoring the feel of the cloth and leather of their covers bumping lightly under my fingers. Traveling book merchants were my favorite visitors to Fernweh, and I usually tried to buy enough books to last until the next merchant came through. I'd already read most of the books in Fernweh's own small library, even though winter was the only season I really had time to read on the vineyard.

I tried some of the books on the lower shelves of the Citadel's library first, but most weren't in a language I understood. I looked further up the shelves until I thought I saw titles in the common language on higher shelves. There was a rolling ladder attached to the shelf, so I climbed up several feet to see what might be up there.

A dark purple book caught my eye off to the left. I couldn't read the spine from my angle, but it looked to have embossed grapes on it. I reached out, but the book was too far away.

I wondered if I could move the ladder without having to get off of it, and I reached out on either side of me to grasp the chest-high shelf firmly. Pulling with one arm and pushing with the other, I tried to roll the ladder a few inches to my left, but it didn't budge.

"You need to release the brake," said an amused voice directly below me.

I shrieked in surprise and almost fell as I turned automatically to see who was in the room with me. I grabbed the ladder with both hands just in time and flattened myself against it before looking behind me. Bressen stood below me with his arms outstretched as if ready to catch me.

Blood pounded in my head, and my heart seemed to be in my throat as I said, "My lord, I didn't hear you come in."

Bressen chuckled. "That's normally a skill I pride myself on, but I'm sorry I startled you."

I started to step down the ladder, but he stopped me. "Don't forget

130

your book."

"I can get it later," I said, very aware that he was looking up at my backside.

"You're already up there, so you might as well get it now. I'll help you. Just flip the brake release. It's the handle below your right hand."

I looked down and saw the handle he was talking about. I flipped it up and immediately felt the difference in the mobility of the ladder.

"Hold on," Bressen said.

I grasped the ladder, and he pushed it gently a couple feet to my left. I relocked the brake, grabbed the book, and climbed down. I wasn't sure what book it was, but I just needed to get off this thing.

I thought Bressen would move when I got to the bottom, but he didn't, and I descended right into the circle of his arms. I turned quickly and pressed myself back against the ladder.

His turquoise eyes caught my gaze and held it. Being this close to him was unnerving, and my heart hammered in my chest for an entirely different reason. My nose caught that intoxicating scent of his, and I inhaled deeply before realizing what I was doing. Fortunately, he didn't seem to notice.

"Thank you, my lord," I said when he didn't move. "I appreciate your help."

He appeared to be studying my eyes again. There was about a foot of space between our bodies, and the air prickled with an energy that made me want to lean toward him. I pressed myself further back against the ladder instead.

Finally, Bressen broke our gaze and pulled the book gently from my grasp.

"*Viticulture of the Hiraeth Territory*," he read on the cover.

My eyes flew to the book. That was indeed the title. I opened my mouth to say something, but Bressen only smiled and handed me back the book. He let go of the ladder and walked over to sit down in an armchair, then motioned for me to sit in a chair opposite him. His manner suggested nonchalance, but I felt that omnipresent tensity that followed him everywhere.

"Have a seat," Bressen said. "I'd like to talk to you."

I groaned inwardly at the prospect of another interrogation, but I sat down opposite him and put the book on the table between us. When I looked up at him, I realized something was different, but it didn't come to me immediately.

Bressen cocked his head at me. "Is there a problem?"

Then I knew what it was.

"You had some kind of dark halo around you in the Great Chamber. I couldn't focus on it, but I don't see it at all now."

I realized he hadn't had the halo at dinner the other night either.

"Ah, yes," Bressen said. "That's a glamour I sometimes wear. I put it up when I don't want people staring at me too closely. It tends to make them dizzy if they look at me too long. I also put it up if I really need to make an impression...or if I just want to piss Jerram off."

I just stared at him. As if he wasn't intimidating enough, the man liked to put up a special illusion to make it worse.

"I don't need the glamour now, though," Bressen went on. "We don't want you getting dizzy, do we?"

I narrowed my eyes at him. "I'd appreciate not being dizzy."

"Indeed. So how was your tea with Glenora yesterday?" he asked.

I wasn't necessarily surprised by the question. It was clear by now that each lord was playing their own endgame and that none of them trusted each other. What was less clear to me was which one of them – if any – I could trust myself.

"It was nice," I said vaguely. "Thank you for asking, my lord."

Bressen smiled as if he knew exactly what I was doing. "Did Glenora happen to mention to you what power she has?"

The question caught me off-guard, and I blinked at him. It didn't occur to me that Glenora had any powers, but in hindsight it was stupid to think she didn't.

I shook my head slowly. "No, my lord. She didn't mention any powers to me."

132

Bressen smiled wryly. "Of course not," he said, more to himself than to me.

"What is her power then?" I asked when he didn't volunteer the information.

"Glenora is a truth seer."

I'd never heard the term before, but I could guess what it was, and something cold gripped my chest. "You mean she can…"

"She can tell if you're lying, yes."

I went pale, and my mind raced to replay my conversation with Glenora. Had I said anything that wasn't true? I'd perhaps glossed over the journey to Callanus with Samhail, but I didn't think anything I'd said was an actual lie.

"Glenora doesn't read minds as I can," Bressen explained. "She can sense a lie, but as far as I know, she has no way to know what the actual truth is."

Bressen waited another few seconds as I finished running through the conversation with Glenora in my head before he asked, "Did you lie to her at all yesterday?"

"I…I don't think so," I said, but I couldn't keep the slight quaver out of my voice. Then anger replaced fear, and I added, "I've told you all before, I have nothing to hide. I have no reason to lie."

"What did Glenora ask you about?"

"I don't know. Many things," I said. "She asked me about what happened at the Priory. I told her about the tigers. She also asked me to speculate on how I might be connected to the seer's vision, but I didn't know."

Bressen's face darkened considerably at the mention of the Priory.

"Anything else?" he asked, and there was an edge to his voice.

I thought for a moment. "She asked me about my journey here with Samhail, and I told her about being attacked by the highwaymen."

The sudden surprise in his expression told me he hadn't heard about the attack. "Highwaymen?" he asked, leaning forward in alarm.

"Twenty or so of them," I said, and I took a perverse pleasure in watching his eyes widen. "Samhail killed most of them. We were fine."

I expected to see shock on his face, but instead he relaxed and sat back in his chair again.

"It seems we might owe Samhail a bonus," he said more to himself than me. "I'm glad you weren't harmed," he added.

"Thank you, my lord." I paused before volunteering, "Glenora asked about you too." I wasn't sure what made me mention it.

Bressen studied my face. "What did she want to know about me?"

I shrugged. "Mostly she wanted to know about your relationship with Samhail. I couldn't tell her much at the time."

"At the time?" he asked, picking up on my phrasing.

I blushed a bit. "I asked Samhail this morning how you met. Glenora made me curious."

A smile tugged at the corner of his lips, and his eyes seemed to flash. Nemesis damn me, he had beautiful eyes.

"Samhail mentioned that you were adopted by your parents," Bressen went on. "Do you remember anything about your birth parents?"

"No, I was only a few months old when my parents took me in."

"And who gave you to them?"

"They never told me, but my brother Jaylan remembers a man coming to our house. He wore a hood, so Jaylan didn't see him well."

"And your brother has no idea who this man was? Whether he was a relative of yours or perhaps someone who kidnapped you?"

I jolted in shock at his words. I'd never thought too deeply about how I'd ended up with my family, but Bressen's questions suddenly seemed like things I should have asked myself – or better yet, my parents – a long time ago. Was the man a relative who didn't want to be burdened with a child? Had he stolen me but given me up because the authorities were closing in on him? Was I the unwanted bastard of some powerful man's mistress who needed to be disposed of before his wife found out?

"I see I've planted some ideas you never considered," Bressen said.

I narrowed my eyes. Could he see from my expression, or was he reading my mind?

"My apologies if I brought up some painful thoughts," he continued, "but the answers to these questions may be important."

"Why?" I asked.

"They may help me determine why you've been brought here. Jerram and Ursan won't let you go home until they're sure you're not a threat to their power or their lives."

I shook my head at the absurdity. "And what about you, my lord?"

"Me?"

"Do you think I'm a threat to your power or your life?"

Bressen just smiled. "I do think you're a threat, but not to my power or my life."

I gaped at him. I hadn't been expecting that answer, nor did I have any idea what he meant. Did he mean I was a threat to Jerram and Ursan, but not to him? Was I a threat to something other than his life or power? Both? My head swam as I tried to interpret his words.

"What happened to your parents?" he went on before I could ask him to clarify.

"They were taken by the Great Flu when I was twelve. My older brother raised me and my younger brother after that."

"I'm sorry to hear that," Bressen said. "The three of you took over the vineyard all by yourselves?"

"We'd all been working on the vineyard since we were old enough to carry buckets of grapes. We knew what we were doing."

"You managed to keep it running through the pandemic?"

I shrugged. "People did a lot of drinking at the time."

"Fair enough," he said with the hint of a smile. "So you've always had powers but kept them secret, and until recently you've never done more than conjure flames or summon water?"

I nodded. "Correct. As I said, I'm no threat to you."

"That's not necessarily true. Ursan was right about one thing. Turning that bear to earth shouldn't have been possible. Even those

135

who have the power to transfigure can't do that."

"Transfigure?"

"Those who can change one substance into another," Bressen clarified. "Living beings, anything with a heartbeat or anything that can breathe or move on its own are complicated things to change. More powerful perimortals can do it. They can, for instance, change a dog into a cat. Or shapeshifters like Ursan can change himself into whatever animal he wants, but to change a living being into something inanimate, and to snuff out its life in the process, that's a power I've never seen. It's the opposite of giving life to something inanimate, which is a power only the Creator has."

When Bressen explained it like that, what I'd done to the bear did seem more extraordinary, and a seed of fear began to grow inside me. I stood up. "If you have no more questions for me, my lord, I really need to go."

He studied me a moment. "I still have lots of questions, but you can go if you want."

I didn't wait to see if he'd change his mind but headed for the door.

"Cyra," Bressen called after me, and I froze. It was the first time I'd heard him use my name, and something about hearing it on his lips made my insides flutter.

I felt him at my back a moment later as that energy crackled in the air between us, and his scent filled my nostrils again. My skin seemed to tingle with anticipation, as if I expected – wanted – him to touch me. His nearness was palpable, although the barest space still remained between us.

The purple book appeared in front of my face in his hand.

"Don't forget this," he said. His mouth was next to my ear, his breath teasing my skin.

I took the book carefully from him. "Thank you, my lord."

I took one step toward the door and then another. When he didn't stop me again, I hurried the rest of the way and slipped out as fast as I could. I broke into a run in the hallway and didn't stop until I got back to my room and flung the door shut behind me. I stood against it for several minutes breathing hard. Being alone in the same room with Bressen was discomforting enough, but he'd told me a number of things that had truly shaken me.

To start, I needed to be more careful about what I said in front of Glenora. The last thing I wanted was to be caught lying to her.

As for the man who'd given me to my parents, I didn't want to think about who he might be. I had my hands full with the lords of the Triumvirate and the threat they thought I posed. If Bressen was to be believed, I did indeed have the potential to be a threat to them. I didn't know how it was possible, but what he'd said made sense.

I sighed. Cyra of Fernweh, Scourge of the Land after all.

Chapter 13

It was past eleven o'clock, and I was still wide awake. I'd gone to bed an hour ago, but I hadn't even been able to close my eyes, let alone fall asleep.

My mind drifted to Jaylan, Brix, and the vineyard, and I wondered if they'd ever received the help Lord Ursan had promised us. They must be mad with worry about me by now, and I thought about asking the lords if they'd let me send them a message so my brothers knew I'd arrived safely in Callanus and hadn't yet been executed.

I sat up in bed. Now that I wasn't on the vineyard, I didn't have hours of physical labor during the day to tire me out. Traveling had been exhausting in its own way, and then I'd faced both the tigers and Glenora yesterday, so that had gotten me to sleep last night. Today the only thing I'd done was talk to Bressen, and that had energized rather than tired me for some reason.

I threw off my covers and got dressed in a pair of pants, a loose tunic, and a pair of slippers, then crept to the door of my bedroom. I didn't have guards during the day, but I wasn't sure about after dark. True to their word, the lords were treating me like a guest so far, so within the Citadel's walls at least, I had the freedom to move about unencumbered.

I opened the door and stuck my head out. The hall was empty. A few torches burned in sconces, casting just enough light to discern the edges of the walls and floors. I stepped out carefully, but no guards rushed to detain me. I took a few steps down the hallway, and when my path remained clear, I began to walk in earnest.

I took the stairs to the top of the central building and then went down a level each time I finished walking a floor. Samhail was up here somewhere, but I hadn't yet learned where his rooms were. I originally thought he stayed in Bressen's wing, but Raina confirmed that Samhail's quarters were in the central building, if only to maintain the illusion he was a neutral party. Of course, everyone knew he wasn't.

Part of me considered knocking on Samhail's door if I found it, and my imagination ran wild at what he might look like when he readied for sleep. I wondered what he wore to bed, or even *if* he wore anything at all. I couldn't determine which rooms were his, though, and that was probably for the best.

When I reached the bottom level again, I turned down a hall that I remembered led toward the Great Chamber. The fortress was peaceful at night in the dark, and I wanted to investigate the chamber when I wasn't being interrogated. I fully intended to sit on all three of the Triumvirate seats.

When I reached the passageway to the chamber, however, I saw a slit of light midway down the hall. I walked silently toward it, realizing that the lights were on in a room across from the chamber, but I froze as I heard Bressen's voice drift toward me. I turned quickly to go. If the lords found me in the hall at this hour, I'd be in trouble.

I'd only gotten a step or two before I heard someone mention my name from behind the door, and I swore inwardly. It would be impossible for me to walk away now.

The door was only open a crack, but it let the sound of three voices into the hall. Just beside it, a large alcove held the statue of a woman in flowing robes, and there was enough space that I could wedge myself behind the statue in the shadows and largely be out of sight. As with the rest of the fortress, only enough torches lined the passageway to allow someone to find their way, so I ducked into the alcove and flattened myself against the wall to listen.

I wasn't sure if Bressen was able to sense the minds of people nearby, but I wasn't taking a chance that my thoughts might give me away. I'd somehow put up a wall in my head that first day in the Great Chamber, so I concentrated now on trying to re-erect that barrier.

"You should have been there when the seer told us of her vision, Bressen," Ursan was saying. "She was frightened."

"My guess," Bressen said, "is that she was frightened because she had to tell two Triumvirate lords they were probably going to die. That would make anyone a bit nervous."

"Exactly!" Ursan insisted. "If she's right, then only one of us is going to survive the next few weeks or months. If you'd heard her vision, you wouldn't take this so lightly."

"I take this lightly," Bressen said, "because we're talking about a girl from the outer lands who, according to Samhail, can barely wield a negligible amount of elemental powers."

I felt a pang of betrayal at the words. I'd always been a bit proud of my powers. They'd made me feel special in Fernweh, but here in Callanus where magic was more prominent, my powers were barely more than parlor tricks.

"What about the bear?" Ursan asked.

"The bear was an anomaly. She was threatened and somehow managed to draw on a power beyond her normal abilities. She's unlikely to do something like that again, as you yourself found out when you sent tigers after her and almost killed her." Bressen's voice had risen, and I heard the anger in it as he continued. "If either of you ever do anything so reckless again, you'll have *me* to deal with."

Someone scoffed, likely Jerram.

"Now, now, there's no need for threats, Bressen," Ursan said placatingly. "There was no permanent harm done. I had everything under control."

"You and I have very different definitions of what constitutes 'under control,'" Bressen said, menace still lacing his words. "You left the girl there with nothing but a bit of fire and water to use against three tigers, and she nearly had her leg torn off."

"Samhail vastly exaggerated the situation if that's what he told you," Ursan said.

"And don't be so quick to dismiss elemental powers," Jerram added bitterly.

"I'm not dismissing elemental powers," Bressen said. "I'm dismissing *her* elemental powers. I'm fully aware that *some* elementals wield a prodigious amount of power." He seemed to emphasize the word *some*, and I had the sense this was an insult thrown at Jerram. I still didn't actually know what Jerram's powers were, and it made me wonder if he was an elemental.

"Regardless of her level of power," Jerram said, "the seer believes Cyra is inextricably involved in whatever happens to two of us."

"Then perhaps you should've left her in Fernweh where she was less likely to do any harm," Bressen said. "If she's involved in the downfall of the Triumvirate, then the only thing you've done is let your doom in by the front door. By the gods, just send her home!"

"It's too late for that," Ursan said. "We can't send her home now. She needs to stay until we figure out how she's involved."

"Nemesis take you both," Bressen swore.

"Give her to me for an hour," Jerram said. "I promise you I'll find out what she's hiding."

"We're not torturing the girl," Ursan said.

Out in the hall I swallowed hard.

"Fine," Jerram said, "then give her to Bressen and see what he can find out. You have at least tried to read her mind, haven't you?" This last was obviously addressed to Bressen himself.

"Of course," Bressen said. "I saw nothing of consequence. She's just a frightened young woman."

I wasn't sure what angered me more, his easy dismissal of me or his offhanded confirmation that he'd invaded my mind at some point.

"And you're sure she's not hiding anything?" Jerram asked. "If she's more powerful than we think, perhaps she's blocking you or playing you for a fool. She's clearly stoked your sympathies. Who knew the great Nemesis Incarnate could be made impotent by a pretty face and some flashy eyes."

There was a pause before Bressen spoke, his voice ominous. "Be careful, Jerram."

"Easy now," Ursan cut in, ever the peacemaker between the two. "Let's not let things get out of hand."

"Has it occurred to you," Bressen said, "that maybe Jerram and I will just kill each other arguing over what to do about the girl, and that's the extent of her involvement in this vision?"

"It's not helpful to say such things," Ursan admonished him. "Don't jest."

"I'm not jesting," Bressen said. "In my experience, that's how these visions work. You're both assuming Cyra will suddenly show some enormously dangerous power and destroy us. It's just as likely she'll spill something on the floor and two of us will die by slipping and breaking our necks. Send her home before she takes us out with a glass of water."

"You're an ass," Jerram growled, then added, presumably to Ursan, "Do we really have to involve him in this? He seems happy to let us all die for the sake of this girl."

"Not all of us," Bressen said. "Just you, Jerram."

Ursan sighed loudly. "This is getting us nowhere, and we're not going to settle the issue tonight. I need to get to sleep."

"Fine," Jerram said. "We'll pick this up tomorrow."

"There's nothing to pick up," Bressen said. "Just be done with the girl already."

"Are you offering to kill her for us?" Jerram asked silkily.

Something twisted in my gut, and I clamped a hand over my mouth to stifle the small cry that threatened to escape my throat.

"No," Bressen said, and his voice was cold. "I'm offering to send her back to Fernweh. She can't destroy us if she's not here."

"You're more confident about that than we are, I'm afraid," Ursan said, "but let's not start this whole thing again."

Chairs scraped on the floor, and panic skittered up my spine. I stepped forward, intending to hurry back to my quarters, but light flooded the hallway as the door to the room swung open, and shadows on the wall told me the lords were exiting.

I flattened myself back into the alcove and pressed behind the statue as far as I could, then sent a silent prayer to the Protector that

Bressen wouldn't sense my presence. I still wasn't sure how his power worked, but I had a feeling he didn't need to know I was nearby to be able to read my mind.

Ursan and Jerram both passed by the alcove without stopping, and I held my breath as I waited for Bressen to leave as well. It was a few seconds later before the light finally went out in the room and he walked by. He didn't even pause as he passed me, and I slowly let out the breath I'd been holding.

I sagged against the wall, but I didn't dare move yet. I needed to be absolutely certain all three of the lords were on their way back to their own wings before I came out.

I waited close to five minutes without moving before I finally leaned out from behind the statue and looked down the hall. It was empty, but my blood was still pounding as I stepped out and started back toward my chambers.

I'd taken no more than three steps before Bressen materialized in front of me, leaning against the wall with his arms crossed over his broad chest. I cried out as I staggered back a step, and my hand flew to my heart. I gasped for breath as I looked in horror at the man smirking at me in the faint torchlight of the hallway.

"I was starting to think you planned to hide there all night," Bressen said. "A few more minutes and I was just going to tell you to come out."

"Nemesis take me!" I said between gasps, still holding my hand over my chest. "Have you been there this whole time?"

"Of course."

"But...I didn't see you."

"Obfuscation glamour," he said, and he suddenly disappeared from view again.

I stared at the spot where he'd been standing. There was a slight fuzziness to the space now that I knew he was there, but I hadn't noticed it at all when I thought the hall was empty.

Bressen reappeared and pushed off the wall to stand in front of me. I'd finally gotten control of my breathing, but my heart raced again as he approached me. I couldn't bring myself to look up at him, but staring down at his chest wasn't much better. His scent enveloped me, and I had to close my eyes as my head swam a little. It was like he made me half drunk, and I swallowed, trying to clear my mind.

"When did you realize I was here?" I dared to ask.

"Not until I was about to leave the room."

"You sensed my mind?"

Even in the dim hallway I saw his grin widen. "I smelled you."

My mouth fell open in indignation. "You what?"

He leaned forward a little so his nose was near my hair, and he inhaled deeply. "Almond and jasmine. I'm not sure what you use when you bathe, but I approve."

He winked at me and my stomach fluttered violently. I knew I must be blushing.

"How much of our conversation did you hear?" he asked.

I swallowed again. "A few minutes," I said, hoping the answer was suitably vague to keep me out of trouble.

He smiled, obviously guessing my intention. "And why are you out of bed so late?"

"I couldn't sleep."

"You're worried about what's going to happen to you."

I let out a mirthless laugh. "Yes, of course I am."

His face grew serious. "I won't let Jerram and Ursan harm you."

"Why not?"

He quirked a brow at me. "What do you mean?"

"I mean, why would you protect me? You're just as much at risk if the seer's vision comes to pass as they are. Why aren't you worried that I'm going to destroy you all?"

"I told you this morning that I don't believe you're a danger to us."

"I remember, but I don't understand why. Is it because you can just kill me with a thought anytime you want?"

His head snapped back as if I'd slapped him, and I suddenly

regretted my bluntness.

"Is that what you think I'd do?" he asked. "That I would just kill you instantly if I thought you were a threat?"

"Wouldn't you?"

"No," he said, and the conviction in his voice made me wince. There was something dark in his eyes, and I realized he was angry.

"I'm sorry." I tried to step back from him, but he caught my arm so I couldn't retreat. I gasped, but more out of surprise than fear.

"I need you to hear me when I tell you this," Bressen said. "I don't believe you'll ever intentionally be a danger to the Triumvirate, and if it somehow becomes apparent you are, it'll be because we put you in that situation to begin with. Do you understand what I'm saying?"

I didn't, but I nodded anyway.

"Regardless, if you do become a danger," he went on, "I wouldn't just kill you without first exploring every other possible option."

He meant it to sound reassuring, but I heard only that he was willing to kill me if necessary. I tried to move, but he held me firmly.

"That didn't come out the way I meant it," he said. "I meant-"

"It's fine, my lord," I cut in. "I understand. I don't expect you to promise you won't act in self-defense if by some impossibility it seems I might harm you or the other lords."

He dragged his free hand through his hair. "No," he said finally. "I can't promise you I won't act as necessary if there is a clear danger to my life or the lives of others, but what I'm trying to say is I don't ever foresee you being the cause of that danger."

"You can't know that, my lord."

He smiled at me, and his grip on my arm eased. "Here I thought you've been trying to convince us this whole time you aren't a threat, and now you're trying to convince me you are."

I opened my mouth to deny it, but he was right, and I willed myself to be smarter about the things I said in the future.

Bressen stepped closer so his body was almost touching mine. If I inhaled deeply enough, my breasts would press into his chest, and I had the urge to lean forward and let them.

Unnerved by the impulse, I was about to pull away to put some distance between us again when Bressen's other hand slipped around my waist, as if he'd known I was going to step away. He pressed forward so our bodies met, and I lost all ability to think. His hand on my arm moved up to brush a stray lock of my hair behind my ear, and my entire head tingled at his touch.

"I…I should go back to my room, my lord," I said, but he didn't let go.

Bressen leaned down to graze his lips boldly along my temple, and I closed my eyes as a shudder of expectation ran through me. My breasts had hardened into peaks, and my head turned toward his of its own accord as if offering my lips for him to kiss. Every nerve in my body was alive, yet I couldn't move. I knew I should go, but I was rooted to the spot. I wanted to believe Bressen was mentally holding me in place so I couldn't leave, but I knew it was my own mind that imprisoned me there, not his.

Bressen's hand slid down to my hip, and reason finally came crashing down. I stepped back out of his reach, and my body screamed in protest, as if I'd somehow torn away a piece of myself. The feeling of loss was a bucket of icy water. Across from me, Bressen straightened as well, looking as though he'd just been pulled from the same trance.

"I need to go back to my room now," I said, and I slipped around him to hurry back down the corridor without waiting for his permission to go. I wasn't sure if I was allowed to leave his presence until he told me I could, but I needed to get out of there quickly before I did something I'd regret.

There was only silence behind me, and I resisted the urge to look back to see what Bressen was doing. If there were any consequences to my sudden departure, I'd face them later.

Unfortunately, I was more wide-awake now than ever, and I wondered if I would ever get a restful night of sleep again while Lord Bressen of Hiraeth was around.

Chapter 14

I awoke with a purpose the next morning. It had indeed taken me a long time to fall asleep with the ghost of Bressen's touch dancing on my skin, as well as memories of everything I'd overheard. When I did finally drift off, I was plagued by nightmares about Jaylan and Brix, but the nightmares at least reminded me that I needed to send a message to my brothers to let them know I was okay. I resolved to find a way to contact them, even if they wouldn't be able to respond, and inspiration struck when I met Samhail leaving the dining room that morning.

"I need a favor," I said, laying a hand on his stomach to stop him in the hall.

He looked down at my hand and smiled wickedly. "What kind of favor?"

I took my hand away and shot him an admonishing look. "Not that kind of favor."

He gave an exaggerated sigh of disappointment. "Then what can I do for you?"

"I need to send a message to my brothers to let them know I'm safe," I said, adding the words 'for now' in my head. "Do you have any more of that paper you used to send Ursan a message back at the vineyard?"

"I don't have any myself, but Bressen does. I'll get it for you."

I shook my head. "You can't tell him I asked for it. What if he thinks I'm trying to call for help or send coded messages?"

Samhail gave me a look that told me exactly how ridiculous he thought that was. "If you want the paper, I need to get it from Bressen. And I'm not stealing it from him," he added, when I opened my mouth to suggest exactly that. "You need to trust me that he's on your side."

Part of me knew that, but I was having trouble letting go of all the frightening things I'd heard about him over the years. It was safer to think he was evil and stay away from him.

"Fine," I said, "but if I end up locked in the dungeons because of this, you're responsible."

"At least I'll know you're staying out of trouble that way," Samhail said, winking at me.

I gave him a withering look, but he just smirked and strode off.

I didn't see Samhail the rest of the day until dinner. He didn't give any hint he remembered my request, and I was too afraid to ask him about the paper with everyone else around. I went back to my room disappointed, but I resolved to ask him again tomorrow and every day thereafter until he gave me the paper.

At nine thirty that evening, though, a loud thumping at my door made both Raina and I jump. I was already in my nightgown, and Raina was brushing my hair.

Raina pulled open the door and then stepped back when Samhail strode in without waiting for an invitation as usual.

I got up and went right over to him. I forgot that I was wearing only a silk nightgown with thin straps that left little to the imagination until I saw him stop dead and rake his eyes up and down my body. I motioned for Raina to hand me my robe, and she helped me slip it on before I got any closer to him.

"Remind me to visit in the evenings more often," Samhail said, ignoring Raina as she cowered behind me.

"I hope you have something for me, or you're never allowed to visit again," I said.

"I do," he said huskily. "It's in my pants."

Raina inhaled sharply, but I just crossed my arms over my chest and gave him a look that said I wasn't going to play this game with him with my lady's maid standing right here.

Samhail sighed and reached into the pocket of his pants to pull out a thick stack of the paper rectangles. He held them out to me, and my eyes went wide. I took the stack from him carefully so as not to crumple them.

"Bressen let you have all of these?" I asked.

"He wanted you to be able to stay in touch with your brothers," Samhail said. "He said you can have more if you need them."

I looked at him incredulously. "Thank you for getting these for me, and please tell Bressen…Lord Bressen, that I said thank you as well."

Samhail nodded and turned to go.

"Wait," I said. "I'm not sure how they work."

I'd seen him use them before, but I didn't know if there was a trick to it.

Samhail turned back. "After you write your message, just hold the paper between your forefinger and middle finger and think about who you want to send it to. Say their name in your head, but make sure it's only one name. If you try to send it to both your brothers at once and they're in different places, the message will tear itself in half."

I nodded my understanding.

"Some of those are for your brothers," he said. "Hold the blank ones in your hand and send them the same way so they can write back. Just make sure to give them the directions."

"Thank you again."

"Give Jaylan and Brix my regards, and let me know if they have any Eddin issues," Samhail said as he headed again toward the door. He looked back when he got there and let his eyes roam over me once more before he left.

"My lady," Raina said, "are those message leaves?"

I looked at the papers in my hand. "I'm not sure what they're called, but, yes, they're for sending messages."

"There has to be about fifty of them there."

I looked at the stack of papers in my hand. "Probably. Why?"

Raina shrugged. "Magical items like that are expensive, and that's a large stack of them. From Lord Bressen, no less."

I furrowed my brows at her. "Why does that matter?"

"It…it just surprises me is all."

I looked down at the papers again. It surprised me a little as well.

Bressen surprised me a lot lately in general. He'd shown himself to be on my side at every turn, and I wondered if the abundance of message leaves in my hand was yet another effort to prove that to me.

"What should I say to my brothers?" I asked Raina. I went to the writing desk and pulled out the first pen I found.

"I don't know," Raina said. "I didn't even know you had brothers. Are they handsome?"

"I don't think I'm really the best judge of that myself, but I've been told they are."

"And are they married?"

I chuckled. "Are you planning a visit to Fernweh sometime soon?"

"Just keeping my options open," Raina said crossing her arms over her chest.

"What about that guard you know?"

Raina spoke often about a guard who worked in Bressen's wing of the Citadel. She was sweet on him, and the feeling seemed mutual, but the man was shy around her. She got most of her information about what went on in the fortress from him, but romantically she'd been unable to get more than a kiss thus far.

"Damian?" Raina said with a huff. "Don't get me started on Damian. Tell me more about your brothers."

"Jaylan is all but engaged, and Brix is probably too sweet and naïve for his own good."

"I can work with sweet and naïve," Raina giggled.

"What should I tell them? I feel like it's been ages since I've spoken to them," I said.

"Tell them you arrived here safely for one."

I nodded and began to write. I addressed the message to both of them, although I'd send it straight to Jaylan.

"Should I tell them about the vision? I don't want to worry them."

"Tell them..." Raina said, thinking, "tell them that you were brought here because of a vision and that you just need to help the lords sort out some issues."

I didn't think the explanation would satisfy my brothers, particularly not Jaylan, but I wrote it down anyway. I could figure out a better way to spin the truth later. I ended the note with directions on how to use the message leaves I was going to send. I'd written as small as I could on both sides of the paper and just barely had enough room to fit everything.

"That should at least ease their minds that I'm alive," I said as I stood up from the desk and divided the stack of message leaves in half. I put my message on top of the blank ones and held the whole bunch up between my forefinger and middle finger.

Jaylan, I thought. *Get to Jaylan.*

The stack of papers between my fingers vanished in a puff of smoke, and I looked at Raina. She looked back at me expectantly.

"Well, it seems like it worked," I said.

"How long do you think it will take them to write back?"

"I have no idea."

"Do you want me to leave while you wait?" Raina asked tentatively.

I knew she didn't want to go until we'd heard back, and I didn't really want her to leave either. I needed the company, or I'd drive myself mad waiting for a reply.

"Stay," I said.

"Shall we play cards while we wait?" she asked.

"I don't know many card games," I admitted.

"I can teach you. Do you know how to play poker?"

I shook my head.

Raina went to a square table in the room with four chairs set around it. She reached under the top of the table and pulled out a drawer I hadn't even realized was there. She came out with a deck of cards and motioned for me to come over.

"The guards usually place bets when they play poker," Raina said, "but we'll play for fun since you're learning the game. You've seen a deck of cards before, I hope?"

I sat down. "Of course. We're not completely cut off from

151

civilization out in Fernweh."

The cards slapped smartly against each other as Raina expertly shuffled them in a way that made me think I might be in over my head trying to play with her. She dealt us each five cards.

"The object of the game is to collect cards of the same suit, the same number, or in consecutive numbers," Raina told me. She briefly went over the possible combinations of hands and which combinations beat other combinations.

"If you don't have a good hand," she said, "you can turn in up to three cards, and I'll deal new ones for you. Do you want any new cards?"

I looked at the cards in my hand. Two of diamonds, three of hearts, five of hearts, nine of clubs, and ten of spades. I returned my nine of clubs and ten of spades facedown to Raina, and she dealt me two more cards before taking three for herself.

Before I could look at my new cards, though, a piece of paper appeared in a puff of smoke before me and floated down to the table.

"They wrote back!" I said, laying down my cards and snatching up the paper. My eyes welled with tears as I recognized Jaylan's neat handwriting on one side and Brix's chicken scratch on the other.

"What did they say?" Raina asked, laying down her own cards to look over my shoulder.

I held the paper up and read Jaylan's side of the letter first out loud.

Dear Cyra,

Thank the Protector you're okay! What was this vision about, and how can you possibly help the Triumvirate with it? You need to come home soon. Brix has completely lost his appetite. He only eats four meals a day now instead of seven.

I wiped furiously at the tears running down my face, even as I chuckled at the joke about Brix's appetite.

"Your brother Brix likes to eat, I take it?" Raina asked as she laid a hand on my shoulder.

I nodded. "Half our money goes to fill his plate. I have no idea how he stays so lean."

"Are you going to answer your brother's question about the vision?" she asked.

"No, it'll only worry them."

"Read the other side."

I turned the paper over and read Brix's half of the note with a bit of difficulty.

Cyra! What took you so long to write? Jaylan's been stalking around the house for days since you left. He was ready to ride up to Callanus himself if we didn't hear from you soon. How's the food at the Citadel?

I sighed and shook my head. I knew Brix was completely serious in wanting to know about the Citadel's food.

"Are you going to write back?" Raina asked.

I didn't want to use too many of the message leaves so soon, but there was at least a little more I wanted to say. I went back to the writing desk to grab the pen and a few more sheets of paper and wrote:

Dear Jaylan and Brix,
The food here is both abundant and delicious. They also serve our wine at the Citadel. The vintage from three years ago has matured well. Did you receive the help we were promised on the vineyard?
Love, Cyra.
PS – Samhail sends his regards and wants to know if Eddin has been a problem.

I held up the paper, and it vanished in a puff of smoke.

"This is so exciting," Raina said. "I've never used message leaves before. It's like waiting to open a gift. I hope they report back that Eddin's balls have fallen off."

I smiled. Raina and I had grown close quickly, and I'd shared my story about Eddin after she'd told me about Damian.

"Do you have any siblings?" I asked Raina, realizing that I knew very little about her.

"Not that I know of."

"What do you mean?"

"My mother was a servant here at the Citadel many years ago, a lady's maid to Glenora," Raina said. "She was sent away from the fortress when she became pregnant with me, and she raised me in Rowe. We had a falling out when I decided to return a couple years ago to seek employment here, and I haven't spoken to her since."

"I'm sorry," I said, then asked hesitantly, "And your father?"

"Someone she met here at the Citadel. They had a brief affair until she became pregnant."

"Does he still work here?"

Raina smiled sadly and picked her cards up from the table. "I see him from time to time, but he wants little to do with me."

I felt a pang of sadness for Raina. "How awful. Does it bother you to see him?"

"No, I enjoy being a reminder to him about how he used my mother then just let her go."

I nodded. "Is that why you fought with your mother?" I asked, picking up my cards as well. "She didn't want you around your father?"

"No, she didn't, but I wanted to meet him."

Raina put her cards down on the table to reveal two kings, two fives, and a ten. I grimaced and laid down my cards. My new cards were an ace of hearts and a seven of diamonds.

"They're all red," I said. "Does that count for anything?"

Raina smiled. "Unfortunately, no, although you would have beaten me if you'd gotten a four in any suit instead of the seven. Do you want to try again?"

I nodded, and Raina shuffled the cards.

"Once you get better at it," she said, "you can play variations of the game. Or you can play for clothing instead of money with the right company." She grinned wickedly.

"What do you mean you play for clothing?" I asked, imagining people going into their closets to find dresses or shirts to throw onto the table as bets instead of money.

"If you lose a hand you have to take a piece of clothing off. Only the winner gets to stay dressed," she explained.

My eyes went wide. "And you've played this way before?"

"Once or twice with a few of the guards."

"How did you do?"

"I usually keep most of my clothing. Some of the guards aren't good at hiding their tells."

"And Damian?"

Raina shook her head. "I haven't been able to get him to play yet. He's a little...reserved sometimes."

Before I could respond, the next message from my brothers fluttered down to the table. I grabbed it up and read it to Raina. Jaylan and Brix were surprised and pleased to hear that our wine had the honor of being served at the Citadel, and Jaylan confirmed that three apprentice winemakers arrived from the vineyard in Gendris a day after I left. He also reported that Eddin hadn't said a word about me. Rather, the rumor around Fernweh was that the owner of a nearby gaming house hired Samhail to collect gambling debts from Eddin while he was in town, and it was a rumor that the owner was happily encouraging.

Raina and I stayed up for almost another two hours talking, playing cards, and exchanging messages with my brothers. I'd gone through almost half of my remaining message leaves before I told Jaylan and Brix that we should save the rest. After assuring my brothers that Samhail and I were now friends and that Bressen was not the terrifying monster everyone thought he was, I agreed to send them a message every two or three days just to check in.

When Raina finally left my room at close to midnight, my heart was lighter than it had been in days, and for the first time since I arrived at the Citadel, I fell into a deep, peaceful sleep.

Chapter 15

I managed to catch Bressen's eye the next morning at breakfast to mouth 'thank you' to him for the message leaves, and he gave me a brief nod before returning to his food. Despite myself, the dismissal gnawed at me. He'd been so bold the last time we were alone together, pulling me against his body and running his lips over my temple. My stomach still fluttered at the mere memory, and any question I'd had about his interest in me had vanished in that moment.

Yet my interactions with him were uncomfortably familiar. Eddin too had been sensual and affectionate behind closed doors while giving me very little attention in public. I assumed Bressen ignored me when others were around because he didn't want to give Jerram and Ursan reason to think I'd 'stoked his sympathies,' but the difference in how he treated me was a painful reminder of Eddin.

I tried to remind myself that nothing good could come of getting too close to Bressen. He was a Triumvirate lord, and I was…no one.

I avoided interacting with the residents of the Citadel altogether for several days after that. I went down to breakfast as late as I dared in the hope of missing them, and most of my other time was spent either in the library looking for books, or in my room reading. The only time I saw anyone was at dinner, which was the one meal served at a set time.

Dinners overall were more subdued affairs than that first evening. Jerram didn't speak to Bressen or Samhail if he could help it, and the two of them were happy to ignore him in kind. Ursan and Glenora tried to engage me in occasional conversation, but they got tired of making the effort when they found I wasn't inclined to chat.

There'd been no change in my situation. Raina told me that, based on what she'd heard, a seer's vision usually came to pass within a few weeks of when the seer had it. Perhaps a month or two at most. I wasn't sure how much I could rely on Raina's understanding of seer magic, but if she was right, then the lords appeared content to simply wait everything out.

In the meantime, I was slowly going stir-crazy. Back home I'd be doing hours of labor on the vineyard, and my newly sedentary life of reading was getting to me. My body wanted to be up and doing things, so a nervous energy that was ready to snap at any moment was coiling itself up inside me.

I missed Samhail's company, but I decided it was best not to get used to spending time with him. I'd learned from Raina that his room was two floors above mine, and I'd been tempted to go looking for him once or twice, but wisely decided against it.

Today I was in my room trying to be interested in a novel about a wizard on a quest to find some magical sword that would help him save the world from destruction. It wasn't as good as the novel I'd finished yesterday about a sorceress queen on a journey to find a magical jewel that would save her kingdom from certain doom.

After an hour, I gave up on the novel and grabbed my cloak. I threw it over my shoulders before stepping out onto my balcony, and the chilly outdoor air hit my face as I passed through the magical barrier. Several of the pigeons that always sat on my railing scattered in a flap of wings, but a few others stayed to watch me, obviously hoping for a few crumbs from breakfast.

"Sorry, nothing for you today," I told them. A couple cocked their heads at me, and I sighed. "Gods, I need to get out of this room. I don't suppose any of you know a way out of the fortress so I can walk around the city for a bit?"

Some of the pigeons ventured closer, unconvinced that I hadn't brought them anything to eat.

I still entertained half-hearted notions of escaping back to Fernweh. I visited my horse, who I'd named Ghost, in the Citadel stables at least once a day. I wasn't allowed to ride her, but I talked to her, brushed her, and fed her treats so she continued to know me. I brought the Citadel stable hands treats as well, in the form of desserts

I poached at meals. If I ever did decide to escape, I'd need Ghost, and getting to her would be easier if the stable hands knew me and, more importantly, liked me.

The other thing I'd needed to know was where the guards were usually stationed and when they changed shifts. A few trips up to the outer walls told me that they changed at midnight, six in the morning, noon, and six in the evening. Surprisingly, none of them questioned me the times I'd climbed the battlements to walk around. The only time I'd ever been stopped was when I wandered a little too close to the front gate of the fortress. The two guards closest to the entrance had immediately crossed their spears in front of me to bar my way, and several other guards drew their swords. None of them said anything to me, but the sharpened steel pointing my way spoke volumes, and I'd backed away quickly.

Unlike the stable hands, who were friendly and willing to be bribed with gifts of food for small liberties, the Citadel guards were all business. I'd tried to speak to some of them on more than one occasion, and they'd all pointedly ignored me. It became my game to stand next to them and start talking to see if they might react. I'd even teased one guard unmercifully after a little too much wine at dinner when I lowered my voice to a soft purr and told him about the different ways I liked to pleasure myself in bed. He hadn't so much as blinked when I'd described running my hands over my breasts and between my thighs, but the bulge in the front of his britches told me he'd heard every word.

Deciding I needed another walk now, I bid the pigeons goodbye and headed for the battlements overlooking the training yard. The yard was one of the more interesting places in the Citadel, as there were often guards practicing their hand-to-hand combat or their sword fighting. There were several men practicing when I arrived on the wall, and I was looking for a good spot to watch them when I realized the guard I'd teased the other day was just a few feet from me.

I sidled up to him as close as I dared. "Hello. It's nice to see you."

The guard didn't move, but a muscle ticked in his jaw, and a slight bulge appeared at the front of his britches a moment later.

"I see you remember me," I said.

The knot in his throat bobbed.

"I should apologize for last time. It wasn't nice of me to tease you."

No response.

"I just don't have many people to talk to, so I have to make my own fun."

A small commotion in the training yard drew my attention as the guards there quickly put away their swords and vacated the space. I saw why a moment later as Samhail and Bressen strolled in together.

"Do you know Samhail?" I asked. "He's the tall one."

No response.

"Do you know they call Lord Bressen the Nemesis Incarnate?"

I was finally rewarded with a flinch from the guard, and he blinked.

The sound of clanging metal drew my eyes back to the training yard where Bressen and Samhail had begun exchanging blows with swords. Samhail used two swords, although they weren't the razor-sharp blades he normally carried, while Bressen fought with a single sword. Bressen was tall, but Samhail still had several inches on him, and he was more solid. Samhail was also fast, especially for his size, but I was relieved to see Bressen was just a little bit faster as he blocked several blows from Samhail's swords that sent ringing echoes across the yard.

I looked around and realized that more than a few of the guards had lingered to watch Bressen and Samhail fight, and even a few female servants had found some task to put them within viewing distance of the training yard.

I myself spent my nights fantasizing about both Bressen and Samhail. I was sure the feel of my own hands roving over my body would never compare to having Samhail's large hands on me. Nor could the brush of my fingers mimic the light scratch of stubble on Bressen's face against my skin, but I nevertheless had a good enough

159

imagination to give myself some powerful climaxes the last few nights.

I looked behind me at the guard I'd been teasing and found that he'd somehow multiplied into two guards. One was still looking out over the wall while the other was now watching the training match below with an expression that didn't quite reach the look of cool disinterest he must be going for.

I looked back to the yard to see Bressen roll to one side in order to avoid vicious swipes from Samhail's two blades. Bressen came up swinging, and the blow from his blunted sword caught Samhail in the side of his ribs. Samhail grunted and inclined his head toward Bressen to acknowledge the hit before they circled each other once more.

Samhail attacked again immediately, and Bressen was forced back several steps as Samhail's blades sliced through the air from opposites sides. I gasped, and my heart skipped as one of the blades knocked Bressen's sword to the side, forcing him to dodge again as Samhail's second blade came around for a follow-up blow. Bressen pulled up short for some reason, though, and this time Samhail's blade connected, coming down on Bressen's shoulder.

My hand flew to my mouth as I remembered the highwayman's arms parting from his body, but Bressen only grunted as the blow from the blunted sword on his leather training vest forced him down onto one knee. His eyes flicked up to me on the wall for the briefest second, and I backed away so I was no longer at the balustrade. I wanted to watch, but somehow I knew Bressen had sensed my fear for him, and I was now wary of my presence being a distraction.

"Who's winning?" I asked the two guards as the sound of swordplay resumed.

Neither one of them answered.

"Remember that Samhail is the tall one," I offered helpfully.

They both remained silent, but I saw the lips of my guard twitch up as he fought to keep from smiling.

I spent the next half hour listening to metal meet metal and taking brief peeks at the fight before the clanging finally stopped. I peered over into the training yard. Samhail and Bressen had put their practice swords back on the rack and removed their leather vests. I was about to ask the guards a question when I saw a flash of copper and realized one guard had passed the other a coin.

I looked back into the training yard and swallowed. Both Bressen and Samhail had taken off their shirts despite the chilly air and were preparing to do some hand-to-hand fighting. I'd pulled my cloak tighter around me at one point while I was listening to the sword fighting, but I suddenly felt a lot warmer as I watched the two men move below. Their bodies were nothing short of masterpieces, and even from up here I could see every sinewy muscle flex and strain as Bressen struck a straw-stuffed pad that Samhail held up for him to hit. When they switched places several minutes later so that Bressen was holding the pad for Samhail, I realized I'd been biting my lip.

Bressen's punches had been fast and vicious, but I was shocked to see the strength behind Samhail's blows. It seemed to be a workout in itself for Bressen to hold the pad steady enough while Samhail hit it, and I thought I could feel the reverberations all the way up here. Samhail's fists seemed like hammers, and something clenched in my heart a while later when Bressen put down the pad and he and Samhail squared up to spar. I was certain one blow from Samhail would be enough to kill me if I ever accidentally found myself in the path of his fist. Bressen could likely take a punch better than I could, but I still had visions of him with a broken jaw if one of Samhail's hits ever really connected.

I watched wide-eyed as the two men circled each other, throwing jabs and punches every now and then when they saw an opening. Here again, Bressen was a little faster than Samhail, but when Samhail did land a blow, it usually sent Bressen staggering back. I moved away from the rail again, unable to fully watch the match.

"So who do you have in this fight?" I asked the guards.

They both stiffened, but neither said anything.

"Or do you only bet on their swordplay?"

No response.

"How do you decide who wins when you bet on them?"

Neither guard moved an inch.

"I'll let them know we've got two silver marks on Samhail up here," I said sweetly. I strode to the railing and had just opened my mouth to inhale when one of the guards spoke.

"Don't. Please."

I turned around to see the guards looking at me. I wasn't sure which one had spoken, but both were watching me desperately. I was relieved they hadn't called my bluff. There was no chance I would've shouted down to interrupt a sparring match between Samhail and a Triumvirate lord, but luckily they weren't willing to take that risk.

"How do you decide who wins?" I asked again.

"We don't bet on who wins," the guard I teased said. "Not exactly."

I frowned. "Then what exactly do you bet on?"

"My lady," the other guard said pleadingly, "if anyone ever found out about this, we'd-"

"I have no interest in getting you in trouble. I won't tell anyone about your side bets."

My guard sighed. "It's not just a physical battle they have. It's a mental one as well."

I frowned. "What does that mean?"

"Samhail puts up a mental shield when they fight," he explained, "and Lord Bressen tries to break it down. If he succeeds, he immobilizes Samhail so he can't move."

My mouth fell open, and I stared at them.

"You bet on whether or not Lord Bressen immobilizes Samhail?" I asked, and their sheepish looks were confirmation enough. "How often does Lord Bressen break through Samhail's shield?"

"They're about even," the other guard said.

"And this is what passes for entertainment around here?" I asked, my tone teasing.

"It's about all we have up here while on duty," the other guard said. "This is the most coveted shift because it falls during their training time when Samhail is here."

The guards both stiffened then, and one marched off along the wall, while the other turned back toward the city to resume his watch.

I turned to see that Bressen and Samhail were putting their equipment away and gathering up their things. I didn't see if Bressen had immobilized Samhail, but Bressen appeared to be brooding while Samhail's expression seemed smug.

The Priory bells rang out in the distance, and I realized I'd been standing out here for over an hour. I felt the cold creep back in around me, and I descended the stairs down from the wall to hurry along the corridor that led back to the rotunda. The training session had given my imagination some new fuel for tonight, and I was so engrossed in replaying the action that I didn't see the door at the end of the corridor swing open until Bressen and Samhail stepped into my path.

I pulled up just in time to avoid colliding with them, and my mind went blank as I took in the fact that they were both still shirtless. A thin sheen of sweat covered their chests, and they smelled of sweat too, but the sight and scent of them sent fire through my blood.

Bressen was closer. I'd almost run straight into him, and they both looked down at me with expressions that held a mixture of amusement and something else I couldn't read.

"Out enjoying some fresh air?" Bressen asked me.

I smiled pleasantly at him. "I can only spend so much time in my room reading before I need to escape for a while."

"How is the view from up on the wall nowadays?" Samhail asked. He smirked at me, and I shot him a glare.

"Only slightly more interesting than staring at the walls in my room," I said.

Samhail made a sound that was equal parts grunt and laugh, and Bressen quirked a brow at me. The corridor felt tight, as if there wasn't enough air for the three of us to occupy the same space. Both men

163

where huge compared to me, and my breasts tightened as I stood between them.

"Sometimes it depends where you look," Bressen drawled. "Some views are better than others." He inclined his head toward Samhail as he said "others," and Samhail grunted again.

"You're welcome to watch our training anytime you like, Cyra," Samhail said, dropping all pretense. I knew the comment was more for Bressen, who growled at it. Yes, I'd definitely distracted Bressen during their fight, and Samhail knew it.

"I need to go take a bath," Samhail said. "I'll leave the two of you to debate the views."

Samhail tossed his shirt over his shoulder and strode off toward the rotunda leaving me alone with Bressen. I wanted to follow him, but I'd already left Bressen standing in a hallway once before without getting his permission to leave. Doing it again didn't seem like a good idea. I certainly wasn't staying because I wanted to be near him…

There actually seemed to be even less air in the corridor now that Samhail was gone, and I wished Bressen would put his shirt back on. His chest was only inches from my face, and that bare golden skin called to me. I kept my eyes resolutely upward, though, and tamped down the urge to touch him.

"I'm told you spend quite a bit of time in your room these days," Bressen said. "It seems you only do your sneaking around in the dead of night."

My mouth dropped open in indignation, and it was on the tip of my tongue to ask him who was giving him information about how much time I spent in my room, but I realized the Citadel guards probably reported my whereabouts to all three lords regularly.

"I trust your quarters are adequate?" Bressen went on.

"More than adequate, my lord," I said, recovering myself. "I'd half-expected to occupy a dungeon cell when I first got here."

Bressen shrugged, and I marveled at how many muscles in his upper body flexed in that one simple movement. "Samhail wanted to put you in the dungeons, but Jerram, Ursan, and I talked him out of it," he said.

He was teasing me. The Nemesis Incarnate was actually teasing me.

"Are you sure you weren't in favor of the dungeon too, my lord?" I asked. "I believe you were expecting some sort of monster when I arrived."

I'd thought to tease him back but regretted the words as soon as they were out of my mouth. Bressen's lips curled into a grin, and he looked at me from under heavy lashes. I knew exactly what he was going to say before he said it.

"As I recall, so were you."

He leaned toward me, and I had to stop myself from leaning forward as well. I wasn't sure how many of my thoughts he'd read that first day, but I hoped he didn't know how attractive I'd found him, *still* found him. Gods above, his face and body were nearly perfect.

"You'll have to forgive me for that, my lord," I said. "The stories they tell of you in Fernweh aren't flattering, and Samhail wasn't forthcoming with anything to ease my mind."

"I'm not surprised. Samhail seems to enjoy the shock people feel when they meet me."

I tried to be annoyed at the arrogance of the statement, but there was too much truth in it. People did fear Bressen, and they were undoubtedly surprised to find he was young and beautiful when they met him.

"You seem to enjoy it too, my lord," I said, holding his stare. I had no idea where my insistent boldness with him came from. There was an energy that sparked between us whenever I was near him, and that energy fueled a recklessness in me I was powerless to stop.

Bressen's face was only inches from mine now, and I couldn't for the life of me remember how he'd gotten so close. I thought about stepping back to reclaim some space between us, but my foot went forward instead as I raised my head to lock my gaze with his. Surprise flickered in Bressen's expression, but he didn't move. We'd somehow gotten into a standoff, and neither of us was inclined to back down.

Our bodies were nearly touching now, and I felt the warmth radiating off him like a stone that's been absorbing the sun all day. The smell of his sweat curled in my nostrils, and there was something primal and raw beneath it that made every nerve in my body sing.

A cool fog settled on my skin suddenly, muting Bressen's heat, and I frowned.

"I do enjoy surprising people," Bressen said, his voice husky, "but I enjoy it more when *they* surprise *me*. That's hard to do since I usually know what they're thinking before they do."

My chin went up a notch. "And I suppose you know what I'm thinking right now?"

His brow arched at the challenge, and in a belated attempt at self-defense, I willed myself to make my mind blank.

"You're thinking," Bressen said, grinning at me, "that you find my arrogance charming."

I scoffed.

"You're thinking," he went on, "that you don't know how you let me get this close."

My eyes widened. That was too near the truth for comfort.

"And you're thinking," he said, his voice just barely above a whisper now, "how much you want me to touch you."

A thousand tiny butterflies took flight in my stomach as Bressen's hands slipped up to my waist, and he leaned in. He held me in place as he had the other night, but I had no thoughts of pulling away.

"It's alright," Bressen said, his voice tickling my ear. "I was thinking the same thing." He dipped his head lower to kiss my neck, and any denial I'd been about to make died on my lips as liquid heat trickled down my back. I should admonish him for his brazenness, but the words wouldn't rise any higher than where his lips moved along my throat.

Bressen pulled me closer, and I grabbed his arms to steady myself.

I remembered he wasn't wearing a shirt only when I was met with smooth bare flesh, and I couldn't help running my hands up his arms to feel the steeliness of his muscles under my fingers. Then my back was against the wall, and I inhaled sharply as Bressen's tongue flicked lightly at a spot just below the back of my ear. I ran my hands up over his shoulders and threaded one hand into his hair. It was still damp with sweat, but I didn't care. I didn't care about anything but his lips on my throat and the bliss they were making me feel.

My eyes flickered open when Bressen's teeth grazed my neck, and I realized we were still in the middle of the corridor where anyone could see us.

"My lord," I said, moving my hands down to press against his chest. Nemesis take me, that was hard as steel as well.

"Yes?" he asked, not budging an inch.

"We're in the middle of the hallway."

"No one can see us. I put up an obfuscation glamour. You probably felt it earlier," he said. His lips never left my skin, and the warm tickle of his breath was making my knees weak.

"The cool fog?"

"I suppose it does feel a bit like a fog," he conceded.

Bressen pressed his mouth harder against my neck, and I gasped but kept my hands on his chest. I forced myself to push on him again.

"My lord, please, I can't."

He was silent, and I realized he probably wasn't used to anyone telling him no. Finally, he nodded and pulled back so that he no longer pressed me against the wall. Where I'd found the will to stop him, I had no idea.

In truth, my objection was less about where we were and more about the danger of my situation. This man and the other two lords held my life in their hands. I wasn't too proud to admit I would've willingly shared Bressen's bed if I wasn't in danger from him or the other lords, but I didn't delude myself into thinking that letting him have me might keep me safe.

"I'm honored by your attentions, my lord," I said, "and under different circumstances, I'd be yours to command, but letting this go any further would be dangerous for me."

Bressen frowned at me. "Mine to command?" His voice had the same edge to it as the other night when I'd reminded him that he had the ability to kill me whenever he wanted. "I'd never command anyone to my bed," he said sharply, "nor do I need commands."

I started to apologize, but he cut me off.

"Your body responds to my invitations just fine," he said.

The sureness in his voice annoyed me, but when I looked into his eyes, I was shocked by the raw desire I saw there. I blushed and tried to look away, but he grabbed my chin and brought my face back around to look at him. "But you're right that this isn't a good idea," he said. "I'll leave you alone from now on."

He stepped back from me, and I felt the cold fog of his glamour lift. His words should have relieved me, but they only made me miserable, more so when he turned on his heel and strode down the corridor back toward the rotunda. I sagged against the wall as I watched him go, cursing myself at every ripple and twitch of the muscles in his back.

Only now that I couldn't have him, did I realize how much I truly wanted him.

Chapter 16

Bressen resolutely ignored me at meals after our encounter outside the training yard. I told myself it was better this way, but the twisting in my chest every time I saw him kept insisting that I'd made a huge mistake. I didn't understand why I felt this way. I'd only known Bressen a short time, but something thrummed in my body when he was around, like I was a harp and his presence plucked at my strings. I even caught Samhail watching me closely at breakfast one morning, as if he could see the energy vibrating inside me.

I'd been at the Citadel for about two weeks, and the monotony wore on me a little more each day. I looked forward to my time with Raina at night when we talked and played cards, but the rest of my hours were painfully dull.

The Citadel's ball should have been an opportunity to dispel the tedium, but as I stood in the ballroom among the bustling throng of people who were there for an event that was supposedly being thrown in my honor, the only thing I felt was misery. I'd never seen this many people in my life, and the instinct toward flight hummed louder inside me every second I was there. Fernweh boasted a population of a few hundred, but even at town gatherings, there'd never been this many people in one place at the same time.

Each person was dressed in clothing and jewelry that probably cost about what our vineyard profited in a year. Women shimmered from head-to-toe in dresses of silk and satin as glittering gems hung from their hair, ears, necks, wrists, and fingers. Men wore fine suits or doublets of black, navy, or dark brown with the occasional pop of color from a vest or cravat.

If I'd thought the rest of the Citadel was opulent, it was nothing compared to its grand ballroom. Floor-to-ceiling windows curtained in deep blue velvet lined the long sides of the room, and twenty chandeliers with thousands of twinkling crystals lit by candles hung overhead. Tables of food practically groaned under the weight of their many platters, and servers slalomed among guests with trays of drinks. An orchestra tuned their instruments near a dance floor that accessed a huge balcony through a set of double doors.

Under different circumstances I might have been impressed or even excited to be here, but I'd arrived at the ballroom ten minutes ago and had already had enough. I turned to go but immediately came face-to-face with a broad chest. I wasn't at all surprised to find Samhail looking down at me when I raised my head. I seemed destined to continually meet him like this, my face almost running into his chest.

"Leaving already?" Samhail asked in amusement. "I went to your room to escort you down, but your lady's maid said you'd already left."

I took a moment to look him over. "I didn't even know you owned clothing that wasn't black," I said brushing my hand down the arm of the dark indigo jacket he wore. It was embroidered with gold accents and looked at once both impeccable and foreign on him. Aside from dinner the first night I was here, I hadn't seen him in anything besides his warrior's clothing, and I couldn't wrap my mind around him dressed up like this, ripples of muscles straining under the fabric of his jacket. He wore what everyone else here wore, but he clearly wasn't one of them.

"Shall we get something to eat?" Samhail asked, extending an arm. I took it, and we headed toward the tables of food.

I realized right away that being with Samhail in a crowd like this was a boon. People parted for him as if pushed by some invisible force, and I breathed a sigh of relief. Years ago, I'd looked over a bluff to see a shark swimming in the middle of a school of fish. Every time the shark turned, the fish made way for it, keeping a cushion of space between them and the predator. Such was the case as Samhail and I cut through the crowd toward the food tables.

"People certainly take notice of you when you're in a room," I said to Samhail as murmuring rose around us.

"It's not me they're looking at," he said.

170

I furrowed my brows and looked around. Indeed, most eyes did seem to be on me rather than my giant companion, and I now regretted letting Raina dress me in the pale silver gown I wore. It had an underskirt of soft flowing fabric with a sheer overlay featuring thousands of tiny gemstones embedded in it like stars. Strands of clear gems also hung around my hips, which emphasized their sway.

Raina said the gown enhanced my eyes, but it seemed to almost do that too well. Between the gown, the strands, and the other pieces of jewelry Raina had fastened on me, I sparkled like a diamond. Had I wanted to be noticed, the look would have been perfect, but attention was the last thing I wanted right now. I felt like a curiosity on display, and I pressed closer to Samhail.

We finally made it to the tables of food, and I took in the vast array of fruits, cakes, meats, and cheeses that sat overflowing on them. I speared a piece of fruit with a toothpick and turned to Samhail. He'd already piled food onto one of the tiny plates in a feat of balance that rather impressed me.

"Where did all these people come from?" I asked.

"Some are from the city, but others came in from the territories for the ball," he answered. "They'll stay at inns around Callanus tonight. Most come to catch up on gossip or to make business connections. The rest come just to say they've been here. Word has gotten around that Bressen is in residence right now, so they're here to catch a glimpse of him."

"He's really that much of a draw?"

Samhail grunted in disgust. "It's a status symbol in some circles to say you've been in the same room with him and not had your brain leak out of your head."

I had to throw a hand over my mouth to keep from spitting a bite of cake across the room. I choked but managed to force the cake down my throat.

"Really?" I asked as my eyes watered.

He sighed. "I wish I could say that I made that up."

As if in confirmation, guests began to buzz at the other end of the room, and I felt Bressen's presence before I saw his dark head just above the crowd. The very air in the space pulsed with his power, and I stepped closer to Samhail.

If I'd thought the crowd parted for me and Samhail, it was nothing compared to the wide berth they gave Bressen, his dark halo once again undulating around him. Bressen had admitted he only wore the halo to make an impression, and I wondered if the same was true for the sense of power that preceded him. I'd only felt it now and that time in the Great Chamber. I'd been oblivious to his presence when he snuck up on me in the library, which led me to believe he was letting his power loose on purpose now for the benefit of those assembled.

Like Samhail, Bressen usually wore mostly black, and he hadn't bothered to deviate from that tonight. Even the shirt under his jacket was black this time. The clothing was even finer than he normally wore, and his shoulders gleamed with ornate silver embroidery.

I saw Bressen catch Samhail's eye above the crowd, and Samhail nodded to him.

"I'm needed," he said. "I trust you'll be fine here?"

I didn't really want him to go, but I nodded, and he headed off toward Bressen.

I moved to a table of drinks next to the buffet and was pleased to see that wine from my family's vineyard was once again being served. I poured myself a glass and savored the notes of blackberry and dark chocolate I tasted.

The crowd was no longer paying me any heed, and I inched back toward the window behind me figuring that I might go unnoticed for the rest of the night if I...

The orchestra struck up their first song, and as if summoned by the music, Jerram materialized at my side. His appearance was so sudden that I jumped back in alarm.

"Cyra, you look beautiful," he said. "I must have your first dance."

I held up my wine, ready to protest, but he cut me off. "I insist.

Your wine will be fine on the windowsill."

He tugged on my hand, urging me to follow him. Instead of leaving the wine, though, I downed it quickly and set the empty glass on the sill as he led me to the dance floor.

Jerram took my hand in his and put an arm around my waist. Couples were already swirling around us, and I cringed as I saw what they were doing. I'd danced before, but never like this. There seemed to be specific steps, and all the dancers knew them. I did not.

"Just let me lead you," Jerram said.

His arm tightened on my waist, and he whirled me into the eddying couples. I immediately regretted downing the wine as all of the spinning threatened to send it back up. Admittedly though, Jerram knew what he was doing, and he kept me moving in the right direction as we turned around the floor.

When the dance ended, I managed to beg off a second one despite his entreaties. No sooner had I made it off the dance floor, than Ursan was at my side.

"Are you enjoying the ball, Cyra?" he asked.

"It's lovely."

"I used to be a pretty good dancer in my day," Ursan said, and I groaned inwardly as he held out his arm to me. "Allow me the pleasure?"

I forced a smile onto my face and let Ursan lead me out onto the floor. I didn't expect him to be as light on his feet as he was, but Ursan was just as good a dancer as Jerram. Dance lessons must be standard for Triumvirate lords.

When the dance again ended, I thanked Ursan and made straight for the open doorway onto the balcony. I prayed no one was out there. I needed time to regroup away from the crowd and to purge the memory of my less-than-inspiring turns on the dance floor.

I paused at the threshold but didn't see anyone outside. I crossed the large balcony to the edge and rested my hands on the cold stone balustrade. The quiet enveloped me as the music and general clamor of the crowd faded away, as though the noise didn't dare spill out past the doorway of the balcony. My mind cleared, and I reveled once again in the solitude under the halfmoon nestled among the stars.

I stretched my neck and arched my back to ease the stiffness from trying to hold my posture during the dances. Between the wine I'd gulped and the dancing, I felt warm, and I savored the chilly night breeze on my skin. I wondered how long I could stay out here before I either got too cold or anyone missed me.

"Hiding from anyone in particular?" a familiar deep voice drawled from behind me.

I whirled at the sound but couldn't see anyone in the darkness as the light pouring out of the ballroom kept my eyes from adjusting.

A moment later, Bressen emerged from the shadows in a corner of the balcony I hadn't seen. My stomach somersaulted at the sight of him, and I wrapped my arms around myself to hide the shiver that had nothing to do with the cold.

He walked over and put a hand on the balustrade as well. My body felt his presence even from a few feet away, as if my blood flowed a little faster in my veins. Samhail's words from earlier resurfaced, and I pictured my brain leaking out of my head.

I thought I saw Bressen smile in the dark. "You *are* hiding, I assume?" he asked.

"This seems to be the popular place to do it," I said, giving him a pointed look.

Bressen chuckled and took a step closer to me. "The difference is that I'm hiding more for their benefit than my own. They think they want to see me, but the fear coming off them is...tedious. I make my appearance at these balls so the city elite will have something exciting to discuss tomorrow, and then I make my exit and let them get on with their nights."

You need me to come because my presence will stoke fear in the guests, and you want them to be afraid, Bressen had told Ursan at dinner that first night.

"I also come so Glenora won't scold me," he added with a wink.

174

He took a couple steps closer as he spoke and was now only inches from me. He'd promised to stay away from me, but he seemed to have given up on that already.

"You like their fear from what I can tell," I said. My heart thundered as I said the words, but Bressen surprised me by laughing.

"Fear has its uses," he said, "although apparently not on you."

He was amused rather than angry, so I shrugged. "I suppose I have a new tolerance for fear since I jumped off a cliff with Samhail before I knew he could fly."

Bressen's brows lifted, and his smile widened. "Oh, he didn't tell me that story. I'll have to pry that one out of him later."

I had no idea where the impulse to tease Bressen came from, but he seemed to enjoy it. My brain hadn't leaked out of my head yet, in any case. I was about to wish him goodnight, but I froze at the voice from the doorway of the balcony.

"There you are, Cyra," Jerram said coming toward us. "You owe me another dance."

No. Please, no.

"Cyra already promised the next dance to me," Bressen told him.

Even in the darkness I could see the scowl on Jerram's face, but then Bressen's hand was in mine, and he led me off the balcony and back into the bright light of the ballroom.

I blinked as my eyes tried to adjust, and I heard audible gasps of surprise as Bressen steered me through the crowd toward the dance floor. Then we were in the middle of the floor, and I was staring into the piercing depths of his eyes.

"I don't know any of these dances," I warned him in a whisper.

"You'll be fine," he said, his lips hinting at a smile.

Bressen's hands were warmer than I expected, especially considering he'd been outside in the cold, and I felt a small thrill as he placed a hand on my shoulder blade. It surprised me since Ursan and Jerram had both held me by the waist. I'd managed to keep some space between me and the other lords when we danced, but I was acutely

175

aware now of my hip pressed into Bressen's, and the muscles between my legs tightened.

Then the music started, and we were moving.

From our very first steps, Bressen swept me gracefully around the floor as if we'd been dancing together for years. Somehow I seemed to know exactly which way to move, and I strongly suspected Bressen had something to do with that. The skirt of my gown billowed out around me as Bressen swirled me across the floor, my feet stepping deftly in time with his. The music held us together, as if each note was a shared understanding between us, and his hips pulled me along with him as if we were stuck together like magnets. I felt a lightness in my legs as if I was held up by air.

My eyes never left Bressen's. With Jerram and Ursan, my attention had darted around to see what other couples were doing so I could follow their moves, but I felt no compulsion to do that now. I was confident every step I took was the right one. My body moved of its own accord, as if I'd been a dancer in some other life and muscle memory had taken over.

I was almost certain Bressen had implanted the steps in my head. I should be angry he invaded my mind, but there was something so beautiful and freeing about moving around the floor with him that I couldn't bring myself to be upset. I'd chastise him later if I dared, but for now I wanted to enjoy this feeling for as long as it lasted.

I didn't realize we'd stopped moving until Bressen's hand fell from my shoulder, and I blinked up at him.

"I should make my exit now before we give the gossip mills too much fodder for tomorrow," he said.

He led me off the floor, and I almost stopped walking when I realized we'd been the only two dancers out there. Whether the other couples had fled to be away from Bressen, or whether they'd yielded the space to us in deference to his skills as a dancer – skills that had temporarily been extended to me – I didn't know. Regardless, a flush bloomed on my face to think everyone had been watching us.

176

"Thank you," I said when we reached the side of the room again. "Not just for the dance, but for rescuing me."

"It was my pleasure," he said as he gave me a quick bow, and then he was gone.

The heaviness settled back in my legs as I stood there. For the few minutes we'd danced together, we'd seemed like two parts of a whole, and now I felt like I'd lost something important.

A glass of wine appeared under my nose.

"I thought you might need some refreshment after all that dancing," Jerram said, his voice clipped. "I believe this wine is from your vineyard?"

I took the glass and thanked him.

"You should be careful around Bressen," he said.

"Oh?" I took a sip of the wine. Something seemed slightly off about the taste, and I made a mental note to hunt down the bottle before I left to check it for possible faults.

"I'm sure you've heard how dangerous he is," Jerram went on.

"I've heard rumors."

"They aren't rumors," he said.

I took another sip of wine but didn't say anything.

"Bressen can be charming when he wants to be, but I've seen him do things to his enemies I'd rather forget," Jerram said.

"Should I consider myself his enemy?" I asked.

Jerram smiled wryly. "Maybe not yet, but if we learn something about your connection to the vision, and he suddenly thinks you're a threat…"

He let the thought hang in the air. It was the first time in days anyone had mentioned the vision to me. I'd almost managed to forget why I was here, but my situation suddenly came crashing back.

I took a big gulp of wine and laughed off his suggestion. "I'm sure I'm no threat to a man who can kill with his mind."

"You've heard the stories then. I wasn't sure they'd made it out as far as the outer lands," Jerram said, sipping his own wine. "So then at least you know what you're up against."

"Up against?" I asked in surprise. "You sound like he's already marked me for death."

"No, of course not. You're a beautiful woman. There are probably other things he wants from you first," he said, giving me a pitying look. "He'll only use you and then discard you."

I stared at him, completely bewildered by his temerity. "I have no interest in Lord Bressen," I assured him, "and I'm sure he doesn't have any interest in me either."

"No? That was quite a dance the two of you just had," he said.

"I also danced with you and Ursan. Should I add you both to my list of suitors?"

Jerram just lifted a brow as if to say, *Why not?*

"Ursan is married," I said obtusely.

"Not very happily from what I've seen."

I was a little shocked to hear Jerram say it so baldly, but I'd seen myself that there was some tension between Ursan and Glenora. On the other hand, I'd also seen how she seemed to worry for her husband. Jerram was trying to sow seeds of discord, in any case, and I wasn't about to let him pull me in, so I took another sip of my wine instead.

I was starting to feel a little faint. All the spinning on the dance floor plus the wine must have gotten to me. I turned to Jerram to excuse myself, but my vision blurred, and I swayed.

"Are you alright?" he asked me.

"I'm...dizzy," I said. I tried to focus, but things only got blurrier.

"Maybe you've had enough wine for tonight," he said pulling the glass from my hand.

"I only had two," I said as the room started to spin. I was a winemaker for gods' sake. I usually drank more wine than this when taste-testing from our barrels.

"Two seems to be your limit tonight," Jerram said as he snaked one arm around me and put a hand under my elbow. He steered me toward the door of the ballroom. "Let's get you outside where you can get some fresh air."

I let Jerram guide me through the ballroom, and moments later the brightness faded away as we exited into the dimly lit corridor.

"Where are we going?" I asked, fighting the haze overtaking me.

"Don't worry. I'll take care of you," Jerram whispered. "We have to be quiet now."

Something was wrong, but I couldn't clear my mind enough to figure out what.

"Wait." I tried to stop walking, but Jerram was insistent, and I couldn't summon enough resistance to halt him.

"Jerram!" A voice boomed through the corridor and echoed around in my addled head. Both Jerram and I jumped at the sound, and then I was falling. Time seemed suspended as my body took forever to reach the floor, but I eventually hit the ground with a loud thud, and pain shot through my hip and limbs as they connected with the stone. My eyes fluttered wildly as I tried to stay conscious, and I saw someone coming toward me. Two glowing red spots, like eyes, flashed from somewhere in the darkness of the hall, and I felt an anger that was not my own. No, not anger. Unfettered rage.

My limbs were leaden as I tried and failed to move. I had to flee, but my body wouldn't obey me. Then I was being lifted off the floor and cradled in someone's arms. We were moving, and I tried to cry out, but I couldn't.

I wasn't sure how much time passed before brightness once again filled my vision, and I had the sense of being in my own room. I heard voices, but I didn't understand them.

My knees touched down gently on a cold marble floor, and I vaguely recognized that I was in my bathing chamber. A strong arm was anchored around my waist while another held my head. My eyes fluttered again, and I realized I was kneeling in front of my toilet.

"I need you to vomit now, Cyra," a deep accented voice said into my ear. No sooner had I heard the words than I pitched forward and heaved the contents of my stomach into the toilet. Purple bile swirled in front of me, and I vomited some more. When I had nothing left in my stomach, I fell back from the toilet into a pair of waiting arms.

I felt myself being lifted and carried again. More voices sounded, and then I was on my bed. I was so tired, but there was too much light. It hurt my eyes.

As if in answer, the lights dimmed, and I relaxed.

When had I lost my tolerance for wine? The question rattled around in my head, but the darkness was calling to me. Someone tugged at my dress, trying to remove it, and alarm filled me until I heard Raina's voice. "I'm just getting you ready for bed, my lady."

"Is the ball over already?"

"It is for you. It's time to sleep."

"I danced," I said. "It must have made me dizzy. And I had too much wine."

A pause. "You can tell me all about it in the morning."

Raina's voice came to me through a fog, and I gave up trying to keep my eyes open. My body felt heavy, as it had at the end of the dance with Bressen, and I let myself sink into sweet oblivion.

Chapter 17

My mouth was bone-dry, and my body hurt.

Those were the two thoughts I had just before opening my eyes to a cold, gray sky outside my windows. My tongue felt oversized and fuzzy, and I smacked my lips together to get the saliva flowing, but it was slow in coming.

I started to sit up but groaned as pain shot through my limbs. My knee, hip, and elbow on one side all ached sharply, and I vaguely remembered falling last night. I was in my room at the Citadel, but I didn't remember climbing into bed after the ball. There were too many gaps in my memory, signs that I'd had too much to drink last night.

I groaned into my pillow. It had been a long time since I'd been drunk enough to vomit and pass out. The last time was the previous winter at the vineyard when more than a foot of snow had already fallen outside with no end in sight. Jaylan, Brix, and I had ended up playing a drinking game out of sheer boredom. It had started out as a normal game of dice to give us something to do, but the three of us were too competitive for our own good, and we'd decided the losers of each round should have to drink. By midnight, we'd all passed out in the living room and woken up the next morning to find that one of us had thrown up in the fireplace. It was still hotly debated who.

I'd felt wretched that morning, but it didn't quite compare to how I felt right now. By the Nemesis, how much had I drunk to feel this bad?

The better question was whether I'd done anything stupid last night in front of the Triumvirate lords and all those people. I buried my head deeper into my pillow, but that only made my head pound harder.

"My lady?" Raina's voice came tentatively from somewhere beside the bed.

"Go away," I said into the pillow.

181

"Thank the Protector! You're awake!" Raina shrieked, and the sound pierced my brain like she'd shoved a dagger through my eye.

"Raina, please…" I mumbled. "Not now."

"Are you alright, my lady?" Something in her voice made me frown. She seemed afraid.

I turned over and groaned as every muscle in my body objected. "What's wrong?"

"Don't you remember? Lord Bressen brought you in last night."

"What?" I tried to blink the last fog of sleep from my eyes. "Lord Bressen?"

Realization dawned, and I bolted upright in bed, which sent another throb of pulsing pain through my head. "Oh gods, what did I do last night? How drunk was I?"

I now remembered hearing Bressen's voice last night and that I'd thrown up right after.

"Please tell me I didn't throw up on Lord Bressen," I moaned as Raina pressed a cup of tea into my hand.

I looked up when she didn't answer. She was at the side of my bed wringing her hands.

"Raina, just tell me. How bad was it? What did I do?"

"You…you didn't do anything, my lady. Lord Bressen said you'd been drugged. He tried to make you vomit it all out."

"What?" I heard her words but couldn't wrap my brain around them. Then my eyes flew open, and I was suddenly very awake. "Drugged! What do you mean I was drugged?"

"I don't know. Lord Bressen just came in last night carrying you in his arms. He was angry…So angry." She seemed to shiver. "After he made you vomit, he put you in bed and told me to get you into your night clothes. Then he stalked off. He looked ready to murder someone."

Raina pressed three fingers to her lips and kissed them as an offer of prayer to the Trinity.

I just stared at Raina. My mind was having a tug-of-war between relief that I hadn't gotten drunk and embarrassed myself, and horror at the idea that I'd been drugged and carried to my room half-unconscious by Bressen.

"I need to get dressed." I threw off the blankets and set the tea on the nightstand so quickly that it clattered loudly and threatened to tip over.

Raina bolted into action and went to pull clothes from my closet. I made my way into the bathing chamber to splash some water on my face, and twenty minutes later, I was dressed and heading toward the dining room.

My entire body ached, and I still had a splitting headache. Cold tendrils crept through me at the idea that someone had tried to drug me last night, for the gods-only-knew what reason. My stomach knotted tightly every time I thought about what could have happened if Bressen hadn't been there to…save me? He *had* saved me, hadn't he?

I almost ran right into Samhail as he was leaving breakfast, and I peered around him to see who else was in the dining room. Only Ursan and Glenora were at the table.

"Where's Bressen? I need to speak with Bressen," I told Samhail.

He nodded. "Come with me."

Samhail headed into Bressen's wing of the Citadel, and I followed behind him, trying to keep up with his long strides. I'd never been to Bressen's private wing of the building, but the halls looked much like those in Ursan's wing, minus the menagerie of animals.

Samhail led me to a pair of large double doors and waved me inside. It was a library with large windows spaced between shelves of books on two sides of the room. The other two sides of the room were covered from floor-to-ceiling with books, and I marveled to see that Bressen's library was almost as big as the Citadel's central one.

Bressen, however, was not in the room.

I turned to Samhail. "Where is Bressen?"

"Bressen is taking care of an issue right now, but I can tell you what you want to know."

I crossed my arms over my chest. "And what is it you think I want to know?"

"You want to know what happened to you last night."

I went still. "And you know what happened to me?"

"Maybe you should sit down."

"I'll stand," I snapped. "Just tell me."

Samhail exhaled and nodded. "We believe Jerram drugged you last night. Bressen caught him trying to lead you away. You seemed only half-conscious."

My arms came uncrossed, and I reached for the back of one of the cushy reading chairs to steady myself.

"What...what was he trying to do? He wasn't...Was he going to...?" I couldn't finish the sentence.

"It might have been that," Samhail said, seeming just as hesitant to mention rape as I was, "or he might have been trying to question you without anyone else around. Maybe both."

I felt as if I wanted to throw up again. Stars burst in my vision as I went lightheaded, and I felt Samhail's arms come around me as I swayed.

"Sit," he ordered, helping me down into the chair.

"What happens now?" I said when I'd quelled the nausea enough to speak.

"Unfortunately, probably not much. We can't prove Jerram drugged you. Whatever was in your glass was destroyed. Jerram ran when Bressen confronted him about dragging you through the hallway, but Jerram is a coward, and he's afraid of Bressen on a good day, so seeing him flee last night isn't proof of anything."

"So then nothing happens? I get drugged and almost...attacked last night, and nothing happens?"

"Not entirely nothing. Jerram disappeared last night, but Bressen is looking for him now, and guilty or no, Jerram will regret it when Bressen finds him. There are limits to what Bressen can do to a fellow member of the Triumvirate without solid proof of wrong-doing, but

184

Jerram won't find the confrontation pleasant regardless. In the meantime, we need to be more vigilant. Jerram has shown he's a threat, and we need to proceed accordingly."

I let that sink in, then stood up. Samhail eyed me with concern and stepped toward me.

"Is...is there anything I can do?" he asked.

I'd thrown myself into his arms before he finished the question. Tears trickled down my cheeks, but I managed to hold back the sobs that threatened to escape my throat. I leaned my head against his chest as my tears disappeared into his shirt.

Samhail's arms came around me hesitantly, and he patted one large hand clumsily on my shoulder.

The awkwardness of his attempt to soothe me almost made me laugh. "You're really bad at hugging," I said in a quavering voice, and his chuckle rumbled against my cheek.

"My kind doesn't do much hugging. I'll work on my technique."

I lifted my head off his chest and stepped away from him. He wiped the wetness from one of my cheeks with his thumb.

"Actually, there is something you can do," I said.

"What is it?"

"Will you teach me to fight?"

Samhail frowned. "What do you mean teach you to fight?"

"I mean, I don't want to be at someone's mercy ever again. You and Bressen practice your combat in the training yard. I want you to teach me how to fight like that. To punch, to wield a sword. Any of it, all of it."

I could see it was on the tip of his tongue to say that fighting wouldn't help me if I was drugged again, but he apparently thought better of it and just nodded once.

"Let me discuss it with Bressen."

My brows knit. "Why does he get to decide if I can learn to fight?"

Samhail paused. "I trust his judgment. I want to see if he has any concerns."

185

"What kind of concerns?"

"I'll know that when I talk to him."

I glared at him. "Fine. Let me know what he says." In truth, his answer was more promising than I'd expected.

Samhail nodded. He turned to leave but then stopped suddenly. The hair on the back of my neck stood on end for a moment, and I felt the prickling at the base of my skull that I'd felt a couple times before.

"Bressen is back," Samhail said. "He's in his study. I can take you to him if you still want to talk to him."

"Yes! How did you know he was back?"

"I just got a message from him."

It didn't surprise me Bressen could send messages with his mind, but it did surprise me that I'd apparently been able to sense it. I assumed the prickling in my neck was my body somehow detecting the message when Samhail received it.

Samhail led me out of the library and up some stairs before stopping in front of a large, ornately-carved mahogany door. He knocked loudly, and a call to enter sounded from within.

I wasn't sure what I'd expected the study belonging to a lord that everyone called the Nemesis Incarnate to look like, but it was not this. The room was light and airy with high ceilings and sheer white curtains that billowed gently in the breeze coming in from the open doors of the balcony off to the left of a desk that sat in front of a large window. The walls were a soft shade of jade green, and the artwork that hung there had clearly been done by a master. A bookcase stood against one wall, and a long table with six chairs around it sat on another side of the room.

Samhail walked straight in and stopped before Bressen's desk, which was also mahogany, although not quite as ornate as the door. I followed at a slower pace as my eyes roamed around the room.

Bressen looked up from his desk and nodded to Samhail. "I see you found her," he said.

"*She* found *me*. I told her everything you told me this morning."

Bressen nodded again. "Jerram has been dealt with for the time being. He denies doing anything untoward, of course, but I impressed on him what will happen if I find out he's lying or if he tries anything so stupid again." He looked back down at his desk and signed a paper.

"Were you able to read his mind?" Samhail asked.

Bressen frowned and looked up again. "Either he's telling the truth, and he was just trying to help her back to her room," he scoffed to indicate that he didn't buy it, "or he's gotten much better at mind shielding lately. I tried to read his mind, but I felt…" He seemed to search for the words to describe it.

Samhail cocked his head questioningly. "Felt what?"

Bressen shook his head. "I'm not sure. It was almost as if my powers were…off."

"Off?"

"I can't explain it. Something felt wrong, but I'm not sure what."

"And the other thing we discussed earlier this morning?" Samhail asked. "Were you able to confirm…?" He trailed off.

Bressen went still and braced his arms on the desk. "Gone," he said quietly, and I thought I heard Samhail growl.

"How?"

"I don't know yet. They found the issue and took care of it, but we're not sure how it happened in the first place."

"And you're certain he's gone?"

"Yes."

The two men stared at each other a moment longer before Bressen spoke again. "We'll talk about this later. Give me half an hour," he said to Samhail, inclining his head toward me.

Samhail nodded and strode from the room, closing the door behind him.

I suddenly felt very conspicuous standing in the middle of Bressen's study. I must be taking him away from something important if even Samhail seemed worried about whatever news Bressen had just given him. I felt guilty for taking up his time with a problem that now seemed minor by comparison.

I took a step back toward the door, but Bressen's eyes locked with mine, and I froze. He came around the front of the desk to lean against it, and my eyes slipped to the floor. This man had seen me vomit last night, and a flush warmed my cheeks.

"How are you feeling?" Bressen asked gently.

I almost laughed. I didn't know how to answer that question. I wasn't even sure if he meant physically, mentally, or emotionally, although I wasn't feeling very well by any of those measures. I gave him the first answer that popped into my head. "I'm angry."

He nodded.

"But grateful," I continued. "I'm told I have you to thank for saving me, so thank you."

He nodded again but waited to see if I had anything else to say.

I felt the need to fill the silence between us. "It seems as though you were meant to spend your evening rescuing me from Jerram."

His face went serious. "You have my word he'll never have an opportunity to do anything like that again."

Something in his voice sent a chill down my spine, and I nodded.

"I know it might be uncomfortable for you to remember," Bressen said, "but can you recall anything about your interaction with Jerram before you started to lose consciousness? Any details you can think of might be able to help us determine what he was up to."

"It sounds like you already know what he was doing," I said hesitantly.

"I have my suspicions. I'm not sure if you overheard the night you were eavesdropping, but Jerram has been wanting to question you further about the vision, preferably without Ursan and I there. I suspect that's the main reason he tried to sneak you away, but I wouldn't trust him not to take advantage of you in other ways while he had you."

I shuddered and wrapped my arms around my chest. Bressen

pushed off his desk and seemed for a moment as if he might come to me, but he didn't move any further. Instead, he just asked, "Do you remember anything he might have said to you?"

I thought for a moment. I remembered talking to Jerram before my mind went foggy, but what had we been talking about?

"He tried to pull me into some gossip about problems in Ursan's marriage," I said finally.

Bressen nodded. "Anything else?"

My mind played the conversation backwards. "He warned me to stay away from you."

Bressen raised an eyebrow, but there was amusement in his voice when he said, "Well, that's just good advice in general. Did he say why? Was it my penchant for biting the heads off live chickens, or has he confirmed I drink the blood of children to maintain my devastatingly good looks?"

Bressen's turquoise eyes held mine, and for a moment I was just as paralyzed as I'd been last night, but for a very different reason. I finally tore my gaze away from his. "It...might have been the chickens. My memory is still a bit fuzzy."

Bressen came forward to stand in front of me. He opened his mouth to say something but then seemed to think better of it.

"What is it?" I asked.

"If you think there might be something else important, I can help you try to remember."

My eyes narrowed. "What do you mean?"

"I can...look into your mind. If you want me to."

I remembered dancing with Bressen last night and how I'd known the steps without having ever done the dance before. I remembered how we'd moved together as if our minds were connected...and they had in fact been connected. I was certain of that now.

Then another memory came back to me of my head hanging over a toilet and Bressen's voice telling me to vomit. The words had barely left his mouth when I'd thrown up the entire contents of my stomach into the toilet. That had been him in my mind as well, I realized now.

Given that he'd already been in my mind twice yesterday, I didn't know why he was bothering to ask permission to do it now. Whether Jerram was right or not about trusting Bressen, though, I recoiled at the idea of willingly letting this man into my head, and I felt a wall slide up in my mind the way it had two weeks ago in the Great Chamber.

Bressen leaned back as if he sensed the barrier I'd just erected.

"The offer stands," he said. He lifted his hand as if to touch me, but then put it back down.

I was surprised by the acute pang of disappointment I felt when he dropped his hand. While my mind balked at the idea of letting him in, my body seemed to crave his touch.

"Let me know if I can do anything else for you," Bressen said.

"There is," I said quickly. "There is something you can do."

"Of course. What is it?"

"I want Samhail to train me to fight," I said.

Bressen frowned. "You want Samhail to do what?"

"Train me to fight. I want to learn hand-to-hand combat, sword fighting, and anything else he'll teach me."

Bressen's frown deepened. "Have you asked Samhail about this?"

"I did. He told me he'd need to ask you, so I'm asking you myself."

I sighed in frustration when Bressen just continued to frown at me.

"I don't understand why this is such an issue," I said. "If Samhail's work for you won't allow him enough time to train me, then let me train with someone else."

"Samhail doesn't work for me," Bressen said. "Not directly anyway. He's not bound to me or the Triumvirate."

Samhail had said as much to me, but he was still clearly involved with something Bressen was working on.

"It just seems like Samhail does a lot for you."

"He *does* do a lot for me, and I'm extremely grateful for it all. I give him money when he lets me, but he does much more than I pay him for," Bressen explained.

"Why?" I asked.

"I don't think he considers it appropriate to take money given our history."

"Your history? Samhail said you were friends."

Bressen smiled. "More like brothers." There was genuine affection in his voice.

"Then Samhail can train me if he wants to?" I asked, trying to bring the conversation back around.

Bressen exhaled deeply and crossed his muscular arms over his chest. "Do you know what Samhail is?"

I frowned. "I'm not sure what you mean."

"Do you know what kind of being he is? You've seen his wings, but I'm not sure you truly understand what he is."

"He...he told me he has a dormant beast form," I offered.

Bressen seemed surprised. "He did?"

I nodded. "Yes, but he didn't tell me what kind of beast."

Bressen seemed to wrestle with himself for a moment. "Samhail is a gargoyle," he said finally.

I blinked. "A gargoyle? Like...the stone monster statues on the roofs of temples?"

"Sort of. Those statues are modeled after Samhail's kind, but Samhail is the real thing."

"What does that mean?"

"It means that while Samhail normally maintains a human form, he can transform into a giant beast at any time, one that is essentially as hard and as strong as stone."

When Samhail told me about his beast form, I'd pictured something a little more...mundane. Part of me imagined that he just transformed into a giant bat. I had trouble picturing anything truly monstrous, but I found that it didn't matter to me regardless. I knew Samhail, and I trusted him.

"What does that mean in terms of having him train me?" I asked, trying to figure out why Bressen thought it was important to tell me

191

this. "Do you think I won't be able to keep up with his training?"

Bressen didn't take the bait. "I'm sure you'd be a great student."

"Then what's the issue?"

"Samhail is a battle-hardened warrior who has trained plenty of other warriors, but those warriors have either been other gargoyles, or at the very least, strong and powerful men who didn't...break easily."

I gaped at him, my ire rising. "So you think I'm too breakable?"

"Compared to Samhail, yes," Bressen said flatly. "Even in his human form, Samhail is exceptionally strong and fast. I'm not sure he'd know how to train you without hurting you, or even..." He trailed off, but I understood.

Well, that was something to think about. I was certain Samhail would never purposely hurt me, but the possibility he might hurt me accidentally had never occurred to me.

I was quiet for several seconds more before I spoke. "I want to learn how to fight. I need to learn."

Bressen let out a long sigh. "Let me talk to Samhail. If there's a way to make it happen that keeps you safe from egregious bodily harm, then I'll allow it."

The idea that he'd "allow" me to do something I wanted to do grated on me, but I at least understood why both he and Samhail were hesitant to agree to my request. I tamped down the stubbornness my brothers had complained about often and vowed to wait and see what Bressen's final determination was before I did anything.

"Fair enough. I'll await your decision."

Bressen nodded. "Is there anything else?"

I shook my head.

"Then I'll call someone to escort you back to the central building."

"There's no need. I can find my own way back."

He looked at me as if he might insist, but then he gestured toward the door to indicate I was free to leave.

I turned to go without another word and made my way back through his wing.

Anger roiled within me as I got back to the rotunda. I was furious at Jerram, frustrated with Bressen and Samhail, and chafing under the monotony of living in the Citadel. I needed an outlet.

I also needed to do something about what had happened last night. Bressen assured me he'd confronted Jerram, but I didn't want others to fight my battles for me. What would happen the next time I had to see Jerram at dinner? Was I supposed to ignore him? Pretend as though nothing had happened? Let him think I was content to hide behind Bressen? That sure as hells wasn't going to happen.

I looked at the four doors in the rotunda that led to various parts of the Citadel and steeled myself before I headed for the one that led to Jerram's wing.

Chapter 18

I thought the doors to Jerram's wing might be locked, but they weren't. I assumed my next problem would be tracking Jerram down, if he was even there after Bressen confronted him this morning, but I was wrong there as well. My next problem was the pair of spears leveled at my throat the moment I threw open the doors and tried to walk inside. I gasped and pulled up just short of impaling myself on their blades.

The spears relaxed when the guards saw me, but they didn't completely lower.

"What's your business?" one of the guards asked me.

"I...I'd like to see Jerram," I said, then corrected myself. "Lord Jerram."

"And you would be?"

"Cyra of Fernweh."

The guards exchanged surprised looks and pulled up their spears.

"This way," one of them said, and I followed him down the hall.

There were stark differences in the décor of Jerram's wing from the other two. Bressen's style leaned toward minimalist, but Jerram's halls were congested with rugs, paintings, statues, vases on pedestals, and even the occasional taxidermied animal head.

The guard stopped in front of a surprisingly plain-looking oak door and knocked.

"What?" Jerram's voice barked from inside.

The guard pushed the door open, and I followed him in.

"My lord, Cyra of Fernweh to see you."

Jerram's head jerked up from where he stood behind his desk. He looked at me in surprise, possibly panic, but he schooled his features, and a bright smile spread across his face. I saw even from across the room that he had a black eye, a split lip, and an ugly red welt on his cheek that I assumed were Bressen's doing. Apparently he hadn't yet had time to see a healer.

"Cyra, my dear!" he said coming around the desk, and I noticed he walked a bit stiffly as well. "I'm so glad to see you. I despaired of ever being in your company again. Come in!"

He shooed the guard away with a hand and pulled out a chair in front of his desk, motioning for me to sit.

"Thank you, but I prefer to stand," I said.

"Whatever makes you comfortable. Can I get you something to drink?" He motioned to a side table with an assortment of crystal bottles on it.

I looked at him as if he were mad.

"You're offering me a drink after what you did last night?"

He looked confused. "What did I do last night?"

I blinked at him. Was he really going to play dumb? "You drugged my drink!"

Shock showed on Jerram's face before his features softened into a knowing expression. "So that's what he told you happened?"

I just stared at him.

"Bressen told you that I drugged your drink," he clarified.

"You *did* drug my drink."

"Did you see me do it?"

I paused. "No."

"Then how do you know I drugged it?"

I didn't answer.

"Bressen told you I did, and you just believed him," Jerram said.

I frowned. "If you didn't drug my drink, who did?"

"No one."

My mouth fell open at the ridiculousness of that statement. "Then why was I ready to pass out last night at the ball? I only had two glasses of wine."

"Isn't it obvious?" Jerram asked, and his look was pitying. "Bressen knocked you out himself."

I just gaped at him. He seemed to be blushing, and I held onto that as evidence that he was lying. Not that I needed it.

"When we spoke last night after you danced with Bressen, I saw you fading," Jerram explained. "I knew instantly he'd done something to you, invaded your mind. I tried to get you out of there, but he caught me in the hall helping you escape."

Jerram's blush seemed to deepen, and I shook my head slowly. He was insane.

"I'm so sorry I left you there at his mercy, Cyra. Admittedly, I'm no match for Bressen's powers, and he would've killed me if I tried to challenge him, so I took the coward's way out and fled."

I stepped back in alarm as he advanced on me, but he grabbed my hands and pulled them to his chest. I tried to yank them back, but he held them fast.

"Can you ever forgive me?" he asked.

I shook my head. "No, it wasn't Bressen. You drugged me."

He looked crushed and let go of my hands with a mirthless laugh.

"He told me he'd do this," Jerram said. "When Bressen came to see me this morning, he beat and tortured me for trying to help you last night." He motioned to his face as evidence. "He told me he'd blame me for everything."

"Because you *are* to blame," I whispered.

"Because that's what *he* told you?"

I didn't say anything.

"You know what they call him, don't you? All those nicknames people have for him?" Jerram asked. "The Nemesis Incarnate?" he supplied. "The Lord of-"

"The Lord of Lies," I finished for him, remembering the little-used moniker I'd heard once, a reference to Bressen's mind powers that could make you think and feel things that weren't real.

Jerram nodded. "I know you don't want to believe me, but the most dangerous monsters often come in pleasing forms, and Lord Bressen is a very dangerous monster."

I didn't believe him. Or was he right, and I just didn't want to?

Bressen's power was a terrifying one, and I had no way to know for sure he hadn't attacked my mind and made me think Jerram drugged me. He'd manipulated my mind at least twice yesterday alone.

My whole being rebelled at the thought. Bressen was arrogant and teasing and unquestionably dangerous, but he'd never been cruel to me. Or was that part of the lie? Was my reluctance to believe Jerram all part of Bressen's mind manipulation?

"I need to go," I said as my stomach lurched violently.

Jerram nodded. "I understand. But think about what I said carefully. You can't trust a thing Bressen says."

I turned and left without saying anything else to him. The guard who'd escorted me there was still outside the door when I opened it, and he led me back through the halls to the main door of Jerram's wing. I exited, and the doors closed solidly behind me.

My head hurt from trying to reason out the issue. My mind was telling me Jerram drugged me and Bressen saved me, but how could I trust my mind given what I knew about Bressen's powers? Or maybe it was my heart that wanted me to believe Bressen over Jerram.

I was suddenly very tired, and I returned to my room hoping a nap might bring some clarity.

"Bullshit!" Samhail thundered later that afternoon when I told him what Jerram said.

Well, first Samhail raged at me for five minutes about confronting Jerram on my own without protection, then he yelled at me some more when I gave him Jerram's explanation of what happened.

He'd come to check on me and found me reading in the library after my nap. I admitted to him where I'd gone that morning after leaving Bressen's study. He'd been shocked, then angry, then reluctantly impressed that I'd sought Jerram out to confront him. Everything had turned back to rage again when I told him Jerram blamed Bressen for my blackout.

"You don't have to believe Bressen," Samhail said standing over me where I sat curled up with a book. "You can believe *me*. Jerram is a snake, and he's the one you shouldn't trust."

"But how can I trust anything I know anymore? How can you? How do you know we're not all just walking around like Bressen's puppets, thinking whatever he wants us to think? How do you know he's not controlling what you think too? How do you know-"

Samhail reached down and placed a hand over my mouth to cut off my words. I glared at him over his hand, and he put it down.

"I understand how hard it can be to trust your own mind, especially after what you experienced last night," he said gently. "Trust me. I know from experience. But you can't live the rest of your life questioning the very fabric of your reality. It will paralyze you."

I knew Samhail was right, but my visit to Jerram had turned me upside down, and I now half-regretted confronting him. I'd been certain this morning that Jerram was behind my blackout, and I wanted to believe Bressen rescued me, but Jerram's version of events hadn't been easy to dismiss.

"Look," Samhail said, "I can't give you back the peace of mind you had yesterday before all this happened. I can only tell you that you make your own reality. If you feel like someone is pulling your strings, pull them right back."

I didn't know exactly what that meant or how to do it, but it sounded nice.

"I have news, by the way," Samhail said. "Bressen agreed I can train you. We'll start tomorrow morning."

I sat up straight. "Really?"

"Don't make either of us regret this," he said.

"What made him allow it? He said he was afraid you wouldn't know how to train someone like me."

"We'll have to be careful for sure, but I assured him I could practice restraint."

I smiled widely and shot out of my chair to throw my arms around him for a hug. Samhail wrapped an arm around me and patted me on

198

the back as he had before.

"You still need to work on your hugging," I said.

Samhail shrugged as I pulled back. "Maybe it can be a quid pro quo. I'll give you fighting lessons, and you can give me hugging lessons."

I quirked a brow. "One of us definitely has their work cut out for them, and it's not you."

"We'll see if you're saying that tomorrow morning after your first training. I expect you in the yard at nine o'clock sharp. Tardiness will be punished."

"Going to spank me?" I joked, but I regretted the words instantly as the look of lustful promise Samhail gave me sent heat flushing down my face.

"Nine o'clock sharp," I confirmed.

He feigned disappointment but turned and left the library.

I looked at the book I'd been reading, but I didn't have a head for it anymore. The news about my training had energized me, and I suddenly needed to get out of here. Not just out of the library, but out of the Citadel itself. I knew my way around the fortress well by now, but I hadn't yet found any way out. Maybe if I asked permission…

I shook my head. I knew the lords would never allow it, and after everything that had happened with Jerram, I wasn't about to ask. I may be living in luxury here, but I was still a prisoner. Even the servants had more freedom than I did.

I gasped as something clicked into place in my brain. I knew how I was going to get out of the Citadel tonight.

"Please don't do this, my lady," Raina said later that night as I pulled on my cloak over a simple pair of pants and a shirt.

It was about half-past nine, and Raina had come to my room to help me get ready for bed as usual. She wasn't pleased when I'd told her what I really planned to do that night.

"No, absolutely not," she'd said when I told her my idea.

I'd raised a brow at her, and she immediately looked contrite. I wasn't actually a lady, but she was supposed to obey my commands, even though she and I both knew my status here at the Citadel wasn't all that much above hers.

"I'll be punished if they find out," Raina insisted.

"They won't find out. I'll only be gone a few hours. Everyone thinks I've gone to bed, and I'll be back well before anyone comes looking for me."

"But what if you get caught?"

"If I get caught, I promise I won't tell anyone you helped me. I'll say I found the way out on my own."

Raina looked at me miserably. "If Lord Bressen-"

"Lord Bressen is not the monster everyone claims he is. He won't punish you for something like this."

"How do you know that?"

"I just know. You have to trust me on this."

I might have lingering doubts about Bressen's mind control powers, but I knew he wasn't malicious. He wouldn't hold Raina accountable for my actions. Or I was pretty sure he wouldn't.

"Please Raina. I've been a prisoner here for two weeks now."

Raina's face fell, and I saw the sympathy in her eyes. I honed in on that and pressed my advantage.

"I was torn from my home, made to face the Lords of the Triumvirate, almost killed by tigers, and last night I was drugged. And in between all that, I've had nothing to do but sit on my ass and read. I need to get out of here, if only for a few hours. Please."

Raina's face looked pained, but I knew now that I'd won.

"I'll owe you a huge debt," I said. "Just show me how the servants and guards get out of the Citadel."

Raina sighed heavily. "Alright. Come with me."

I trailed Raina to the door of my room, and she looked out into the hallway. Seeing no one there, she motioned for me to follow her. At the end of the hall, she opened a small door that stood inconspicuously in an alcove I'd never noticed before.

The door led to a tight passage that ran behind the walls of the main hallway. I'd been right in thinking the Citadel's servants had ways of moving about the building unseen. In all the time I'd been here, I rarely saw servants in the halls, even though I knew there were hundreds that worked in the fortress. Now I knew how they were all getting around.

"Put your hood up, my lady," Raina said as she led me through hidden hallways and down sets of stairs. I flipped my hood over my head and kept my eyes down as we emerged into an open space with other people in it.

"I'll just get my cloak," Raina said brightly, not bothering to lower her voice.

I felt her leave my side, and I glanced up quickly to see that we were in some kind of common room. Three other women were there, but they seemed engrossed in their own affairs.

Raina returned a minute later with her cloak, and I followed her as she led us out a back door that emerged into a courtyard.

"This way," she said.

We hurried across the courtyard to another door that was set into the outer wall of the fortress. Inside, a set of stairs went up toward the battlements, but another set that I'd never seen before went down under the wall. I wondered if the doors and stairs the servants used to get around the Citadel were concealed to anyone who wasn't looking for them.

"Where does this let out?" I asked Raina as we reached the bottom of the stairs and started down a tunnel. We passed under a portcullis that could be lowered to close off the tunnel in case of attack, and at least two more were built into the ceiling ahead.

"Just outside the wall," Raina said. "There are guards posted, but just keep walking. They don't usually stop anyone going out."

"Will they let me back in later?"

Raina came to a dead halt, and I grunted as I ran into her back.

"Nemesis take me," she breathed. "I never thought about how to get you back in." She turned around to face me. "We have to go back."

I shook my head emphatically. "No, I'm not going back now."

"You have to. I don't have any way to get you back in."

"I'll figure out something later."

"There's no other way unless you walk through the front gate."

"What if I'm with you? The guards will let you in, right?"

"Yes, but I'm not allowed to just bring guests into the Citadel, and if they recognize you, we'll both be in trouble."

There was pleading in Raina's eyes, but I wasn't willing to go back. I couldn't spend another night sitting in my room.

I sighed and put on an expression of resignation. Raina relaxed, and that's when I bolted around her and ran for the door.

"No!" she yelled after me, and I heard her footsteps thudding behind me on the ground. I reached the door at the end of the corridor, yanked it open, and launched myself through it.

I emerged from the tunnel onto a sidewalk and pulled up a little ways outside the door as Raina came flying out after me. She grabbed me by the arm before I could go any further.

"Stop!" a voice yelled behind us, and we both froze.

"Let me do all the talking," Raina said in a strangled whisper as she turned around to face the guard that had yelled at us. She positioned herself in front of me, and I shrank down, ready to run if she wasn't able to talk us out of this.

"What in the three hells are you doing running out of here like that?" the guard thundered as he advanced on us.

"Damian?" Raina said, sounding surprised.

The guard pulled up short and looked at us. "Raina?"

Raina pulled back her hood, and I saw a smile tug at the guard's mouth before he schooled his features. This was the shy guard Raina liked, I realized. From what I could see, he was attractive in a boyish sort of way with thick wavy brown hair and full lips that Raina had told me more than once she wanted to devour.

"Where are you going in such a hurry?" Damian asked, trying to sound serious.

"We're just going out for a night on the town," Raina said, her voice sweetening.

"You know better than to run out of the tunnel like that," Damian scolded, but there was no menace in his voice.

"I'm sorry," Raina said, her voice still unnaturally honeyed. "We were just eager to start the night. What are you doing down here? I thought you only worked in Lord Bressen's wing?"

"They needed someone to fill in tonight, so I volunteered. If I'd known you had some time off and were going out…" He let the thought drift off.

Raina seemed lost in Damian's gaze, and I tugged on her cloak.

"We should go," Raina blurted out. "I don't want to keep you."

"Who's your friend?" Damian asked, leaning around Raina. She tried to sidestep to keep me hidden, but Damian's face went serious. "Raina, who is that?"

"Damian, I…" Raina's voice went hoarse as she fumbled for an explanation.

I tried to edge around the other side of Raina so that Damian wouldn't see my face, but there was a second guard stationed outside the gate, and he appeared ready to move if Damian needed his assistance. I ducked my head back around Raina and found Damian peering around her shoulder. He jolted back as our eyes met.

"Raina! Is that-"

She reached up quickly and put a finger on his lips. Damian instantly stopped speaking, and he looked a bit dazed to have her touching him.

"Please," Raina whispered desperately, "if you say anything I'll be in so much trouble."

"Are you helping her escape?" he asked, narrowing his eyes.

"No! Of course not! She just wants to get out for the night. She'll be back in a few hours."

"Please," I said, giving Damian a beseeching look. "Just a few hours. I promise."

"Please," Raina said, echoing my tone. "As a favor to me?"

Damian looked like he was about to refuse my request, but his face softened at Raina's plea, and he sighed heavily. "You need to be back by midnight," he told her. "That's when my shift ends. If you get here later, you're on your own."

Raina paused. "I...I wasn't actually going to go with her," she said.

I grabbed her arm. "Yes, come with me! I don't know the city."

She hesitated.

"You can't go back in now," Damian said. "Roland will be suspicious." He cocked his head toward the other guard.

"He already is," I said, seeing the guard walking toward us.

"Raina, we need to go now or we'll both be caught," I said, pulling her hand.

"What's going on here?" Roland asked as he came up behind the three of us. I was about to bolt when I recognized the voice.

I poked my head around Raina and saw my guard, the guard who I liked to tease and the one who I'd caught gambling on Samhail and Bressen's training fights.

"Roland," I said, coming out from behind Raina. "Your name is Roland."

Raina and Damian froze, but Roland stepped back in shock as he recognized me.

"What in the three hells is going on here?" he asked. His hand went to the hilt of his sword, but Damian put himself between us so that he was blocking me and Raina.

"Easy, Roland," Damian said. "It's not what it looks like."

"Really?" Roland said, looking at me. "Because it looks like she's trying to escape."

"No!" I said over Damian's shoulder. "We're just going out for a few drinks. We'll be back before midnight."

Roland made to say something, but I cut him off.

"You and I keep each other's secrets, and this night out will be our little secret. Right?"

Roland flinched as he understood the threat in my words. He hesitated, and I knew he was weighing how much he'd be in trouble for gambling while on duty compared to how much he'd be in trouble if someone learned he let me leave, especially if I didn't come back.

I reached out and put my hand over Roland's where it still rested on the hilt of his sword. "I promise I'll be back before midnight. You have my word."

Roland's eyes seemed to go glassy for a moment, but he refocused on my face a second later and nodded. "Go," he said, although he didn't look happy about the capitulation.

"Thank you," I said, nodding gratefully. "Raina, let's go."

Raina looked at Damian, and he nodded. I grabbed her hand and pulled her away before the two guards changed their minds.

"They're going to have me whipped for this," Raina said miserably as we hurried down the sidewalk. "What have I done?"

I turned around and gripped her shoulders. "Raina, what you've done is set me free. Maybe not for long, but for the first time in two weeks, I don't have anyone looking over my shoulder or telling me where I can and can't go."

Her look was one of grim acceptance.

"Where do you go on your nights off?" I asked, excitement welling in my chest at being out of the Citadel.

"There's a tavern downtown I like."

"Perfect! Let's go get a drink."

"I may need more than one," she said resignedly.

"Absolutely. I'm buying," I said as I patted my coin purse. "We'll have fun. I promise."

Raina sighed. "It'll probably be the last night I spend outside of a dungeon, so we might as well make it good."

And with that, we headed off to see what the night would hold.

Chapter 19

The tavern Raina suggested was on a main thoroughfare in Callanus, one of a number along the well-lit street. The whole area was alive as patrons meandered between establishments, the atmosphere outside seeming just as social as it was inside. Everyone seemed to be out and about tonight, and Raina and I made our way to the counter as we entered.

"Thank you, my lady," Raina said when I'd given the barkeep our order and laid down some coin to pay.

"Please, call me Cyra," I said. When she looked at me uncomfortably, I added, "At least for tonight."

"Yes…Cyra," she said, trying it out.

We settled on some stools at the bar to wait for our drinks, and I studied the crowd packed into the tavern. Small groups of people of all ages clustered around, while couples tucked themselves into private tables in more secluded parts. Raina and I had been fortunate that two young men were leaving their seats at the bar when we'd gone up to get drinks, and we usurped their places before anyone else stepped in.

"There are a lot of people out tonight," I observed.

"It's the week before the Harmilan. The celebrating starts early," she said.

We didn't celebrate many holidays in the outer lands, and I remembered that people in Fernweh eschewed the Harmilan, although I couldn't recall exactly why. I'd ask Raina about it later, but there was something else I wanted to talk about first.

"So that was Damian," I said silkily. "He's very handsome. Remind me again why the two of you aren't together?"

Raina blushed and sipped the drink the barkeep set in front of her.

"He's just a friend," she said.

"But you want him to be more."

"I do, and I think he wants more too, but he's very shy when it comes to anything romantic."

"You've kissed him, though?" I thought I remembered her telling me that.

"Only once," she admitted. "It was…wonderful." Her eyes glassed over as she lost herself in the memory.

"Have you spent any time together?"

"A little. We had dinner once, and we've gone for a few walks. It's been hard to find time together with our schedules."

"And he hasn't tried to do anything other than kiss you?" I asked.

Raina shook her head.

"What's he waiting for?"

Raina heaved an exaggerated sigh. "I have no idea."

We both sipped our drinks. I'd watched the barkeep pour my drink closely and hadn't taken my hand off the glass since he set it down.

"What about you and Samhail?" Raina asked.

"Me and Samhail?" I asked in surprise.

"The two of you seem close, and he obviously wants you. The look he gave you when he brought the message leaves could have set the room on fire."

It was my turn to blush now, but I waved a dismissive hand. "Samhail is just a friend as well." I took another sip of my drink too quickly for the half-truth to be believable.

Raina raised a brow at me.

"Fine, part of me wants to tie him to my bed and do unspeakably dirty things to him," I admitted. "Are you happy now?"

Raina stared at me and then laughed. "Alright then. Have you kissed him yet?"

I blushed and took another sip of my drink.

"You have!" Raina exclaimed, poking a finger into my shoulder.

"It was more like *he* kissed *me*."

"And how was it?"

"Toe curling," I admitted, and Raina clapped her hand to her mouth to stifle the giggles that erupted.

"Tell me everything!" she said when she'd gotten herself under control.

I gave Raina the brief version of my journey with Samhail, including sleeping up against him, our kiss, and flying in his arms. Raina sat wide-eyed and open-mouthed when I was done.

"How romantic," she breathed.

I blinked at her. That wasn't quite the word I would've chosen.

"Nothing's happened since?" she asked.

"No. I teased him about spanking me today, and he gave me a look that nearly melted my clothes off my body, but that's it."

"You asked him to spank you?" she asked incredulously.

"Not exactly. He threatened to punish me if I was late for training tomorrow, and I...might have suggested the manner of punishment."

Raina giggled again. "By the gods. I'd love to have Damian spank me, but I'd never have the nerve to suggest it to him."

"I didn't suggest it per se."

"But you want to take him to your bed, right?"

I started to say I did, but Bressen's face flashed into my mind, and the words caught in my throat. Part of me still held onto the idea of being with Samhail, but I was no longer sure he was the man I really wanted. At some point, thoughts of being with Bressen had started to replace thoughts of Samhail, although I wasn't sure exactly when.

"I don't know," I said to Raina. "Maybe."

"Maybe?" Raina asked in disbelief. "Cyra, that man is magnificent, and if he looked at me the way he looks at you, my clothes would fall off every time I saw him. He's also huge. I can't even imagine what his cock must look like."

"Raina!" I said in mock admonishment, my face flushing. I'd wondered the same, of course, but hearing her say it out loud only put ideas back into my head, ones that made my thighs clench.

We ordered another drink and continued to swap stories about the men we'd been involved with as well as Raina's hopes for Damian. I tried to give her what advice I could, although I was hardly an expert on love. She probably would've been better off doing the exact opposite of what I told her.

We finished our second drink and decided to try another tavern a little farther down the way that someone had recommended to her. The number of people outside had grown considerably since we'd first come in, and I stuck close to Raina as I followed her through the crowd. It would've been handy to have Samhail there, I thought sardonically, and I wondered belatedly if he would've agreed to chaperone a night out on the town if I'd asked him. Perhaps the lords would've allowed me out if Samhail was watching me.

On the other hand, going drinking with Samhail seemed like a very dangerous idea if I wanted to keep our "only friends" status intact. I did want to keep it that way, right? I still wasn't entirely sure.

Unbidden, thoughts of Bressen swam through my head, and I found myself biting my lip. I was so confused about what…or *who* I wanted right now. That was presuming I could have either of them, of course, which I couldn't.

I shook my head to clear my lustful thoughts, but a familiar prickling drew me up short in the middle of the road, and several people swore as they had to swerve around me quickly.

My head darted from side to side looking for black hair and turquoise eyes, but I didn't see Bressen. Had I just imagined the prickle because I'd been thinking about him, or was he really here? Worse, did he know I'd left the Citadel, and he was coming to find me?

My stomach knotted, and I looked around again. If Bressen was around, then surely Samhail would be too, and Samhail was easy to spot. I surveyed the crowd slowly, but there was no giant with white hair in their midst.

I realized a moment later that I also didn't see Raina anymore. She must've pushed on ahead thinking I was behind her, and now I couldn't see her anywhere among the throng. She hadn't told me how far up the street we were going, but I figured I'd find her eventually if I kept moving.

I started walking, but as I passed an alley, I felt the prickle on my neck again. The alley was darker than the main street, but there were several open taverns down it as well.

I should keep going. If Bressen was down that alley, I didn't want to get caught by him outside the Citadel. I should definitely go.

Instead, my feet carried me down the alley.

A few people stood outside the taverns there and eyed me as I walked by, but no one spoke to me. It wasn't a good idea to be down this way, but I was powerless to make myself go back. I waited to feel the prickle again. It was almost there, as if something barely brushed the hair on my neck, but I didn't feel that distinct sensation again.

I reached the end of the alley to see that it opened onto a wharf. This must be the Scion River that flowed through the city, and I walked to the edge of the dock to look down into the dark water lapping at the pylons.

I loved the water, but it had been a long time since I'd been anywhere near a sizable body of it. Fernweh was on the coast of Polaris, and my family visited the beach often when we were children, but my brothers and I hadn't gone since our parents died. Brix brought up the idea once, but Jaylan made excuses about how much work we had to do on the vineyard, and we didn't bring it up again. Brix and I understood that the idea of going without our parents had been painful for Jaylan, and we'd both quietly acquiesced to his refusal.

I found something about the water peaceful, though, and I promised myself that the first thing I'd do when I got back to Fernweh was go to the coast, regardless of whether Jaylan decided to come.

Something swirled in the water below me, just breaking the surface, and I leaned over carefully to see what it was. I saw nothing but inky blackness, though. It might simply have been the back of a fish, but it could also have been the hand of a nixie, the half human, half fish creatures that were said to live in the river and lure people to their deaths in the water. I leaned back, wary of getting any closer, and looked out over the ships rocking gently in their berths. A soft breeze ruffled my hair, but whatever prickling I'd felt at my neck earlier was gone now.

"My lady! Cyra!"

Raina's voice echoed down the alley as she hurried toward me.

"Cyra, what are you doing?" She grabbed my arm and tried to tug me back toward the alley. "We need to return to the main road right away. Why did you come down here?"

"I…" I started to speak, but I wasn't completely sure why I'd come down this way. If Bressen really was close by, it was foolish of me to have come here for so many reasons.

"Cyra, we need to go. Please." She tugged on my hand, and I turned to follow.

"I think you may be lost, my lovelies," said a voice behind us. Raina and I whirled around to find a man in well-worn clothes with his hands crossed over his chest. There were crates stacked all along the docks, and he seemed to have snuck up on us from behind them.

"We don't usually get the likes of you two down here," the man said, coming closer.

Something about him set me on edge, and I stepped in front of Raina so I was between her and the man. I dragged a smile onto my face. "Yes, sir. We are a little lost. Could you point our way back to the Citadel?" I asked.

Surprise bloomed on the man's face, as I hoped it would when I mentioned the fortress.

"The Citadel?" the man said. "Now why would you need to get to the Citadel?"

"I'm staying there," I said. "I'm a guest of the Triumvirate, and this is my friend. They're bound to miss us soon, so we should head back."

I turned around and pressed Raina back toward the alley, but we found our way blocked by another man.

"Cyra!" Raina cried when she saw him, and I swore inwardly that I'd insisted she call me by my name tonight. It might have helped our cause for her to refer to me as "my lady."

211

I pushed Raina behind me so our backs were to the river. I glanced down at the water and saw it swirl again, but I still couldn't make out what was causing it. If I knew for sure it was just fish, Raina and I might be able to jump in and swim for it. If the churning water hid a nixie, however, we'd be in just as much danger in the water as we were on the wharf right now.

"They can't be missing you that much if they let you wander around down here," the man said. "What do you think, Silas?" He looked to the newcomer who was now blocking our path back toward the alley.

"I think the Citadel's loss is our gain," Silas said. "If I had such pretty guests, I don't think I'd be letting 'em walk alone in these parts. It ain't safe."

I caught movement to our left as two more men emerged from the shadows. Nemesis take me. Our situation had gone from questionable to ominous. Our only hope was that maybe these men were mortal, and they weren't prepared to deal with some magic.

I stood up straighter before I sent a silent prayer up to the Protector that there were no more than four of them. "Sirs, we appreciate you taking an interest in our well-being, but I assure you that the only thing we need from you is directions back to the Citadel."

"Look at her eyes!" one of the men exclaimed. "I never seen eyes like that before."

"Stay behind me," I whispered to Raina. "We'll jump in the water if we have to."

Raina shook her head vigorously in my periphery. "Nixies!" she hissed back.

"We can help you back to the Citadel," the first man said, "but our services aren't free."

Fear trickled through my limbs, but anger flowed as well. "I was under the impression that providing directions to lost strangers was a common courtesy, not something that required payment."

"Ah, but it's not directions you'd be paying for," the first man said.

"It'd be our protection. We can't let the two of you wander around in these parts alone without an escort. Far too dangerous. Don't worry, though. If you don't have any money, we accept other types of compensation for our time."

The men all laughed. They were slowly closing in on us, and I'd need to act soon. I still hadn't tried to throw my fire, but maybe a small show of it would be enough.

I clenched my hands before throwing them open before me. Flames roared to life in my palms, and the men all took a step back. Raina gasped behind me, and I felt her step back as well. The flames were the largest I'd ever conjured, but in light of our current situation, they still seemed disappointingly small and feeble.

"She's a fucking perimortal!" Silas spat, and I realized our situation had just gotten worse rather than better. Perimortals were more abundant in cities, but that didn't mean they were any more well-liked in some circles than they were in Fernweh.

"Stay back," I snarled at the men, "or you'll learn what the scent of your own charred flesh smells like."

Pure bravado. It was the most violent thing I'd ever uttered, but it had the desired effect. The men growled at me but moved a little further back. I looked around for an escape route, but they were still blocking our path back to the alley. If Raina and I could just get past them, we could run for it back to the main road.

Raina's shriek drew my attention as Silas lunged toward us. I threw a hand out toward him, and my flames flared brightly before sputtering and dying. Silas pulled back to avoid the fire, but he lunged again when it went out. I splayed my palms once more, and this time a wind roared up. It turned over crates on the dock and rattled nearby window shutters. It blew Silas back as well, and he swore as he landed hard on the dock.

Emboldened by their companion, though, the three other men closed in.

"She can't take us all at once!" one of them yelled.

213

"I'm going to fuck the fire right out of that perimortal bitch!" another hissed.

Terror jolted through my body, and I tried to harness it. I held my hands out and fire bloomed again, but I only had two hands, and there were four men as Silas had regained his feet and was moving toward us again.

"Run when I tell you to," I told Raina.

"No!" she cried and grabbed my arm.

"Don't argue with me! Just do it!"

"I won't leave you!"

Nemesis damn her. Now was not the time for Raina to be loyal, and I almost laughed as I suddenly understood Samhail's frustration with my refusal to flee when he'd told me to. I owed him an apology if we got out of this alive.

Silas rushed us again, and I swung my hands to meet him, but he wasn't going for me. He knocked me sideways onto the dock as he pushed past me to get to Raina. She screamed as Silas's hand closed on the neckline of her shirt, and he pulled her forward. She jerked back, and her shirt tore partially down the front. Raina flailed her arms at Silas, raining her small fists down on his head, and he lost his grip on her shirt. Raina stumbled backward and landed on the dock perilously close to the edge. She cried out again and rolled away from the water when she realized how close she'd come to falling in. She rolled toward Silas, though, and he reached down to haul her to her feet.

The other three men rushed toward me, and I threw out both hands in front of me to conjure more wind. A gale instantly swirled up and sent them all sprawling back on the dock.

I picked myself up and turned back to find Silas holding a knife to Raina's throat.

"Stop right there," Silas said, "or I'll gut her like a fish."

I stopped, but my eyes darted to the water at Silas's back, and I sent up a silent prayer to the Protector that what I was about to do wouldn't get Raina's throat cut. I flared my hands at my sides and willed the water to do what I wanted.

A wave splashed up and hit Silas from behind, sending him stumbling forward onto his knees. The knife flew out of his hand at the impact of the cold water, and I grabbed for Raina to pull her toward me. I threw out my hands again and more water splashed up and curled around Silas to pull him backward toward the edge of the dock the way the tide drags sand and rocks with it back toward the sea. I was about to call the water again when a clawed, webbed hand shot up and grabbed Silas's ankle. He screamed as he was yanked toward the edge of the dock, and Raina and I both scrambled backward in horror.

Silas tried to grab for the pylon, but he didn't have a grip, and he was pulled over the side into the dark, churning water. His screams died as he went under, and violent sprays of water shot into the air as Silas thrashed against whatever was holding him. The splashing stopped seconds later, and the water once again stilled to an eerie calm.

"Fucking bitch," one of the men growled behind us.

They'd picked themselves up off the docks and looked at us with loathing. Silas was dead, and now they were going to make us pay.

Chapter 20

I pulled Raina toward the alley, but it was too late. The men surrounded us again, and we retreated as they grabbed for us. A meaty hand closed around my forearm, and I jerked back, but the man held me fast. I willed a flame into my palm before clamping down on the man's arm. He screamed and pulled his hand back as my fire seared his skin, but the other two men were on us.

One man locked his hands painfully around my wrists so I couldn't burn anyone. I tried to yank my hands free, but his grip was too strong. Beside me Raina screamed as a second man looped an arm around her waist and started to drag her away.

"Cyra!" she cried out as she reached for me.

"Raina!" I yelled back as I struggled against the man holding my wrists, but his grip on me was like a vice.

Then suddenly his hands slackened and fell away, and I looked up to see his eyes were vacant before he crumpled to a heap on the ground. Around us, the other two men dropped as well, falling in unison like stringless marionettes.

I was breathing hard as I surveyed the bodies sprawled on the ground around us for any sign of movement. The man holding Raina had let go of her when he fell, and she now whimpered softly behind me. Her hands clamped onto my shoulders, and I stood anchored to the spot ready to fight if one of the men sprang back up to attack us.

A flash of something caught my eye, and I turned to see two points of red light glowing in the darkness of the alley. I froze as I remembered similar flares last night in the corridor when Jerram had dropped me and fled.

The red glow disappeared, and two large forms emerged from the darkness of the alley. I recognized Samhail's giant silhouette instantly, and I realized a second later the other one was Bressen's.

I almost sagged to my knees in relief. I took a step toward them but stopped when I saw the look of fury on Bressen's face. Sparks of red lit his eyes briefly, and I took a step backward instead.

"Protector save me," I breathed.

Raina let out another cry and huddled behind me, and I found her hand to squeeze it. "Hush. We're safe now."

At least I hoped we were. The look on Bressen's face sent a shudder down my spine.

He surveyed the men lying in a tangle of their own limbs on the ground. I looked to see if they were breathing, but I couldn't tell. I wouldn't shed any tears over them, but the thought that my escape into the city might have cost four people their lives made me a little sick.

I looked at Bressen. His eyes were no longer glowing, but he didn't look any less menacing for it.

"I can explain," I said, but he cut me off.

"Are you alright?" he asked. The fury in his voice belied the sentiment, but I nodded.

"We're fine," I said as Raina whimpered again.

Bressen seemed to relax. "Samhail," he said, "would you take our friends for a walk and explain to them where they erred in their treatment of our guest and her lady's maid?"

I could tell he was fighting for control.

"My pleasure," Samhail answered, and I heard the rage in his voice as well.

I gasped and stumbled back as the three bodies lurched to their feet together and turned to Samhail, their eyes empty and unseeing. I shivered and wrapped my cloak tighter around me. Behind me, Raina shook uncontrollably, and I moved to pull her against me.

Samhail turned toward another part of the wharf and began to walk away as the three men fell into synchronized step behind him. It was one of the most horrifying things I'd ever seen, and I now fully understood why Bressen terrified everyone so much. It was one thing to know that he could kill with a thought or make someone do anything he wanted, but it was another thing entirely to see it happen,

217

to see a person's autonomy completely stripped from them.

"Just a minute, Samhail," Bressen said, and Samhail stopped to look back while the men continued to march into the darkness. "Can you bring Raina back to the Citadel first? I think she's had enough excitement for one night. Our friends will still be waiting when you return."

Samhail nodded and came back to me and Raina.

"No!" Raina cried, pulling away to step back from Samhail.

I turned and grabbed her shoulders, but she was trembling all over as the shock of the ordeal overtook her. She clutched the torn halves of her shirt together, and I briefly caught a glimpse of a birthmark between her breasts.

"Raina!" I said, shaking her. "You're safe now. Samhail will take you back to the Citadel."

But Raina was beyond reason. She shook her head violently and tried harder to pull away from me as I held her tight. I was about to shake her again when she suddenly went still, and I recognized the blank stare in her eyes. My head snapped to Bressen, who hadn't moved.

I stepped back as Samhail approached and picked Raina up. She slumped in his arms as his wings flared out behind him, and a moment later he shot into the sky with a giant rush of air.

I was alone with Bressen, but I couldn't look at him. Instead, I looked into the darkness where the three men had disappeared to await Samhail's return.

"What's Samhail going to do to those men?" I asked quietly. I wasn't sure I wanted to know, but I couldn't stop myself from asking.

Bressen looked into the shadows as well and shook his head. "Truthfully, I don't know, but they'll regret touching you long before he's done with them."

I winced at the matter-of-factness in his voice.

Bressen motioned to the water where Silas was dragged down. "That one got off too easily."

I didn't realize Bressen and Samhail had arrived in time to see Silas go under, and I shuddered to remember him being pulled down by clawed hands.

"And what about me?" I asked.

Bressen looked at me questioningly. "What about you?"

"Am I in trouble?"

A smile curled the corners of his mouth. "You *were* in trouble." He inclined his head to where the men had disappeared. "Not anymore."

I exhaled the breath I'd been holding. "So what now?"

"Now we return to the Citadel before anyone realizes you're missing. How did you get out anyway?"

"I…found a back door."

I wondered how much trouble Raina would be in considering it was obvious she must've helped me get out.

Bressen considered my answer and smiled. "The servant's entrance. Clever."

"Don't punish Raina. Please. I made her take me."

"She'll be fine," he assured me.

I looked into the sky where Samhail had disappeared with her. "Will she?"

"I sedated her for now so she can rest. She may be anxious tomorrow when she remembers what happened, but this will get her past the initial shock."

I nodded.

"We should get back now," Bressen said, holding out a hand.

I was still wary of his mood, but his anger seemed to have ebbed, so I stepped toward him. I didn't take his hand, though. I could walk without him leading me.

Bressen grasped my wrist gently as I tried to walk by him.

"We're going to take the short way," he said.

I was about to ask what the 'short way' was, when huge feathered wings sprung from Bressen's back. They were pitch-black, darker than Samhail's, and where Samhail's had a dull leatheriness about them,

219

Bressen's bore the soft sheen of a raven. I gasped and tried to step away, but his hand tightened on my wrist.

"Are you a gargoyle like Samhail?" I asked in awe. I wasn't sure if the question was rude, but I couldn't help it.

"No, I'm an angelus. We're fairly rare."

My eyes came back to his. "What's an angelus?"

Bressen thought for a moment. "It's a bit hard to explain. The feathered wings are a prominent feature, but what defines us is a certain capacity to harness that which is most light and most dark in the world."

I frowned. "Is that why you always wear black? You harness the darkness?"

Bressen grinned at me. "I wear black because I look damn good in black, and because white is so hard to keep clean."

I opened my mouth to say something else, but he cut me off. "You can ask more questions later. Right now, we need to get you back to the Citadel."

"We're flying?" I asked, resignation coloring my voice.

Bressen arched a brow. "You object?"

"It didn't go well last time," I reminded him.

He nodded knowingly. "Gargoyles aren't known for their gracefulness, but the experience is also better when you don't begin by jumping off a cliff first."

I didn't move. The cliff aside, flying with Bressen would mean being in his arms, and I wasn't sure how to react to that.

I sighed. "Fine. I'll let you try to change my mind about flying."

He quirked an eyebrow at me again, and I realized the unintended challenge I'd issued. I started to correct myself, but he pulled me toward him and scooped me into his arms before I could say anything else. A moment later, he'd launched us into the air, and I wrapped an arm tightly around his neck.

Bressen was indeed a much smoother flyer than Samhail, and I watched the lights of lamp posts and shops twinkle below us like stars in an upside-down sky. The powerful wings on his back beat occasionally to propel us forward, but mostly we glided along above the city.

The more I relaxed, though, the more I became aware of other things, like how my body pressed up against his, how close his lips were to mine, and how strongly he held me in his arms.

Bressen touched down a few minutes later on the balcony off my room. His landing was light, and he set me down gently, keeping an arm around my waist until I had my feet under me. I looked up at him and saw the question dancing in his beautiful eyes.

"Not bad," I said. "You're a better flier than Samhail, but don't tell him I said that until he's done training me."

Bressen laughed. "I can't make any promises, but I'll try to keep it a secret."

I stepped out of his arms, but he made no move to leave.

"Thank you for rescuing us and flying me back," I said, inching away from him. I was flushed from being so close and needed to get some air between us. He grabbed my hand and stopped my retreat.

"I'd like to speak to you for a moment. May I come in?"

I looked into the room, and my eyes lit on the bed. No, that was out of the question…

"Those should do fine," Bressen said, gesturing to the plush chairs near the fireplace.

I nodded and led the way. I removed my cloak and threw it over the back of one of the chairs before sitting down.

Bressen shrugged his shoulders, and his wings folded back into his body as Samhail's had. He sat in the other chair and crossed one leg gracefully over the other.

"What did you want to speak to me about?" I asked.

"I'd like to know why you have this habit of courting danger."

I blinked at him. "What? I don't court danger."

"Just going off the last couple weeks, you attacked a bear, confronted a powerful perimortal lord who likely drugged you, asked

Samhail – of all people – to train you to fight, and then snuck off into the city tonight without an escort. And," he added as an afterthought, "you've let yourself be alone with me several times."

My stomach fluttered at his last words, but I had to admit that when he put things that way…

"I didn't attack the bear I was only trying to shoo it away," I argued. "And as for Jerram, I…" I trailed off, unable to think of anything to say on that count.

Bressen only watched me fumble for an explanation.

"The training," I said, giving up, "is because I don't want to be helpless. And I left tonight because I'm going mad cooped up here. I needed to get out, and I didn't think I'd be allowed out if I asked, so I didn't ask."

He just watched me, and I again felt the need to fill the silence.

"I'm used to being busy. If I were home right now, I'd be working long hours to make wine and prepare the vineyard for winter. I can't sit here and do nothing anymore while you and the other lords decide if I'm a threat to the fate of the world."

His face grew serious, and he nodded in understanding.

"As for being alone with you," I said, sitting back and crossing my arms over my chest, "I fail to see how that counts as courting danger."

He grinned and uncrossed his legs to lean forward. "You don't?"

My stomach flipped, but I crossed my arms tighter. "No, I don't."

"You're really not afraid of me, are you."

"Should I be?"

"Everyone else is."

I scoffed. "I'm not like everyone else."

"No, you're not. You're candid about what you think, and you take liberties in teasing me that no one else but Samhail has dared to take."

He leaned back in his chair again. "It's refreshing, to be honest. I've grown weary of people plying me with platitudes because they're afraid I'll melt their brains out of their heads."

I opened my mouth to say something but thought better of it.

"And yes," he said, "I'm aware people find it a status symbol to get near me without dying."

Something in his tone made me feel sorry for him, and I recalled he wore his halo glamour to keep people away. It suddenly seemed like a lonely way to live.

"And what about me?" I asked carefully. "Do you think I find some kind of thrill in teasing you?"

"I think you enjoy teasing me, but you don't do it for the prestige of getting away with it."

"What makes you think I enjoy it?"

"Don't you?"

"No," I said, perhaps too quickly, and he smirked.

I stood up. His arrogance was beginning to annoy me, and I needed to sleep.

"Rest assured my teasing has nothing to do with you," I said. "It's just my way. When you have two brothers, you need to learn to hold your own."

His eyes seemed to twinkle with amusement as he looked up at me, and I felt compelled to show him I wasn't afraid to be near him. I put a hand on the arm of his chair and leaned forward to look him in the eye. "As for being alone in the same room with you," I said, "I don't consider that-"

I let out a cry as Bressen's arms shot up and pulled me down on top of him. One of his hands threaded through my hair while the other rested on the small of my back. He didn't hold me tightly, and I could've risen if I tried, but I couldn't move. My entire body had gone liquid, and gooseflesh rose on my skin.

"Please, continue," Bressen said. "What were you saying again?" My lips hovered just above his, and I felt the brush of his warm breath across them.

I didn't know what I'd been saying. My mind had gone blank. Every nerve in my body was acutely aware of being pressed against him, and I suddenly couldn't form words.

"I…" I said but couldn't get any further.

The hand on my back slid lower to graze lightly over the swell of my ass, and I inhaled as his hand kneaded gently. My eyes dipped to the dimple in his chin, and I bit my lip as I fought the urge to lean forward and kiss it.

"You what?" Bressen asked huskily.

I opened my mouth to speak but nothing came out. Bressen leaned up and brushed his lips over mine with just the barest touch. A small, involuntary moan escaped my mouth, and my head dipped down toward his, but he pulled back out of my reach.

"Now admit, you like teasing me, because I," he leaned up again and nipped my bottom lip with his teeth, "certainly like teasing *you*."

I was working up the will to deny everything, but a gentle pressure from his hand on the back of my neck brought my mouth down on his, and then there was no more room for words. His tongue slipped into my mouth, sending a jolt of fire straight down my body, and my hand curled in his jacket as I met his kiss willingly.

Gods above, I'd wondered what kissing him might be like, but nothing I imagined prepared me for the way every nerve in my body came alive as his lips closed over mine. I tasted the wine he must've been drinking earlier as his tongue moved in my mouth, and my breasts peaked against his chest. His warmth felt like the sun after the clouds part, and I melted into him so my softness pressed against his hardness, including his groin. One of my legs rested between his, and I felt the hard length of him against the top of my thigh.

I nestled my body more fully onto his, and he groaned against my lips. His arm moved back up to my waist to crush me down against him, but he loosened his hold a moment later and lifted me gently away from him. I whimpered in protest, but he shook his head.

"I'm supposed to be staying away from you," he rasped. "I shouldn't have given in to your little challenge."

"Now who's afraid?" I taunted him.

Bressen growled, and I shrieked as he suddenly stood up from the chair, taking me with him. He held me against him with only one arm before he let my body slide slowly down his. His other hand brushed lightly down my cheek before he leaned in to capture my mouth again, and I fought the urge to jump back up and wrap my legs around him.

Every one of my senses was alive as I took in the fine fabric of his jacket under my fingers, the gentle scratch of the stubble on his face, the taste of his mouth on mine, and that strange but intoxicating scent of musk mingled with hot cinnamon. Desire rampaged through my veins as he held me there against him, and I couldn't imagine wanting to be anywhere else right now but in his arms.

A memory of the last time I'd been kissed intruded suddenly, and I tried to lean back from him. "I kissed Samhail," I blurted out. "On our journey to Callanus."

Bressen frowned down at me, still holding me against him. "That's not the usual reaction I get when I'm kissing a woman. Is there a reason you needed me to know that?"

"It…it doesn't bother you?"

"Should it?" he countered, leaning down to brush his lips against mine again.

"In my experience, most men get…territorial about such things."

Bressen laughed. "I'm not most men. Besides, it wouldn't be the first time Samhail and I shared the same woman. Occasionally we share one at the same time."

My eyes widened as mischief flashed in his gaze.

"You mean…"

"Samhail and I have taken women to bed together, yes. Quite a few times in fact."

I realized my mouth was hanging open when his eyes fell to my lips. I closed it quickly. "I see," was all I could think to say.

Bressen's grin widened, and he leaned in close to my ear. "Maybe someday you will."

His breath tickled my ear and gooseflesh rose on my arms again as the promise in his tone sent a jolt of anticipation through me.

"Unfortunately, I need to go," he said. "I should check in with Samhail about our friends. I didn't expect to stay this long, but I never could resist a challenge."

He ran a thumb over my bottom lip, and I had the urge to bite it, but that would be counterproductive to him leaving. And I did need him to leave. I'd let things go too far, and I needed to stop them before they went any further. Getting involved with Bressen had trouble written all over it.

Also, I needed a cold bath.

Bressen leaned down to kiss me again, gently this time. His lips parted just enough to let his tongue flick playfully into my mouth, and I couldn't bring myself to pull away. I put my hands on his chest and willed myself to push him back, but I couldn't seem to do that either.

"There's somewhere we can visit tomorrow if you still want to get out of the Citadel," Bressen said when he finally broke the kiss.

Somewhere *we* can visit. I weighed the pros and cons of spending more time with Bressen against the prospect of getting out of the fortress for a while again.

"I'd like to go. Where is it?"

"It's a surprise. We'll leave after lunch."

Bressen kissed me once more and then released me to walk to the balcony. I followed him to the threshold and leaned against the stone doorway.

"Most men would take the stairs," I said, nodding to the bedroom door.

Bressen winked at me, and the two giant black wings unfurled from his back before he was gone in a rustle of feathers and whoosh of air.

My legs gave way, and I slid into a heap on the floor as I replayed the last few minutes of the night in my mind. It was a while before my heart stopped racing and my legs felt steady enough for me to stand.

Bressen was right. Being alone in a room with him was very, very dangerous.

Chapter 21

It had taken me a while to fall asleep after Bressen left last night. I was entirely too wound up from both the attack and the things his kiss had made me feel afterwards. Then I'd remembered I had my first training with Samhail this morning, and excitement for that had kept me up even longer so that I lay awake in bed for at least two hours before I calmed enough to finally drift off.

I came down to breakfast dressed in my leather pants and a simple cotton shirt that would be easy to maneuver in. My hair was swept back into a ponytail, and I'd pinned down the loose tendrils that normally curled near my face to keep them from flying around. I wasn't giving Samhail any excuse to back out of training me.

Samhail, Ursan, and Glenora were in the dining room. I assumed Jerram's absence was an attempt to avoid Bressen, but I thought Bressen himself would be there, and I was disappointed to see him missing.

"Ready for our training this morning?" I asked Samhail as I sat down across from him with a plate of food.

He grunted. "Isn't that supposed to be *my* question?"

"Training?" Ursan asked, looking up nervously.

"Samhail agreed to teach me how to fight," I said brightly. He couldn't back out if there were witnesses.

"What kind of fighting?" Ursan asked.

"Hand-to-hand combat," I said. "Maybe a little sword fighting." I turned to Samhail. "Do you think I can handle a battle axe, or should we leave that until lesson two?"

"We'll see if you survive lesson one before planning additional lessons," Samhail said.

I rolled my eyes at him, and Ursan seemed to relax.

Samhail stood up and put his plate in a bin near the kitchen.

"I'll be down to the training yard at nine sharp," he told me on his way out. "Run ten laps and be stretched and ready by the time I get there."

"Yes, sir," I said, inclining my head toward him with a mock salute.

"Nine o'clock," he said over his shoulder.

Thirty minutes later, I'd finished breakfast, made my way to the training yard, run my ten laps, and stretched most of my muscles. I'd just finished my last stretch when the Priory bells signaled the top of the hour, and Samhail strode toward me before their last tones echoed across the yard.

"All ready," I said to him.

"We'll see. Give me your hands."

I extended my hands to him. He reached into his pockets, pulled out two rolls of cloth, and began unrolling them. I blanched and pulled my hands back.

"What are you doing?" I asked in alarm.

"It's to protect your hands and wrists. Relax. I'm not planning to tie you up." He winked. "Unless you want me to."

I narrowed my eyes and tamped down the flutter in my stomach.

"Do you want to train or not?" he asked.

I nodded and extended my hands to him again.

Samhail took one hand and wrapped the cloth around it, weaving it between my thumb, over my knuckles, and around my wrist. "This will help keep your wrist straight so you don't injure it when you punch, and it'll help cushion your knuckles."

"Do I need to carry these with me in case I need to fight?" I asked, still a little confused.

Samhail chuckled. "You won't have time to wrap your wrists if you get into a real fight, but these will protect you while training until you can strengthen your muscles and your body gets used to the impact."

I nodded. Samhail tied off the cloth on my first wrist and began to wrap the other.

"How does that feel?" he asked when done. "Not too tight?"

I flexed my wrists a little and nodded. "It's fine. I can't bend my

228

wrists much, though."

"That's the point. Now make a fist."

Samhail balled his own hand into a fist to show me. I tried to copy him, but he shook his head. "Thumb outside the fist, not inside."

I corrected my fist and he nodded.

"Now show me a punch."

I pulled my fist back and threw it forward as hard as I could.

"Not bad. You're not as hopeless as I was afraid you'd be."

I threw him a glare.

"Not quite right, though. Your wrist needs to be perfectly in line." He adjusted my hand so that it wasn't hanging down.

"See?" he said, running a finger along the top of my hand and wrist. "Straight. That's important or you can break your wrist."

I nodded again.

"Now punch," he ordered.

I threw my fist out again but had to correct the position of my hand once more so that my wrist was straight.

"Again."

I punched again, and my wrist was straighter this time.

Samhail continued to have me throw punches several more times, making adjustments as we went, until he was satisfied with my form.

"Now, we'll try it with this," he said, picking up the straw-stuffed pad I'd seen him use with Bressen.

My arms were already starting to tire, but I didn't dare complain.

Samhail held the pad out, and I punched it. It stung a bit but wasn't bad. I looked at my arm to confirm that my wrist was straight.

"Harder," Samhail said.

I threw another punch, and the impact reverberated up my arm.

"Better. Again."

"What the hell is going on here?" came a voice from one of the upper walkways that circled the yard.

I looked up to see Jerram frowning down at us.

"Samhail is teaching me to fight," I said.

"Why?" Jerram asked, his voice dripping with scorn.

"So I can defend myself if attacked," I said, locking eyes with him.

He flinched, and we stood looking at each other for a long moment before he shook his head. "Just make sure this brute doesn't hurt you, or he'll have me to answer to."

He turned and left without another word.

I looked at Samhail. His expression said he could beat Jerram to a pulp with little effort and really wanted to do so now.

"Do you want to continue?" he asked.

"Can I draw his face on that pad?"

Samhail grinned and held up the pad. "Just use your imagination. That's what I do."

For the next hour I punched, kicked, and even elbowed the pad over and over again as Samhail yelled directions and coached me on my technique. My entire body hurt when Samhail called time, but I'd worked off both my anger at Jerram as well as some of my frustrations from last night with Bressen.

"Not bad at all," Samhail said as he unwrapped the cloth from my wrist. "Once you've had a little more practice, we'll add in some sword training."

"Thank you. I appreciate this."

He nodded. "You'll be sore tomorrow. I recommend you put something cold on your knuckles and your muscles."

I watched him unwind a wrap and shove it back into his pocket before I mustered enough courage to ask what I'd been wanting to know since I first saw him this morning.

"Samhail...what did you do to those men last night?"

His hands stopped moving for a moment.

"Only what they deserved," he said as he resumed unwrapping. "They're not dead, if that's what you're afraid of."

"Are they in one piece?"

"They are. Some of their bones may not be."

I gasped, but Samhail jerked my wrist, making me look up at him.

"Don't feel sorry for them." It was a command, and I shivered at the look in his eyes. "They would have raped you and your maid and left you for dead."

"You don't know-"

"I do know," he cut in. "Bressen looked into their minds and saw exactly what they planned to do to you. They're lucky I left them with their pricks somewhat intact."

I flinched and wiped furiously at the tears that welled in my eyes.

Samhail finished unwrapping my other hand and shoved the second cloth back into his pocket. I looked down at the ground, unable to meet his eyes, but he gripped my chin and forced my face back up to his.

"Don't feel sorry for them," he repeated. "They suffered and will continue to suffer for a while, but they got better than they would have given you."

I nodded, and he released my chin.

"Thank you for saving us last night. I'm not sure how you found us, but I'm grateful."

"Bressen found you. We were having a drink in one of the taverns on that alley, and he sensed your presence. We were settling up our bill to go look for you when he felt your fear. I don't think I've ever seen him move that fast before."

I'd been lured by some unexplainable force down that alley last night, and I wondered now if I'd been drawn toward Bressen somehow.

"I kissed Bressen," I told Samhail suddenly, not sure why I kept confessing these things.

Samhail raised a brow.

"Last night," I went on, "when he brought me back, I kissed him. Or he kissed me."

Samhail smiled. "I know."

I frowned. "What do you mean you know?"

"He told me this morning," he said, clearly amused. "He said you

231

confessed to kissing me as well." He was trying not to laugh.

"Or maybe you both kissed *me*, and I'm innocent in all this," I snapped at him.

His look said I was in no way innocent of anything.

I shook my head in bemusement. "It doesn't bother you either, does it."

"Should it?"

I grunted in frustration. "Bressen said the same thing last night."

"You seem like you want it to bother us."

I thought for a moment. "No, I don't want you to be bothered by it. I just don't understand why you aren't. Most men in Fernweh would be jealous over something like that."

Samhail grinned. "I'm not most men."

I grunted again. "Do the two of you have a script for this?"

"Bressen said the same thing?"

"To the word."

Samhail shrugged. "I can't speak for Bressen, but my kind doesn't form romantic attachments easily. I suppose Bressen and I don't get jealous of each other because our liaisons with women are usually just a matter of satisfying a physical need. There's no reason for jealousy."

I felt a pang of disappointment that their interest in me was purely physical. I hoped I might mean more to them than that, but I told myself not to be stupid. The idea of a relationship with either of them was ridiculous.

I tried to hide my hurt, but Samhail realized his mistake and lifted a huge hand to brush his fingers tenderly down my cheek.

"If it makes a difference," he said, "I very rarely meet women that I enjoy spending time with outside of a bedroom. You're an exception to that rule, Cyra."

I cocked my head at him. I wasn't sure whether to be flattered he thought so highly of me, or offended on behalf of all womankind. He again realized his mistake.

"I'm really not good at these conversations," he said, shaking his head. "What I meant to say is that I consider you a friend, and my kind doesn't make friends easily either."

"Your kind. You mean gargoyles."

He looked a little surprised. "Bressen told you."

"He wanted me to understand what I was getting into when I asked you to train me."

"And you still wanted me to train you after you knew what I was?"

"Of course. Why wouldn't I? Like you said, we're friends."

He still seemed surprised but nodded. "So we are."

I gathered up the things I'd brought down with me, a cup for water and a cloth to wipe my face. "Just for the record, though," I teased him, "you wanted me that day we kissed in the Soundless Woods. Admit it."

His eyes smoldered, and he grinned wickedly at me. "I still want you," he said huskily.

I inhaled sharply.

"Gargoyles are a lusty bunch," he continued, "and you're a very beautiful woman. I'll always be open to taking you to my bed."

All the muscles in my lower body tensed, and my face flushed with heat.

"I'll keep that in mind," I said, my voice a little unsteady.

I turned to go, but he called me back.

"Cyra," he said, his face serious again. "You should train your magical powers as well. You weren't prepared to fight those men."

"Will you help me?"

He shook his head. "I don't know anything about elemental powers. I'd be useless to you."

"Not true," I insisted. "You'd make a pretty good target." I threw a hand toward him, and a jet of water sprayed into his face.

Samhail blinked in surprise, then growled under his smile. He lunged for me, but I clutched my things with a cry and ran from the yard. I heard him chuckling behind me, but I didn't stop running until I reached my room and closed the door behind me.

A knock sounded a moment later, and my heart skipped as I wondered if Samhail had followed me, thinking the jet of water was a playful invitation.

"Who is it?"

"Raina, my lady," came the answer from the hall.

I exhaled in relief and opened the door.

Raina was back to addressing me formally after our trip into the city. She'd been quiet this morning when she helped me dress, and I assumed she was still in shock from the night's events. She'd started to cry as she brushed my hair, and I'd pulled her into my arms for a long hug as she sobbed into my shoulder. When her sniffles had subsided, I'd apologized for putting her in danger, and she forgave me. She remembered Bressen and Samhail arriving but then nothing more until she'd woken up in her bed this morning.

Raina took in my sweaty face and dusty clothes as she entered the room now. She sniffed me and wrinkled her nose.

"Do you...need a bath, my lady?" she asked carefully.

I leaned my head down and sniffed as well. The smell of sweat assailed my nostrils, and I recoiled from it. Samhail really had given me quite a workout.

I followed Raina into the bathing room.

"How are you doing?" I asked her as the tub magically filled itself with water.

She shrugged. "Better. I didn't thank you earlier for trying to protect me, so thank you."

I huffed a mirthless laugh. "I didn't do much. We would've been in trouble if Lord Bressen and Samhail hadn't arrived when they did."

"I saw Damian. He came to find me this morning because we didn't return to the guard station before midnight."

Nemesis take me. I'd forgotten our promise to Damian and Roland. If I ever saw them again, I'd owe them an apology as well.

"What did he say?" I asked.

"He thought you tried to escape. I had to admit we were caught

234

outside the fortress, but he already suspected as much."

"Why?"

"Lord Bressen walked by him this morning, and Damian heard the lord say, 'Don't let it happen again,' into his mind."

I sighed. "It could have been worse. I'm really sorry for everything."

"Damian's mad at me now."

"He should be mad at me, not you. I can talk to him if you want."

"No, I'll handle it. I made the decision to help you last night. I need to take responsibility for it."

I smiled weakly at her as Raina helped me pull off my clothes.

"I'm never letting you leave the Citadel again, by the way," she said.

I grimaced. "Actually..." I said, giving her an apologetic smile.

"No! Forget it. I'm not taking you out again."

"I have permission to leave today," I clarified. "Lord Bressen is taking me somewhere after lunch."

"He's taking you somewhere?" she asked incredulously. "Even after he caught you outside the Citadel last night?"

I shrugged. "I told him I was going crazy shut up here, and he offered to take me out, but I don't know where." I stepped into the tub and sank down into the hot water. "How do I dress for that?"

"Are you sure he's not taking you to Revenmyer?" she asked, and my eyes flew to her.

"Nemesis take me, I hope not."

I doubted that was Bressen's plan, but now I was a little wary of our trip.

"Raina, you need to make me look good enough that Lord Bressen won't even think about bringing me to Revenmyer."

"So just to be clear, first you needed a look to make the lords tremble, and now you need one that says, 'Please don't throw me in prison, my lord,'" she teased.

"Yes, please."

"Fine, I have some ideas, but I'm going to need a raise after this."

"If I can make it happen, I will."

Raina just scoffed.

"Actually, I have another favor to ask you."

"You're running up quite a debt, my lady," Raina said.

"Can I pay you in wine?"

Raina thought for a moment. "I'll take a deposit in wine. What do you need?"

"If Damian ever starts talking to you again, can you ask him something for me? Lord Bressen and Samhail spoke the other day about something that happened. They were very vague, but it sounded important. I want to know what they were talking about."

"Damian may need more details than that. If he ever speaks to me again, that is."

"Samhail asked Lord Bressen if he was certain a man was gone from somewhere, and Lord Bressen said yes. He said they found the issue and took care of it, but they weren't sure how it happened in the first place."

Raina frowned. "That's not a lot to go on."

"I know, but it's all I've got."

Raina sighed. "I'll see what I can do, but you're going to owe me."

"I already owe you more than I can ever repay," I said, smiling at her. "You have no idea how much I appreciated your help last night, despite how things turned out."

Raina's face softened. "That's sweet," she said. "I really hope you make it back from Revenmyer now."

She squealed and ran for the door as I shot magically propelled jets of water at her.

Chapter 22

I arrived at lunch a couple hours later, bathed and dressed in an outfit Raina swore would keep me out of Revenmyer. I wore flowing teal pants that sat low on my waist and were just full enough to look like a skirt when I was standing still. My top was a fitted blouse of the same color that accentuated my breasts and showed some of my midriff. A teardrop diamond pendant encircled my throat while a small diamond comb held my hair back from my face on one side.

I was again disappointed to see Bressen wasn't in the dining room, nor was Samhail. Ursan and Glenora were there, as was Jerram, and my stomach twisted to see him, even more so when he noticed me.

"Cyra!" Jerram exclaimed, standing as I approached the table. "You look lovely." He grabbed my hand and kissed it, and I recoiled inwardly.

I thanked him and went to get my food. My usual seat was next to Jerram, and I wondered if there was a way to sit in a different place without making it too apparent that I didn't want to be near him. I didn't really care if he knew, but I didn't want to answer questions if Ursan or Glenora noticed. Unfortunately, Jerram pulled out the chair next to him as soon as I turned around with a bowl of soup, so I clenched my jaw and sat down.

"I'm glad you survived your training with Samhail," he said. "I hope the brute didn't hurt you. I'd hate to have to teach him a lesson."

Jerram's tone said he'd love to teach Samhail a lesson, but I knew he'd never have the courage to challenge Samhail to a fight. At least not a fair one. What angered me the most, though, was his continued insistence on calling Samhail a brute.

"He isn't a brute," I said. "He's a good teacher. I learned a lot."

Jerram scoffed but didn't argue with me.

I'd only eaten one spoonful of my soup when Damian entered the dining room in his guard uniform and came right over to stop next to my chair.

"My lady, Lord Bressen wishes to speak with you."

"Then tell Lord Bressen to come lunch with the rest of us," Jerram growled at Damian. "Can't you see the lady's eating?"

Damian looked uncomfortable. "My orders are-"

"Fuck your orders!" Jerram spat out. He slammed a hand down on the table, and Damian flinched. Ursan and Glenora stopped eating to look at him.

I put my spoon down and rose from the table. "I'll go."

"Cyra," Jerram began to protest, but I held up a hand.

"If I don't go, this man will be in trouble for not bringing me. You know how Lord Bressen can be. I don't want to see anyone punished on my account."

Jerram hesitated but then nodded. "Of course. We don't want anyone subjected to Bressen's cruelty. You're kind to indulge his whims and spare this guard his wrath."

I gave Jerram a knowing look and followed Damian out of the room. I rolled my eyes at him when we were safely down the hall, and Damian smiled.

"Thank you for last night," I said softly to him. "I'm sorry if I got you in trouble."

"My lady," he acknowledged with a small nod.

I followed Damian to Bressen's study where he knocked. Bressen's voice sounded an invitation to enter, and I stepped inside. Bressen was behind his desk, and he stood as I entered.

"Are you ready to…" His voice trailed off as he looked me over, his gaze lingering on the expanse of bare waist below my shirt. Appreciation lit his eyes, and I decided Raina had once again found the right look.

"I didn't know how to dress since you didn't tell me where we were going," I said.

Bressen smiled. "It's perfect." He wore his usual black pants and jacket, but the shirt beneath it today was the color of red wine.

"I thought we were leaving after lunch."

Bressen came around the desk toward me. "Change of plans. It occurred to me we could have lunch where we're going, so I made some arrangements."

"And you still won't tell me where you're taking me?"

"It's a surprise, although I should warn you we're leaving Callanus and heading into my own territory. I'm breaking a few rules to do this. Jerram and Ursan will be furious if they discover I took you out of the city, so if you have any objections, say so now."

I shook my head.

"Raina's been told to say you weren't feeling well after your meeting with me and that you retired to your room."

I nodded again, and Bressen led me toward the balcony. He pulled a cloak from one of the hooks and wrapped it around my shoulders. I was enveloped by his scent, and my stomach fluttered, as it now did regularly around him. He picked me up and strode to the edge of the balcony before his wings unfurled, and he launched us into the air with a few powerful beats. I felt a heavy mist settle over my skin as we rose.

"Obfuscation glamour?" I asked, recognizing the feeling.

"At least until we're out of the city."

I nodded, then tucked my head tighter into the crook between his neck and shoulder.

"How did your first training with Samhail go?" he asked as we soared out above the city.

"Samhail says that I'm not as hopeless as he was afraid I'd be."

Bressen chuckled, and the deep rumble of his voice vibrated against my body.

"That's high praise indeed coming from him," he said.

"Jerram saw us training and was rude to Samhail."

"Jerram is a petty, spiteful man. Ignore him. Samhail does."

I paused. "Does Jerram know what Samhail is?"

"That he's a gargoyle? No, I don't think so. It's not common knowledge. Ursan might know since he and my father worked together

239

closely during the war with Rowe, but I don't think Jerram ever had occasion to see Samhail in his gargoyle form."

"How often does Samhail change into that form?"

"Not often. As far as I know, he hasn't fully changed since the war. He usually just manifests his wings."

I glanced down and noticed that the tightly packed buildings of the city had thinned out as the land changed over to green and yellow plains and patches of tufted forest. The Scion River that ran along Hiraeth's western border wound along to our left.

"Are we in Hiraeth already?" I asked.

"We just flew over the border. Welcome to my territory."

I watched the land roll by below and decided flying with Bressen wasn't bad at all. I'd never had a problem with heights and being pressed against him kept me surprisingly warm against the chilly air flowing all around us.

Almost an hour later, though, I was finally starting to get cold despite the warmth of Bressen's body.

"How much longer until we get where we're going?" I asked.

"You should be able to see it over this next ridge."

I looked down and saw jutting gray rock formations passing beneath us. Out ahead, the edge of a cliff loomed, but at least I was already in the air this time.

The cliff fell off below us as the landscape changed to rolling green hills, and I gasped as I realized the hills were striped with rows of grape vines that extended for acres.

My eyes welled with tears, and I tried to blink them away. "You're taking me to a vineyard."

"One of our best."

Bressen tipped his wings, and we descended, the rows of grapevines seeming to fly up to meet us. A stately manor house sat in the midst of the fields, and behind it were several barns.

I closed my eyes as the ground suddenly seemed only feet away, but Bressen landed smoothly, touching down with a few steps that brought us to a walking halt on the stone patio in front of the manor.

I opened my eyes again, and Bressen set me down gently on the patio. I marveled at the stamina he must have to fly here while carrying me in his arms the whole time.

I looked around, and my mouth fell open in awe. Our vineyard back home was large, but it was dwarfed by the vastness of the fields before me now. My brothers and I also never put much effort into keeping the vineyard tidy, since it was just the three of us, and aesthetics weren't a priority, but these fields and vines were impeccably manicured.

"Worth the trip?" Bressen asked, looking at me expectantly.

I swallowed down the emotion in my throat and nodded.

Bressen slipped his hand into mine and led me across the patio into the manor house where we passed through a large serving room decorated with plush carpets and ornate metalwork chandeliers. We emerged behind the house where a table for two was set under a pergola that trellised four grape vines. Their canopy of leaves crawled over the top of the pergola to shade the table underneath, and bunches of grapes hung heavily down from the underside.

It wasn't as cold here as it was in Callanus. There was a slight nip in the air, but back home in Fernweh we sometimes had snow by now. An additional layer of magic also seemed to warm the space under the pergola itself.

A woman from the manor house helped me remove my cloak, and I took a seat at the table while Bressen sat down opposite me. A large plate of cheese, bread, and fruit was already laid out. I was ravenously hungry by now, so I reached out to pull some food onto my plate.

"I'm sorry. I didn't realize how hungry I was until just now," I said.

"By all means," Bressen said, filling his own plate.

A server appeared with a bottle of wine and poured us each a glass. Bressen requested samples of several other wines, and the man hurried back into the house to pull the bottles.

"What do you think?" Bressen asked after I'd taken a sip.

I smelled the wine and took another sip. "It's young, but I can taste its potential. In another year or two it should drink very nicely."

Bressen inclined his head to acknowledge my assessment.

"What do you think of it?" I asked him.

"It's good, but I've had better." He winked at me, and pride swelled in my chest as I understood the compliment.

"Is this your vineyard?" I asked.

"No, it's owned by an acquaintance."

"How were you able to arrange all this?"

He lifted a brow at me. "Being the Lord of Hiraeth does have its perks sometimes," he said as he extended his glass in a toast.

I clinked my glass against his. "To knowing people in high places."

What followed was an almost never-ending stream of the most exquisite foods I'd ever eaten and samplings of some of the best wines I'd ever tasted. An hour later, my stomach was almost bursting, and my limbs felt pleasantly light under the influence of the wine.

"Shall we take a walk through the vineyard to help our lunch settle?" Bressen asked.

He rose and held out a hand to me. I took it and let him lead me down a row of vines. I tried not to think of how giddy it made me to be here with him like this.

My brothers and I had already harvested our grapes, but most of the vines at this vineyard still had all of their fruit. I supposed the ripening season came later up here. I stopped at the end of one row and looked at the sign nailed to the trellis post with the name of the grape on it.

"How much sun does this region get during the growing season?" I asked.

Bressen shook his head. "I don't know. Why?"

I slipped my hand from his and searched under the leaves of the vine to examine the fruit beneath.

"These vines are vigorous growers. The leaf canopy is covering all the fruit."

Bressen looked at the vines and nodded.

"If the fruit doesn't get enough sun under the leaves, it won't ripen as well," I went on, looking back at the vines. "I remember tasting this varietal at lunch, and it was a little acidic. The fruit probably needs more sun. If the vineyard has enough workers to do it, trimming the leaf canopy back a couple times a year on these vines will make the grapes sweeter and help control that acidity."

I looked behind me when Bressen didn't say anything. He was just smiling at me.

"What?" I asked.

"Would you like to talk to the winemaker? You should tell him what you just told me."

"I'd love to talk to the winemaker!" I said. There were no other winemakers close to us in Fernweh, so I didn't usually have an opportunity to compare notes.

Bressen took my hand again to walk back toward the barns behind the manor house. We found the head winemaker there, and Bressen introduced me. Caymus was a good-natured older man, and he listened with interest as I made my suggestion about trimming back his vines. He assured me he'd try it next year.

"Would you like to see our cellar?" Caymus asked me.

I looked at Bressen, not wanting to drag him all around the vineyard while Caymus and I went on about winemaking, but he nodded to the winemaker. "Lead the way."

We spent the next couple hours exploring everything in the vineyard. I felt bad for Bressen, but he seemed content to let me and Caymus share notes and swap winemaking stories for the better part of the afternoon. Caymus did still have work to do, though, so we eventually said our goodbyes.

"Thank you," I said to Bressen as we walked back toward the house. "For all of this."

"It was my pleasure."

"I'm sorry you had to spend all afternoon listening to Caymus and

I carry on about winemaking."

"Not at all. It was fascinating to learn from a master."

"Caymus certainly is very knowledgeable," I agreed.

"Yes, but I was talking about you," he said.

I stopped, and he did too. I saw only sincerity in his beautiful eyes, and a warmth spread through me. I was surprised at how much it meant that he appreciated the work I'd dedicated my life to, but it also made me homesick. I missed that slightly sweet smell that hung in the air for days after the grapes were pressed, and I missed the excitement of that first taste of the wine once the fermentation stopped to see what flavors the yeasts brought out. I missed doing what I loved.

"We need to return to Callanus soon," Bressen said, "but I'm told the sunset on the vineyard is spectacular."

Bressen and I went back through the manor house so I could retrieve my cloak. It was beginning to get chilly as the sun dipped toward the horizon, and Bressen wrapped the cloak around my shoulders as we climbed one of the hills to get a good view. The day had been one of the best of my life, and I didn't want it to end.

I wrapped the cloak tighter around me as we sat next to each other on the hill, and I leaned against him just slightly. For warmth, I assured myself. Bressen reached an arm around to pull me closer, and I tried to remember that he was the Lord of Hiraeth, and it was dangerous to feel the things I was feeling. There was no future for me with him.

"How much longer will I need to stay at the Citadel?" I asked, and I felt his body stiffen.

"Samhail and I are trying to figure out what we can, but the seer's vision didn't give us much to go on."

"Samhail said you trained together in your father's army," I said, changing the subject. I decided I didn't want to think about how much longer I'd get to see Bressen.

"I met Samhail when I began my military training. He was already the star soldier in the training camp for obvious reasons, and I wanted to distinguish myself as something other than just the lord's son. He and I were bitter rivals to start, but then it became a friendly rivalry, then a friendship, and then a brotherhood. Even once we were friends, we still competed for just about everything, though."

Bressen smiled as if remembering those times fondly.

"Including women?" I asked.

Bressen went still, but he answered, "We were young, lusty, and reckless. Perhaps a bit stupid too. I'm not proud of how we handled ourselves at times, and neither is Samhail. We discovered we didn't always have to compete for women if they were interested in us both, and we broke a few hearts early on."

"Is it normal up here to…be with more than one person?"

"Not common, but it's also not frowned upon the way it is in some places. Three is a sacred number, especially in Callanus."

I'd noticed. Thasia's three ruling lords loosely mirrored the country's three gods, but the number three was also used whenever possible in other things. I'd started to notice features in the Citadel that came in threes. Three chandeliers hung over the dining room table, three portcullises guarded the tunnel under the battlements, and three paintings adorned most large walls.

The number figured prominently in other ways as well. Raina told me Damian was one of three children, for instance, which was considered an ideal number for many families.

"Amorous encounters between three people are sometimes considered a way to honor the Trinity," Bressen went on, "although Samhail and I can't really claim we did it for any kind of divine purpose."

"Did?" I asked.

"We haven't done so recently. Samhail is away a lot. This is the longest he's been in Callanus for a while."

"Last night when you and Samhail went to the tavern, were you…" I trailed off. I wasn't sure how to ask the question, but more importantly, I wasn't sure I wanted to know the answer.

"Were Samhail and I looking for women?" he supplied.

I nodded.

"No. At least, I wasn't. We were just catching up. It's been a long time since he and I went out drinking together."

I suddenly felt bad that I'd interrupted their night by getting into trouble so they had to come rescue me.

"You said Samhail is like a brother to you."

"He saved my life."

I looked at him sharply. "When?"

"During the war. I'd been using my powers for days to try and gain an advantage over Sandrian's forces, and I was drained."

"You were...killing men with your mind?" I asked, not sure why I felt the need to confirm this.

Bressen shook his head, though. "Not at first, or at least not directly. I turned the enemy forces to our side. I took over their minds and made them fight for us. It's more draining than killing them because it requires maintaining control of the soldiers for long periods, but it also meant slightly less blood on my hands. Or that's what I told myself anyway."

I looked at him in surprise. It wouldn't have occurred to me to use his power that way, and I was amazed he'd gone to so much trouble to avoid killing people, even in war.

"It worked? Turning people to your side?" I asked.

"For a little while. Unfortunately, Sandrian had a mind wraith like me on his side named Morland who was doing the same. I was turning his soldiers, and Morland was turning ours."

Bressen's face went dark as he remembered that time.

"I didn't know Morland had turned Samhail until I saw him across the battlefield," Bressen said, and I gasped.

"He was in his gargoyle form, and he was tearing through our soldiers, just ripping them apart. He was dripping in their blood. He charged me when he saw me. I tried to get through to him, but I was weakened, and Morland's hold on his mind was too strong."

"How were you able to bring him back?"

The sun had just started to dip below the horizon, and I shivered, partly at the idea of Samhail's mind not being his own and partly from the growing chill.

"You're cold," Bressen said, almost hesitantly, as if he wasn't sure what to do with that knowledge.

"I'll...be fine," I assured him, but another shiver belied the words.

Three seconds dissolved into the air along with my misty breaths, and then Bressen suddenly pulled me across his lap so I was seated between his legs. I squeaked in surprise but sighed when he slipped his arms around my shoulders and drew me against him. His warmth cloaked me as my skin cataloged every place we were pressed together.

The pinks and oranges of the sunset painted a spectacular tableau across the sky before us, but I barely noticed them as my entire world narrowed to the feel of Bressen's soft breaths fluttering the whisps of hair near my ear. I turned my head toward his instinctively, and he brushed his lips across my cheek in a soft kiss.

I closed my eyes and tried to commit this moment to memory so I could recall it when I was back in Fernweh trying to keep warm some winter night. Gods above, my body sang to be this close to him, and I leaned back, allowing myself to sink into his warmth.

"Samhail brought himself back," Bressen said, answering my question. "He'd been fighting Morland's mental hold the whole time, and he managed to break it right before he would've killed me. I'd been so sure I could get through to him that I didn't even try to defend myself when he attacked. He broke half of my ribs when he backhanded me across the field. I couldn't move, and he was about to crush my skull when he finally broke out of Morland's control. After the war, Samhail made me teach him how to build an impenetrable mind shield so no one could ever control him like that again."

I nodded, but Bressen wasn't done.

"That's only part of how he saved my life, though," Bressen said.

"There's more?"

"Morland was watching from the side of the battle. He hoped

either to see Samhail kill me, or to watch me kill Samhail to save myself. When neither happened, he turned all the men in the area to attack us. Samhail saw Morland on the side and picked up a spear. He threw it, and the spear went straight through Morland's head. All the soldiers Morland was controlling regained their minds, and the battle turned in our favor. Then Samhail picked me up and flew me back behind our lines so the healers could fix my ribs."

I shivered again, and Bressen drew me back even harder against him. His forehead leaned against my temple, and his breath caressed my cheek. I wasn't sure how we'd gotten to the point where I could sit like this with him, but I never wanted it to end. Two weeks ago, I'd been terrified at the thought of being in the same room as this man. Now, I couldn't seem to press myself close enough to him, and I didn't feel an ounce of shame for trying.

The last sliver of the sun disappeared below the horizon, leaving only fading pink and purple streaks in its wake, and something intangible shifted around us as the world came back into focus.

"We need to get you home," Bressen said. He uncurled his arms from around me and stood up. My body shrieked in protest at the loss of his warmth, but he pulled me to my feet and into his arms again.

"You mean you need to get me back to the Citadel," I corrected him with a weak smile.

His face fell a bit. "Yes, of course. My apologies."

I shrugged. "I knew what you meant. It's just getting harder and harder to be away from home, from my brothers."

Bressen paused. "It wasn't my choice to bring you to the Citadel. If I'd been there at the time, I wouldn't have agreed to summon you, and I'll do everything in my power to help get you home. You have my word on that."

"Thank you," I whispered, my face lifting toward his instinctively.

"I sincerely hope that's an invitation to kiss you," he said, his voice husky, "because that's what I'm about to do."

My lips parted as he lowered his head, and then his mouth was on

248

mine, and I nearly forgot how to breathe. His kiss was gentle at first as his tongue slipped in to caress my own, but the urgency grew quickly between us as our mouths melded together. Bressen wrapped his arms around me, pinning my body inside the cloak, and his lips roved hungrily over mine until we finally parted in a gasp. He took my face in his hands and pulled back to look at me.

"Gods above, you're so beautiful," he said, his voice fraying. "I don't think I've ever…"

I trembled at his words. "Ever what?" I asked, but he just shook his head.

"Never mind. It's not important. Just know that you're beautiful."

I didn't know what to say to that. That this gorgeous, powerful man thought I was beautiful made no sense to me. I'd fantasized about being with Bressen, but the idea I might actually be able to have him hadn't been real to me until just now.

Bressen kissed me again, and his hand slipped inside the cloak to steal over the bare skin at my waist. His thumb brushed in slow sweeps just below my breast, and I couldn't help the moan that left me as my nipples peaked sharply against the fabric of my shirt. His hand drifted higher so his thumb grazed the underside of my breast, and wetness gathered between my thighs. I tried to savor every second of his touch, every sweep of his lips over mine as time lost its meaning. I had no idea how long it had been when Bressen finally lifted his head again.

"We really do need to go now," he said as he pressed his forehead against mine. His hands moved back to my face, and his thumbs brushed lightly across my cheeks.

Bressen lifted me up as his wings unfurled behind him, and with a few heavy beats, he propelled us into the sky. The rows of grape vines faded below us into the darkness, and as I laid my head against his shoulder, I only hoped the rhythmic beating of his wings drowned out the frantic thundering of my heart.

Chapter 23

I awoke to the feeling of falling. I'd dozed off in Bressen's arms on the flight back, and I couldn't see anything in the dark. Bressen's grasp had gotten tighter around me, though, and even in my just-waking fog, I could tell something was wrong. I felt weightless again as we dropped in the sky, and I cried out in alarm.

"Hold onto me!" Bressen yelled, and I felt him bank hard.

My arms were trapped in the cloak, and I struggled to free them so I could hold onto him. I finally managed to pull one loose and threw it around his neck.

"What's happening?" I yelled.

"Someone is shooting arrows at us."

"What!" I was fully awake now.

"It's my fault. I didn't put up the obfuscation glamour because I didn't think anyone would see us in the dark. The glamour is up now, but they seem to be shooting randomly into the sky on the chance they'll hit us."

I looked down and saw the lights of Callanus twinkling below us. To our left, the glow of the Citadel's torches told me we were close.

An arrow whizzed by us a few feet away and Bressen barrel-rolled in the sky. I yelped and clung tighter to his neck.

"Sorry about that," he said.

"That arrow came from the Citadel," I noted.

"I know. Probably a guard on the outer wall who isn't sure what he's seeing."

As he spoke, my skin prickled in a way I'd never felt before — not just at my nape, but all over — and I sensed the next arrow cutting through the air toward us. I threw out a hand and a strong wind swirled past us. Orange from the arrow's fletching flashed in my vision before the gust knocked the arrow off course…but not far enough.

The tip of the arrow nicked one of Bressen's wings, and he grunted in pain as we dropped in the air again. His grip slackened briefly, and I slipped in his arms. I yelled and held onto him tighter as I glanced down at the city still far below.

Bressen tightened his arms around me again. "I've got you."

"Are you alright?"

"I should be able to stay up," he grunted.

I looked down and saw the Citadel growing larger. I closed my eyes and summoned all the strength I had to focus it into an updraft we might be able to ride all the way down.

By some miracle, it worked. I felt the air rise up to meet us, and so did Bressen. He adjusted his wings to catch it, and we glided down toward the Citadel. The arrows had stopped coming, but our approach was still precarious. Bressen tilted to let us circle down some more, and I kept my eyes tightly shut as I focused all my energy into letting the wind keep us aloft.

"Drop the wind," Bressen said after a few more seconds of gliding.

I open my eyes and cut off the wind. We were just coming in toward my balcony and the sudden loss of the updraft dropped us the last few feet onto the stone. Bressen tripped forward as he landed hard but managed to keep his feet. He let go of my legs but kept his other arm anchored around my waist as the two of us stumbled to a halt on the balcony.

We stood still for a moment doing nothing but trying to catch our breath as we held onto each other. I gripped the solid bulges of his biceps as his hands rested on the small of my back.

"You were hit," I said, putting a hand on his chest.

"I'm fine. It was just a graze."

I looked his wings over and found where the arrow had nicked the bone. Blood trickled down the wing, and a couple of feathers were also damaged, possibly from an earlier shot before I'd woken.

"Come in and let me clean that for you."

"Cyra," he said, starting to protest, but I cut him off.

"Be quiet and let me clean the wing."

Bressen raised a brow but then smiled. "Yes, my lady."

I took his hand and brought him over to sit on the corner of the bed, then ran into the bathing room to see what I could find for towels. I came back with several small towels doused with warm water. I sat down on the bed next to him and dabbed at the wound as I examined his wings up close. They were sleek and powerful with long raven-black feathers, and they emerged right through the fabric of his jacket without a hole, which I assumed was some kind of magic. One wing hung off the edge of the bed while the injured one flexed out across the mattress.

Bressen sat completely still as I worked, and I wondered if he was as cognizant of being on my bed as I was. I'd been in his arms half the day, but this was the first time I felt free to touch him, and I let my fingers trail over him perhaps a bit more than necessary. The rigid set of his body told me he was well aware of everything I was doing, and I tried to refocus my thoughts onto my task. A few minutes and several bloody towels later, the wing had stopped bleeding.

"It doesn't look too deep," I said. Indeed, the wound already seemed to be mending. "The blood is clotting now, but you should have a healer look at it."

Bressen stood up and flexed his wings a bit to gauge their mobility.

"Be careful. The wound will start bleeding again," I said.

With a shrug, Bressen retracted the wings into his back.

I sighed. "Or you can just do that."

"Your wind saved us from a harder landing," he said. "Thank you."

"The arrows were still getting very close, even after you put the obfuscation glamour up."

"I'll look into it tomorrow. For now, I should go."

He started toward the balcony but remembered the state of his wing and thought better of it. He turned back toward the bedroom door, but I'd been following him, and we bumped into each other when he turned. My hand pressed against his chest, and his arm came around my back to steady me.

"Maybe...I'll take the stairs tonight," he said, but he didn't move.

I held Bressen's gaze, not wanting to tear myself away from those stunning pools of turquoise. My mouth parted ever so slightly, and I leaned against him. He lowered his head so that his lips hovered just above mine, and I stretched up to meet him. A small shock leapt between our lips as they touched, and he pulled back suddenly, dropping his hand from my waist. I sucked in a ragged breath and fought the urge to throw myself back into his arms.

"I need to go," he said, his voice a husky rasp.

He stepped to the side to leave, but I grabbed his wrist. It was pure instinct. I didn't even realize I'd grabbed him until I looked down and saw his wrist in my hand. Our eyes locked, and there was pure searing heat and an unspoken promise in his gaze that sent anticipation skittering over my skin. I gripped his wrist tighter than I intended, but both my mind and my body were screaming at me not to let him leave.

"Stay." The word was both an order and a plea.

Bressen shut his eyes tightly for a few seconds before answering. "Cyra, you were right the other day. Letting this go any further only puts you in danger. I've been selfish to-"

"I don't care. I don't want you to leave," I interrupted him.

Bressen went still, and I felt him fighting for control. His arms twitched as if he wanted to reach out for me, but he resisted the urge and closed his eyes again.

In that moment, a boldness I didn't know I possessed took hold, and I started unbuttoning his jacket. His eyes flew open again, but he didn't try to stop me. I held his stare as his chest rose and fell heavily. I worked my way down the buttons and then opened his jacket to reveal the wine-red shirt I now realized should've been a clue as to where he was taking me today.

I pressed my palms flat against his stomach, and the muscles clenched under my fingers. A smile curled my lips, and I ran my hands slowly up his chest. I felt the hard knot of each sinew through the soft fabric of his shirt, and I ached to touch the skin beneath. When I

253

reached his collarbone, my hands moved across his shoulders to catch his jacket and pull it down his arms. His breathing was still deep, but its rhythm had steadied.

When I'd pulled the jacket halfway down, he shrugged his shoulders to let it fall the rest of the way as I began to unbutton his shirt. I yanked it from his pants when I got to his waist and heard his sharp intake of breath. I'd never been this forward with a man before, and I was rather enjoying myself.

I tugged his shirt open when I'd freed the last button, and I bit my lip as my eyes roamed over the beautiful expanse of muscled torso and tanned skin that lay beneath. I ran my fingers along a scar under one of his ribs, and he flinched. He was still watching me when I looked up, but his breathing was ragged again, and his chest heaved with each effort. My own breathing was growing deeper now as well, but I forced myself to take my time.

I gave Bressen a coy smile and walked behind him.

I tsked. "So disappointing," I said as I ran my hand over the taut swells of his ass, and his back stiffened.

I leaned up on tiptoes so my lips reached over his shoulder just under his ear. "No tail," I said, and he exhaled a breath that was part sigh, part laugh.

I pulled his shirt down his back and dropped it onto the floor with his jacket. My hands splayed across his back, and I ran them over the smooth skin there between his shoulder blades. He had a few other scars here and there, but I couldn't tell where his wings emerged from at all. I planted a light kiss in the center of his back, savoring the feel of his smooth skin under my lips. Bressen drew in another sharp breath, but I only moved my hands to his sides to rest on those curving sinews just above each hip that made me suddenly want to learn the name of every muscle in his body.

I moved back to stand in front of Bressen, letting my hand trace a light trail around his waist as I went, and I felt him tremble. I caught his gaze again when I was in front of him. His eyes were darker than usual, almost teal, and the knot in his throat bobbed as he swallowed.

I reached out for the fastenings of his pants, but Bressen grabbed my wrists, startling me. He was breathing heavily, and he seemed to be wrestling with himself. His hands were firm but not painful around my wrists. I felt the strain in his body as he held me there.

"Cyra," he breathed.

"Yes, Bressen?" I asked innocently, and his eyes widened slightly to hear me use his name for the first time.

"What are you doing?"

"Exploring."

"You need to stop," he said, the pain of every word evident in his voice. "I can't do this. I can't let myself…I won't be able to stop if I touch you like this."

"I want you to touch me."

I tried to move my hands, but he held them firmly. I leaned into him and the hard length inside his pants bulged against my stomach.

I'd been afraid he was resisting because he didn't want me. I thought perhaps I'd misread his teasing or the way he'd held me against him at the vineyard, but the clear evidence of his desire was there now, pressed into me. I smiled and moved my hips slowly against him. He groaned and pulled back a few inches from me.

"Cyra, you don't understand," he said, his voice barely above a whisper. "I need you. I need to be inside you like I need air in my lungs, and if I take that first breath…"

"Take that breath," I urged him. "Take *me*."

He closed his eyes and his hands tightened for just a moment on my wrists. He was wound like a crossbow, and I was about to pull the trigger. I stood up on my toes so that my tongue flicked at the dimple in his chin and then licked along the length of his jaw, his stubble rough on my tongue.

Bressen's eyes flew open, and he let out a low growl. I squeaked as he picked me up roughly and swept over to the bed to toss me down on top of it. His body came down to cover mine as he grabbed my hands again to pin them next to my head.

"That was a dangerous thing to do," he rasped, and my breath caught at the heat raging in his eyes. Yet it was nothing compared to the heat of his body as he pushed a thigh between mine.

I looked up at him defiantly. "I've been told I court danger."

He growled again, and his lips came down to claim mine. I tried to arch off the bed under him as his tongue delved into my mouth, but his body pressed me down. His kiss was raw and urgent, and I groaned my consent to the onslaught. Tension coiled in my stomach and quickly worked its way lower in my body. Desire burned through my veins, and I tried to free the hands Bressen had pinned at my head, but he held them fast.

"I want to touch you," I said as he lifted his lips.

Bressen shook his head. "You had your chance. It's my turn now."

He laid a trail of kisses down my neck then lowered his head all the way to the neckline of my shirt. I looked down in surprise as I felt him pop the first button of the shirt open with his teeth. Two more buttons followed, and he pressed his face between the flaps of my shirt to nudge it open so his tongue could lick a path between my breasts.

I moaned, and his hands finally let go of mine so he could finish opening the buttons. My fingers threaded through his hair as he opened one side of the shirt to bare my breast. His hand covered it, and my nipple instantly pebbled under his warm touch. I moaned again as he gently squeezed the breast, letting his thumb flick over the peak.

His hot mouth replaced his hand, and I cried out as he began to suck, his tongue teasing the nipple. My hands clenched in his hair, and his mouth redoubled its efforts on my breast. I tried to bow off the bed again, but his hand wrapped around my waist to hold me down. Bressen pushed back the fabric of my shirt from the other breast, and his mouth closed over that one next.

I was going out of my mind as the heat from his mouth seared my skin and radiated down my body. The tension building between my legs was quickly becoming unbearable as I writhed beneath him.

"Bressen!" I gasped as his tongue circled my nipple.

"I like hearing my name on your lips," he said.

"Bressen, please!" I begged as he lowered his head again to suck my breast deeply into his mouth, sending lightening through my veins.

"Please what?"

"I need you!" I breathed.

"You need me to what?" he asked as his teeth closed gently over my nipple.

I cried out and grabbed his shoulders. Gods above, I'd never felt anything like this. "I need you inside me now. Please!"

Bressen moved up so he was looking into my eyes. One of his hands trailed lightly down my stomach and pulled the tie at the waist of my pants, but he didn't move to take them off. Instead, his hand slipped down into the pants and moved between my legs. I gasped as he slipped a long finger inside me and moved it slowly in and out.

"Is this what you want?" he teased.

"I want *you*," I insisted. I tried for the fastenings of his pants again, but his hand slipped back out to catch mine.

"Cyra, I don't think you know what you're asking of me."

"I'm asking you to fuck me," I rasped. My tone was just short of a growl, but my patience was fading as the ache between my legs grew.

"Such a wicked little mouth," he purred, tracing his thumb over my bottom lip. "I bet it would feel incredible wrapped around my-"

He cut himself off and shook his head, but I knew well enough what he'd been about to say. I ran my tongue over the bottom of my lip where he'd traced his thumb. His eyes fixed on my mouth, and I saw the knot in his throat bob again as he swallowed.

Bressen lifted himself off the bed to undo the fastenings of his own pants. He never took his eyes from mine as he kicked his boots off and stepped out of the trousers. My own eyes dipped to the swollen shaft between his legs as it sprung free, and I inhaled sharply. His cock was already rock-hard and ready for me. My eyes ran down his muscled thighs, and I bit my lip again as my gaze came back to rest on that part of him I wanted most right now.

I sat up, and Bressen pulled my shirt off before he pressed me back down with a gentle hand to the middle of my chest. He looped his fingers at the waistbands of my pants and undergarment together and pulled them off. He didn't move for a moment but just stood looking down at me laid out naked before him as if I were a feast and he was famished. He tossed my clothes aside and lowered himself back onto the bed to cover me with his body. His hands pressed my thighs open, and he settled between them. Pure need flashed in his eyes, and his smile was sultry as I felt him push at my entrance. I arched up to meet him, but he pulled back, denying me.

"Is this what you want?" he breathed, pressing himself forward again so I could feel the tip of him part me.

"Yes!" I gasped, trying to grab for his hips to pull him into me.

"Are you sure this is what you want?" he asked, and this time the question wasn't teasing. He was asking for permission to unleash his desire, and I felt the strain between our bodies as he held himself back, waiting for my answer.

"If I let myself have you," he said, "if I let myself fill you now, I won't be able to hold back. I'm not sure I can be gentle with you."

"You don't need to be. I want you," I insisted. "I want all of you."

Bressen's eyes flashed, and his restraint broke then. He entered me swiftly in one quick thrust, and I cried out as my body closed around him, like I was joining once again with something I'd lost. I welcomed his filling presence as relief washed over me, not the explosive relief of release, but the promise of the pleasure inherent in his surrender.

Bressen let out a low groan, and he pulled back slowly before burying himself in me again. I wrapped my arms around his neck, and my hips arched up to meet him as he thrust into me. Despite his earlier warning about not being gentle, he was taking his time, and the throb building at my core was threatening to shatter me into a million pieces.

"Nemesis take me, you feel so fucking good," Bressen breathed against my ear. He slid into me again, achingly slow, and I dug my nails into his shoulder as I felt every inch of him fill me.

"Bressen, take me harder," I begged.

He thrust into me a little harder, but still too carefully.

"I don't want to hurt you," he said. "I've wanted this too much. If I let myself go now…"

I reached up and touched his cheek, drawing his eyes to mine. "You won't hurt me. Let yourself go."

There was only a moment's more hesitation before he plunged into me so hard that I cried out in ecstasy, and my hands came around his back to dig into the muscles there. The feel of my fingernails made Bressen groan, and he moved in earnest now, pushing harder and faster into me with each thrust. He slipped his arms under me, and I wrapped my legs around his hips, urging him deeper. He obliged, and that exquisite tension built steadily in my core. The pressure of his body against the whole length of mine was a teasing torment against my overly sensitive skin. I was all too aware of every place we ground together, and shockwaves jolted through me, pooling between my thighs where Bressen continued to bury himself inside me again and again. I lost all sense of time as pleasure took over, and each drive of his hips brought me closer to a precipice.

My release broke over me like nothing I'd ever felt before. It was as if a new sun burst into fiery existence between us, and Bressen groaned as my body clenched around him. I held onto him as he continued to thrust, sending aftershocks of rapture through me before his body seized a few strokes later, and he roared with his own climax.

Bressen's wings sprang out from his back as he spilled himself into me. They unfurled in a full stretch behind him, knocking one of the bedside lamps off its table. The lamp shattered on the floor, and the wings shuddered, still fully stretched out as if he was flying.

It was several seconds before the tautness in Bressen's wings eased and they folded back against his body. He relaxed on top of me, and we lay for a long time entwined in each other's arms as our breathing eased. I savored the heaviness of him on top of me, but I knew he was still holding himself up so I wasn't taking his full weight.

Bressen pulled his arms out from under me, and he leaned back to withdraw himself from between my legs.

"Are you alright?" he asked, and I nodded. He ran a finger down my cheek. "You are a wicked temptress."

"And you're a teasing scoundrel," I answered.

I looked over his shoulder at his wings tucked against his back.

"I've never had that happen before," he said, following my gaze.

My eyes found the spot on his wing where the arrow had hit him, and they widened in surprise. "Your wing is almost fully healed."

Bressen glanced upward, but I doubted he could see the wing. "I've always been a quick healer," he said as he lifted himself off me and got up from the bed.

I moaned in protest, but he only pulled down the covers and picked me up to tuck me under the sheets. I was afraid he was going to leave, but he retracted his wings and crawled into the bed after me, letting his body curl around mine. I relaxed against him, and moments later, we were asleep.

I awoke later that night to gentle kissing, and we made love again, much slower and more sensually this time, but no less passionately. My body craved Bressen's, and I fell asleep only reluctantly after he'd coaxed my pleasure from me several more times. Close to dawn, I woke once more to his hand on my cheek.

"Again?" I asked sleepily. "You're insatiable."

He smiled but shook his head. "Not this time. It's almost dawn, and I can't be caught in your bed. I need to return to my own room."

I gave him my best doe eyes, and the look wasn't lost on him, even in the dark.

"By the gods, don't look at me like that. If I don't leave now, I'll never go."

"Is it really so bad for you to stay?" I asked seriously.

"I tempted fate enough yesterday by taking you out of the city. If Ursan – or worse, Jerram – found out I shared your bed, they'd view

260

it as you taking a side. The only thing that keeps you safe for now is their belief that you have no allegiance to any of us, especially me. Your friendship with Samhail already makes you suspect because they know he and I are friends. They can't learn what we did, and," he said, taking a deep breath, "this cannot happen again."

My body went cold, and I shook my head. Now that I'd been with Bressen, my body only wanted him all the more. To abstain now was unthinkable.

"No, that's not fair," I said.

"I don't want to put you in danger," he said softly.

"I've been in danger since the moment I arrived."

He looked at me but didn't say anything. He was fighting with himself, and it gave me hope.

"We'll see," he said finally. "For now, I need to leave. At the very least, no one needs to catch us tonight."

I nodded, and he kissed me gently before climbing out of bed. I watched him pick up his clothes and get dressed. By the Creator, he was magnificent.

"Your wing," I reminded him as he headed toward the balcony.

Bressen swore and turned for the bedroom door instead. He opened it quietly and looked back at me once before slipping out.

The door had barely closed before I already missed the sound of his steady breathing and the heat of his body next to mine. My encounters with Eddin and the merchant back in Fernweh had been mostly quick ruts in convenient places when others weren't around. We didn't wake up in the same bed together like a couple, but I wanted that feeling of being with someone, of being able to say they were mine. I wanted it desperately.

Nemesis take me, I wanted Bressen.

I slept fitfully for the next couple hours and felt wholly unrested when Raina threw open the curtains to let the sun in. I'd changed into my sleeping clothes after Bressen left so Raina didn't find me sleeping naked. I wondered what she thought about the fact that I hadn't called her to help me get ready for bed last night.

"Your tea, my lady," Raina said setting the cup down on my bedside table.

I picked it up and took a sip. There was a slight pink hue to the tea that wasn't usually there, but whatever had been added gave it an extra zing I enjoyed.

"You threw your clothes everywhere last night," Raina muttered as she went around picking up the pants, shirt, and undergarment I'd worn the day before. "And what happened to the lamp?"

My eyes flew open, and I bolted upright. Raina was bent over picking up pieces of the lamp that Bressen's wing had knocked over.

"Nightmare," I said quickly. "I must've had a nightmare and knocked it over."

"There's glass all over the floor. Don't get out of bed until I get this cleaned up, my lady."

I looked around the room for any other evidence of Bressen's visit I'd forgotten about. His cloak was still in a pile near the balcony – but worse – the bloody towels I'd used to dab Bressen's injured wing lay on the floor at the foot of the bed. I launched myself toward the end of the bed and shoved the towels under it.

Raina looked up from her cleaning to see what in the three hells I was doing. "My lady? Are you well? You seem…restless this morning."

Oh, she had no idea. Bressen and I had spent half the night having sex, and I still wanted him. Just thinking about him made me ache to have him above me, thrusting inside me, but if he had his way, I'd never again fulfill that desire.

I shuddered. I couldn't even consider that possibility right now. The thought of never kissing Bressen again or having him in my bed, of never feeling that pleasure I'd only ever felt with him was anathema. I'd go mad.

"It was a long night," I told Raina.

And I was in for many more long nights of a different kind if Bressen stayed away.

Chapter 24

I was prepared for Bressen's usual aloofness at breakfast the next morning, but my heart sank to see he wasn't there at all when I arrived. I ate in silence and then met Samhail for my training an hour later. That kept my mind off Bressen for a time, but my thoughts quickly strayed back to him when we were done.

I went to the library in the central building to get a book, but I didn't find anything that spoke to me. A voice in my head kept insisting that Bressen's library might have something better, so I finally gave in to the urge and headed toward his wing of the Citadel. I wasn't sure how often he even used his library, but just walking into his wing made me feel better, as if I was closer to him already. I thought the guards at the door might stop me, but they let me pass without a word.

Once in the library, I began sifting through books, but I found myself reading and rereading each title several times without taking in a word. My ears were attuned to the slightest sound in case Bressen happened to enter. I'd pulled a book at random and had been staring at it without seeing anything for ten minutes when I heard a shelf groan behind me.

I spun around to see Samhail leaning against one of the bookshelves with his arms crossed over his chest. I fought down my disappointment at seeing it was him and not Bressen.

"He's not here," Samhail said.

"Who's not here?" I asked, playing dumb rather unconvincingly.

"Bressen."

"Yes, I can see he's not here," I said. "I was just looking for a book." I held up the book in my hand and shook it.

Samhail's look said we both knew that was bullshit.

"You were distracted at training today," he said.

I frowned at him. Really? I'd felt like it was a good training. I'd thought about Bressen somewhat, but not nearly as much as I was thinking about him now.

"No, I wasn't," I said, deciding on outright denial.

Samhail smiled. "If you say so. In any case, Bressen isn't here."

"If I wanted to see him, I'd go to his study," I said, flipping casually through the book. "That's usually where he is around this time of day, isn't it?"

"Usually, yes, but not today."

My gaze snapped up to Samhail, but I looked quickly back down at my book, pretending disinterest. I waited for him to offer more, but he didn't.

Damn him. He was going to make me ask.

"Fine," I said, closing the book. "Where is Bressen then?"

He smirked, and I had the urge to throw the book at his head.

"He went back to Hiraeth. He had some business at Revenmyer."

"Wait, so he's not here?"

Samhail raised an *Isn't that what I've been saying?* eyebrow at me.

"I mean, he's not in the Citadel at all?"

He shook his head, and I felt a knot form in the pit of my stomach.

"When will he be back?" I asked, then added quickly, "I'm just curious."

Samhail shrugged. "He didn't tell me. Maybe tomorrow."

That meant I wouldn't see Bressen tonight. My legs suddenly felt weak, and I grabbed the back of a nearby chair to steady myself. I'd only known Bressen for a little over two weeks. How could thoughts of him affect me this much? For that matter, had he really gone all the way back to Hiraeth just to avoid me?

Samhail pushed off the bookcase and came over to me. "Are you alright?"

I waved him away. "I'm fine. Just a little tired from training. I should lie down."

"I'll walk you back to your room," he said, but I heard the other offer below the surface as he caught my gaze. His hand slipped gently around me to rest at the small of my back, and his eyes held me fast.

I remembered his words to me after our first training well enough. *I'll always be open to taking you to my bed.* I knew that look. It was desire, and for the briefest moment I imagined inviting Samhail into my room.

The thought was there, but I shook it away. Right now, I only wanted Bressen.

"No need. I'll be fine on my own. Thank you for letting me know about Bressen."

Samhail didn't move for several seconds, and I very nearly changed my mind. Finally, he gave me a nod so slight I would have missed it if I hadn't been looking directly at him. He pulled his hand back from my waist and stepped back from me.

I put the book I'd been holding back on the shelf and left the library, leaving Samhail alone. I went back up to my room and stayed there for most of the day. I didn't come down for lunch, and I only came down for dinner on the remote chance that Bressen might be there. He wasn't, and I returned to my room after eating very little.

I was annoyed at myself for letting Bressen's absence affect me this much, but I couldn't help it. It was like being together had opened a door that I was powerless to shut again. I'd had two other lovers, but I'd never felt this kind of pull toward either of them. Yes, I craved Bressen's body, but I craved the feeling of wholeness I felt when I was near him more. Now that we'd crossed that line into being lovers, I felt like a puzzle with one piece missing when I wasn't with him.

Around ten that night I began to regret not eating more today. I was already dressed for bed in a silky nightgown, but I put on my robe and slippers and crept out of my room and down to the kitchen.

The only guards on duty at night in the Citadel were on the outer walls, so I didn't encounter anyone on my way down. I entered the dining room and headed straight for the door where the servants usually came out. I pushed on it lightly, and it swung open.

I opened my palm and let a flame flicker to life in my hand. I looked around the kitchen and saw a basket of apples on the counter in one corner. I wiped off one of the apples and took a bite. It was sweet and juicy, and my stomach growled its approval.

I was going to leave with my apple, but I didn't want to go back to my empty room, and the kitchen was peaceful in an odd sort of way. Once the sun came up, it would be a cyclone of activity from dawn to well after dark, but for now I enjoyed the calm.

I found another door at the back of the kitchen, but it was locked. I remembered seeing a set of keys on a counter near the entrance and went back to get them. One of the staff had likely left them there by accident. I threw away my apple core and brought the keys over to the door at the back of the kitchen. The third key I tried worked, and the mystery door swung open.

It opened to a set of stairs, and I started down, making sure to take the keys with me.

I pulled my robe tighter around me as the temperature dropped. The stairs were narrow and curved around in a circle. I came to another door at the bottom, but this one was unlocked. I pushed the door open and shined my flame inside, then smiled as I saw where I was.

The wine cellar.

I lit a couple of torches and surveyed the barrels that lined one wall and the racks of bottles that covered two others. I inhaled the familiar cool, damp air that smelled of old wine, and a pang of homesickness hit me.

I wandered around the room looking at the various bottles and barrels to see what their labels said. The Citadel had an impressive collection of wine from all over Thasia and even some from outside the country, including bottles from Rowe.

I remembered some of my wine should be down here and expanded my search. I found several crates labeled "Fernweh" off to one side and pulled the lid off one. Sure enough, the crate contained bottles from our vineyard tucked safely in between layers of straw. I pulled out a bottle and looked around for something to remove the cork. I needed a drink.

I found a corkscrew on a table and opened the bottle. I smelled near the mouth of it and was pleased to catch aromas of dark berries and licorice. I looked around again for a glass but didn't see one, so I put my mouth to the bottle and tipped it back to take a long swig. I coughed a little as the alcohol hit the back of my throat but followed it quickly with another deep drink. This wasn't the way wine was meant to be drunk, but I didn't care right now. I just needed to numb my mind a little.

I took the lid off another crate and found a bill of sale on top of the straw. I took another drink of wine but almost choked on it when I saw the numbers on the paper. The Citadel had paid almost four times the amount for each bottle than we normally sold them for.

The name at the top was a merchant we sold about half of our stock to every year. I knew he marked the wine up to make a profit when he resold it, but I'd never dreamed he marked it up this much or that people were even willing to pay so much for our wine. I made a mental note to tell Jaylan we should start charging more for our stock.

I took several more swigs of wine and put the lids back on the crates. I was getting lightheaded already. I'd lost some tolerance for drinking since I'd been here, and with my empty stomach, the wine was hitting me fast. This is what I wanted, though. If I got drunk, maybe I'd forget about Bressen long enough to fall asleep.

"Are you going to share, or should I get my own bottle?" a voice drawled from the door.

I almost dropped the bottle in my surprise but managed to hold onto it. I swung around and saw Bressen leaning against the doorframe with his arms crossed. His hair was tousled in a way that I didn't usually see it, and I was completely disarmed by this one instance of…imperfection? No, even with his hair slightly out of place, Bressen still seemed perfect.

"What are you doing down here?" I asked.

I shouldn't have been surprised. The man had an uncanny knack for sneaking up on me when I least expected it.

"I might ask you the same thing," he said. He uncrossed his arms and pushed off the doorframe to walk toward me. His lips held the slightest curve of a smile.

"Samhail said you went back to Hiraeth," I noted.

"I did. I just got back a little while ago."

I frowned at him. How was that possible? It took Samhail and I three days to ride here by horse from Fernweh, and I knew Revenmyer was on the outskirts of Hiraeth. Bressen could have flown, but that seemed like a long flight, especially one to make twice in one day.

By the time my wine-soaked brain finished considering the logistics of Bressen's trip, he was standing in front of me, and my body reacted instantly to his nearness, spreading warmth through me that had nothing to do with the wine.

He was entirely too close for me to be able to think. Instead, my eyes just roved over his face, settling on his sensuous lips that I ached to kiss.

Bressen pulled the bottle from my hand and took a long drink.

"Very nice," he said running his tongue over his lips.

Unconsciously, my mouth parted, and I leaned toward him. I'd wanted to jump into his arms and wrap my legs around him all day, but now that he was here, I suddenly felt shy.

"Samhail said you had business at Revenmyer," I said, trying to fight the giddiness seeping through me.

Bressen frowned. "Samhail has been awfully forthcoming with my whereabouts. You didn't mention to anyone else that I left the Citadel today, did you?"

"No. I didn't see anyone besides Samhail."

"Good. I'd appreciate it if you didn't tell anyone I left."

"No, of course not."

He tipped the bottle back again for another drink.

Before I could react, Bressen's arm wrapped around my waist, and he pulled me hard against him. His lips came down hungrily on mine, and the wine he'd just sipped ran into my mouth. I drank it down and

268

grabbed for his arms to steady myself. He ran his tongue inside my mouth as if to taste the wine he'd just offered me.

Every part of me was suddenly alive. Bressen's body pressed up against mine was somehow both intoxicating and sobering.

"I promised myself when I got back here that I'd go straight to sleep and not seek you out," he breathed against my ear before trailing kisses down my neck, "but then I got this urge to go looking for wine in the middle of the night, and here you are."

"How odd," I murmured. I barely knew what I was saying as his tongue traced lazy circles on my collarbone. "Maybe…maybe we should go back up to my room, and you can tell me all about this strange urge."

Bressen chuckled. "That's not going to happen."

My heart dropped at the refusal, but his lips came back up to claim mine again even more urgently than before, and I frowned in confusion.

"You don't understand," Bressen whispered. "I plan to have you right here, right now."

White-hot desire shot through my veins at his words, and I clung to his arms.

"This isn't appropriate attire for a wine cellar," Bressen said, running his finger along the strap of my nightgown. He brushed lower to graze my breast, and my nipples peaked at his touch.

Bressen pulled my robe off my shoulders, and I squeaked in protest.

"What are you doing? It's cold down here," I said as I wrapped my arms around myself.

"You'll be warm enough in a minute," he said.

Bressen laid my robe on a nearby wine rack then pulled my nightgown over my head. I made another noise of protest as the cold air of the cellar caused gooseflesh to rise on my naked skin, but Bressen was already unfastening his jacket. He took the jacket off and pulled it around me, helping me to put my arms into the holes. The jacket was warm from his body, and his familiar scent of hot cinnamon and musk made my head swim even more.

"Better?" he asked, and I nodded.

He scooped me up in his arms and brought me over to lay me on top of a wine barrel. My slippers fell off my feet as my legs dangled from the barrel, and my spine curved over the arch of it, splaying me out before him. His jacket fell away from my chest to bare my breasts, and I didn't have time to protest before his mouth came down on one to suck at it. I cried out as the wet warmth of his tongue teased my nipple.

"Do you want some more wine?" Bressen asked.

I nodded, and he leaned over to hold the bottle carefully to my lips while I drank.

"My turn," he said, pulling the bottle away from me.

Instead of bringing it to his own lips, though, Bressen tipped it over my chest. I gasped as a trickle of the cold liquid ran over one breast and down my side, but Bressen's lips and tongue were there a second later to catch the drops that ran off my skin. I writhed on top of the barrel as his mouth roved over me hungrily, and I felt the roughness of his tongue run up the side of my body as he caught a droplet of wine that threatened to drip onto his jacket. His mouth was hot, but everywhere he licked left a wet trail that intensified the cold air in the cellar.

Bressen raised the bottle again and poured a trickle of wine down my stomach, where it pooled in my navel. His mouth was there a second later to drink the wine and then trail his tongue up over the path of the drip.

I was panting now. The alternating sensations of hot and cold were making my skin especially sensitive so that every brush of Bressen's fingers or inadvertent graze of his shirt pushed me closer to the edge of what I could endure.

"Bressen," I breathed.

"One more drink," he whispered huskily.

Bressen knelt down at the end of the wine barrel and pulled my hips toward him. He lifted my legs and hooked them over his shoulders then reached up over me with the wine bottle.

Nemesis take me, he wouldn't...

He did.

Bressen poured the wine at the apex of my legs so that it ran down between them and over my sex. I cried out again as his mouth and tongue delved in to lick and suck at the wine and at me. My legs curled up toward my body as I lay sprawled across the barrel, the arc of its shape laying me open for Bressen and his sweet torture.

I'd taken my two previous lovers into my own mouth before, but neither had ever bothered to reciprocate, and I nearly came undone at the sensations Bressen's tongue coaxed to life between my thighs. He'd already given me more pleasure in two days than Eddin and the merchant had given me together in months.

Bressen put the bottle of wine on the floor, and his hands held my hips in place so that I was a prisoner to his tongue's attentions. I tried to grab onto something as his tongue licked straight up my center and then flicked the knot of nerves at my core. My hands clawed for purchase, but they only scraped across the top of the barrel as I came closer and closer to falling over that chasm that awaited me.

I screamed as I went over the edge, but Bressen only pressed his mouth to me harder, pushing me over one wave, then another, then another until I was weak and trembling. My body finally went limp as my limbs hung uselessly over the barrel.

Bressen stopped and gently moved my legs off his shoulders. He stood up and took my hands to help me sit up on the barrel. I was breathing heavily, but I steadied myself as I tugged at his shirt. He didn't move but just watched as I undid each button with fumbling fingers. I freed the last button and reached up to push the shirt over his shoulders. It slipped down his arms but caught on his wrists. He moved to pull it off, but I put my hands on his arms to stop him.

"Wait. Let me," I said. I slid off the barrel but had to take a moment before my legs remembered how to stand after Bressen had turned them to jelly.

When I had my feet back under me, I walked around him, trailing a finger across his shoulder. I ran my hands slowly over his arms as I kissed a trail down his back, alternately running my tongue over him as I went. He exhaled deeply, and I imagined that he was feeling the same small chills I'd felt where the skin was wet.

My hands were at his wrists now, and I pulled them behind him quickly. I grabbed the tails of his shirt and wrapped them over and around his hands before tying the ends in a knot. The hastily tied ball of cloth wouldn't hold him for long if he wanted to free himself, but I was counting on a couple minutes of cooperation from him.

"What are you doing?" he asked, surprised and intrigued.

"Payback."

I came back around to face him, and he grinned at me. I lowered myself to my knees and reached for the fastenings of his pants. His eyes flared, but he didn't move. I pulled his pants down his legs, and he helpfully kicked off his boots and stepped out of the pants. He was already erect, and I bit my lip at the sight of him. Gods he was beautiful. So hard, so full of promise.

I grabbed the bottle of wine he'd left on the floor and took a drink. I looked up to see him watching me intently. His breathing had gone shallow, and he swallowed. I smiled up at him sweetly and poured wine slowly over his cock. He gasped and jerked back as the cool liquid dripped over him, but I grabbed his hips and pulled him toward me.

"Cyra!" he growled as I slid my mouth over him as far as I could. The muscles of his legs tightened as I pulled my lips back over him slowly, then licked up and down his length. He groaned as I swirled my tongue over his head and pressed my mouth onto him again.

"Nemesis fucking take me," Bressen gritted out between his teeth. "How can your mouth feel that fucking good?"

I continued to take him in and out, sucking at him and closing my lips tightly around his cock as he thrust his hips gently, pushing himself deeper into my throat. His groan of pleasure set my own body on fire again, and I gazed up at him as my mouth slipped over his shaft.

The look in his eyes was almost feral, and he let out another growl as I pressed him into my throat as far as I could go. The fabric of his shirt ripped as he pulled his hands free, and I slid my mouth slowly back from him, letting my lips feel every bump and ridge of the soft skin over his steely length. Bressen pulled the sleeves from his wrists and bent down to grab me and lift me by the elbows.

"That's enough," he rasped as he seized me around the waist and lifted me quickly back onto the edge of the wine barrel. I gasped as he sheathed himself into me as far as he could go, and I wrapped myself around him, trying to take him into me impossibly further.

"Keep your legs wrapped around me," he ordered.

I had no intention of disobeying, and he lifted me effortlessly off the wine barrel to bring me over and press me up against one of the walls. His hands were cupped under me, holding me in place as he began to thrust, his jacket soft and warm around me as it protected me from the roughness of the stone. The wall was hard, but I liked the feel of its immovable presence at my back while Bressen drove into me with increasing fervor.

I moaned as I felt that sensation of quickening between my thighs, and I wrapped my legs and arms tighter around Bressen. I relished the feel of him inside me as my body glided up and down his cock, so slick from my wetness.

"I can't hold out," Bressen breathed against my neck as he pushed into me, each drive eliciting a grunt from me as my back met the hard, unyielding stone. I liked the pressure of being trapped between the wall and Bressen's body, the latter so hard in its own ways, and I only wrapped myself around him tighter until finally the pressure coiling inside me snapped.

I screamed my release as liquid heat burst through my veins, and Bressen followed a second later as my body pulsed around him. He roared into the silence of the cellar as he came inside me. He collapsed against me, so I was pinned between him and the wall, but I didn't care. I couldn't have stood now if my life depended on it.

I tried to keep my legs wrapped around him, but they'd gone limp again and slipped down his hips. We panted against each other as the wall held us up before he finally lifted me off him and set me gently on the floor.

"Despite my best efforts not to," Bressen said between breaths, "I've been thinking about doing that to you all day."

"Even the part with the wine?" I asked, trying to bring my own breathing under control.

He chuckled softly against my ear. "The wine was an unexpected but welcome addition."

Bressen pulled away from me, and I felt the heaviness of my body as my legs were once again obliged to support it. I stood leaning against the wall as Bressen went around the room to retrieve our things. He folded his pants and my nightclothes into a pile and then balled up the torn remnants of his shirt on top of them. He brought the pile over to lay in my arms.

"Hold these, please, and put your slippers back on."

I arched a brow at him, but I found my slippers and pushed my feet into them. Bressen slipped his own boots on and then bent to grab the half-empty bottle of wine from the floor.

"This too," he said adding the bottle to the bundle he'd been piling into my arms.

I was about to ask him what in the three hells he was doing when he scooped me up. I had to adjust the bottle of wine to keep it from spilling down my chest.

"*Now* we can go to your room," Bressen said.

"We're naked. Or at least you are." I still had Bressen's jacket wrapped around me.

"That's what obfuscation glamours are for," Bressen said, and I felt the fog of the glamour envelop us.

"They're going to know someone was down here," I said.

274

"I'll take the blame. The good thing about being me is that people are usually too afraid to scold me about anything. You're the exception, of course."

"Someone needs to scold you occasionally, or your arrogance would go unchecked."

He started up the stairs. "Speaking of scolding, you shouldn't be out of bed so late."

"Do I need to go to *sleep* or just back to *bed*?" I asked him teasingly.

"Oh, you're not going to get much sleep tonight," he answered.

I laughed and laid my head on his chest before closing my eyes. Two minutes of sleep as he carried me back to my room and his body pressed against mine were all I needed anyway.

Chapter 25

Bressen was right that I didn't get much sleep. He'd made love to me again the moment we'd gotten back to my room and then a few hours later when I'd accidentally rolled into him in bed. He'd woken instantly, flipped me on my stomach, pressed between my thighs, and pumped into me until I'd screamed into my pillow. Just before dawn, as he tried to slip out to his own room, I'd wrapped myself around him once more and pulled him back into bed. He'd been more than happy to oblige me, and I marveled at how quickly we were both ready for each other by the fourth time that night.

I had no regrets until Raina woke me the next morning. I buried my head under my pillows to shut out the bright morning light and Raina's even brighter disposition. The usual morning tea she gave me didn't help a bit, and I walked down to breakfast dead on my feet.

Bressen, Samhail, Ursan, and Glenora were there, and I was annoyed to see Bressen didn't look nearly as bad as I felt. He seemed fully awake, and there were no signs of dark circles under his eyes as there were under mine.

I must've looked worse than I thought because Glenora put her teacup down when she saw me. "Are you alright, my dear? You don't look well."

I smiled weakly at her and forced myself not to look at Bressen. "I'm fine. I just didn't get much sleep last night."

I remembered to make sure my words held enough truth so that Glenora didn't question their veracity.

I fixed myself a plate and sat down across from Samhail as usual. When I looked up, he was watching me intently.

"Maybe some fresh air might help you, Cyra," Ursan suggested. "I can take you riding today if you want. The stable hands say you visit your horse frequently."

Several days ago when I'd been chafing under my confinement, the offer would've been a balm to my soul. Unbeknownst to Ursan, of course, I'd already managed to escape the Citadel twice since then, but I wouldn't turn down another opportunity. I was about to answer Ursan when Bressen's voice sounded in my head.

Don't go. I don't trust him.

I was startled to hear his voice so clearly in my mind, as if he'd spoken aloud. I knew he'd read my mind before, but this was the first time I'd heard his voice in my head, and it was a bit unsettling. I assumed he could read my thoughts if I was inclined to answer him, but I wasn't.

"Some fresh air might help, my lord," I said. "I've been wanting to ride my horse again."

I forced myself not to look at Bressen, but I could tell even out of the corner of my eye that he was frowning.

"Shall we leave after breakfast?" Ursan suggested.

"She has training with me after breakfast," Samhail said.

My eyes flew to Samhail. He rarely spoke at the dining table when people other than Bressen and I were present if he wasn't being addressed directly.

Ursan seemed a bit shocked as well but said, "Very well. After lunch then?"

"Yes, my lord. That sounds wonderful." I turned to Glenora. "My lady, will you be joining us?"

Glenora opened her mouth to answer, but Ursan cut in before she could say anything.

"I think just you and I this time, Cyra." He turned to Glenora. "You don't mind, do you, my dear?"

Glenora's smile was tight and didn't reach her eyes. "Of course not, Ursan darling. I need to make preparations for the Harmilan. I should probably take my leave now anyway."

Glenora stood and excused herself.

"I should be going too," Ursan said. "I'll see you at the stables after lunch, Cyra."

I watched Ursan and Glenora leave. I was afraid to look at Bressen, but Samhail moved first. He stood silently and brought his plate to the bin for dishes before going to the sideboard again. I speared a piece of egg and ate it as I waited for either Bressen or Samhail to say something to me.

A cup clunked down on the table next to me, and the sound seemed to resonate in the stillness of the room. Samhail's large hand rested on the cup of dark brown liquid as he leaned over me. Coffee, I realized. I'd never had coffee before because the beans were hard to come by in Fernweh, and it was more expensive than tea.

"Try this," Samhail said to me. "I have a feeling you're going to need something stronger than tea to get you through training today."

He didn't wait for me to respond but strode from the room, leaving me and Bressen alone. I picked up the coffee to take a sip but instantly choked on the strong, bitter liquid.

"Try it with cream and sugar," Bressen said. "It's more palatable that way."

I went over to the side table to add the cream and sugar as he suggested, testing the flavor now and then. When I sat down again, I felt Bressen watching me, and – realizing I couldn't avoid him forever – I met his eyes.

I expected to see anger, but only amusement shined in them.

"I suppose your brothers are used to this stubborn streak you have," he said. "I'm not sure why it continues to surprise me."

It was on the tip of my tongue to make a comment about domineering lords expecting people to jump when they issued orders, but I decided it was wiser to keep it to myself. Not that it mattered. Bressen apparently read the thought and chuckled.

"Just promise you'll keep your guard up," he said. "Ursan didn't invite you to go riding out of the goodness of his heart. He's up to something."

"Do you know what?"

"Not unless I break into his mind, and I can't risk doing so without overstepping boundaries and creating a lot of problems."

I nodded and took another sip of coffee.

"If you get into trouble," Bressen said, "just call for my help and I'll find you."

"How do I do that? I don't have mind powers."

"I seem to be able to sense when you're in danger. I'll know if you need me."

My one-path mind seized on the idea of needing him, and I pressed my thighs together under the table. The movement didn't go unnoticed by Bressen, and he inhaled deeply.

"Cyra," he breathed.

"Yes, my lord?" I asked innocently, but my voice caught.

Bressen stood abruptly. "I need to go, or I'm going to fuck you on top of this table, and that's just inviting trouble."

I leaned back in my chair and bit my lip as my breasts tightened at his words. Bressen growled and turned on his heel to stride out of the dining room.

I sipped my coffee and finished breakfast before heading out to the training yard to meet Samhail. He obviously knew something was going on, either because he'd guessed or because Bressen had told him, and I felt a pang of guilt for choosing Bressen over him.

Choose was the wrong word. My gravitation toward Bressen was less of a conscious choice and more like an inevitability I'd been powerless to avoid. It was as though our first meeting set a boulder rolling down a hill, and we'd only gathered speed since then, crushing every obstacle in our path. I regretted that Samhail was one of those obstacles, but I couldn't roll the stone back up the hill at this point if I wanted to.

By lunchtime I'd decided that coffee must have powerful magical properties because I'd never been as invigorated in my life, especially given how I'd felt earlier. I was practically vibrating with energy by the end of my training with Samhail. Indeed, he'd grumbled about only letting me have half a cup in the future after I'd hit the straw pad so unexpectedly hard that it had flown out of his hands.

I resisted the urge to have another cup at lunch and instead went back to tea. Ursan was at lunch as well, so we walked to the stables together when we were done. He'd given the stable hands advanced notice because my mare and three other horses were already saddled and ready to go when we arrived. Two of Ursan's guards mounted up with us, and minutes later we'd passed through the front gates of the Citadel and were navigating our way through the streets of Callanus toward the edge of the city.

It felt strange to be leaving, especially after the hostile response I'd gotten the last time I'd wandered too close to the gates. It was the first time I'd passed through them, I realized, given that Samhail and I had flown in when we first arrived. I knew I'd be returning again, but it nevertheless felt as though I was escaping, if only for a little while.

I wondered what it would feel like to leave Callanus for good, but I was surprised to find the thought made me sad rather than pleased. I'd miss Bressen, Samhail, and Raina if I left. I'd become close to all of them since I'd been here, and Bressen had become so much more very quickly.

Back in Fernweh, I'd spent most of my time on the vineyard with Jaylan and Brix. There were people in town I was friendly with, like Rodrick, but there wasn't anyone I was as close to as I was now with Samhail, Raina, and Bressen. Growing up, the isolation had been necessary to keep anyone from learning of my powers, but I didn't need to hide who I was here.

Ursan set a brisk pace to start when we reached the city limits but then slowed once we'd put some distance between us and Callanus. He was, of course, an excellent rider, and I wondered if he actually used the reins or if he was just telling the horse what to do. Ursan rode next to me while his two guards trailed a little ways behind, and the lord chattered on about an array of topics, from his life in Gendris, to the repercussions of a recent millworker strike in Callanus, to what kind of grass the rabbit that just hopped past preferred to eat. I let him talk, offering brief interjections every now and again to let him know I was listening.

"Do you keep animals on the vineyard?" Ursan asked, and I jerked to attention when I realized he'd asked me a question.

"Two horses, my lord. They pull our wagon."

"That's all?" He sounded disappointed.

"In all honesty, we spend more of our time chasing animals away."

"Like the bear," Ursan said, and I stiffened. There wasn't any judgement in his tone, but I was treading on dangerous ground.

"Yes, my lord." I paused a moment before trying to explain. "I was just trying-"

Ursan put up a hand to cut me off.

"I don't blame you for what happened to the bear," he said, but there was sadness in his voice. "You did what you had to do to protect your harvest and your own life."

I nodded but didn't say anything else to him.

"You should consider getting more animals for the vineyard, though," Ursan said, shaking off his brief melancholy. "A vineyard near Gendris keeps dogs to help chase off pests."

It was a good idea, and I wondered how my morning might have gone differently a few weeks ago if I'd had a dog with me when I confronted the bear.

"I also know of a vineyard in Rowe that uses ducks to keep the bugs and snails off the vines," Ursan added.

My brows went up in surprise. "That's a unique idea."

Rowe now had a queen since King Sandrian had been imprisoned after the war, but there were still some tensions between the two countries, even twenty-five years later. I remembered seeing Rown wine in the Citadel's cellar, though, and I wondered if that was the vineyard Ursan spoke of.

"Animals can be very helpful," Ursan said.

I smiled as I imagined Jaylan and Brix trying to herd a flock of

281

ducks among our vines. I could probably talk Jaylan into a dog, but definitely not the ducks. We'd had a cat living in our barn for a few years until it died, and the animal had been helpful in keeping the mice and other pests away.

"My lord!"

The shout came from one of Ursan's guards, and we both reined up. We'd been riding along a wooded area, and riders were emerging from the trees around us. There were nine in all, and each one held a crossbow aimed at us.

Not again. I couldn't be this unlucky.

"Throw down your weapons or you all die," one of the riders said. He pointed his crossbow at the guards, and they instantly unsheathed their swords and threw them on the ground.

"Off the horses!" another of the riders yelled.

"Do you know who I am?" Ursan asked indignantly.

"You're a dead man if you don't get off the horse," the rider said, turning his crossbow on Ursan.

Ursan threw his hands in the air. "Fine, fine," he said and slid off his horse.

"Everyone else too," one of the other riders chimed in.

The two guards and I dismounted, but I held onto Ghost's reins. I'd send her running to the Citadel before I let these men have her.

"Now your coin," one of the riders said.

Ursan reached for a pouch at his belt, and I frowned at the ease with which both he and his guards had given in to the demands of these riders. We were outnumbered, of course, but not by that much, and Ursan had powers. The only time I'd seen him use his powers was to control the tigers at the Priory, but he must be able to do something to help us.

Now that I looked at the riders, something seemed off about them. All nine were mounted, and their horses looked well-fed and well-groomed. The last time I'd encountered highwaymen with Samhail, the band of almost twenty men had only had four harried-looking horses

282

between them and one crossbow. These men each had their own crossbow and a sword at their hip, and while they were all dressed like commoners, their clothes lacked the wear and fading of the other highwaymen I'd seen.

I was instantly suspicious. Ursan was likely trying to test me again to see if I would use my powers to save us. It was a ridiculous plan. Ursan himself was more powerful than me. He could, for instance, shift into something that had lots of claws and teeth, or he could perhaps summon something from the woods that did.

"My lord," I said to Ursan, and he looked at me questioningly. There was no fear in his eyes, nor was there any anger that these men had dared to stop a lord of the Triumvirate and demand his money and his horse. "You can control their horses, can't you?" I said to him softly. "Make their horses rear up or run away."

Ursan's eyes widened the slightest bit. "I..."

"Can't you shift into something that will get us out of this?"

"I..." Ursan said again, struggling to explain why he hadn't acted.

"Or you can just admit that you staged this encounter to test me again," I said baldly.

Ursan's chin went up a notch, and he finally let out the lordly disdain I'd expected to see from him long before now.

"How dare you accuse me of such a thing, girl?" Ursan thundered in real indignation.

I didn't care. I was certain he'd planned this. I turned to Ursan's guards and walked toward the nearest one to pick up his sword and then face the riders again.

"What do you think you're doing, woman?" the lead rider asked, but I could see the uncertainty in his eyes now.

"Fighting you," I said as I held the sword up in front of me.

The riders all chuckled and turned their crossbows my way, and my stomach dropped as it occurred to me that maybe Ursan hadn't brought me out here to test me but to kill me. It would've been convenient to say we'd been attacked by highwaymen and that I'd been slain. I took a step back, gripped by the sudden fear that I'd horribly misread my situation.

I looked at Ursan, but his face was indecipherable.

"Cyra, put the sword down," Ursan said. "You're going to get yourself hurt."

"Listen to the old man," the lead rider said, but I just gripped the sword tighter and took up a fighting stance.

I wondered if I should call Bressen, but if he came and the situation turned out to be nothing, there'd be questions about how he knew where to find us. There was still a slim chance my initial judgement was right and that Ursan was simply trying to get me to use my powers again. Regardless, my powers were useless against nine men with crossbows, so I waited with the sword to see what would happen next.

"Disarm her," Ursan ordered his guards, impatient with my refusal to obey.

The two guards advanced on me as the second one picked up the sword he'd thrown onto the ground. I swiveled to keep both the riders and the guards in view as I held up the sword in front of me. Samhail had only just started teaching me to use a blade, and how to hold it was the first lesson. Unfortunately, we hadn't gotten much farther than that, so it would become apparent quickly that I didn't know what I was doing if I was forced to fight.

"Stay where you are!" the lead rider yelled to the guards, and they halted before looking at Ursan.

The lead rider was also looking back and forth between the guards and Ursan, ostensibly caught between playing the part Ursan had assigned him and letting Ursan give the orders.

The thwack of a crossbow broke our silent standoff, and we all looked around to see who'd fired it. One of the riders pitched forward on his horse and tumbled off the side of the animal to fall at its feet. The animal whinnied in alarm and shied away from the body that now lay with a crossbow bolt in its back.

"Who-" Ursan began to ask, but his question was cut off as a collective cry came from the woods and dozens of men suddenly poured from the trees running toward us.

The men were all on foot, but there were twice as many as Samhail and I had encountered on our journey here. It crossed my mind that maybe Ursan had planned for a second wave of 'bandits' to sell the idea we were being attacked, but I dismissed it almost immediately. The situation was much more real this time, and I felt the urgency in the air. The shouts the men gave as they ran toward us with swords, daggers, axes, and wooden staffs sent chills through me.

Another thwack from a crossbow sent a second of the riders tumbling from his horse, and there was real fear in Ursan's brown eyes as he looked back at me.

No, this new group of marauders were definitely not part of Ursan's plan.

Chapter 26

The sword I held was pulled from my grasp as the guard next to me reclaimed it and ran toward the mass of men now charging toward us. The riders with crossbows had already turned their horses and were firing into the oncoming attackers, but they didn't have time to reload before the horde was upon them. The riders all drew their swords, and the clanging of metal on metal and the clacking of wooden staffs lifted above the shouting and battle cries.

"Cyra! Get on your horse and ride back to the Citadel!" Ursan yelled to me.

My gaze met his as his eyes turned from brown to gold, and his body began to grow and hunch over. His nose and mouth stretched into an animal snout, and coarse gray fur sprouted from all over his body as his clothes receded away. Large claws grew from the tips of his fingers which curled into padded paws, and his teeth extended into sharp fangs.

A giant gray wolf with a white patch on its chest now stood where Ursan once did. The wolf gave a howl that raised every hair on my body, and then it bounded toward the oncoming men. I was stunned at how quickly it had happened.

I stood frozen for a moment, caught between Ursan's order to flee and the realization that there were too many men for Ursan, his two guards, and the now-seven riders to handle. Samhail had told me to flee once in a similar situation, and my failure to do so put us both in danger, but Samhail wasn't here now to take care of these men. It occurred to me that he *could* be, though.

Help! We're being attacked! I let the thought ring out in my mind. I had no idea if the message would reach Bressen or not, or if he could sense the fear and panic now pounding in my chest, but I said the words in my head several times before running to my mare and heaving myself back into the saddle.

Stay to fight or flee? The question rattled in my brain again, but another look at the current situation had me wheeling Ghost around toward the Citadel. The newcomers were quickly overtaking Ursan's men, and I could no longer see Ursan himself in the melee. As much as I wanted to help, there was little I could do against such overwhelming odds.

My decision to flee was too late, though. Before I'd swung Ghost fully around, hands grabbed at my arms and at the reins, and I was pulled off the mare. I cried out as I crashed to the ground and found myself in the middle of a circle of boots. More hands grabbed me brutally under my arms and hauled me up. I struggled against them, but I was surrounded on all sides by several men as they pressed in around me. The smell of their sweat and sour breath almost made me gag, and I tried to lift my head to draw air from above me.

"Hold her hands!" one man yelled, and I cried out as my arms were jerked behind me.

"Are you sure this is her?" another man asked.

"It has to be," said the first.

I tried to pull my arms out of the grip that held them, but a coarse rope bit into my wrists, and I struggled harder, kicking and pushing against my attackers. I saw the blow coming only a second before one of the men's fists connected with my cheek.

Stars burst behind my eyes as pain radiated through my head. I stayed conscious, but my vision blurred for several seconds, and I fell to my knees on the ground. A kick to my stomach knocked the breath from me, and I curled forward to protect my body. The rope on my wrists slackened, and I pulled my arms back around in front of me to renew my thrashing as the men hauled me to my feet again.

"Hold her still, gods damn you!" one of the men yelled.

"No!" I yelled, and I felt a surge of power gather in my chest. A knot concentrated there, growing as my panic did, and before I knew what was happening, the power erupted. I screamed, and the men that held me were thrown back several feet as a wave of energy blossomed out from my body.

I looked around in shock at the men now laying on the ground several feet away from me and wondered if I'd somehow summoned a new kind of wind power. It didn't feel like wind, though. Whatever I'd done seemed closer to the forcefields Samhail used back in the Soundless Woods. I had no idea how I'd managed to imitate him, though, if that's what it was.

I didn't have time to contemplate it since the men on the ground were already beginning to stir. I looked around for Ghost, but she'd run off in the chaos. All of the horses had scattered except for two whose riders had somehow remained mounted.

A terrible shriek rent the air, and I turned to see the huge gray wolf lunge for one of the men and fasten its jaws on his neck. The man's scream was cut short as the wolf ripped his throat out and blood sprayed both the wolf and the men closest to him. Even more dark red blood covered Ursan's chest, and it dripped from his muzzle as he whirled to slash his claws at the attackers.

I heard another howl then, but it didn't come from Ursan. I looked toward the woods as a dozen more wolves emerged out of the trees to head toward the fight. The men at the edge of the fray screamed as the animals bore down on them, and within seconds the pack tore into them. I heard the pained yelp of one of the animals as the men fought back with swords and axes, and I looked around for a way to help.

The wolves were a welcome addition to our side, but there were still too many attackers. At least one of Ursan's guards lay on the ground covered in blood, and only three of the riders, whoever they might be, were still alive that I could see. I needed to stay and fight.

I tried to call my wind power, and a gale rose around me as dirt and debris swirled into the air. Everyone in the area shielded their faces, but the wind lacked the power to knock anyone off their feet. I let it fall and tried instead to summon my flames. Fire burst into my palms, but when I reached out to try and throw it at the nearest attacker, the fire only flared up before flickering back down.

Nemesis take me. One of these days I had to figure out how to wield my powers as weapons, as this seemed to be a growing need.

Frustrated, I looked around for a sword instead. I saw one next to a fallen body and ran for it. I bent to pick it up, but something crashed into me before I could get my hand on it. Breath whooshed from my lungs as I landed flat on my stomach with the man who'd tackled me on top of me. He grabbed my wrist and wrenched my arm behind my back, and I screamed in pain as I tried to free myself. I bucked under him, hoping I might be able to throw him off, but he was too heavy. I waited to feel that power I'd used before gather in my chest again, but only cold dread remained. The coarse rope was at my wrists again, and I thrashed as hard as I could against the man as he tried to bind me.

"Stop struggling or I'll knock you unconscious!" he yelled.

I heard a growl, and the man's strangled cry sounded in my ears before his weight was suddenly gone from on top of me. I inhaled deeply to fill my lungs before I rolled over to find the giant wolf snarling at the man, who cradled his torn arm against his chest. Ursan clamped his jaws onto the man's neck and shook him violently. I blinked as drops of blood hit my face, and the memory flashed in my mind of being similarly splattered when Samhail cut the highwayman's arms off. I looked back at the man Ursan held in his jaws, and I could tell by the flop of his head that he was already dead.

Something heavy thudded beside me, and I scrambled backward on the ground. When I looked up, though, Samhail was standing above me with his wings flared out behind him.

"Thank the Protector! It's about time!" I yelled at him.

"Get behind me!" Samhail ordered as he drew the two swords from his back. He stepped toward the wolf, but I threw one of my hands out to stop him.

"Samhail, no! It's Ursan!"

Samhail stopped, and his eyes locked with the wolf's. They both gave each other a curt nod before Ursan turned and bounded back into the fray.

Samhail reached down and pulled me to my feet as Bressen landed next to us. Bressen folded his wings in behind him and immediately came over to look me up and down.

"Are you alright?" he asked. His hand brushed the spot on my cheek where the man had hit me a few minutes before. There was likely the start of a bruise forming there, and I saw Bressen's face darken as he examined the mark.

"I'm fine. It's nothing," I told him.

Bressen pulled his hand back and noticed the blood smeared on it from when he'd brushed my cheek. He grabbed my arms and set me away from him so he could look me over again.

"Are you bleeding?" he asked urgently as his eyes darted around looking for wounds.

"It's not my blood. I'm not hurt."

Bressen's eyes locked with mine as if he was looking into my mind to be sure I wasn't lying, and I wondered if he could see in my memories what had happened. If so, whatever he saw eased his mind because he nodded and turned to look out over the fight, trying to make sense of what was going on.

"I assume the big wolf is Ursan?" he asked.

"Yes, a group of men came out of the woods and just attacked us while we were riding," I said.

There was a lot more to the story, but the details weren't important at the moment.

Several attackers came toward us with weapons drawn, and Samhail stepped forward to meet them. There was no need, though. The men suddenly slumped to the ground before they could reach us. In fact, everyone around us but Ursan and the wolves fell where they stood. At the far end of the field, the pack of wolves growled and continued to tear at the now-prone bodies, but Ursan stopped and let go of the man whose arm his jaws had locked onto.

Samhail sighed and re-sheathed his swords. "I really could have used the workout, you know," he said to Bressen. "Battles are no fun

290

when you're around."

"Sorry," Bressen said with an apologetic shrug. "Next time."

Ursan padded back toward us, and Bressen stepped forward to meet him. Just as quickly as Ursan had shifted into the wolf, he transformed back into a man and stood before Bressen.

Ursan was covered in blood. His mouth dripped with it, and his shirt was crimson in front. The effect was chilling as I remembered him tearing the first man's throat out and then shaking the other attacker to death.

Even after Ursan sent his tigers after me, I'd never considered the affable older lord all that threatening, but I had a new appreciation for both his power and the danger he posed. I also realized Ursan could have killed me at several points since we'd left the Citadel, but instead he'd saved me when one of the attackers tried to tie me up.

"How did you know?" was all Ursan said to Bressen.

"The lady sends out a strong distress signal when she's in trouble," Bressen said, and his tone was the one of cool disinterest he usually used around Ursan and Jerram. "What in the three hells happened here, Ursan?"

Ursan glanced at me, and I knew he was wondering if I would tell Bressen about our initial encounter with the nine riders. I just looked back at him impassively. I had no intention of contradicting anything he said right now, but I would fill Bressen in on everything eventually.

"We were attacked while riding," Ursan said. "They came out of the woods without warning, and I told Cyra to ride for the Citadel."

Samhail huffed a laugh next to me. "Cyra doesn't follow directions well," he mumbled, and I elbowed him in the ribs.

"I tried to go," I insisted, "but I was pulled off my horse."

The pack of wolves had wandered over to us and were now sitting patiently around Ursan's feet. Like their master, their muzzles and feet were stained crimson with blood. At least a few seemed to be missing from the original pack, but I couldn't bring myself to survey the field and find their bodies among the fallen.

"Who are they?" Bressen asked. "Highwaymen? There are dozens of them."

"I have no idea," Ursan said with a bit of irritation. "They didn't bother to introduce themselves before they attacked."

Something crashed in the woods, and we all turned to see a large shape emerge from the tree line. My eyes widened in horror as I took in the monster that lumbered toward the bodies strewn about the field, and I vowed silently that I was never going to leave the Citadel again if there were things like that roaming the countryside. Clearly riding with me was bad luck.

The beast was nearly ten feet tall and lanky, with long arms that almost brushed the ground. Each finger on its hands ended in a massive claw that was nearly a foot long, and its head was bulbous with black orb-like eyes, sharp fangs, and whisps of wiry hair. It was something I couldn't have dreamed up in my wildest nightmares, and the shriek it let out when it saw us set my teeth on edge.

"Protector save us," I breathed, taking a step back. "What in the three hells is that?"

"It's a swarax," Samhail said, drawing his blades again. "There's a few in these woods."

The wolves at Ursan's feet stood and bared their teeth, growling low in their throats at the monster. They seemed to be waiting for Ursan to give them his order to attack, but Samhail spoke first.

"I'll take care of it," he said. He cracked his neck and beat his huge wings to launch into the air straight toward the beast.

Ursan held up a calming hand, and the wolves all sat down again to watch as Samhail landed across the field in front of the swarax to engage it.

"Shouldn't we help him?" I asked anxiously, looking between the two lords.

"No need," Bressen said. "Samhail can handle this."

I looked across the field again and gasped as Samhail barely dodged a vicious swipe from the swarax's huge claws. He slashed out with a sword, and one of the claws went flying into the air. The swarax roared, a terrible high-pitched sound, and Samhail was thrown back by the force of its cry. He was on his feet again a second later and paid the creature back in kind with a blow from one of his own forcefields.

"The creature must have smelled all the blood and come to investigate," Ursan said.

I just stared at the two lords who were quietly watching Samhail fight across the field with their arms crossed. My stomach was in my throat as Samhail took on the swarax, which towered over him by several feet, but neither Ursan nor Bressen seemed alarmed in the slightest at the deadly brawl playing out nearby.

"How many of these men are yours?" Bressen asked, turning back to Ursan.

Ursan's eyes darted to me again, but I just crossed my own arms over my chest and waited for him to answer. That was a question I wanted to know the answer to as well.

"We brought two guards with us," Ursan said, and I raised a brow at him.

Well, it was the truth anyway. I imagined that, being married to Glenora, Ursan had a lot of practice twisting his words so he could say the bare minimum without lying.

Ursan glanced at me to see if I would accuse him of staging the initial attack with the other riders, but I didn't say anything. Not out loud anyway.

I think at least nine other men here were Ursan's, I said in my mind, hoping for once that Bressen was reading it. The slightest tick of his head toward me told me he'd gotten the message, and I quickly filled in the details of what happened.

"At least one of your guards is dead," I said to Ursan as I pointed to a man covered in blood.

Another screech echoed across the field, and my eyes flew back to where Samhail grappled with the swarax. Samhail was big, but the monster was bigger, and Samhail had lost his swords somehow.

"Let's see just how many are still alive," Bressen said, drawing my eyes back to him.

This time I was prepared as about half of the men on the ground lurched to their feet. The wolves beside Ursan raised their hackles and growled their displeasure, but Ursan quieted them with another wave of his hand.

"Some of these men are from Rowe," Bressen said in surprise.

"Rowe? How do you know that?" Ursan said.

Bressen approached one of the men and examined his shirt. He bent to pick up a knife that lay at the man's feet and turned it over in his hands before reaching inside the man's coat pocket to pull out a bag of coins and dump them into his hand.

"For one," Bressen said, holding up the bag he'd pulled off the man, "some of these coins are Rown sovereigns. There are also some subtle differences in their clothing and weapons I recognize from my time there."

Bressen held up the knife he'd taken off the ground and ran his finger along the back of it to trace the slight curve of the blade. "Look at the way this knife curves. It's a common style for Rown blades."

"But why would men from Rowe be hiding out in the woods here?" Ursan asked. "And why did they attack us?"

"I'm not sure why they're here," Bressen said, "but maybe they recognized you and decided to strike a blow at the Triumvirate."

I remembered then that the men seemed to be looking for me, or a woman they thought was me. I sent a message into Bressen's mind to relay what I'd heard them say, and his head snapped to me.

At the far end of the field, Samhail was on the ground with the swarax on top of him, and I cried out in alarm. Samhail grabbed the creature's hands and was trying to hold them back as the monster attempted to swipe its huge claws at him.

"Cyra?" Ursan asked, seemingly confused at my cry.

I looked at him incredulously. "Samhail is in trouble! We have to help him!"

The two men looked to where Samhail was on the ground fighting the swarax.

"He's just toying with it," Bressen said. "He's fine. He'll be angry if we interfere."

My mouth fell open, but he just smiled and winked at me.

Across the field, the swarax screamed, and I looked over to see Samhail pull one of his swords from its side.

"See?" Bressen said. "All under control."

I continued to stare at Bressen as he turned back toward Ursan. This day had officially replaced all the ones before it as the most ludicrous experience of my life.

"I'll get these men back to the Citadel," Bressen said. "I can read their minds later."

The men all stepped forward as one and began to march back in the direction of Callanus, merging into a single-file line as they went. I watched them file past and couldn't help the shudder that ran up my spine. The sight of the men marching away covered in blood was disturbing enough, but it reminded me of what occurred on the wharf, and I wondered if the same fate now awaited these men.

"Is that your guard?" Bressen asked Ursan. He pointed to a man dressed in a Citadel uniform, and Ursan nodded.

The man stepped out of the line and awoke from whatever trance he'd been under. The guard looked around in confusion, but understanding dawned on him when his eyes found the three of us. He came over and stood at attention as he waited for Ursan to give him an order.

"I trust you can round up the horses and ride back to the Citadel?" Bressen asked Ursan.

Ursan pursed his lips into a thin line, but he nodded again. "I'll take care of it."

The wolves at Ursan's feet stood and padded back toward the woods. Horses whinnied in the distance, and I saw at least two of them already heading back this way. I didn't see Ghost, though, and I hoped she was unhurt.

"Samhail, can you bring Cyra back to the Citadel?" Bressen asked.

My head snapped around to see Samhail stepping over bodies as he crossed the field toward us. His swords were re-sheathed in their scabbards, and he was covered in a viscous, purplish substance I assumed was the blood of the swarax. It matted his hair, dripped down his face, and soaked into his clothing, but he didn't seem injured.

Samhail came up to stand before us and nodded.

"Enough of a workout for you?" Bressen asked him with a smirk.

"For now," he said before turning to me. "Are you ready to go?"

I eyed his blood-soaked body. "You can't be serious."

Samhail looked down at himself and shrugged. "It washes off. Some apothecaries even swear swarax blood is good for the skin." He grinned at me, and I glared back at him.

I looked from Ursan to Bressen, but neither offered an alternative.

"Can't I ride back when we find the horses?" I asked.

Bressen shook his head. "If these men are from Rowe, we need to get you back to the Citadel as soon as possible."

"Rowe?" Samhail said, suddenly grave.

"Yes," was all Bressen said, but he and Samhail exchanged a meaningful look.

"Let's go, Cyra," Samhail said, his attention whipping back to me. It was just short of an order, and I wondered if Bressen had said something else into his mind.

I looked at Bressen pleadingly. *You can fly me,* I said in my mind, hoping he was listening.

It's better if Samhail takes you.

I closed my eyes and sighed. Samhail's arms were crossed over his chest, and he was smirking. I had the urge to hit him, and the look I gave him vowed revenge. "Fine," I said.

Samhail scooped me up, and I wrapped an arm around his neck. I groaned as the swarax blood squished against me, seeping into my clothes, and I shot Bressen one more look that promised retribution before Samhail beat his leathery wings and launched us into the sky.

We were well up in the air where we wouldn't be overheard before he spoke. "I hear Bressen is a better flyer than me." There was only amusement in his tone, but I winced anyway.

"He wasn't supposed to tell you that."

"Angelus like Bressen were made for smoother gliding, but others of us were made for more dynamic maneuvers," he said casually.

I shrieked as Samhail plunged toward the ground and then swung back up to loop around in the air. I tucked my head into the crook of his neck and fisted my hand in his shirt as I held onto him tighter. I groaned again as the sticky purple blood squelched against my temple.

"It's not going to end well if you do that again," I told him.

Samhail chuckled, but something twisted in my stomach as I recalled the first time I'd flown with him and what we'd been doing just before that.

"I'm sorry," I said quietly.

"For what?"

"For...insulting your flying." I wanted to apologize to him for choosing Bressen, but I didn't know how to say it. I wasn't even sure he cared, but I was certain there'd been more to his offer to walk me back to my room from the library the other day. "I'm sorry for...putting you up against Bressen." It was the closest I could get.

To my surprise, Samhail's body tensed against mine.

"It's fine," he said so quietly I almost didn't hear him, and his hand tightened around my back.

I looked up at him, but he stared resolutely forward, refusing to meet my eyes. I sighed and wrapped my arms tighter around his neck, no longer caring that I was as covered in swarax blood as he was. His muscles tensed again, but I didn't loosen my grip.

I was suddenly finding it very hard to let go of him.

Chapter 27

Bressen came to my room later that night, and I asked him as he held me tucked against him in bed after sex if he'd learned anything about the men who attacked us on our ride. He confirmed they were from Rowe but assured me it was nothing to worry about and that I must have misunderstood their comments about a woman they were looking for.

I wasn't sure I believed him that I'd misunderstood the marauders about the woman, but I couldn't imagine why they might have been looking for me. Then he'd reached around to slip his hand between my legs again, and any further questions I might have asked him scattered in my mind like birds taking flight.

Bressen had also confronted Ursan about the first nine riders, and Ursan admitted he'd tried to get me to use my powers again. Unfortunately, there wasn't much Bressen could do besides warn Ursan to stop testing me unless all three lords agreed to it. Six of the nine men had died in the attack, so Ursan was contrite enough to promise he'd stop.

Bressen was still looking for whoever had been shooting arrows at us on our way back from the vineyard as well. He redoubled his efforts to find the archer today when he learned that a man in the city had almost been killed when one of the arrows that missed us came down and hit him in the shoulder. By some miracle, the other arrows seemed to have missed anyone else and were now likely lodged in the roofs of houses or lying on the street somewhere. The recklessness of firing the arrows into the air and the near tragedy of the one man made Bressen determined to figure out who'd been firing at us. The guards on the wall all used standard white fletching for their arrows, not orange, though, so the archer remained a mystery.

I was almost afraid of Bressen when he'd arrived tonight and told me what he'd learned about the man's injury. I'd felt the fury roiling inside him and saw the red flash in his eyes that promised his wrath.

He'd calmed a little when I climbed into his lap and wrapped my arms around him, but our sex was rougher than we'd ever had. Knowing he needed an outlet – both for his anger at the man's injury and his frustration with Ursan – I'd teased him into a near frenzy, then urged him to drive into me harder and faster until I was sure I'd have bruises. It made me feel useful to absorb his anger this way, especially since there was little else I could do to help, and he held me tenderly the rest of the night after he'd spent his rage and frustration inside me.

Bressen came to my bed nightly for the next week after the ride with Ursan. He arrived shortly after Raina left, and we fucked until the wee hours of the morning. He returned to his own room just before dawn, and I fell asleep to catch a couple hours of rest before Raina came in to wake me.

I lived happily in a permanent state of exhaustion now. I drank at least two cups of coffee in the morning to keep me awake, and it energized me long enough to make it through my training with Samhail until I could take a nap later in the afternoon to prepare myself for another night in bed with Bressen. I rarely saw him during the day, except at the occasional meal, and he continued to give me as little attention as possible, but it no longer mattered to me. I came alive each night when he slipped into my room.

Samhail seemed back to normal after the awkwardness of our flight to the Citadel, so I followed his lead and pretended as though nothing had happened.

We always began my training with a basic warmup and then some punching with the straw pad. I worked my way through a regular routine of punch sequences, and then Samhail called out combinations he wanted me to do.

After a couple of lessons, Samhail also showed me how to dodge blows. In other words, every now and again he would swing the pad at me, and it was up to me to avoid getting knocked on my ass. The first several times he swung the pad, I ended up in a heap at his feet, but I eventually recognized the signs he was about to swing.

I wasn't even aware of it at first. I ducked on instinct the first time I successfully dodged the pad, and I was so stunned at my triumph that I was knocked over by the backswing as Samhail brought the pad around again. Finally, I realized I was subconsciously noticing the way Samhail's shoulders tensed when he was about to swing at me.

When I explained to Samhail after our training why I'd gotten so much better at dodging his blows, he was impressed and congratulated me. The next day, however, he masked his tell, and I was back to being knocked on my ass every couple minutes. After that, I learned not to confess such things to him.

When we added sword work into my training, I donned a leather vest and a pair of leather vambraces to help protect me. The swords we used were heavily blunted and unlikely to slice an apple, let alone a person, but the leatherwear still provided a layer of protection from bruising.

Finding that the vest and vambraces fit perfectly the first time I wore them, I expressed surprise to Samhail that the Citadel had them in my size. He grinned and told me they were for young boys. Then he smiled and handed me the small, light-weight sword I would use for training, and I glared back at him.

For sword work, we started with defense rather than offense. Instead of teaching me how to attack with the sword, Samhail first showed me how to block strikes from an opponent. I started with a wooden sword just to get the feel of the movements, but Samhail moved me to one of the blunted metal practice blades soon after, since I picked it up quickly enough.

Even with the small sword I'd been given, it took me a while to build up the strength to wield it. I was used to lifting and carrying things on the vineyard, so I was fairly strong, but the sword movements were different from anything I was used to. My arms were brutally sore after the first few days, and we'd gone back to hand fighting for a while to give my muscles a chance to recuperate and adjust. My body finally started to get used to the weight of the sword, as well as the unfamiliar movements needed to wield it, and Samhail let me add in attack moves.

I found attacking much easier than defending. While Samhail tried hard to rein in his power when he swung his sword, even his light-effort blows were backed by his incredible strength, so part of my soreness the first day was from the unusual force of the blows I attempted to block.

Samhail used a smaller blade like mine, but the drawback to a lighter blade for someone like him was that he had a hard time controlling how fast he could swing it without the added resistance provided by a heavier blade. It was in those first few days of sword fighting that I finally understood why both Samhail and Bressen had been reluctant to agree to my training.

Gradually I built up my strength, and Samhail learned how to wield the lighter sword without almost slicing me in half, so our training sessions became much more effective. I was getting the hang of the motions and could transition back and forth between offense and defense with decent fluidity. The movements reminded me of a dance, and I sometimes got lost in the rhythm of it.

I was so lost in training one morning, in fact, that I was completely unaware of our audience until Jerram spoke.

"Cyra," Jerram said when Samhail and I paused after a volley. "You almost look like you know what you're doing with that sword."

I blinked and looked around for the voice. Jerram stood to the side of the yard with one of his guards. Both were dressed for training.

Jerram's words finally caught up to me, and I frowned. Samhail had said almost the same thing to me the day before, but while Samhail's words conveyed understated pride in my progress, there was a sardonic strain to Jerram's statement.

"Thank you," I said anyway. "My apologies, my lord. I didn't see you there."

Jerram came toward me, and Samhail withdrew to the side to wait.

Lord Jerram of the Triumvirate wanted to speak to me, so apparently everything needed to stop, I thought resentfully. Samhail, of course, was practiced enough in dealing with Jerram to know it was better just to fade into the background and wait for Jerram to say whatever he wanted to say.

Bressen told me a while back that Jerram thought Samhail should eat with the rest of the Citadel staff and guards when he was there, but Bressen was adamant that Samhail's status entitled him to eat with the lords. Afraid of angering Samhail and losing his valuable services, Ursan agreed with Bressen, and Jerram's objection was overruled. Jerram, however, continued to treat Samhail as second-class, and Samhail ignored it to keep the peace. It was enough for Samhail to know he could squash Jerram like a bug if he wanted to.

Jerram circled around to stand between me and Samhail, and I noted the move for what it was, a claim to my attention. I wasn't sure if he even realized the myriad ways he flexed his power like this. Bressen flexed his power all the time as well, but it was Bressen's prodigious magical power that really spoke to people from under his mysterious dark aura. Jerram's power was concentrated in his title and the perceived authority it afforded him, so he took pains to bolster his image in other ways whenever he could. Unfortunately, those ways often involved reminding Samhail he was not Jerram's equal.

"I remember those little practice blades well," Jerram said, looking at the sword in my hand. "I myself have graduated to something a little bigger and more dangerous."

He unsheathed the sword that hung from a scabbard strapped to his hip and held it up for my inspection. It was admittedly a beautiful weapon with fine detailing in the handle and a sharp blade polished to a mirror shine.

"Her name is Harpy's Bane," Jerram said.

My eyes flicked up to meet Samhail's over Jerram's shoulder. A smile tugged at the corners of Samhail's mouth, and I had to purse my own lips to keep from catching his grin.

"That's quite a name, my lord," I said, steeling my face into a serious expression.

"Indeed. Legend has it that this sword was used to kill a giant harpy that was terrorizing a village in Derridan centuries ago. One of my ancestors – an unparalleled warrior – had the sword specially made and slew the harpy. The sword has been passed down to the eldest in my family ever since."

I glanced over Jerram's shoulder again and caught Samhail's eye roll. Seeing my glance, he shook his head almost imperceptibly.

"What an intriguing story that must be," I said.

"I'll tell it to you sometime," Jerram promised.

He re-sheathed the sword and unbuckled the belt that held his scabbard. He laid everything carefully on the bench near the weapons rack and selected a practice sword from it.

"You're not going to use Harpy's Bane?" I asked.

"Oh no. She's far too sharp for practice. I'd slice my guard in half."

I looked quickly to the guard Jerram brought with him, but the man remained motionless and didn't meet my eyes. It was on the tip of my tongue to ask Jerram why he'd brought the sword with him if he wasn't going to use it, but then the answer occurred to me. He'd wanted an excuse to show off the blade to me. By now, everyone at the Citadel knew Samhail and I trained in the yard at this time, so Jerram's presence here was intentional.

"Your lessons appear to be going well," Jerram said.

"I'm learning a lot from Samhail."

"I could probably teach you a lot more myself, but my Triumvirate duties don't allow me extra time for things like that."

"Of course not. I'd never expect you to use your valuable time training me."

Jerram shook his head. "I'm still not sure why you want to learn to fight anyway."

"My lord, up until a few weeks ago I'd have told you myself I didn't need to know how to fight, but since then I've been attacked by a bear as well as two separate groups of brigands. Knowing how to wield a sword seems like it might be a good skill to have."

Jerram nodded knowingly, and I bristled inwardly at the pity in his expression.

"I promise you're perfectly safe within these walls," Jerram said. "Harpy's Bane is here to protect you, and so am I."

My jaw clenched, but I dragged a smile across my face.

"I really should get back to practicing now," I said, then added, "just in case you're not around when the next bear attacks."

"Actually, I was hoping to have a quick word in private with you."

I glanced at Samhail who nodded his head a little to the side to indicate I should go speak with Jerram.

"Of course, my lord."

Jerram put his hand on the small of my back to steer me toward a vacant corner of the yard. I tried to pull away from his touch, but he only pressed more insistently. Behind us, the sound of clanging metal told me Samhail and the guard were practicing so they could give us some privacy.

"How much do you know about the Harmilan?" Jerram asked.

I shrugged. I'd almost forgotten the holiday was tomorrow.

"Not a lot. I've heard of it before, but we don't celebrate it in the outer lands," I said.

Jerram nodded. "I'm not surprised. The Harmilan is a ceremony that reminds people of the Triumvirate's status as emissaries for the Trinity. It reinforces the divine nature of our authority in the mortal realm, and from what I understand, there's little respect for authority in the outer lands, divinely-bestowed or otherwise."

I kept my face impassive. Jerram seemed to think the outer lands were a lawless, godless wasteland. It was true we relied more on local authorities to govern ourselves, but that was because the Triumvirate seemed loath to send resources our way. That we'd ultimately imposed our own order in the absence of their involvement wasn't surprising, but I kept all this to myself.

"The Harmilan is about union," Jerram went on. "It celebrates joining. On any given day, Bressen, Ursan, and I are three lords who oversee three separate territories, but those three territories are still part of one country. When needed, we come together to rule Thasia as one entity. At least, that's how it's supposed to work. The Triumvirate mirrors the divine Trinity, and the Harmilan is a reminder that each of us has an obligation to serve at once as a creator, a protector, and an enforcer in the realm. Bressen, of course, likes to channel the Nemesis a little too much for my taste, but there's usually no harm in his little role play, so I try not to complain."

My smile tightened even more.

"In any case, union and joining are prominent themes of the day, and the people of Callanus honor those themes in a number of ways. It begins in the morning with the Ceremony of One at the Priory where the lords renew our oaths to serve Thasia as ambassadors of the Trinity. From there, the day is full of celebrations of all kinds. Many people take their marriage vows on the Harmilan to engage in a very real and binding union. The Priory usually has a full schedule of weddings from morning until late into the night."

I frowned, suddenly afraid of where he was going with this.

"Others choose less permanent ways of joining to show their reverence." Jerram paused to look at me meaningfully, and my eyes widened just a little as it became clearer what he wanted from me.

"I'm not sure I understand, my lord," I said, feigning confusion. By the gods, if he wanted what I thought he wanted, I was going to make him spell it out.

Jerram smiled. "The sexual act is another way to celebrate joining on the Harmilan. People go home and make love all night, and the brothels are usually full until morning."

I blinked at him. "My lord, are you asking me to share your bed tomorrow night?"

"I am," he said, and my heart fell into my stomach.

"As Triumvirate lords, we're all expected to take someone to our beds tomorrow night," he went on. "Ursan always takes Glenora, although he's not obligated to. As for Bressen, the Trinity only knows what deviant carnalities he gets up to. In any case, I need to choose a companion for tomorrow night, and I've chosen you."

My mouth was hanging open when he finished, and it was several seconds more when I finally managed to stutter, "I...I'm honored beyond belief, my lord, but I have to decline your generous offer."

Jerram's face darkened, and it occurred to me that it hadn't been a request but a statement of intent. He believed he was bestowing an honor on me, and he hadn't expected me to refuse it. My mind raced for something to tell him that would get me out of this. I wondered if he could punish me for refusing to go to his bed on the Harmilan, or any time for that matter.

I considered telling him I was a virgin and was saving myself for my husband, but something told me that might only make things worse if he decided to claim my maidenhead.

"My lord, I humbly beg your forgiveness, but please find someone else to bestow this great honor on." I looked at him as contritely as I could, but he was still frowning at me.

"The customs you have up here are still very...new to me," I continued, "and while I'm trying to learn more about Callanus and its people, this particular custom might be too big a leap for me. Surely you'd rather spend your night with a woman who can appreciate the importance of this rite more than me. I'm sure many women will be vying for your attention tomorrow."

I held my breath, hoping flattery might convince him to keep his options open until I could find a way to avoid him.

Jerram continued to look at me, and fear crept up my spine. Finally, he sighed. "I understand. Our customs must seem strange to you."

I nodded vigorously. "Yes, very strange."

"I only ask," Jerram went on, and my heart fell again, "that you try to immerse yourself in the celebrations tomorrow. Perhaps by evening you may be ready to...try something new."

It was the best I was going to get at this point, and I forced myself to smile and nod at him. "I'll do my best."

Jerram inclined his head to me. "Very well. Until tomorrow."

He turned and headed back into the training yard. Samhail and the guard were still practicing, but they stopped when Jerram returned. Samhail looked at me, but I shook my head quickly at him.

"We should let Lord Jerram have the training yard now," I called to Samhail. "I don't want to get in his way."

Samhail nodded and gathered our things to bring them over. "What did he want?" he asked softly when he reached me.

"Not here. Inside."

I took my things from Samhail and led the way back into the Citadel. When the door was safely shut behind us, I turned to him as tears welled in my eyes.

His brows narrowed sharply. "What's wrong? What did he say?"

"Jerram wants to take me to his bed tomorrow night for the Harmilan," I squeaked at him. The panic I'd been holding in was threatening to break free. "Apparently the best way to celebrate joining is with lots of fucking."

Samhail raised a brow at my language, but his face grew serious as he realized what I'd said. "He asked you to share his bed tomorrow?"

"Not asked. He thinks it's an honor he's bestowing on me."

Samhail's face darkened even more. "Nemesis take me, not if I have anything to say about it," he growled, and the menace in his voice sent a shudder through my chest.

I shook my head. "I managed to put him off by claiming a wariness of strange customs, but he hasn't given up completely. I need to find a way to avoid him tomorrow."

Samhail nodded, but his face was still contorted in anger. "Bressen can help with that."

My mind flashed back to what Jerram said about how the Triumvirate lords were expected to take someone to bed with them. He'd also said Ursan wasn't required to take Glenora, even though they were married. I couldn't help but wonder who Bressen spent his last Harmilan with. Was he expecting to spend this one with me, or would he welcome the opportunity to take someone new to his bed tomorrow night? The thought made me queasy.

"Cyra, are you alright?" Samhail put a large hand on my shoulder and patted it awkwardly in a way I imagined he thought was comforting. It made me smile despite my worry.

"Just let me know if Bressen has any ideas about keeping Jerram away tomorrow."

"Don't worry," he said. "Bressen and I will keep your bed Jerram-free."

Chapter 28

The day of the Harmilan dawned bright and unusually warm for the season, which was good for the festivities that would be held outdoors in the vast gardens of the Priory. Raina was in especially high spirits as she explained how the balmier weather made people more amorous, and she warned I might need to step over couples having sex by the end of the night. I hoped she was exaggerating, or I'd need to make my exit early to avoid this tripping hazard.

Raina herself hoped to finally convince Damian to take her to bed, since they'd patched things up after the night Raina and I snuck out of the Citadel. She'd also asked him about the information I requested, but he didn't yet have anything to share.

"If he doesn't try to lift my skirts tonight, I'll toss the man down and jump on him myself," Raina vowed as she fixed my hair.

I smiled at her in the mirror. "You should."

"It wouldn't be too forward of me?" she asked earnestly.

"Of course not. Don't wait for him to make the first move if you know what you want."

My advice was bolder than I would've normally given, but Bressen and I were only sharing a bed because I'd been audacious enough to insist that he stay that first night. I'd also listened to Raina complain for weeks now that Damian wouldn't just 'shut up and fuck her already,' so I too was looking forward to a change in their situation. I felt bad about Raina's unwilling abstention from sex while I myself was having so much of it that I woke exhausted on most mornings. I also felt a bit guilty that I still hadn't told her I was sleeping with Bressen when she was sharing so much with me about her and Damian.

Last night had been an exception to my usual activities with Bressen. With the Harmilan imminent, he'd stayed in his own room to prepare, and I'd gotten a good night's sleep for once. Unfortunately, I hadn't seen him or Samhail recently, so I didn't know if there was a plan for keeping me out of Jerram's bed.

"And…all done!" Raina said, putting the last jeweled comb into place in my hair.

I looked in the mirror and had to admit I was impressed. The Citadel's clothiers had been working on my gown for a week now. It was a pale seafoam green interwoven with glittering silver threads that shimmered with every move I made. The bodice laced low in the back, and then fastened at the neck. A keyhole cutout on the chest dipped low enough to display the tempting mounds of my breasts where the corseting pushed them up. A necklace of diamonds from the Citadel's vault sat at my throat while matching hair combs added dazzle to my dark waves of coffee-colored hair.

I was to accompany the three lords to the Priory as their guest and would be sitting with Glenora in her designated area. As such, I represented the Citadel in all its power and grandeur, so I needed to dress the part. That my place in the Citadel was still very much up in the air was immaterial right now. We all had our parts to play.

Bressen, Jerram, and Samhail were already in the rotunda when I arrived. Similar to what he'd worn to the ball, Bressen's ink-black jacket was adorned with silver embroidery that rolled like thick, thorny vines across his shoulders. The effect was striking, and I stopped to stare at him before remembering myself.

Samhail wore the same deep indigo jacket embroidered with gold that he'd worn to the ball, but this time his two swords crisscrossed his back. His official function was to serve as personal guard to the Triumvirate, although it was largely ceremonial. According to Raina, Samhail usually came back to Callanus for the Harmilan, and his presence was part of some ancient tradition. Given the lords' collective powers, or even Bressen's power alone, it was unlikely anyone would attack them. Nevertheless, Samhail's looming presence in our entourage made for an impressive effect.

Jerram, Bressen, and Samhail turned as I entered, and all three gaped as they looked me up and down. I thought I saw desire in all their eyes, but it was Bressen's gaze that caught and held mine. He seemed unable to look away as he let his eyes rake boldly up and down my body before giving me the hint of a smile.

"You look beautiful, Cyra," Jerram said, recovering his voice first.

"Thank you, my lord."

Further talk was cut short as Ursan and Glenora arrived.

"Apologies," Ursan said as he hustled into the rotunda. "I needed to call the tailor for a last-minute alteration. Shall we go?"

Thousands of people had gathered at the gates of the Citadel and also lined the street to the Priory, and the roar of the crowd met us as soon as we exited.

Six horses waited outside in the courtyard for us. I saw Ghost, who'd been found safe, and I also easily recognized Samhail's giant black stallion. To my surprise, Bressen mounted a brilliant white stallion, and the stark contrast of his dark form on the horse was a striking picture.

I scanned the crowd as we rode, interested to see if the cheering masses reacted to Bressen differently than they did to Jerram or Ursan. If anything, they seemed to cheer louder when he passed, but some people also shrank back from him or kissed their fingers in prayer.

We arrived at the Priory to much fanfare. In addition to the crowd outside, several hundred others had received invitations to witness the ceremony within. About half the invitations were reserved for important people and their families, but the other half were determined by lottery and given to citizens of Callanus from all classes. Raina said she'd won an invitation a few years ago, but she found the ceremony rather boring. It was the festivities and feasts afterward that made it worth going.

We all dismounted near the front steps of the Priory and made straight for the main hall. The crowd inside fell into a hush as the doors opened and music filled the room, and I shuddered slightly as I remembered the last time I'd been here.

Glenora entered the hall first, followed by me and Samhail. We received polite applause as we made for a small seating area to the side of the central dais. Then Ursan, Jerram, and Bressen entered together to thunderous cheers from the crowd. They walked to the central dais and filed around it. The crowd only quieted when two priestesses and a priest entered from a side door behind the dais and proceeded to the center where they stood so that each of them faced one of the lords.

Together, Ursan, Jerram, and Bressen all dropped to one knee, and the voices of the priestesses and priest filled the room as if speaking as one. I tried to hear what they were saying, but I couldn't make out the words. I furrowed my brows and concentrated harder, but it didn't sound like any language I recognized.

"It's ancient Arystrian, the language of the old continent," Glenora leaned over to whisper to me. "It's a dead language now. No one uses it but those here at the Priory, and even most of them only repeat the words without really understanding them."

I didn't know the entire continent once had its own language. Many people now spoke the common tongue, which borrowed from the languages of several countries, but its use wasn't universal.

"No one knows what they're saying?" I whispered back.

"Ursan does because he loves languages and finds things like this fascinating, but him and maybe the priest and priestesses are the only ones."

"Ursan knows ancient Arystrian?"

"He explained the whole speech to me once. It starts out with something about acting as one to protect and rule the land through shared wisdom, compassion, and valor, or some such nonsense." She waved a dismissive hand. "The last part was about joining that which was once separate to make it whole. To be honest, it almost sounded like our marriage vows," she said with a soft laugh. "The lords have a response toward the end, but I think Ursan is the only one who understands the words. I know Jerram has no idea, and one never knows with Bressen."

As if on cue, the voices of the three lords rang out, reciting words

I didn't understand.

I watched as the priest anointed each lord with something in a bowl, then he and the priestesses withdrew behind the dais. The lords stood simultaneously and walked to the center where they clasped hands with each other. They recited more words I didn't understand and turned to face the crowd, which erupted into a deafening standing ovation.

Samhail and Glenora both stood as well, and I followed them half a second later.

"Is it over?" I asked Glenora.

"Yes and no," she shouted into my ear above the crowd. "The Ceremony of One is over, but we need to stay for the first couple hours of marriage ceremonies. The lords don't leave until there's a break for lunch, so, unfortunately, we can't leave either."

The crowd settled once again, and the lords retreated to chairs on the opposite side from us. The priestesses and priest had returned to the center and were awaiting the approach of a young couple making their way toward them from the main entrance.

"It's a great honor to be the first couple married after the Ceremony of One," Glenora whispered in my ear. "It's supposed to mean the couple will have a long and happy marriage."

"Do you think it's true they will?" I asked, looking at the joy in the faces of the couple.

Glenora gave me a small smile. "Two hundred and one years ago, Ursan and I had the honor of being the first couple married."

My head snapped to her. "Really?"

She nodded, and I looked back at the couple who were saying their vows to each other. Several minutes later, they kissed and made their way with huge smiles to a side exit as the next couple approached the dais from the main entrance.

Almost two hours and the-gods-only-knew how many marriages later, my eyes were glassy and my backside was asleep as the last couple before lunch finally kissed and left the hall. I understood now why

Raina thought the ceremony was boring, and, knowing her as I did, I wasn't sure how she'd managed to sit through it.

Next to me, Samhail hadn't moved a muscle the entire time.

"How do you do that?" I asked him as we stood.

"Do what?"

"Sit so still."

"You mean, sit as still as stone?" he asked, quirking a brow at me.

I rolled my eyes. "Never mind. Forget I asked."

He grinned at me. "Let's go get lunch."

A lavish meal for the six of us was set up in the private dining room of the Priory, and I wished, not for the first time, that Jaylan and Brix could see the array of food laid out.

The lords then went into a series of private business meetings that would take up most of the rest of the afternoon, as marriages weren't the only unions secured during the Harmilan.

Once we were done eating, Glenora, Samhail, and I were free to do as we wished until the meetings broke up in the evening. There were games and small shows on the grounds for the rest of the day and even a large hedge maze to wander through.

Glenora planned to leave the Priory to visit a few ladies out in the city with whom she'd made friends over the years. She'd met the women at other Harmilans, and they now gathered as a group each year to celebrate.

Samhail needed to stay on the grounds in his official role as guard for the lords, although he didn't need to be in their meetings with them. I'd already been told not to leave the Priory, so Samhail and I wandered out onto the grounds together after lunch to partake in the festivities with the hundreds of others who'd been in the hall.

"Is there a plan for tonight?" I asked Samhail as we strolled through the gardens.

"It's taken care of. Jerram will be in meetings all afternoon, so you're free until they get out. The lords all exit their last meeting at the same time and come out onto the grounds to circulate among the crowd. As soon as Bressen gets out, he'll cast an obfuscation glamour over you so Jerram can't find you. That will happen around 7 o'clock, so you just need to be alone and out of the way at that time."

"What then? Will Jerram just give up and choose someone else if he can't find me?"

"He'll have to. You just need to stay out of sight. Ursan usually leaves right after the meetings get out, and I need to escort him back to the Citadel."

"I can't go back with you?"

"Bressen will find you and bring you back himself."

"Won't he be looking for someone to take to bed?" I asked as nonchalantly as I could.

Samhail stopped and looked down at me. I stopped too and returned his gaze.

"Where did you think you'd be spending the night if not with Bressen?" he asked.

I blinked at him. "You know."

I'd suspected he knew, but this was the first time we'd openly acknowledged that I spent my nights with Bressen.

Samhail grinned at me. "Bressen and I haven't spoken about it directly, but I know enough to guess why he looks so tired every morning, or why you do too, for that matter."

I blushed furiously. "How long have you known?"

"I assume it started the night he brought you home from the vineyard?"

I nodded, and we resumed walking.

"I'm sorry," I said softly after a few seconds.

He was quiet a moment before he said, "You don't owe me anything."

I huffed a laugh. "I owe you a lot. Just maybe not that."

Samhail chuckled. "No, maybe not."

"Are you sure Bressen plans to spend the night with me? I didn't want to assume anything when he'll...have more options than usual."

315

Samhail stopped again and frowned at me. "Is that what you think? That Bressen comes to your bed because you're convenient?"

I looked down, but he caught my chin and lifted my face to his.

"I've known Bressen a long time, and he's never done anything simply because it was convenient," he said. There was anger in his voice. "You're a beautiful woman. A maddening woman to be sure, but I promise you Bressen doesn't sacrifice his sleep every night to be with you just so he can take someone new to bed the first time the opportunity presents itself. Understand?"

He released my chin, and I nodded. I started walking again, and he fell back into step beside me.

"Will you find someone to spend tonight with?" I blurted out, hating myself for asking. I felt him look at me, but I kept my own eyes straight ahead.

"At some point, yes."

"Any idea who?" Nemesis take me. I needed to stop talking.

I realized I'd been hoping Samhail might take me to his bed if Bressen didn't want me tonight. The thought made me flush with shame. I hadn't even known what Bressen's plans were, and I'd already been making other arrangements in the back of my mind. I couldn't deny a part of me still desired Samhail, regardless of my feelings toward Bressen, but I shouldn't have been that quick to consider other plans.

"Never mind. I shouldn't have pried," I said.

"You're not prying. One of the priestesses is usually willing to warm my sheets. Sometimes more than one."

My head jerked toward him, but I quickly set my eyes forward again at his grin.

"I'll come back to the Priory after I return Ursan to the Citadel. The priestesses aren't free to find a companion for the night until after their duties for the Harmilan are complete, but I've never had trouble finding a soft pair of thighs to spend my night between."

I winced a bit. The question about Samhail's plans had been burning in me all day, but now that he'd answered, I wanted nothing more than for him to stop talking about it.

"Good. I hope you find someone nice," I said, but even to my own ears, my voice sounded false and strangely high-pitched.

Mercifully, Samhail let the subject drop, and we spent the rest of the day walking the grounds. We watched the shows and games taking place, and he answered all the questions I'd been wanting to ask him. I learned he was a hundred and twenty-four years old and that Bressen was a hundred and seventeen, although both looked to be around Jaylan's age. Gargoyles were a type of perimortal, he said, so they followed the same aging process.

Samhail came from a relatively large family by both gargoyle and perimortal standards. He was one of five siblings, although he wasn't close with any of them. He explained that gargoyles by nature didn't form bonds easily, and family attachments were considered somewhat artificial. Rather, gargoyles valued the bonds they chose for themselves more than the "arbitrary" ties of blood. According to Samhail, Bressen was his oldest and still closest friend, more of a brother to him than his two actual brothers, their bond forged through the shared experiences of training and battle.

"Bressen told me how you saved his life," I said to Samhail.

He grunted. "His life was only in danger in the first place because of me."

"He doesn't see it that way."

"Yes, well, Bressen is stubborn."

"I'm sure he'd say the same about you."

It was starting to get dark by now, and the Priory staff were out lighting the hundreds of lanterns and lamps stationed throughout the garden. I hadn't been paying much attention to the crowd around us until now, but people had started to pair off rather than congregate in groups.

I saw from the Priory's clock that it was around half past six, and the lords would be getting out of their meetings soon. It was also dinnertime, but I wasn't remotely hungry. Servers with trays of food had been circulating among the guests all day, so Samhail and I had been continually eating in small bites. It was a long day, but Samhail's company had made it bearable, and I felt a wave of affection for him.

"Thank you for keeping me company today. I imagine there were more entertaining things you could've been doing besides shepherding me around."

He shrugged. "The orgies and underground fighting rings will still be there next year."

I turned and narrowed my eyes at him, but he just winked at me. I was about to say something more when I felt the now-familiar prickling at the back of my head. Samhail went still for a moment, and I waited for him to tell me what message he'd just received from Bressen.

"The meetings are over. The lords are on their way out," he said.

"They're early."

He nodded. "I need to go meet Ursan. Bressen will find you when he can."

Samhail strode off toward the main building while I looked around for somewhere to hide. I saw a large marble Pegasus on a plinth and made for the statue, increasingly aware I stood out as a solitary person in a garden full of couples.

I reached the statue and went around behind it only to be brought up short. Two women had already laid claim to the statue's privacy and were wrapped in each other's arms kissing behind the plinth.

A small cheer went up near the Priory, and I looked around the statue to see the lords emerging from the building. Samhail was already there, and Ursan made straight toward him. Jerram and Bressen both seemed to be surveying the gardens.

I felt the obfuscation glamour fall into place around me and breathed a small sigh of relief. I might be able to stay behind the Pegasus after all since the couple wouldn't notice me now. Or perhaps not, I thought as I listened to their lips smacking loudly behind me.

I peeked around the statue again. Jerram had started down the stairs and was on his way out into the lawn. Bressen had just taken a few steps to do the same when a woman grabbed his arm to stop him. She let go of him immediately, apologetic for her boldness in touching him, but then she stepped closer to speak to him. In the light of the lanterns, I recognized it was Jemma. I knew what she must want with Bressen, and I felt a pang of jealousy.

I saw with rising panic that Jerram was slowly heading this way. He scanned the grounds carefully, and I knew he was looking for me. What if the obfuscation glamour failed at the wrong moment? I looked around wildly and saw the entrance to the hedge maze.

I spared a glance back toward Jerram, and when I saw his gaze sweep away from me, I ran for it. I reached the entrance to the maze in a few seconds and ducked inside. I looked back around the corner, but Jerram hadn't seen me. I wasn't sure how long it would be before he decided to head this way, though. I needed to hide in the maze until Bressen found me.

If Bressen was still planning to look for me, that was. Maybe Jemma had changed his mind about his bedmate for the night.

I shook away the thought and turned into the maze but immediately found my way partially blocked by another couple entangled in each other's arms.

There were two ways to go, but both were obstructed by couples wrapped around each other. I didn't yet see anyone I'd need to step over, but Raina hadn't been kidding about what happened on the Harmilan after dark. I made a quick decision and chose the path that had more couples blocking it. If Jerram entered the maze, hopefully he'd choose the other path with fewer obstacles.

I skirted around couples without touching them as I made my way down the path. I brushed up against someone once or twice, but no one seemed to notice. I turned down another path, but it was much the same everywhere, even as I moved deeper and deeper into the maze. I had no idea how big it was or if I'd ever be able to find my way out, but at least all the paths were lit by lamps.

I turned another corner and suddenly found myself at a dead end. The path widened into a small open area with a stone bench, and I thought this might be a good place to stop and wait a while. As I approached the bench, however, I realized I wasn't alone. On the other side was a couple, half naked and fully engaged in the act of making love on the ground.

I was about to apologize when I realized the couple had no idea I was there. Even without the obfuscation glamour, they were too bound up in passion to care that they had an audience. I knew I should leave and give them their privacy, but I couldn't move. The woman writhed and arched her body into her lover's as she cried out softly with each of his thrusts. The man braced himself above her, grunting in pleasure as he pushed into her over and over again. He quickened his rhythm one moment, then pulled out slowly only to thrust into her hard the next time.

I'd never seen others have sex before, and I was captivated by their rhythmic movements. I felt a tightening between my own legs and knew it was arousing me. I needed to go.

I took a step back but met with something solid. I opened my mouth to gasp, but a hand clamped gently over it to cut off any sound. Alarm rose quickly in me but then died a second later as I inhaled the scent of hot cinnamon and musk.

"Sshh," Bressen whispered in my ear, and I relaxed against him.

His hand fell from my mouth but didn't go far. He wrapped one arm across my shoulders while the other snaked around my waist to pull me against him. I felt the bulge of his manhood pressing against my backside, and I inhaled deeply as his mouth brushed all the way up my neck.

"You've turned voyeur, I see," he whispered huskily in my ear.

The hand on my shoulder moved down to cup one breast while his thumb ran slowly over the peak of my nipple through the fabric. I groaned and pressed back against him.

Bressen started to pull up my gown, and I knew I should object, but I couldn't bring myself to stop him. When he'd pulled the back of the skirt over my hips, he hooked his fingers on the waist of my undergarment and yanked it down to my knees.

"Open wider for me," Bressen breathed into my ear as his foot nudged mine.

I shimmied my knees so the undergarment fell to my ankles, and I pulled one foot out of the leg so I could widen my stance. I hoped the obfuscation glamour was still in place.

"Good girl," Bressen groaned into my ear, and I felt him tug at the closure of his pants. A thrill ran up my body, and the ache between my legs grew more insistent.

My eyes found the couple on the ground. Their lovemaking had grown more fervent, and the woman cried out in pleasure as the man drove into her with great pounding thrusts.

I almost climaxed as Bressen entered me hard and quick from behind. He thrust up inside me as I closed around him, and I threw my head back against his shoulder, trying not to scream. I reached behind me to find his thigh, and Bressen groaned as my fingers dug into the steely muscle there. Then he was driving into me, each thrust burying him to the hilt, and it was all I could do to hold onto him as pleasure scorched my blood. His hand went to the apex of my thighs to tease the knot of nerves there, and my legs nearly gave out at the exquisite torment.

I found my release at the same time as the couple on the ground, bliss rocking my body as I clenched around Bressen. His hand came back up over my mouth to cover the cry I'd forgotten to stifle, and the couple on the ground instead gave voice to the explosion of ecstasy that jolted through me. A few thrusts later, Bressen shuddered with his own release as he pressed his mouth against my shoulder to muffle his own moan. I sagged against him, completely spent, and his arms tightened around me as we stood breathing hard for several minutes.

In front of us, the couple stood and righted their clothing without speaking. The woman finished first and smoothed her skirt. She smiled at the man, then turned and disappeared back into the maze, walking right past Bressen and I without noticing us. The man sat down on the stone bench and continued to catch his breath.

"They're not together," I whispered.

Bressen shook his head against my neck before withdrawing himself from inside me. My body felt the loss of him, and I whimpered quietly in protest.

"Many who share a night together on the Harmilan never see each other again," he said.

I pulled away from Bressen. His arms loosened, but he seemed reluctant to release me. When I leaned down to pull up my undergarment, though, he bent quickly and snatched it from under my foot. I had to grab his shoulders to keep from falling over.

"What are you doing?" I whispered to him.

Bressen grinned at me as he refastened his pants and shoved the garment into his pocket.

"You won't need these again tonight," he said. "That couple may be done with each other, but you and I are just getting started."

Chapter 29

The flight from the Priory to the Citadel was short, but I dozed in Bressen's arms for the couple minutes it took to get back. It was a long day punctuated at the end by panic and then rapture, and my body didn't know how to handle it.

I awoke when Bressen set me down, and we stood in each other's arms for several seconds while he brushed tender kisses across my lips.

"What did you think of your first Harmilan?" he asked me.

"Shouldn't I answer later?" I asked. "I was told it isn't over yet."

Bressen laughed. "That's true, but I was wondering about everything before the maze."

"Do you understand ancient Arystrian?" I asked him.

He blinked at me. "That's what's on your mind?"

I nodded, and he shrugged.

"I don't know a lot," he said, "but if I'm going to take an oath in another language, I make it a point to know what I'm agreeing to."

I nodded. "It was a long day," I admitted.

"It was. Now just imagine if you had to sit in meetings all afternoon listening to Ursan drone on about fishing tariffs when all you can think about is coming back here to spend the night making love to the most beautiful woman in Thasia."

Bressen drew me close again and buried his head in my hair. He pulled out one of my jeweled combs and inhaled deeply as a lock fell over my shoulder.

"Mmm," he said. "Jasmine and almond. I can't get enough of your scent."

"I wasn't sure I'd see you tonight," I ventured. "It looked like Jemma wanted your company."

Bressen frowned down at me. "Jemma?"

"The red-haired priestess. She was the seer who had the vision about me."

"Ah, I didn't realize it was the same priestess. She did ask me to come with her, but I told her I was already spoken for tonight."

I grinned teasingly at him. "That was rather presumptuous of you, my lord."

He arched a brow at me. "And here I thought you sounded jealous I might share a bed with someone else tonight."

I blushed but held his gaze. "We'll see if I invite you in then."

He looked amused, and I turned to go but stopped dead as I saw the room I was about to enter.

"This isn't my room," I said dumbly.

Bressen put his hands on my shoulders. "No, it's mine."

He plucked two more jeweled combs from my hair that sent locks tumbling down my back.

In the weeks I'd been here, I'd never seen Bressen's bedroom. He'd always come to mine. What I saw now was jaw-dropping in its magnificence and grandeur. It was everything that my room was, magnified tenfold. Ornate chairs gilded with gold and upholstered in rich brocades sat around the room in various seating nooks, and breathtaking artwork hung on walls painted in a deep shade of emerald that almost matched the dress I'd worn my first night here. The most eye-catching feature, though, was the huge bed that stood against the wall near the balcony. It could easily have slept five people of Bressen's size and was piled high with fluffy goose-down pillows, soft blankets, and warm furs. A crackling fire already glowed in a giant tiled fireplace that sat across from the bed.

Another lock dropped over my shoulder, but I just stared at the bedroom as Bressen freed the rest of my hair, then pushed it aside to remove the diamond necklace around my throat.

"Remind me to remove the necklace first next time," he said as he fumbled with it through my hair that kept falling back into his way.

I turned to face him just as he freed the necklace. "This is your room."

He smiled. "You are full of useful observations tonight."

"You didn't say we'd be in your room."

"Does it matter whose room we use?"

"It's just…all this time, I've never seen your room."

His eyes softened. "You're seeing it now."

I turned to go inside, and Bressen followed me, dropping the combs and necklace onto a table next to the bed. The lamps went out so that only the fireplace lit the room, and I watched him approach me in the dancing light, hunger swirling in his eyes.

"I had no idea everyone in Callanus was so licentious," I said. "People in Fernweh won't believe it when I tell them what goes on here."

Bressen had been bending to kiss me, but he stopped short and frowned.

"What is it?" I asked.

"I've gotten used to having you here. I said I'd help you get home, but I haven't actually considered what it would be like to let you go back to Fernweh."

I didn't say anything. Truthfully, I hadn't thought about going back to Fernweh myself in at least a few days, and the thought of leaving Bressen made my stomach twist painfully.

"It's where I belong," I said quietly.

Bressen gathered me in his arms. "Not tonight. Tonight, you belong here with me." His mouth covered mine for a deep kiss, and I moaned against his lips. We were both breathing hard when he finally pulled away a little.

"Who do you usually take to bed on the Harmilan?" I asked him.

He frowned. "What kind of question is that?"

"I'm just curious. Jerram said you're expected to take someone to bed tonight. I'm just afraid I made it too easy for you this year."

I tried to step back teasingly, but Bressen grabbed my hands and pulled them around behind me to hold them at the small of my back. His mouth came down again on mine in a demanding kiss that threatened to buckle my knees.

"You are the only woman I want in my bed. Do you understand?" he growled when our mouths parted. I nodded against his lips before he crushed them back down onto mine and his tongue invaded my mouth. I tried to pull my hands free to wrap them around his neck, but he held them fast behind me, and I whimpered a little.

"Let me touch you," I begged.

He didn't. Instead, he teased me by brushing his lips over mine and then retreating. My mouth tried to follow his, but he pulled back out of reach.

I pouted at him. "Cruel man."

He chuckled and brushed my lips again, but I was ready for him. I caught his bottom lip between my teeth and bit it gently before releasing it.

His tongue ran over the spot I'd nipped. "Mmm, she bites."

"Afraid of me?" I teased.

Bressen pressed his forehead to mine. He released my hands only to drag me against him so hard that I sucked in a breath. "Everything about you frightens me," he said seriously. "You're...dangerous."

"I thought you said I *courted* danger."

He shook his head. "You *are* danger." He grinned. "Maybe I should call Samhail in to protect me."

Whether he intended it or not, I recalled what he'd said about sharing women with Samhail, and I fought back jealousy at the idea of other women getting to enjoy a night with both of them.

Bressen seemed to read my thoughts and cocked his head in question. "*Should* I call Samhail?"

I opened my mouth to say something, but I wasn't sure what. I bit my lip as I considered what he was offering, but it seemed outlandish. Be with both Bressen and Samhail? I couldn't. Could I?

"You can," Bressen said softly. "You can if you want to, but only if you want to." He searched my face for a moment. "Do you want to be with both of us?"

I knew he was reading my mind, and I'd need to speak to him

about that eventually, but right now I didn't care. I remembered Samhail kissing me, remembered being pressed against him, and how he'd looked with those strong, beautiful wings stretched out behind him. I saw myself alone in a room with two of the most powerful and alluring men I'd ever seen, and I knew that I did want to be with them both, more than I could ever remember wanting anything.

Before I even knew I'd made a decision, I nodded my head.

"I need to hear you say it," Bressen said, his eyes locked on mine.

"You...wouldn't mind?"

He smiled. "I want to do whatever makes you happy, and if this would, then I don't mind at all. Would having Samhail join us make you happy?"

I couldn't move for several seconds. I couldn't think. Then I nodded again and swallowed. "Yes."

I felt the prickle at the base of my neck and shivered with anticipation. Somewhere, Samhail was hearing a voice in his head. I wondered what his reaction would be. I knew Samhail desired me and that he'd done this before with Bressen, but I had trouble wrapping my head around the idea now that I'd agreed to it.

"You summoned, Samhail?" I asked.

Bressen chuckled. "No one summons Samhail. I invited him."

"He knows what you're inviting him to?"

Bressen considered for a moment. "I planted a pretty clear picture in his mind, I think."

"And you think he'll come?"

Before Bressen could answer, a thud sounded on the balcony, and we turned toward the noise together. The shadow of Samhail's hulking form, wings splayed, stood against the dark blue starry sky.

Fear gathered in my stomach, not of Samhail, but fear of what was about to happen.

No, not fear. Shame. It was shame at the realization that I wanted this, that I wanted both these men, and I wanted them together.

Bressen took my face in his hands. "You don't have to do this, but

327

don't deny yourself because you think you *shouldn't* want it."

I looked into his eyes. The light was too dim to see their brilliant color, but I saw the sincerity in them very clearly. There was no judgement there, only desire.

I turned toward the balcony to face Samhail. He'd already stowed his wings and walked a few steps into the room. He'd been watching the exchange between me and Bressen and now waited to be sure he was welcome. I nodded to him, and he walked toward us.

"You got here rather quickly," Bressen drawled to Samhail from behind me.

Samhail stopped a couple steps from us and shrugged. "I hadn't gone back to the Priory yet, so I wasn't far. Plus that was one hell of an image you planted in my head."

I turned to Bressen and frowned. "Exactly what was this image?"

Bressen grinned. "That's between us men."

I turned back to Samhail with a silent plea for explanation, but he put on a mask of innocence. "It was tasteful, but…very persuasive."

I rolled my eyes.

"Am I…still invited?" Samhail asked, half amused, half serious.

In answer, I stepped toward him. The first was hesitant, but my second was more certain, and I closed the space between us. Samhail stood completely still as I placed a hand on his chest. I'd spent the whole day with him but hadn't allowed myself to touch him. Not like this, at least. We spent hours in the training yard, our bodies straining together, but not in the way I imagined they'd be straining soon.

I ran my hand down Samhail's chest to his stomach and felt his muscles clench. I'd wanted to touch him like this for a while now.

Samhail exhaled as I ran my hand back up his chest, savoring the contours of him under my fingers. The V of skin where his shirt sat open drew my hand, and I traced two fingers gently down the middle of his chest until I hit the fabric of his shirt. I looked up and saw he was just watching me, but there was something fierce in his eyes.

I was suddenly very conscious of my lack of experience in this area.

"I'm new at this," I said softly to them. "You probably shouldn't let me lead."

Bressen and Samhail both chuckled, and Samhail reached forward to thread a large hand through my hair. His mouth came down slowly onto mine, and my lips parted for him. His lips brushed mine briefly as if giving me the opportunity to change my mind, but when I didn't object, he deepened the kiss, and I leaned into his body automatically. This was not uncharted territory, I reminded myself.

I felt Bressen's hands on the back of my gown working at the laces. "There are no leaders here. If you want to do something, do it," he breathed into my ear.

I tugged Samhail's shirt free from his pants and started to pull it over his head, but he was too tall for me to manage without help. Sensing my problem, Samhail pulled the shirt the rest of the way.

I ran both hands down his smooth, broad chest and then down his arms and over the dark markings at his wrists. He let me explore his body, and I delighted at the clench I felt in his muscles as I ran my hands over him. He was trying hard to restrain himself, I realized.

Samhail's lips came down on mine again, and I let his tongue explore my mouth a while before I pressed gently away from him. He let me go so I could turn to Bressen.

I tugged at the bottom of Bressen's shirt, and he started to pull it off. It was halfway over his head when I grabbed his hands and stopped him from pulling it the rest of the way. It still covered his eyes but left his mouth free. I stood on my tip toes and nipped at the irresistible little dimple in the middle of his chin. He tried to lean down to find my mouth, but I brushed a teasing kiss on his lips and retreated.

"Minx," he growled and pulled his shirt the rest of the way off.

Behind me, Samhail pushed my hair aside and began working on the laces of my gown where Bressen had left off. The gown loosened around me, and Samhail unfastened the piece that clasped at my neck. The fabric fell from my shoulders to bunch at my waist, and he slid his hands over my hips to help it the rest of the way so that the gown puddled in a gossamer pool at my feet.

He let out a long breath. "Stunning," he whispered.

Gooseflesh rose all over my body as Samhail's gaze raked over me. I'd never considered myself stunning, or even beautiful. Different, certainly. My body wasn't as soft and rounded as the bodies of most of the women in Fernweh. I'd worked on the vineyard since my early childhood, and that meant a lot of lifting, bending, and hard labor, so my body had more muscle tone than other women's. My breasts were round and a decent handful – or so I'd been told – but they weren't as large as Pryn's. When lifted with the right corset, Pryn the barmaid could practically rest her chin on her breasts.

"It's not fair that I'm the only naked one here," I said and began working at Bressen's pants as he toed off his boots. I slid the pants down his legs, and he stepped out of them, his shaft already erect.

Samhail toed off his boots as well, and I turned to give his pants the same treatment. What I saw when I pulled them down his legs took my breath away. It was a truly impressive cock, already hard, with a patch of stark-white hair at its base.

Gods above, I nearly dropped to my knees right there to see what he tasted like, but I wouldn't be able to fit much of him in my mouth.

The enormity of what I was about to do, both literally and figuratively, made me suddenly lightheaded, and I turned to walk toward the bed on shaky legs. The bed was far larger than it needed to be for sleeping, and it occurred to me that its size might serve an entirely different purpose.

Bressen and Samhail followed me, and I turned to take them both in, their beautiful, powerful…naked bodies standing there, the evidence of their arousal so readily apparent. They wanted me.

Desire coursed through my blood, and suddenly I couldn't wait any longer. I pulled Bressen toward me and pushed him down on the bed. His eyes flared at my boldness even as a grin spread across his lips. He moved back until he was lying near the top, his eyes daring me to follow him. I did, crawling toward him like a cat until I hovered over that rigid length of him. I caught his gaze for just a moment before I brought my mouth down on his erection, and he swore loudly.

The bed dipped behind me under Samhail's weight, and I parted my legs to allow him to enter me, but I felt him shift instead. He lay beneath me, his head between my knees. Wetness immediately flooded between my thighs seeing him there, and Samhail grunted in approval.

I concentrated on moving my mouth languidly up and down Bressen, but I bucked in ecstasy when Samhail drew me down to his waiting mouth. I moaned when his tongue delved into me, licking and exploring between the petals of my sex.

I pressed my mouth down harder on Bressen and he groaned, moving his hips up gently to meet me. His fingers threaded through my hair, and I waited for him to push my head down onto him, as Eddin had liked to do, sometimes to the point of choking me, but Bressen's hand just rested lightly on my head as his fingers flexed in my hair.

I came up for air again and cried out as Samhail took the opportunity to plunge his tongue deep inside me. My hips jerked at the sensation, but Samhail's hands held me firmly in place and at the mercy of his onslaught. Gods above, I'd never felt anything like what Samhail was doing to me. The wine cellar had been my first experience with a man's mouth between my legs, and Bressen was damn good at it, but I almost couldn't handle the sensations Samhail's tongue was drawing from me.

It made me want to be filled.

I lifted myself slowly away from Samhail's devouring mouth. He let me go this time and sat up to watch me expectantly. I wasn't sure if this is how things were usually done, but I knew what I wanted now.

I turned to face Samhail and then threw a leg over Bressen's waist so I was straddling him backwards. I glanced back at him and saw the mix of surprise and delight on his face. He grasped my hips and helped guide me down onto his cock. Pleasure coursed up my body as I closed around him. I was dripping wet, thanks to Samhail's ministrations, and

I slid easily up and down Bressen's long, hard shaft while he rocked beneath me.

Samhail knelt in front of me, and I closed my mouth over his considerable cock. His head tipped back with a groan, and he swore under his breath as I took him as deep as I could, my tongue returning his teasing favors. Samhail was huge, and I couldn't get his whole length in my mouth, so I wrapped a hand around his base to squeeze him tightly while I held onto his waist with my other hand. His hips moved gently, meeting my own thrusts to help me take him deeper.

The three of us soon fell into a sensuous rhythm as I rocked back and forth on Bressen while my mouth slid up and down Samhail. Our pace quickened as the ache at my core grew by leaps and bounds. Bressen pulled me down harder onto him, and his hips bucked under me as I rode him. I let him take over as he thrust up harder and faster into me. My hand stroked Samhail, and I pulled my mouth back just as pleasure exploded inside me. I screamed as my body convulsed around Bressen, and he groaned his release a second later, his fingers digging into my hips as he pulsed into me.

Bressen stopped thrusting as he lay breathing hard on the bed beneath me. My body throbbed around him, and I looked up between gasps to see Samhail watching me. The hint of a smile played on his face, but I looked down, and he hadn't come yet.

I slipped off Bressen and lowered my head back down to Samhail, flicking the head of his cock with my tongue. I smiled to feel it twitch against my lips, and I moved to take him into my mouth again, but Samhail's hands curled around my arms. He pushed me down gently onto the bed next to Bressen and knelt between my legs. When he didn't move further, I realized he was waiting for my permission.

I looked to where Bressen lounged on the goose-down pillows in a satiated haze. A smile quirked at the side of his mouth as he nodded, and I took Samhail's hand to tug him toward me.

Samhail pushed my thighs open and settled himself between them. I felt so tiny beneath him as my legs spread wide to accommodate his large, hard body. I reached up to grasp his shoulders as I prepared to take him into me, but he took my hands in his and pulled them up over my head to pin them on the bed. His hands were so big he only needed one to hold both of mine in place. He paused to see if I would protest the restraint, but I didn't, and I looked up at him instead with an expression that told him he could do anything he wanted to me.

Desire flashed in Samhail's dark eyes, and he moved his free hand between my legs to slip a finger inside me. I'd climaxed just moments ago, but my need was building again already, and I moaned softly.

"Still so wet," Samhail breathed, and he removed the finger to push the head of his cock into me. I let out a small cry and arched beneath him. Samhail's hand tightened on my wrists, and I pressed my hips up to meet him, sliding him into me a little more. He was bigger than Bressen, his size proportional to his giant form, and I whimpered a little again as my body stretched to accommodate him.

Samhail went still. "Cyra," he breathed, "I don't want to hurt you."

"You won't," I promised.

He looked down at me, and I gazed back confidently.

Samhail pressed forward slowly to sheathe himself into me fully then, and my body wrapped around him, inch by incredible inch. He barely fit, and I cried out when he was fully inside me. He stopped again, unsure if my cry was one of pleasure or pain. In truth, it was a bit of both, but I threw my legs around his waist and pulled him toward me. Samhail groaned and began to thrust, slowly at first, but faster as my slickness coated him and his pleasure built.

"Tell me if I hurt you," he said, his voice strained.

"Keep going," was all I could gasp out.

My eyes flew open as a slight rocking motion in his hips hit just the right spot inside me. He smiled as I sucked in a hard breath, and he drove into me harder, burying himself deep within me. My hands strained for release under Samhail's grasp, and he let go of them so he could brace his arms on either side of me. My hands clamped onto the steely muscles of his biceps, and I held them tightly as each thrust pushed me closer and closer to another release.

I turned to look at Bressen as he watched us intently. I held his gaze as long as I could, but the sweet ache at my core overwhelmed me, and I closed my eyes as tension strained between my thighs.

Small cries escaped my throat at each thrust from Samhail, and my hips bucked up, urging him deeper. His long hair spilled over his shoulders to caress my breasts, and my fingers bit into his arms as he drove into me faster. He was pushing me toward a chasm, but this time I was ready for the fall.

I felt Samhail's pleasure break through him a moment later, every muscle in his body seeming to clench as he spilled himself inside me. His roar vibrated in my chest, and I moaned as I longed to follow him over the edge. My own climax was close, but I wasn't there yet.

Samhail started to ease himself down on top of me, but my whimper stopped him. My body still needed another release, and he lifted himself back up onto one elbow while his other hand fastened around my hip. He thrust deeply into me again, using his hand to rock my body against him in a way that hit a spot inside me I didn't even know existed. I moaned loudly, and he slid out again before plunging into me hard.

Bressen's dark head appeared over my chest, and he fastened his mouth on one breast while his hand closed over the other to gently pinch the nipple. Heat shot through me as he sucked hard on my breast while Samhail ground into me, and my body surged with pleasure.

"Oh gods, please!" I cried out, writhing beneath them as I savored the decadence of their hard weight above me.

Samhail thrust into me twice more, and my climax finally exploded through me. I arched my head back against the bed as my body seized, and my hand fisted in Bressen's hair, holding him to my breast. Relief flooded through me as I went limp beneath them, and Bressen pulled back, giving my nipple a final flick with his tongue.

Samhail lowered himself down on top of me and brought his lips to my ear. "I told you I only make promises I can keep," he whispered before slowly sliding out of me, and his words that day after we'd escaped the Soundless Woods came back to me.

If I ever do have you, it won't be as payment for anything. You'll let me take you willingly with no other expectations between us.

I smiled at him. "You're an ass."

I would've hit his chest, but I didn't have the strength to do anything besides melt into the bed. My chest heaved in great panting breaths as I tried to wrap my head around what had just happened.

"I think she enjoyed herself," Bressen drawled to Samhail.

Both men were propped on an elbow watching me.

"You're both asses," I breathed.

"I think she's helpless right now," Bressen said as he brushed a hand over my breast. I shivered as my nipple perked to attention.

"Hmmm. You're right," Samhail mused. He ran a finger down the side of my body, and I twitched as it tickled me.

"I'm warning you both, my revenge will be swift, brutal, and when you least expect it."

The two men only chuckled before Bressen got out of bed and shifted me under the covers. He climbed in again and pressed his body against mine, his hand resting on my hip. I reached out to touch his chest. On my other side, Samhail shifted closer, and I felt his warmth flood over me. I reached out my other hand and pressed it to his chest as well. I felt both of their heartbeats beneath my fingers, their steady drumming nearly in sync, and I took a moment to revel in being nestled between these two incredible men. My body sank into the bed as if leaden, and my eyes fluttered under an insistent heaviness.

My last thought as I succumbed to sleep was that I'd never felt as safe and satiated as I did right then.

Chapter 30

I awoke the next morning to an empty bed, but not an empty room. Samhail had slipped out sometime in the early morning hours, but Bressen was on the other side of his bedroom getting dressed.

I sat up but immediately groaned as the soreness between my legs from last night's exertions made its presence known. I'd been woken by Bressen and Samhail again later that night for a second round, and they'd pulled me onto my knees to take turns pounding into me from behind until my voice was hoarse from screaming into the bedding.

I'd gotten another hour or so of sleep after that before they'd teased me awake a third time just before dawn. They'd put me between them then and entered me together, Samhail between the already-tender folds of my sex, and Bressen at my other entrance. They'd taken their time preparing me for the latter, the experience a little painful to start, but I'd adjusted soon enough. The three of us had rocked together, moving slowly and carefully as they both kissed me and worshipped the rest of my body with their tongues and hands until I'd nearly forgotten my own name. The night had been beyond anything in my wildest dreams, even if I was certain I wouldn't be able to walk right for the next week.

"Ah, she lives," Bressen said as he fixed a cuff on his jacket. "I was afraid we put you into some kind of permanent torpor."

I grunted. "Don't flatter yourselves. I'm perfectly fine." The statement was belied by my wince as I swung my legs out of bed.

"I stand corrected," Bressen said with a chuckle.

I stood up and looked for my robe but realized a second later I wasn't in my own room. The only clothing I had was the gown I'd worn the night before, which lay in a wrinkled pile on the floor somewhere. It hadn't occurred to me to return to my room by morning to avoid any questions or awkward encounters since I was used to Bressen coming to me.

He seemed to read my thoughts. "Your lady's maid has been informed you're safe and will be returning shortly. I'll cast an obfuscation glamour so you can get back unnoticed."

I frowned as I remembered I needed to talk to him about the mind reading and went to pick up the gown puddled at the foot of the bed. When I stood back up, Bressen was there.

"What's wrong?" he asked.

I sighed. "There's nothing wrong, but there's something I need your help with."

"Anything. What is it?"

I paused. "I need you to teach me how to…block someone from entering my mind."

He stilled and looked hard at me. "I don't understand."

"You're always reading my thoughts, or at least it seems like you are. I need…That is…" I trailed off, not sure how to explain it without making it sound like an accusation.

Bressen put a finger under my chin and lifted it. "Tell me what you need."

"I need to block people from reading my mind. Even you."

He frowned at me. "I thought you already knew how to do that."

I canted my head in confusion. "Why would you think that?"

"That first day in the Great Chamber, you blocked me from reading your thoughts."

I stared at him a moment, remembering the feel that day of a wall sliding up in my mind.

"I don't know how I did that," I admitted. "I felt something…I felt you, and my mind just closed itself off. It was a survival instinct."

He looked at me seriously. "So all this time I've been reading your thoughts, it's been…" He seemed to search for the words. "Against your will? You haven't been letting me in?"

There was pain in his voice. I wasn't sure if it was pain at realizing he'd been violating my mind, or if it was pain that I didn't want him reading my thoughts. Maybe both.

"Not against my will exactly," I said. "Having you know what I'm thinking has been…helpful at times." I chose the words carefully as thoughts of how he always knew exactly how to touch me swam to the surface.

He smiled a little, and I assumed he'd seen what I was thinking. He realized his mistake and shook his head.

"I'm sorry. I'll try to stay out of your mind unless you invite me in, but you'll need to bear with me. I assumed you were fine with me reading your thoughts because it always feels as though you're calling to me. Other people's minds don't pull me toward them the way yours does. It's unlike anything I've ever encountered. I'm sorry if I misunderstood."

I nodded and brought a hand to his cheek. "You haven't seen anything I wouldn't want you to see, but I should learn to defend against having my mind read. Not from you…or not *just* from you, but from others with similar powers. There are others, aren't there? Like you and Morland?"

He nodded. "It's a rare gift, but I'm not the only one who possesses it. There are varying degrees of mind powers. Most perimortals with the gift can only sense moods or general intentions. More powerful mind wraiths can read specific thoughts in people's minds, but very few can compel others to do things. Morland was the only other mind wraith I knew who could do that, but still not to the degree I can. Regardless, you're right. You should learn to defend against it."

"Is it even possible for me to defend against it if I don't have mind powers?" I asked.

"Yes. Just about any perimortal can strengthen their own mind against attacks, and even some mortals can do it if they have the mental fortitude. Putting up a mind shield is a mental exercise, not a magical one per se, although having magic in general does help. I can usually break past the defenses of others with enough time and effort, but a good mind shield will at least slow me down."

"How were you able to call Samhail last night?" I asked. "I thought

Samhail learned to put up a strong mind shield so no one could invade his mind again."

I remembered what the guard told me about how Bressen practiced trying to get into Samhail's mind during their combat training while Samhail practiced trying to keep him out. I hoped Bressen hadn't had to break into Samhail's mind last night to get him here.

"Samhail does keep up a strong mind shield at all times now. I can't read his thoughts unless he lets me, but he always leaves a small sliver open to me in case I need to send him a message…or an invitation."

He grinned, and I blushed furiously.

"I should get back to my room before someone comes looking for me," I said, suddenly aware I'd been standing there naked.

Bressen leaned down and kissed me. One kiss turned into two, and two turned into our mouths crushed against one another, arousal blossoming quickly between us. Bressen's arms started to go around me, but then he grabbed my shoulders and set me away from him.

"You should go, or we'll never leave this bedroom," he said breathlessly. He took the gown out of my hands and gathered it up to slip it over my head. I turned around and pulled my hair out of the way so he could help me lace it up.

"This is torture," Bressen breathed as he fumbled with the laces. "All I can think about is unlacing this last night." He tugged at what was likely a knot in the laces and swore. "And these things were clearly invented by demons. You're no longer allowed to wear clothes that need to be tied. It gives a man…ideas."

My stomach fluttered, and I forced myself not to think about what he was implying.

Bressen finished tying off the gown and kissed my forehead. "Go. We can start your mind shielding lessons tomorrow."

I didn't kiss him again but headed straight for the door. I felt the obfuscation glamour fall into place like a heavy fog, and I hurried back to my room. The glamour lifted as soon as I was inside, and moments later, Raina entered with my morning tea. My bed hadn't been slept in, and I was wearing the gown she'd put me in the night before, but she didn't say a word about it.

For that matter, Raina looked distracted, and she was humming to herself. Then I remembered.

"Raina…how did last night go?"

Raina looked up as if noticing me for the first time, and her face split into a wide grin.

"Damian finally made his move?" I asked hopefully.

"No, but *I* did."

I smiled widely. "Good for you! What happened?"

Raina blushed but spent the next few minutes spilling all the details about her night with Damian. Despite the extra-sensual atmosphere, he'd still been hesitant to take their relationship to the next level, so Raina did it for him. After kissing and teasing him until he'd almost burst out of his pants, she'd thrown him down behind some bushes and ridden him until neither of them could see straight. At least, that was her account of what happened.

I was afraid Raina might ask about my own night, but she didn't press me on anything. Aside from the time we'd been drinking at the tavern together, where the line between lady and lady's maid was temporarily suspended for the night, Raina never asked me direct questions about my love life. Everything I told her I'd volunteered, and so my night with Bressen and Samhail would remain between the three of us for now.

"Oh, I almost forgot," Raina said as she helped me dress. "Damian was able to find out a little regarding the man you asked about."

My face snapped to hers. "Really? What?"

"He wasn't able to find out the details, but it sounds like an extremely dangerous prisoner escaped from Revenmyer."

"Does he know who?"

Raina shook her head. "A few other inmates found a way out before the guards realized there was a breech in the wards protecting the prison. When they did a full check of the inmates later, they found

340

this other prisoner was gone as well. Someone had put up glamours to make it seem like he was still there."

"Did he escape from inside, or did he have help?" I asked.

"It sounds like the wards were breeched from outside. He must've had help."

"Thank you for asking," I said.

"Damian figured out I was asking for you. He says you owe him two favors now."

I sighed. I was racking up quite a debt here at the Citadel that I wasn't sure I'd be able to repay, but I nodded to Raina. "If he needs something that it's within my power to get, have him let me know."

"Why did you want to know all this anyway?"

In all honesty, I wasn't sure why I wanted to know. I'd told myself the information might be related to my own situation, but it didn't sound like it was.

"Just curious. I heard Lord Bressen and Samhail talking about it and was concerned."

Raina looked at me like she wasn't buying it, but she didn't press the issue.

She finished helping me get ready, and I arrived in the dining room a while later to find Samhail and Bressen already at the table. Jerram was just leaving, and I stopped short when I saw him.

Nemesis damn me. I'd forgotten all about him.

"Good morning, Cyra," Jerram said cheerfully as I met him near the door. "It's a late morning for you, I see. You must have been tired from all that stimulation last night."

My eyes widened in panic, and I flushed down to my toes. He couldn't possibly know how I'd spent my night, could he? No, he'd be much angrier if he did.

"My lord?" I asked, hoping that playing dumb might buy me some time. "I'm not sure what you mean?"

"I was told you weren't feeling well and left the Priory early," Jerram said sympathetically. "I do hope you're feeling better. Such an erotic atmosphere can be overwhelming for someone who isn't used to open displays of carnality."

Behind Jerram, I saw both Bressen and Samhail trying – and failing miserably – to suppress smiles.

"Yes, my lord," I said quickly, trying to hide my embarrassment. "That was certainly much more…carnality than I'm used to. It'll take me some time to recover from yesterday's, uh, stimulation. Overstimulation really."

Jerram smiled and bent to kiss my hand. Behind him, Bressen and Samhail were almost doubled over in silent laughter in their chairs. I shot glares at them before plastering a smile back onto my face just as Jerram bobbed back up.

"Good day, Cyra," Jerram said. "Alas, I must attend to my lordly duties."

I inclined my head and waited for him to pass by me before heading to the sideboard to fill a plate for myself.

"Have I told you that you're both asses?" I asked without looking at the two men.

"Quite recently," Bressen said, and I could hear the grin in his voice. "Samhail, do you remember when that was?"

Samhail considered before he said, "I think I do. Wasn't it la-"

I spun around. "You will regret finishing that sentence," I hissed.

There was no one in the room with us, but guards stood outside the doors, and one of the kitchen staff could enter at any moment to remove or refill a tray. I wasn't willing to take the chance we'd be overheard.

Samhail smiled at what was clearly a threat I had no way to back up, but he said to Bressen, "On second thought, I don't recall when that was."

I still took it as a victory. I put my plate on the table and tried to sit with as much dignity as I could, but my grimace when my backside hit the chair negated any chance of that.

Bressen and Samhail both suppressed grins again, but they didn't say anything. I ignored them and attacked my food.

"You're not dressed for training," Samhail said to me as I took an unusual amount of pleasure in spearing a sausage with my fork.

I looked down at the lavender dress I'd chosen for the day. "No, I'm not."

"We have training in half an hour. Getting up late doesn't mean that we push back your training time."

"But I thought…I mean, we were up all night…," I tried to say as I leveled a pleading look at him.

Samhail's eyes twinkled with amusement. "What's your point?"

"My point is I'm tired and sore. I figured we could skip training today."

"Do you think you'll only need to fight when you're well-rested and feeling good?" Samhail asked. "When you're tired and sore is a perfect time to train. It'll teach you to fight through your pain and exhaustion."

I groaned and looked at Bressen. "Is he serious?"

Bressen smiled sadly at me. "Yes, unfortunately, and he's right. We don't always get to fight under ideal conditions. Sometimes it's a good idea to see what your body is capable of when you're not at your best."

I just stared at him.

"If it makes you feel any better," Bressen continued, "he'll likely drag me out for training this afternoon once he's done torturing you."

I looked at Samhail. His expression said that was a certainty.

Samhail stood and bussed his plate. "I'll see you in the training yard in half an hour," he told me. "You might want to eat quickly."

I aimed a rude gesture at his back as he left and then slumped in my chair.

"You'll be fine," Bressen said. "I can massage your sore muscles tonight if you want, and I'll make sure Samhail lets you rest tomorrow."

"I'm supposed to train with *you* tomorrow."

"Yes, and you'll probably find mental training even more exhausting than physical training."

"Perfect," I said with another sigh.

I ate quickly, then cleared my plate from the table and ran up to my room to change into my training leathers. I arrived in the yard with a minute to spare to find Samhail already there, stretching his muscles.

"Run," was all he said, and I began my warm-up jog.

"I said run!" he yelled at me, and I sped up. I'd never heard him use that tone with me, and it made me shudder a little.

Several laps later as I panted for breath, Samhail finally called me over. He had my wrist wraps ready, and I held out my hands to him.

"You'll do it yourself today," he growled and handed me the wraps.

I took them and began to wrap my wrists the way I'd seen him do. He watched me intently, and I wondered what was wrong all of a sudden. He was fine at breakfast, but something had changed since then. He seemed agitated now. I wanted to ask if he was upset about something that happened last night, but I didn't dare.

Thinking about last night was a mistake, in any case. A shiver of a different kind ran up my body as I remembered the feel of him inside me, of his tongue working its magic on my most sensitive parts…

"Let's go," Samhail snapped. "Start your punches." He held up the straw-stuffed pad we used for training, and I fell into the warm-up routine he'd taught me. My arms and legs were heavy, and I ached between my thighs from last night, but I tried to put as much power into my hits as I could.

"Left, left, right. Right elbow!" Samhail ordered, calling out attack combinations.

My body responded automatically, obeying each call without thinking. I hadn't been this close to Samhail since last night, and something about his presence – irritable as he was – still called to me.

I didn't see the blow coming, and stars burst in my vision as I found myself on the ground. Samhail had swung the pad at me, and in my rote mental state, I hadn't even registered the attack.

"Get up," Samhail ordered as he glared down at me.

I locked eyes with him as I picked myself up. "You're being an ass this morning. A real one this time."

"And you're not paying attention. You're distracted."

"I'm tired."

"Too bad. As I told you earlier, you need to be able to fight when you're tired. You need to be able to focus. You don't want to wait until your life is on the line to learn if you can defend yourself. Now go again."

He held the pad up, and I delivered the hits he called. The next time he swung the pad I was ready and ducked just in time. I didn't anticipate the backswing, though. As I came up from my duck, Samhail swung the pad back around, and I stood up right into it. I again found myself in a heap on the ground as I shook my head to clear it.

I scowled at Samhail as I rose again. He gave me a look that said if I didn't like his methods, I could go to the three hells.

I was getting angry.

We began again, but I was awake now, and I managed to avoid the pad the next several times he swung it, but only just barely. On his last swing, I lost my footing and stumbled forward into his chest.

Samhail's hand grasped my arm brutally as he leaned down to growl into my ear. "You're still not focusing. Pay attention!"

He paused, and his voice turned taunting. "You're still thinking about last night, aren't you. You're still thinking about how my tongue felt between your legs, about my cock buried inside you."

His mouth curled into a sneer, and my blood boiled in my veins. "I can still hear you screaming my name as I fucked your tight little-"

He didn't get to finish the sentence. I brought my hands up between us and shoved him with all my might as a scream ripped from somewhere deep and wounded within me.

I shouldn't have been able to move him, no matter how hard I shoved, but when my hands hit Samhail's chest, a force erupted from me, and he flew backward into the stone wall twenty feet behind us. The sound of the impact reverberated around the training yard, and Samhail grunted loudly as he hit the wall and landed in a heap on the ground. The wall cracked at the impact, and crumbles of stone rained down on Samhail where he lay on his stomach.

The look of shock on my face was nothing compared to the look of shock on Samhail's as he looked up at me from the ground. He seemed unhurt, despite how the wall looked, but I shouldn't have been able to do that to him. We stared at each other in silence for a long time before Samhail finally picked himself up off the ground and dusted the dirt off his leathers. He looked behind him at the wall, which would now need to be repaired, then back at me.

"How did you do that?" he asked.

I shook my head. "I didn't...I didn't do anything. I just pushed you...I..."

"Do it again," he said, and he came over to stand in front of me.

"But I didn't-"

"Do it again!" he ordered.

I brought my hands up as I had before and pushed him with all my strength. I might as well have been pushing on the stone wall itself. He didn't even sway.

"I said do it again."

I shook my head. "I can't!"

"Push me," he said, his voice menacingly quiet. "Push me like you did before, when I was reminding you how you writhed and moaned as I was licking you between your thighs."

My hands balled into fists as I glared at him, suddenly hating him.

He leaned down to growl in my ear. "Remember how you played the wanton for me and Bressen last night while we fucked you until you couldn't stand anymore? Do you remember how you begged us to take you?"

Tears welled in my eyes, and I pushed him again with every ounce of fury I could muster. Still he didn't budge. I waited to see what he would do, if he'd make me push him again, but he just looked at me.

"Let's switch to swords," he said finally, and he went to get them off the weapons rack.

"No," I said.

He ignored me and grabbed two swords, the small one I usually used and a slightly larger one for himself. He came back and held my sword out to me.

I shook my head. "No, I'm done."

"You're not done until I say you're done," he said and handed me the sword.

I took it from him but immediately tossed it across the yard into the dirt. "I said I'm done!"

He looked at me for a long moment then nodded.

"Yes," he said as he lifted his sword, ready to swing it down on my head. "You're definitely done."

Chapter 31

I threw myself out of the way of Samhail's blade just in time and landed hard on the ground. He was on me a second later, and I scrambled back from him as he slashed at me again and again, leaving no time for me to get to my feet.

He wasn't swinging hard, so I knew he wasn't trying to kill me. If he'd wanted me dead, one full blow from him, even with the blunted sword, would have cleaved me in two. The sword wouldn't cut me if I was slashed, though. Not badly anyway.

Regardless, if Samhail brought his sword down on my head as he'd tried to do, the blow would knock me out in the best case, or crack my skull open in the worst. If he did land a blow, even a softened one, I'd have a broken bone or at the very least a nasty bruise, so I struggled to stay out of his reach until I had an opportunity to do more.

That opportunity came moments later on his next upswing. As he raised the sword into the air to bring it down on me again, I lurched forward and dove between his legs. I found enough footing to somersault forward into a crouching position, and then I was up and running toward the sword I'd thrown away. I was almost there when a percussive force hit me from behind, and I went sprawling forward on my stomach into the dirt. I looked back to see Samhail's hand outstretched before him as he stalked toward me, and I realized he'd sent one of his magical forcefields at me.

"That's not fair! You said there was no magic during our trainings."

"You broke the rules first," he said as he advanced on me.

I looked back and saw my sword was still several feet away. I crawled back some more to bring it within reach, but I suddenly felt Samhail's huge form above me and turned back to face him. His sword began its downswing, and I reached out behind me as far as I could, praying I could somehow reach the sword that lay on the ground just feet from my hand.

Then my sword was there. I felt it in my palm, and my fingers closed around the hilt as I brought it up just in time to block Samhail's blow. The reverberation of steel on steel sent a shockwave of pain down my arms, and I cried out as I tried to hold my sword up under the force of his swing. His sword was inches from my forehead, but I'd somehow managed to grab my blade and thrust it between my head and his sword before the blow landed.

Samhail loomed above me, and my body tensed as I waited for him to swing again, but he stopped and lifted his sword off mine. I kept my own sword up, expecting another attack, but he just held out a hand to help me up. I glared at him for another several seconds before taking the hand he offered, and he pulled me effortlessly onto my feet in one swift motion.

Once standing, I dropped my sword and swung my hand, intending to slap him across the face as hard as I could. He caught the hand before it reached his cheek. I tried to swing my other hand, but he caught that one as well. I thought about bringing my knee up into his groin, but he gave me a look that warned me not to try.

I fought back the tears that welled in my eyes again. "What in the three hells was that?" I yelled at him.

He ignored my question. "How did you get the sword?"

"What? That's all you have to say to me?" I asked incredulously. I was beyond furious.

"How did you get the sword? This is important."

I tried to pull my hands out of his, and he released them. "I don't know," I said. "I just reached out for it. It must've been closer than I thought."

He shook his head. "The sword was five feet away. It flew into your hand."

"What?" He had to be mistaken.

"You summoned it."

"That's ridiculous. I don't have that power. I must have…called a wind to blow it to me."

He shook his head again. "The dirt would have kicked up if you'd used a wind. The only thing that moved was the sword."

"Then I don't know what to tell you," I said, throwing my hands up in frustration. "Are we done here now?" I asked when he just continued to look at me.

I turned to go before he answered, but he grabbed my arm to stop me. He stepped toward me so we were face-to-face.

"I didn't mean the things I said to you."

My face was taut as I looked up at him, and I didn't respond.

He went on, "I was just trying to-"

"I know what you were trying to do," I cut in. "That doesn't make it excusable."

"Maybe not, but someday you may thank me for it."

I scoffed. "I doubt it," I said, unable to mask the break in my voice.

I tried to leave again, but he didn't release my arm.

"Cyra," he said, and there was something raw in his voice that made me stop. "You were summoned here to the Citadel for a reason, but neither Bressen nor I have been able to figure out why. We know you're in danger here, though. I'm sorry if I hurt your feelings, but I won't apologize for trying to prepare you to face whatever's coming for you."

A chill ran down my back, and I swallowed hard. "I have to go," I said. I really did, or I was sure I'd start crying.

He nodded and let go of me. I pulled away from him and stalked back toward the door. As I reached the threshold, I heard a whoosh behind me and the booming beat of giant wings. When I looked back, Samhail was gone.

I entered the fortress and sank back against the wall onto the floor. I let out two retching sobs as I sat breathing hard for a few moments. I understood what Samhail had been trying to do, but knowing his intent hadn't made his words any easier. I'd enjoyed the night with him and Bressen, and having him throw it back in my face had hurt, even if I knew he didn't mean it.

My insides roiled as I replayed the training session over in my mind. Samhail was right. I'd been unfocused and distracted, and that was no good for me, as well as a waste of time for him. Maybe tomorrow I'd forgive him, but for now I needed to be angry with him.

I hit my fist on the stone floor in frustration but instantly regretted it as pain shot through my hand. I needed to release some energy, and I knew exactly where to go to do it. I didn't care if I was still walking gingerly from last night as it was. I hoisted myself off the floor, brushed the dirt off myself, and went to find Bressen.

I found him easily enough working in his study. The guards at his door didn't question why I was there, and I assumed Bressen told them I was always to be admitted if I ever came by. I knocked and entered when I heard Bressen's command to come in. I closed and locked the door behind me.

Bressen looked up from his desk when he heard the lock click, and his brows furrowed as he took in my dirty, disheveled state.

"Cyra," he said in alarm. "What in the three hells-"

He stopped when he noticed the look in my eyes and just stared at me. A moment later he began to clear the items he'd been working on off his desk. I strode across the room to him, and he met me on the side of the desk. I jumped into his arms, and he caught me easily as I wrapped my legs around his waist. He brought me back around the desk to sit me on the edge of it.

"Cyra, are you-" he tried to ask, but I silenced him with a finger on his lips.

"Shut up and fuck me," I rasped as I grabbed his neck and brought his mouth down brutally onto mine.

Bressen didn't need to be asked twice. He tore at my clothes as I ground myself against him. My tongue invaded his mouth, and he groaned against my lips as I reached down between us to free him from his pants.

"Fuck," he groaned as I wrapped a hand around his cock and stroked him hard.

351

I'd already removed my leather training vest before seeking him out, and Bressen ripped open my shirt to bare my breasts. I cried out as he took one into his hot, wet mouth, and I wound my fingers through his hair to hold him to me.

"Now," I breathed, and he stepped back far enough to help me yank my pants off.

A moment later he was inside me, thrusting hard. I locked one hand around his neck and gripped the desk with the other. My legs wrapped tighter around his hips to pull him into me. One of his arms anchored around my waist while his other braced us against the desk.

Spurred on by my anger, the strain of my imminent climax built quickly, and I cried out seconds later as it crashed over me in a wave of ecstasy. Colors swam in my vision for a moment before I went limp in Bressen's arms, the orgasm draining whatever energy I'd had left and leaving me fully spent.

It took Bressen several more thrusts to catch up to me, and then he groaned his own release into my neck and collapsed on top of me. We both lay there across the desk breathing hard and clinging to each other to keep from crumpling onto the floor.

"Gods above, Cyra," Bressen said, breathing hard into my neck. "To what do I owe the welcome interruption?"

I couldn't answer him yet. I only wrapped myself more tightly around him.

"Cyra?" he asked, trying to pull back. "Are you alright?"

I still couldn't find my voice, so I just reached up to run my fingers through a few locks of the night-black hair that clung to his temples by a fine sheen of sweat.

"Does...does this have anything to do with Samhail?" he asked.

I stiffened in his arms. "Samhail is not on my good side right now."

My tone made him pull back further so he could see my face.

"What happened? Are you alright? Did Samhail do something?"

I shook my head. "I'm fine. I'm just not very happy with Samhail at the moment."

Bressen withdrew from me and pulled me up to a sitting position. He reached up to gently touch the side of my head. "May I...?"

I knew what he wanted to do, and I didn't have the energy to resist. I nodded and felt the prickle at the base of my head as Bressen looked into my mind to see the training session. I only let him see bits and pieces of it, enough to see why I was upset with Samhail, and he was frowning deeply when he finished.

"Why did Samhail attack you?" he asked, hovering between confusion and anger.

"I was tired, and he was frustrated with me," I said. I'd left out the part where I pushed Samhail into the wall. I knew Bressen would likely have questions about that as Samhail had, and I didn't want to deal with them now. Samhail had been acting strangely before then anyway, so my words were true enough.

"I'll talk to Samhail," Bressen promised.

He stood back to let me off the desk, and we both righted our clothes. I knew Bressen would confront Samhail whether I wanted him to or not, so I just nodded as I pulled my pants back on.

"You'll need to change your clothes first," I said.

Bressen looked down at the dirt smudges that marred the stark black fabric of his usually impeccable ensemble. We hadn't fully undressed, and the dirt from my clothing had marked his in rather conspicuous places.

He smiled, and the dirt vanished. "That's what glamours are for."

I smiled back and left the room, pointedly not meeting the eyes of the guards as I left. I didn't want to know if they'd heard anything, and part of me didn't care either way.

Having expelled my frustration in Bressen's arms, I could now feel every ache and hurt in my body once again. My limbs were so heavy I could barely manage to pull myself up the stairs to my room.

Raina was there when I opened the door, and she gasped when she saw what state I was in. She rushed forward, and I nearly fell into her arms as she led me toward the bathing room.

"By the gods! What happened to you, my lady?"

"Training."

"What kind of training could you possibly need that would put you in such a state?"

I didn't answer, and Raina didn't push the issue. She helped me undress but cried out in horror when she saw the purple bruises starting to darken on my body. I just shook my head when she looked at me for an explanation.

I stepped into the bath and whimpered as I sank into the tub. The water was so hot I almost couldn't stand it at first, but once I settled in, I was grateful for its heat. I could already feel it easing my soreness.

Raina left to give me some private time to soak, and I closed my eyes to sink beneath the surface of the water. I held my breath as its warmth closed over my head, and my mind began to turn over Samhail's last words to me. I'd been brought to the Citadel for a reason, but that reason was still very unclear. The Triumvirate had been given plenty of time to figure it out, though. They couldn't keep me here forever. I needed to find a way to get home.

A pang of sadness shot through me as I thought of home. I hadn't seen my brothers for weeks, and I missed them. We exchanged notes occasionally, but we tried to use the message leaves sparingly.

I also wanted to get home to see how our newest vintage was coming. I wasn't sure how much longer the help Ursan sent from the other vineyard would be able to stay, so I needed to think about getting back soon. The vineyard was hard work, but I missed it.

At the same time, part of me rebelled at the thought of going home. Living in the grandeur of the Citadel had been nice for a time, but it wasn't the idea of losing my large, soft bed here that twisted my stomach. Rather, it was the thought of going back to an empty bed at home that tore at my heart.

I wanted Bressen, and not just in my bed. I'd known for days I was falling in love with him, but I didn't delude myself into thinking a future with him was possible. He was a Triumvirate Lord, and one of

354

the most powerful perimortals to ever exist. I was a winemaker from the outer lands. I might be sharing his bed now, but someone new would be sharing it in the future, maybe a few months from now when I was gone. I closed my eyes tighter at the thought.

Hands plunged into the water and pulled me up by my shoulders.

"My lady!" Raina screamed. "Cyra! By the Protector, please don't be dead!"

My eyes fluttered open, and Raina cried out in relief.

I frowned as I realized I'd been lost in thought underwater for what seemed like minutes, but my lungs weren't burning for air.

"Don't frighten me like that again, my lady!" Raina cried. "Are you alright?"

I nodded. "I'm fine. How long was I underwater?"

"I don't know. I came in a few minutes ago and was getting things ready, but I looked over and realized you'd been under the water the whole time. You weren't moving, and I thought you'd drowned!"

Raina looked like she was a moment away from panicking again, and I put a reassuring hand over hers. "I'm fine. I was just...thinking."

Raina took a deep breath and pushed it out in a rush. "Please do your thinking above the water in the future, my lady. My heart can't handle your underwater thinking. How in the world did you manage to hold your breath so long?"

I remembered trying to hold my breath once when Brix's attempt at a cooking fire went awry and the house filled with smoke. I'd only made it thirty seconds as I opened windows and tried to douse the fire before I'd had to go out into the yard and refill my lungs with air.

I was sure I'd been under the water more than a minute this time, but my lungs didn't protest in the slightest. I might have sat underwater for several minutes more if Raina hadn't pulled me out.

I smiled wryly to myself. No, sitting underwater for several minutes at a time was apparently no problem at all. Rather, it was the thought of leaving Bressen that made it hard for me to breathe.

Chapter 32

As promised, Bressen spent an hour massaging my sore muscles when he came to my room that night. He took care to avoid pressing on my bruises, but that was difficult since they were everywhere.

Bressen had his own bruises I realized when I helped him undress later. He'd gone to train with Samhail, and the session had turned more brutal than normal.

"I was irritated with Samhail because of how his training with you went, so I tried to deliver a little retribution for you," he told me when I asked what happened.

I raised an eyebrow, and he shook his head.

"It didn't go quite as planned," he admitted.

"So you...?"

"We beat the hell out of each other for an hour."

I ran my hand gently over a particularly purple bruise on his chest. "Did the two of you talk at any point?"

"Yes, afterwards." He traced the curve of my collarbone. "Samhail cares for you."

I blinked at him. "Is that supposed to be an excuse?"

"No, it's not an excuse, but it is an explanation."

I gave him a look that said they were one and the same in my book.

"Gargoyles don't do caring well," he said. "The concern Samhail feels for you is new to him, and he doesn't know how to deal with it. I can handle Samhail's belligerence when he's worried or frustrated because I've had a century of practice dealing with him, but he doesn't know how to control his emotions around you yet, and I wouldn't expect you to know how to deal with his...more aggressive side."

I looked at Bressen's bruises and raised a brow.

"We've done worse to each other," he said, following my gaze. "In any case, I gently suggested to Samhail...with my fists, that maybe he crossed a line with you today."

"With your fists?" I asked in amusement.

Bressen shrugged. "He argued back with his own, but I think we came to an understanding. The point is, Samhail sees you as very vulnerable, and that worries him. He wants to make you less vulnerable, so he…overcompensated."

"He told you all this?"

Bressen shook his head. "I convinced him to let me read his mind after we fought, and I saw it there. I doubt Samhail actually understands what he's feeling yet."

I exhaled a long breath and ran my hand down Bressen's chest, stopping only when I got to the hard ripples of his stomach muscles, some purple with bruises.

I moved my hand lower, and Bressen groaned. "Both of us are in bad shape right now," he breathed. "Are you sure you want to do that?"

I smiled sweetly at him. "We don't always get to make love under ideal conditions. Sometimes it's a good idea to see what your body is capable of when you're not at your best."

Bressen's eyes flashed hotly. "That's good advice. Where did you hear it?"

"Oh, it's just something I always say."

I shrieked and then giggled as he rolled over on top of me.

"Let's see what your body is capable of then, my lady," he whispered into my ear.

Bressen spent the rest of the night making love to me, slowly and tenderly, in a way that made me want to cry. As usual, he slipped out of my room just before sunrise to return to his own, and I felt the emptiness in the bed like a yawning void.

I slept fitfully after that, and a few hours later, Raina bustled in and swept the curtains open to fill the room with sunlight. I'd cursed her to each of the Trinity, but she only pulled the covers off and coaxed me to a sitting position. She didn't seem surprised to find me naked, and I wondered again just how much she knew.

"Your bruises look better this morning," she remarked brightly.

I looked down and found my bruises had indeed faded a lot.

"Drink up," Raina said, handing me my morning tea.

I took the cup from her and sipped the hot, sweet liquid. I could feel its warmth slide all the way down my throat.

"Mmm. I love this tea," I said to Raina as I took another sip. "I've been meaning to ask you what's in it."

"Just a little of this and that. I don't know the exact recipe, but there's dried fruit, tea leaves, some lemon verbena, ginger root…"

"You added something a little while ago that made the tea pink and gave it some extra flavor. What is that?"

"Oh, that's the turrow berries."

I stopped mid-sip. "Turrow berries?"

"Of course. We don't want any…unexpected consequences during your stay," she said, holding up a gray gown with accents of deep blue for my inspection.

"The berries, they're a contraceptive," I said, remembering.

I'd been sleeping with Bressen for more than a week without any thoughts of preventing pregnancy even crossing my mind. Perimortals weren't as fertile as mortals, which was part of the reason there were comparatively few of us, but that didn't excuse the utter lack of thought I'd given the issue. I'd used stoneseed root back in Fernweh with Eddin, but I hadn't been taking anything here. The effects of the root were longer-lasting than that of other contraceptives, like the turrow berries, which required one to take them daily, so I was still safe in theory. Nevertheless, it was something I should've been paying attention to for my own sake.

"I thought you knew it was turrow berries and what they were used for," Raina said carefully.

I hadn't been thinking about preventing pregnancy, but someone else clearly was. For that matter, the berries seemed to settle the question of how much Raina knew about my nightly activities.

Raina spoke of consequences, but I didn't believe for one minute that I was the person being protected from those consequences. Bressen was. Whoever decided to add the berries to my tea was protecting him from getting me pregnant and whatever scandal that might cause. Perhaps Bressen himself had even ordered it.

Samhail had thrown my wantonness in my face during our training yesterday, but I'd known somewhere deep in my heart he hadn't meant it. I thought he'd only been trying to motivate me, but maybe my anger came from the truth of my situation. I was being given the berries so I could essentially be Bressen's mistress, his whore.

A knot twisted in my stomach, and I thought I might vomit, but I chugged down the last of the tea in two gulps and fought the lurching in my gut. Raina was right about one thing. I couldn't afford any unexpected consequences right now.

I walked into the central dining room twenty minutes later to find Bressen, Samhail, Jerram, and Ursan all there. I almost turned around and left, but before I could move, Jerram noticed me and called out a greeting. Discussion at the table ceased instantly, and I wondered if they'd just been talking about me.

"Come, sit!" Jerram said as he got up. "I'll fix you a plate."

"I can fix-"

"Nonsense," he said. "You look exhausted. Come and sit."

Jerram pulled out a chair for me next to him and I sat down. He pushed the chair in for me, and my stomach crunched against the table so that I had to push the chair out again after he left to get my plate.

I'd decided a while ago that I much preferred the short-tempered, ever-annoyed Jerram I'd first met when I arrived here to the overly cheerful and unhelpfully helpful one that was now the norm. Whether Jerram had decided that being nice to me was more likely to ensure his survival if the vision ever came to pass, or whether he was hoping to gain my confidence to get information out of me, I had no idea, but I couldn't believe he didn't think I'd notice such a dramatic shift in how he treated me.

Ursan sat in his usual spot at the head of the table, and he wished me a good morning between bites of his toast. Bressen and Samhail sat across from me, but neither acknowledged my presence. I knew it was a ruse to keep Jerram and Ursan from suspecting how close I was to both of them, but I couldn't help feeling hurt after what I'd just learned from Raina. My heart twinged, and Bressen glanced at me.

Jerram returned from the sideboard and set a plate before me. It was piled high with foods I never would have selected for myself, but I thanked him and grabbed my fork to dig through the pile to find something that wouldn't make me feel sicker than I already did.

"I should be getting along now. The three of us will be meeting later anyway," Ursan said, nodding to Bressen and Jerram. "I need to go check on Glenora. She hasn't been feeling well the last few days."

"I should be going now as well," Jerram said. He took my hand and kissed it. "I believe you still owe me a walk in my garden, Cyra. Can I call in that debt this morning?"

I stiffened. Spending time with Jerram was the last thing I wanted to do right now, but I'd already put him off for too many things by this point. I resisted the urge to look at Bressen and nodded. "That would be lovely."

"Wonderful. Shall we say half past ten then?"

I forced a smile onto my face and nodded.

Jerram smiled back and followed Ursan out. I noticed they both left their plates on the table for the servants to clean up instead of bringing them over to the bin near the kitchen.

"What's wrong?" Bressen asked me as soon as they were gone.

"It's nothing." I speared a piece of cheese and shoved it in my mouth. "Homesickness." It wasn't entirely a lie.

Bressen looked at me for a while then nodded. "If you're up to it this morning, we can start your mind shielding lessons."

"I need her first," Samhail said before I could answer.

My eyes whipped up to his. I wasn't sure I was ready to be alone with Samhail again yet.

A look passed between the two men before Bressen nodded.

"Keep me posted," he said.

I turned to him, hurt that he hadn't even asked me if I was willing to do whatever Samhail needed me to do.

His face softened when he looked at me. "Please go with Samhail. He's assured me this is important, and we'd both appreciate your cooperation."

It was as close to a request as I was going to get, so I sighed and nodded my agreement. I tried to poke through my food again to find something I wouldn't mind eating, but I finally gave up and brought my plate to the bin near the kitchen. I hated to waste food, but I couldn't bring myself to eat any of it. I went to the sideboard and pulled a few things onto a new plate before returning to my seat.

"Unfortunately, I have work to get done as well," Bressen said as he rose.

He put his dish in the bin and then came over to crouch down next to me. His obfuscation glamour fell over us as he kissed me gently. I savored the feel of his lips on mine despite myself. I wondered how I was going to tell him we needed to sleep in our own rooms tonight, not just because the lack of sleep was killing me, but because I couldn't accept the idea of only being his mistress. I needed more than that.

"Cyra? Is something wrong?" Bressen asked, frowning.

I was surprised he hadn't seen the thoughts in my head, but then I felt it, that barrier between our minds. I didn't know how I'd put it up, but it was there, blocking him out.

I forced a smile onto my face. "Just tired," I said.

He looked unconvinced but nodded. "I'll see you later this morning. Please do whatever Samhail asks you to do."

I nodded and felt the glamour lift as Bressen walked away.

"So what do you need from me?" I asked Samhail when Bressen was gone.

"Finish your breakfast, then we'll go to the library. We need some privacy."

My eyes narrowed, but he waved a hand. "Not that kind of privacy," he said with a wry smile. "Do you think I'd be dumb enough to call on you for something like that after the way we left things yesterday?"

My expression told him I did indeed think he was that dumb.

He chuckled. "Fair enough. I'm told I handled things badly, so I'd like to throw myself on your mercy and humbly beg your forgiveness."

I crossed my arms over my chest. "That was a rather sarcastic-sounding apology."

"Gargoyles don't do apologies well."

"It seems there are a lot of things gargoyles don't do well," I snapped at him.

Surprisingly, the barb hit. Samhail winced and nodded, and I regretted my words instantly. He was trying to make up with me, and I wasn't making it easy for him.

"Although," I conceded softly, as I turned my eyes back to my plate, "I have to admit there are *some* things they do *very* well."

I was sure I was blushing bright red, and I looked up when Samhail didn't say anything. He had a wicked grin on his face.

When we finished breakfast a few minutes later, I followed him down the hall to the library in Bressen's wing of the Citadel. I assumed we'd go to the Citadel's main library, but Samhail said we needed as few prying eyes as possible.

He opened the door for me when we arrived and then followed me inside. He closed it and turned a key in the lock. The click of the lock sent a shiver of panic through me. After yesterday, I wasn't thrilled about being locked in a room with him. We'd buried the hatchet at breakfast, but I still didn't fully trust he wasn't going to attack me.

My apprehension grew as Samhail walked toward me, but he only took my hand and placed the key in it. "You can leave whenever you want," he said.

I nodded and clutched the key in my hand.

Samhail turned to walk across the room to one of the bookshelves.

He pulled a book off the shelf at random and placed it on a table near one of the large windows. Then he walked a few feet away and positioned himself off to the side between me and the table.

"Summon the book," he said.

I froze.

"Please," he added.

"I don't know how," I said, afraid to make him angry again.

"What did you do or feel when you summoned the sword yesterday?"

I blinked at him. "What did I feel? I felt panic. I was on the ground with no weapon and a giant gargoyle bearing down on me."

He winced again at my tone but nodded. "Try to think beyond the panic. What else was going through your mind?"

I sighed and tried to think back to that moment. There had been fear, panic, terror and all the other synonyms for that emotion, but there was also something else. What was it?

Another memory flashed in my mind of the day on the vineyard with the bear. I remembered thinking I had to do something, or I was going to die. No, the thought was there that I *had* to do something, but so was the thought that I *could* do something. It wasn't just self-preservation, but a strange confidence somewhere deep inside me that I could save myself.

I hadn't recognized it at the time, but that feeling was there again yesterday. I hadn't just hoped I could reach the sword. I somehow knew I could. I'd started to move yesterday to block Samhail's blow before my own sword had even been in my hand because I knew it would be there when I needed it.

"You've got something," Samhail observed.

"Maybe."

"Then summon the book."

I held out a hand and tried to well that confidence up inside me again. I concentrated hard, but the book didn't move, and I dropped my arm with a sigh.

"Try again."

"Tell me how," I said. "You know how to summon. How do you do it?"

Samhail crossed his arms over his chest and thought for a moment.

"You need to picture exactly what you want to happen," he said finally, "and you need to know that it's going to happen."

I'd already realized the latter. Now I just needed to visualize.

I held out my hand again and imagined the book flying into it. I could see it clearly, but I didn't yet believe that it would come to me.

The sword had come, I reminded myself. It came when I needed it. This book would come.

Across the room, the book began to vibrate on the table. I concentrated harder, but it only trembled in place. Samhail moved slowly toward me and stopped a few feet from me. The book shuddered wildly on the table, and I felt my confidence climb.

Samhail took a few more steps closer to me, and the book rose into the air, but it stubbornly refused to begin moving across the room. I could feel it now, though, and I knew it was only a matter of time.

Samhail stepped to my side, and across the room, the book began to move. It floated slowly but surely toward my hand.

When the book was about halfway to me, Samhail reached up to lay a large hand on my shoulder, his fingers grazing the bare skin near the neckline of my dress.

As soon as he touched me, several things happened all at once. The book ceased its lazy crawl across the room and shot straight into my hand. It wasn't the only one, though. All around us, books flew off the shelves heading straight for us, and Samhail pushed down hard on my shoulder. My knees buckled under the force of his shove, and I was thrown to the ground as a deafening din of rustling and thudding echoed around the library. I felt Samhail's huge body cover mine as the room vibrated around us from books hitting the floor. I waited to feel the crushing weight of the tomes on top of us, but it never came.

When there was silence again, I opened my eyes. I was huddled on the floor with the book in one hand and the key to the library in the other. Samhail crouched over me, his body shielding me from the onslaught of books that had come rushing toward us when he'd touched me. His wings were out, and he'd wrapped them around us like a cocoon.

"Are you alright?" he asked from where he hunched over me.

I looked up at him. "Yes. What in the three hells happened?"

Samhail stood up with a grunt, and books slid off his back and wings. All around us, the library stood in devastation. We were half-buried in a pile of books, and books lay scattered everywhere around us as well. Every shelf was bare.

Samhail shook his wings to dislodge a few books that still hung onto them, and I noticed that the wings looked like stone instead of his usual leathery ones. A moment later, the stone coating of the wings seemed to dissolve, leaving the ones I was used to, and Samhail pulled them back into his body. He took my hands and helped me to my feet. We stood in a small well of open space that Samhail had created when the shelves collapsed.

"I hope you know how to reshelve all these books," I said to Samhail.

He exhaled deeply and ran a hand through his long, white hair. "That's the least of our worries right now."

"Why? What does this mean?"

"It means you're in a lot more danger than we thought."

Chapter 33

I hurried to keep up with Samhail's long strides as I followed him toward Bressen's study. I'd tried twice to ask what he meant by his last comment, but he just told me he'd explain when we found Bressen.

We arrived at the study moments later and entered after Samhail knocked. Bressen glanced up briefly from what he was doing to acknowledge us. "Done already?"

"She's a syphon," was all Samhail said after he closed the door behind me.

Bressen's head snapped up, and he and Samhail exchanged looks.

Bressen came around his desk to cross his arms and lean against the front of it, and I tried to keep myself from thinking about what we'd done on that desk yesterday.

"Impossible," he said.

"Extremely rare," Samhail corrected, "but not impossible."

"You're sure?" Bressen asked.

"Reasonably certain. There hasn't been a known syphon in close to four hundred years, so the details on them are incomplete at best, but my experiment suggests I'm right."

At the mention of his experiment, I looked down and realized I was still holding the book I'd summoned. The title read, *A Guide to Human Anatomy*. I blushed furiously and put the book on a shelf near the door.

"But her powers suggest she's an elemental," Bressen was saying as I turned my attention back to the two men.

Samhail shook his head. "Elemental powers are not inconsistent with a syphon. I went to the Priory late last night and consulted a few of their texts. I didn't want to risk asking any of the priests or priestesses, though, so we'll need to double check."

Bressen nodded, urging Samhail to continue.

"Elemental powers are often the earliest ones to develop in

syphons," Samhail explained. "The four basic world elements have an inherent power of their own. That power is all around us, all the time, and elementals have an affinity for harnessing that power and using it. Weaker elementals can wield one element, while stronger ones can wield them all but excel in wielding one element above the others. Syphons, however, can usually wield them all equally well."

"And she can wield them all equally well?"

"That's unclear at the moment," Samhail said, "but what is clear is that she has powers beyond elemental ones, and that's extremely rare in elementals."

Their two-way conversation was beginning to annoy me.

"*She* is standing right here," I interrupted, "and *she* would appreciate it if you didn't speak about her as if she's not in the room."

Both men had the decency to look contrite.

"Now that I have your attention," I said, standing so the three of us stood in a loose circle, "can we back up a bit? What's a syphon?"

Bressen uncrossed his arms and braced his hands on the desk. "A syphon is a perimortal who can draw power from anywhere around them that power exists. They're quite simply some of the most formidable perimortals to ever exist, but because of that, they're also the most feared...and the most hunted."

"Hunted? Why?"

Bressen sighed. "We live in a world where those with some power always fear and envy those with more power. Samhail and I are both constant targets because of the degree of our powers. Samhail is challenged regularly by lesser warriors who want to make a name for themselves by defeating him in battle. He enjoys an exalted position at the Citadel because he's the best, but that position comes at a price."

I looked to Samhail for confirmation, and he nodded once.

"And you?" I asked Bressen.

He chuckled. "I've lost count of the assassination attempts I've faced, both overt and covert. Luckily, being able to read minds means I can usually see them coming."

Alarm spread through me at the thought that Bressen was constantly in danger of being killed simply because he was powerful. Then the secondary implication hit me.

"So that means…" I said.

"It means," Bressen said gently, "if you're a syphon, the threat to your life is greater than Samhail and I put together."

I took a moment to let that sink in. "*If* I'm a syphon?"

Bressen looked to Samhail. "You have evidence?"

Samhail nodded. "I started to suspect something yesterday when we were training. As you may recall, I said some…offensive things to Cyra during our session."

I scoffed.

"And she pushed me into the wall," Samhail finished.

Bressen looked confused. "Cyra…pushed you into the wall?"

Apparently Samhail hadn't told Bressen about the wall either.

"Yes, I went flying across the yard into the far wall, and it cracked."

Bressen's eyes went wide. "Is *that* the reason I have the Citadel's stonemasons breathing down my neck about the giant dent in the training yard wall?"

Samhail nodded.

Bressen looked at me, and I shrugged. "He deserved it."

Bressen blinked and looked between us. "Wind. She blew you into the wall."

Samhail shook his head.

"Are you sure it wasn't just a small hurricane?" Bressen pressed.

Samhail grunted and undid a few buttons at the collar of his shirt before opening it to reveal the top of his broad chest. In the center, among other bruises Bressen had likely given him, were two small and faint but distinctly hand-shaped bruises.

My mouth fell open. I'd bruised Samhail. I'd actually bruised him.

Somehow that made me feel better, and I almost started to laugh but thought better of it.

Bressen had no such reservations. He let out a bark of laughter and pushed himself off the desk to take a closer look at Samhail's chest. Samhail gave him a dark look that said he didn't find this funny, but he allowed Bressen a quick look before he yanked his shirt closed again and re-buttoned it. I managed to close my mouth and was trying to suppress a smile behind one hand when Bressen spoke again.

"So you think Cyra used your forcefield magic to throw you into the wall?" Bressen asked, still smiling, and Samhail nodded. "That is compelling evidence, but I assume you have more than that?"

"We were also training with swords, and Cyra's sword was thrown across the yard at one point," Samhail went on.

I quirked a brow at his creative retelling of our training session, but he ignored me.

"I was advancing on her. She was on the ground and still several feet away from her sword, but she managed to summon it to her."

Bressen went serious again. "You're sure that wasn't wind either?"

"Cyra suggested the same thing," Samhail said, finally looking at me, "but I know what I saw. Moving the sword with wind would have kicked up a lot of dirt, but there was none. The sword was the only thing that moved."

"So that was yesterday," Bressen said. "You said this morning you had a theory to test."

"Cyra and I just came from your library. I put a book on one of the tables and asked her to summon it."

"And the book came to her?"

"Not at first," Samhail said. "At first, she was only able to make it shudder around on the table. I was across the room at the time, so I started moving closer to her. The closer I got, the more the book moved. It started to come toward her when I was right next to her. Then, out of curiosity, I put my hand on her shoulder."

Samhail paused, and Bressen gave him a look that said, *And?*

"The entire library collapsed on top of us," Samhail finished.

Bressen looked at me in alarm. "What do you mean it collapsed on top of you?" He was still looking at me, but the question was directed at Samhail.

"I mean that the moment I touched her, every book in the room came shooting straight for us. We were buried under a pile of them."

Bressen stared at us.

"You should get your librarian over there," Samhail added. "He has his work cut out for him."

Bressen rubbed his eyes with one hand. "When you touched her," he asked Samhail carefully, "do you think maybe it was you who caused the summoning?"

"I took pains to make sure all I did was touch her, but this also tracks with what I read last night."

"How so?" Bressen asked.

"In their early training, syphons aren't accustomed to drawing power from others, so they're often most effective when touching their source. One of the texts suggested a syphon must touch their source to first claim the power, then they can wield it thereafter. That being said, particularly formidable or tricky powers may require them to keep contact with their source for longer as they learn the power. Another text suggested that, as syphons become more powerful and more practiced, they can draw power from farther away. In theory, a truly powerful syphon need only be in the general vicinity of a source to use their power."

"How was she able to summon the sword in training yesterday if she needed to be touching you?" Bressen asked, his brow furrowed.

"As with most perimortals, surges of emotion, especially fear or anger, can sometimes amplify a person's powers. Cyra's heightened emotional state at the time probably let her bypass the need to touch me. That's just a theory, though. In general, the texts at the Priory had very little information on syphons, and half of what they did say was contradictory. I couldn't draw any definite conclusions about how syphoning powers work."

Bressen exhaled deeply. "It would explain a lot," he mused. He turned to me. "You live in the outer lands. There are very few

370

perimortals out there, so the only powers you've been able to draw from are the elements. It would explain why those were the only abilities you showed until now."

"There's a way to test the theory more fully," Samhail ventured.

Bressen cocked his head. "Do share."

"Let her try to read my mind. See if she can syphon *your* power."

Bressen blew out another heavy breath. "That's not a good idea."

"Why not?" I asked. "Wouldn't that help confirm whether or not I'm a syphon?"

"Mind powers can be extremely thorny," Bressen said. "If you tried to syphon my power and something went wrong, you could end up going mad. Permanently."

I swallowed. "Okay, so we can put that on the list of drawbacks."

"On the other hand," Samhail said, "it's the best way to confirm you're a syphon. We can't risk finding someone else for you to practice on. If we're right, the more people who know you're a syphon, the more danger you're in."

"I don't understand," I said. "If I'm this hugely powerful syphon, isn't that a good thing? If I can draw on anyone's power, don't I have a better chance of protecting myself?"

"In some ways, yes," Bressen said, "but it also makes you a target, and it makes everyone you care about a target as well."

I felt the color drain from my face. "My brothers."

Bressen nodded. "If someone got to your brothers, they could make you do whatever they wanted. Not to mention, there are ultimately ways to limit your powers or control them. If someone found a way to control you, they could turn you into their own personal weapon."

I suddenly needed to sit down, and both Samhail and Bressen lunged for me as I swayed. I caught the back of a chair next to Bressen's desk and steadied myself.

"Speaking of her brothers," Samhail said to Bressen, "should we go get them? Put them somewhere safe?"

371

Bressen shook his head. "Not yet. The outer lands are in Ursan's territory. Going in to get them without his permission would be considered an invasion. It's a line I don't want to cross yet, and we can't risk letting Ursan know why we want them. Trying to move them only tips our hand. For now, we have to assume only the three of us know what Cyra is."

"*Do* we know what she is?" Samhail asked. "For certain?"

"Let me try to read Samhail's mind," I said.

Bressen shook his head. "It's too dangerous."

"It's not your decision. If Samhail is willing, then the decision is between me and him."

"That's not entirely true," Samhail said. "You've never done this before, so Bressen may need to touch you for it to work."

We both looked at Bressen.

He glanced between us and dragged a hand through his hair. "This is not the kind of threesome I'd hoped to be invited to today, but fine."

Samhail grinned, and I rolled my eyes.

"Okay, so how does it work?" I asked.

Bressen sighed and came over to stand behind me. "In order to read Samhail's mind, he'll need to lower his mental shields. I'm going to put up all of mine so we're sure I'm not reading his mind for you. I'll let you try it by yourself first. If you can't do it, I'll touch you to see if it helps."

I nodded. "Okay. Is there a trick to it? What do I need to do?"

"You need to merge your consciousness with the person whose mind you want to read," Bressen said. "I'm not sure how to explain it. It's like looking through their eyes and your own at the same time."

I looked at Samhail. "Well, I've always wanted to be taller."

Samhail smirked at me, but Bressen growled.

"Be serious," he said to me. "What we're about to do is very dangerous."

"I'm sorry. I promise."

"Let's start simple," Bressen said. "Samhail, put an image in your mind. No words, just something specific Cyra will be able to see clearly if she's able to enter your thoughts."

Samhail nodded. "I have something."

"Alright, on the count of three, Samhail will drop his mental shields, I'll reinforce mine, and you," he tipped his head to me, "you'll try to see the image Samhail has in his mind. I'll give you about ten seconds to try, and if you don't have it, I'll touch you. Do you understand?"

"Yes."

"Okay. One…two…three."

I closed my eyes and let my mind reach toward Samhail's. I imagined the world from his perspective and thought about what image he might choose to show me. A large gray mass floated into my head, but I couldn't tell what it was, or even if it was something other than a fog in my own mind. I focused my thoughts and willed the gray fog to take shape. At times it seemed as if it was starting to form a silhouette, but then the fog spread again into a formless void.

"Do you have it?" Bressen asked. His voice was close to my ear.

I shook my head. "There's something there, but I can't bring it into focus."

Bressen's hands rested gently on my shoulders. "Does this help?"

I saw a flash of something almost recognizable, but then it was gone. The gray blob still refused to take shape.

I furrowed my brow. "A little, but it's still…just out of reach."

"I think I touched her skin directly," Samhail offered, and Bressen moved his hands higher up on my shoulders so they brushed the bare skin of my neck.

I jolted and gasped as the fog immediately converged and manifested into a huge beast. It was dark gray, with enormous, bat-like wings, and its skin seemed to be made of stone. The beast stood upright on animal-like legs that ended in massive, clawed feet while a tail lashed out behind it. Giant horns curled from either side of its head, and its eyes glowed with an unnatural blue light. A forked tongue flicked between large fangs that extended from both the top and bottom jaws of its huge mouth.

My mind started to retreat, and the glowing blue eyes turned to me as the beast opened its maw wide to let out a roar that set every nerve in my body screaming. I lurched backward into Bressen's chest, and his arms wrapped around me, holding me up. I was breathing hard as I tried to banish the image of the beast that now lingered in my head.

"I saw…" I said, trying to calm myself enough to find my voice.

"You saw me," Samhail said quietly.

I looked up at him, still breathing hard. I knew what he was saying.

"You saw what I look like in my gargoyle form," he clarified.

I knew it for the truth it was and nodded. "Yes."

Bressen grunted. "I told you to show her something memorable, not give her nightmares."

Samhail shrugged. "I actually think that's my better side."

"For the record," I breathed, "that side is not invited into bed."

Both Samhail and Bressen burst out laughing.

Chapter 34

Our levity died quickly as Bressen, Samhail, and I realized our experiment had yielded fairly solid evidence that I was a syphon. Not only was my own life in danger, but all those I cared for were at risk unless we could keep my powers a secret. That Jerram, Ursan, and some of those in the Priory were actively trying to figure out why I was at the center of an imminent threat to the Triumvirate didn't help.

"We need to get Ursan and Jerram to send you home," Bressen said running a hand through his dark hair again.

"No!" The word was out of my mouth before I could stop it, and both Bressen and Samhail looked at me questioningly.

"I...I mean, I should be more powerful here in Callanus, shouldn't I? I'll have more powers to draw on here. Isn't it better for me to stay?"

It was a poor explanation, but the thought of leaving Bressen was abhorrent to me. For weeks I'd wanted nothing more than to go back to my quiet life with my brothers on the vineyard, but now I couldn't bear the thought of going home if it meant never seeing him again. I couldn't help but think that, if given enough time, maybe I could be more to him than just someone to warm his bed.

Bressen looked at me seriously, and I wondered if he could see why I really didn't want to go. There seemed to be understanding on Samhail's face as well.

"Cyra, you're not safe here," Bressen said gently.

I wanted to tell him I didn't care, that the safest place I knew was right next to him, but this wasn't a discussion I wanted to have in front of Samhail.

"I'm not sure I'm any safer in Fernweh," I said instead. "If what you say is true, I'll be hunted anywhere I go."

Bressen's face darkened. "We can discuss this more later. For now, we just need to keep you away from Ursan and Jerram."

"I still don't understand," I said. "What does this have to do with

Jemma's vision? Can't I just convince them I have no intention of harming them?"

"Men like Ursan and Jerram will never understand how someone with a lot of power could pass up the chance to have more," Bressen said. "As it is, they live in constant fear that I'll overthrow them someday and take all of Thasia for myself. They don't believe I'm perfectly content overseeing Hiraeth and being one of the Triumvirate. If they find out you can wield not only my powers, but the powers of anyone around you, their paranoia would be overwhelming. They'd never stop trying to kill you."

Dread pooled in my stomach, but something Bressen said stuck in my mind. I could wield his powers now. Did that mean I could kill people just by thinking it, as he could? My mind was momentarily dizzy at the thought, but just as quickly, the heavy responsibility of such a power brought me crashing back to reality. The potential consequences of that ability were not something I wanted to consider.

"There's no way to convince them Jemma's vision won't come true?" I asked.

Bressen and Samhail exchanged glances, and Bressen looked back at me sadly. "I'm afraid Ursan and Jerram have all-but-guaranteed the seer's vision *will* come true."

I furrowed my brows. "Why? How?"

"It's been my experience," Bressen said, "that visions tend to be self-fulfilling. Once the person in a vision learns something bad will happen to them, they almost inevitably take steps to try and prevent it. In every case I've seen, it's those steps that actually set the events of the vision in motion."

"I don't understand," I said, trying to wrap my mind around it all.

"What would you be doing now if you weren't here?" he asked.

I thought for a moment. "Helping my brothers on the vineyard."

"Exactly," Bressen said. "You'd be home doing what you normally do at this time of year. You'd use your powers to light fires and water crops, but not for much else. In short, you'd still be in Fernweh, and the only powers you'd have access to would be elemental ones. When Ursan and Jerram brought you here, however, they inadvertently gifted you with the means of their own destruction. They sent Samhail to get you, and you syphoned his powers. Then they brought you before us, allowing you to syphon not only my powers, but likely theirs as well."

"But why would I destroy them?" I asked. "Having the means to destroy them and actually wanting to do so are two different things."

"True," Bressen said, "but if they decide you're a threat and come after you, will you defend yourself? Will you kill in self-defense, as you did when the bear attacked you?"

My face went white as I realized the truth of his words. Bressen and Samhail both stepped toward me, but I held up a hand and swallowed as I felt bile rise in my throat.

"So I'm destined to kill them?" I asked. Taking the bear's life had been difficult enough. I couldn't imagine taking a human life.

"Not necessarily. That's only one way this might play out," Bressen said. "Remember that we're also not sure they're the two lords destroyed in the end. The seer couldn't tell us which of us was left standing."

The implication was a gut punch, and if there'd been any color still left in my face, it was now gone. I remembered all the times I'd told the lords how ridiculous it was to think I could destroy them. At the very least, I'd assumed my powers weren't a threat to Bressen, but I had his powers now, or at least the potential to wield them. It was possible I could destroy him.

I'd never seriously considered that Bressen might not be the lord left standing in the end, but now every horrible, stomach-clenching possibility ran through my mind. What if Jerram somehow killed Bressen, and I, in turn, killed Jerram, leaving only Ursan. Because I would attack anyone who hurt Bressen, I realized.

"What time is it?" I asked, suddenly remembering my promise to Jerram.

"About a quarter past ten," Bressen said. "Why?"

"I need to meet Jerram for a walk in his garden."

Red flashed in Bressen's eyes. "No. Absolutely not."

"I have to."

"No, you don't. Even if we weren't trying to hide that you're a syphon, you've seen firsthand what Jerram is willing to do to get what he wants. We can't trust him."

"And what will he think if I cancel on him?"

I suddenly wanted to go see Jerram. If he was planning anything that might harm Bressen, I needed to find out. I could use my newly acquired mind-reading powers on him.

"I don't care what he thinks. You shouldn't be alone with him," Bressen said.

"I've put him off too many times already," I argued. "He asked me for this walk weeks ago, and then I avoided him at the Harmilan. If I try to get out of seeing him again, he's going to get suspicious, and that doesn't help us either. Let me meet him and be done with it."

I looked to Samhail for support, but he crossed his steely arms over his chest. "I agree with Bressen. You shouldn't be alone with Jerram, especially not on his own turf."

I looked between the two men. Both had their arms crossed and looked like they'd made up their minds. Well, so had I.

"I'm going," I said stubbornly. "Maybe if I put Jerram at ease, he'll slip up and say something useful."

"No!" Bressen said, grabbing me by the shoulders. I cried out as his fingers bit into me, and he eased his grip. "Please, Cyra, it's dangerous enough for you to see him alone. Don't try your luck by attempting to play spy as well."

I saw the concern in his eyes, but I also knew I'd won. He'd let me go if I promised not to spy. "Fine. I won't try to get information out of him," I said.

Bressen let go of me, and I was relieved he didn't have Glenora's truth-seeing abilities. I could ask his forgiveness for the lie later.

"I can put an obfuscation glamour over Samhail, and he can keep an eye on you while you're in the garden," Bressen suggested.

"I'll be too self-conscious if I'm being watched, and if the glamour somehow fails, you'll have a hard time explaining to Jerram why you have Samhail watching him."

Bressen looked at Samhail who inclined his head to indicate it was a fair point.

Bressen let out a long growl. "I don't like this."

"I know."

"Don't eat or drink anything while you're there," Bressen said.

"I won't." That was a promise I could keep.

"Then you better go before you're late," Bressen said.

I stood still a moment more. I wanted to kiss Bressen before I left, but I was aware of Samhail watching us. Bressen didn't have any such misgivings, though. After a quick glance at Samhail, he pulled me to him and claimed my mouth for an urgent kiss.

"Be careful," he breathed against my lips.

"I will."

I glanced quickly at Samhail as I left, but his face showed only amusement.

"Not one word," I heard Bressen say to Samhail behind me.

"Of course not, my lord," came Samhail's chuckled response as I closed the door.

I hurried toward the rotunda of the central building and pulled open the door to Jerram's wing. I expected to be met with spears at my throat again, but the two guards stationed there didn't move when I entered. Rather, a third guard stepped out in front of me.

"This way, my lady," he said. Clearly, I was expected.

I followed the guard down a different corridor than I'd taken the first time I was here. We came to a large open door on the first floor, and the guard led me inside.

I remembered seeing a few taxidermied animal heads in Jerram's study and in the halls of his wing, but it paled in comparison to what surrounded me now. Every wall of this room was covered with mounted heads, from deer, elk, and moose to tigers, lions, and rhinos. Giant ivory tusks were mounted over the doorway that led out into the garden, and the head of some fearsome creature with rows and rows of sharp teeth hung above a side table where Jerram stood pouring himself a drink. An impressive array of bows and arrows adorned a large glass case all along the wall behind him.

I did a double take at the case, and my mouth went dry as I noticed arrows with orange fletching sticking out from a quiver there. Somehow I wasn't surprised it had been Jerram who'd been firing at us when Bressen and I returned from the vineyard, and I fought down the rage that rose in my chest.

Had he realized it was us, or did he think it was some kind of giant bird he could stuff and add to his collection? My blood went cold as I remembered how much Jerram hated Bressen. He must've known who he was trying to hit.

"Ah, Cyra," Jerram said genially. "I was afraid you might not come today. I was starting to think you were trying to avoid me."

I did my best to smother my fury and plastered a smile on my face. "No, of course not, my lord."

"Can I pour you a drink?"

"No, thank you."

He looked at me knowingly. "You still don't trust me, do you. You can pour your own drink if it makes you feel better."

"Really, I'm fine."

Jerram shrugged. "Suit yourself," he said and topped off his glass.

Jerram set the bottle down and came over to me. He extended his arm, and I pushed down my disgust enough to loop my hand through it. He took a long sip from his glass, then set it down on a table and led me to the door under the ivory tusks. I was surprised to note how green everything still was outside, but when we passed the threshold, I understood why.

"It's warm," I said in surprise. It was a good thing too, since I'd forgotten my cloak.

"There's an elemental at the Priory who's especially good with air and can create these atmospheric bubbles. I make it worth his while to maintain this one for me."

I looked slowly around at Jerram's garden, which was fully, gloriously in bloom. Bright green grass grew in pathways between flower gardens filled with well-manicured rose bushes in just about every color. There were also lilies, irises, and hundreds of other flowers I couldn't even begin to know the names of. Trees, both large and small, were scattered around the garden to offer shade, and I noticed fruit hanging from several of them. A fountain spouted water from a medium-sized fishpond off to our right as well.

"Is that a vegetable garden?" I asked, pointing several rows over.

"Vegetable and herb," Jerram said, steering me toward it. "Glenora grows all of the plants for her tea and her other concoctions over here. I let her come and go as she pleases, and in exchange she lets me harvest anything I want from whatever she doesn't need."

"Why doesn't she grow everything in her own garden?" I asked.

"To start, all of Ursan's animals eat anything she grows."

I nodded. Given our issues at the vineyard with birds, deer, and bears, I should've realized that.

"Second," Jerram said with a smile, "you of all people should know that elementals create the best growing conditions."

It took a moment for his words to sink in before I stopped and turned to him.

"You're an elemental," I said, finally confirming what I'd suspected since the night Bressen caught me eavesdropping.

Jerram cocked his head. "You didn't know that?"

"No. I mean, I didn't know much about you when I was in Fernweh, and when I got here I just never thought to ask." His expression was unreadable, and I added, "I'm sorry. I hope that wasn't rude of me to say."

"No," he said, smiling. "You've had a lot on your mind since

381

you've been here."

"Yes, my stay here has been…" I searched for the right word but could only come up with, "…interesting."

"You've found things to occupy you at least," Jerram said, and something in his tone put me on guard.

"Not as much as I'm used to doing at home, but I *have* found a few things to do here."

"Yes, he certainly does fill your time," Jerram said casually.

I stopped walking. My heart pounded in my chest as I turned to Jerram, but I forced my face into an expression of confusion. He couldn't possibly know about Bressen and me.

"My lord?"

Jerram's expression was knowing. "Do you think I don't notice all those looks that pass between you? All the time you spend together?" He paused, then added, "The Harmilan?"

I couldn't help the hot flush that rose on my face, but I shook my head and began walking again. "I don't know who you think I've been spending my time with-" I started to say, but Jerram grabbed my arm and turned me back to face him.

His expression was cold. "He's not worthy of you."

"Who's not worthy of me?" I asked, all too aware of the note of panic that had crept into my voice.

"Samhail. He's a freak of nature, a hired mercenary, and someday soon he'll just end up dead in a pool of his own blood. You deserve better than him."

My mouth fell open as I stared at Jerram. Nemesis take me. He thought I was with Samhail.

Relief flooded through me, and I made a concerted effort to keep from laughing. Anger quickly replaced relief, though. I knew Jerram disliked Samhail, but to say Samhail was unworthy of me was too much. It was on the tip of my tongue to tell Jerram I did in fact spend the night with Samhail on the Harmilan, but I bit back the retort. Admitting to anything wasn't a good idea.

"My lord," I said, smiling at him with some effort. "Samhail is just a friend."

Not entirely true, but more accurate than what Jerram thought.

Jerram raised a disbelieving eyebrow at me.

"I promise you, there's nothing romantic between me and Samhail. He trains me to fight, and yes, he kept me company on the Harmilan, but we aren't in love."

Jerram scoffed. "I wouldn't expect someone like Samhail to even know what love is."

I narrowed my eyes at him. "Then exactly what do you think is going on between us?"

Jerram stiffened a little, and I could see he was reluctant to say it out loud.

"Say it," I ordered him, and he scowled at my tone.

"Fine. You've been taking that brute to your bed. I don't begrudge you the need to have someone keep you company at night, but you can certainly do better than him."

"Like you?"

His chin went up a notch. "If I have to say it then, yes. A lord of the Triumvirate is more worthy of you than some filthy warrior."

"I'm a winemaker from the outer lands. What is it you think makes me so special?"

I was seething inside about what he'd said regarding Samhail, but I also didn't understand his reasoning. Something inside me needed to know the answer, not because of Jerram but because of Bressen. I had no idea how I'd managed to attract him. What made me so special that not just one, but two, Triumvirate lords wanted me? More importantly, was there something about me that might give me hope for a future with Bressen?

Jerram lifted a hand to brush some hair away from my face, then ran a finger down my cheek. I forced myself not to recoil from his touch.

"Cyra, you're so much more than you seem to think you are. I could do so much with you by my side, but you choose to debase yourself with *him*."

He said the last word with such contempt that I actually stepped back from him.

"I think it's time for me to go," I said. My voice was quiet, but there was menace in it.

Jerram's face hardened, but he nodded. "Very well."

Jerram motioned for me to go before him, and I strode back along the grass path toward the doors of the parlor. I walked right in and would have kept straight on going, but I stopped dead in my tracks as my eyes locked onto the massive shape off to the side of the room. My blood stopped in my veins, and I screamed as I lurched back and crashed into Jerram, who'd been right behind me.

He grabbed my arms to steady me. "Cyra, what is it?"

"How...How do you have that?" I asked with a shaking voice.

"Have what?"

"That!" I said, pointing into a corner of the room that I hadn't seen on my way in.

Next to a large armoire stood the giant taxidermied body of a black bear with a white heart on its chest. Its mouth was open, teeth bared in a never-ending silent roar, and one paw with five white toes reached out toward me.

"The bear?" Jerram asked. "My apologies. I should've warned you about him."

"How do you have that?" I asked again, reeling around to face him.

He looked confused. "I killed it. I saw it one day while I was out hunting a few years ago and brought it down."

"The heart," I said, barely able to speak. "The heart on its chest."

Jerram smiled. "Ah yes, the heart," he said looking fondly at the bear. "That means it's one of Ursan's."

"What?" I was sure my face had gone white again.

"Ursan likes to send bears into the other territories now and then to spy for him, but they're easy to spot because they all have that white heart and toes. They're the same markings Ursan has when he shapeshifts into a bear himself."

Jerram went to retrieve the glass of amber liquid he'd left on the table when we'd gone out into the garden. He downed the rest of it and looked back at me.

"I'd half-hoped it was Ursan himself when I shot the thing," Jerram went on, "but alas, it was only one of his minions. I had it stuffed and brought here to the Citadel just so I could see the look on his face when he finally noticed it. I'll cherish that look of horror every day for the rest of my life. It's my little reminder to him to keep his spies out of Derridan."

Jerram smiled as he recalled the memory, but then he frowned all of a sudden. "Did the bear you killed look like that?"

"I have to go," I said and turned to head toward the door out of the parlor.

A strong wind blew past me and the door to the parlor slammed shut before I reached it. I whirled around to find Jerram right there. I threw out my hands to ward him off, but he grabbed my wrists and pulled me to him.

"Was that the bear you killed?" Jerram asked again, his voice louder and sharper than before. His hands tightened on my wrists, and I cried out in pain. "Was it?"

"Yes!" I said, and his grip loosened a little.

I tried to read Jerram's mind, but either he had a shield up or I hadn't yet gotten the hang of mindreading without Bressen there, because I couldn't see anything.

Jerram looked down at me, and I saw exactly when the look in his eyes shifted from anger to lust.

"Let go of me," I said to him.

He looked as if he might ignore me, but then he shoved me away from him.

"I hope you don't come to regret your choice," Jerram said.

I looked him straight in the eye. "I won't."

"Then go."

I pulled the door to the parlor open and launched myself through it. Ignoring the guard waiting outside the door for me, I started to run back the way I'd come.

"My lady!" the guard called after me.

"I know my way out!" I called back over my shoulder.

The guards at the entrance to Jerram's wing seemed equally perplexed by my haste, but they just pulled the doors open as I neared so I could hurtle through them.

I had only one thought on my mind. I had to get to Bressen and tell him what I'd learned.

Ursan was behind everything.

Chapter 35

Minutes later I was banging on the door of Bressen's study while the guards outside looked at me in alarm, obviously wondering if they should stop me.

"Bressen!" I yelled, pounding on the door. I turned to the guards. "Is he in there?"

The door flew open before they could answer, and Bressen stood there, his face etched with concern as he looked me up and down.

"Cyra, what's wrong? Did Jerram hurt you? I'll kill him if-"

"I'm fine," I said, pushing past him. "Close the door."

Bressen said something to the guards in the hall before closing the door and following me inside. He raked a hand through his night-black hair. "Nemesis take me, Cyra. You scared the three hells out of me. If Jerram didn't attack you, then what's wrong?"

"It was Ursan," I said.

He looked alarmed, and I felt his power pulse. "Ursan attacked you?" he asked in shock.

"Yes! I mean, no. Not exactly."

Bressen gripped my shoulders as his eyes became bright red embers, and I was suddenly mesmerized by the fire swirling in them.

"Cyra, did Ursan attack you?" he asked me, his voice deadly calm.

I just stared at his eyes. They'd flashed before when he was angry, but I'd never seen them stay red for more than a second or two. Now they glowed like burning suns, and I couldn't pull my gaze from them.

"Cyra!" Bressen demanded, and I blinked, bringing the rest of his face back into focus.

"Not today," I said. "The bear I killed in Fernweh was Ursan's."

The red glow in Bressen's eyes dimmed slowly, replaced again by that deep turquoise.

"What do you mean the bear was Ursan's?"

"I was walking with Jerram in his garden, and when we went back into his parlor, I saw it. I must've walked right by it when we went out, but it was tucked in a corner."

"Saw what?" Bressen asked, his patience wearing thin.

"A giant taxidermied bear, one of Jerram's hunting trophies. It was the exact same bear that attacked me at our vineyard weeks ago. They both had the same markings."

Bressen's eyes narrowed. "I don't understand."

"The bear that attacked me had a white heart on its chest and white toes on one paw. At least, I thought it was a white heart, but maybe it's a U to mark it as Ursan's. Regardless, I saw the exact same bear in Jerram's parlor today. Jerram said Ursan sends bears into the other territories to spy for him, and those bears always have the same markings. Jerram came across one at some point and killed it. Then he had it stuffed and put in his parlor to remind Ursan to stay out of his territory."

Bressen exhaled and crossed his arms over his chest. "And you think the bear you killed was one of Ursan's spies."

"It must've been. It was the same bear Jerram has. I'll never forget what it looked like."

Bressen nodded. "Samhail and I wondered about the bear. They're special to Ursan. It's the animal he turns into most often when he transforms. We were suspicious, but there was never any evidence to suggest yours was anything other than a normal bear."

"Until now."

"Until now," he agreed.

"So what do we do?" I asked, leaning against the front of his desk in his usual spot.

He paced slowly. "We need to look into this now that we have reason to suspect Ursan is more involved than we thought."

"There's something else," I said, remembering the arrows. "I think Jerram was the one shooting at us when we returned from the vineyard."

Bressen's head jerked to me. "How do you know that?"

"He has bows and arrows in his parlor, and some of the arrows have orange fletching."

Bressen let out a growl. "It doesn't surprise me it was Jerram. If he wants to use me for target practice that's fine, but if I find out he knew you were with me, I'll kill him."

I gave him a gently admonishing look. "You won't kill him."

"I will," he insisted. "At the very least, he needs to answer for the injury he did that man."

I took one of Bressen's hands and pulled him gently toward me. His hard expression softened as he looked down at me. I put a hand on the side of his face and ran my thumb over the dimple in his chin. Bressen brought his hand up to lay it over mine.

"Fine, I won't kill him," he said, "but I reserve the right to break into his mind and make him think he's a rooster for the rest of his life."

"That sounds like a reasonable alternative," I said, smiling.

Bressen leaned down to press a soft kiss on my lips. "I'll update Samhail later, but since you're here anyway, we should start your mind shielding lessons."

"Now? I'm not sure I'll be able to concentrate. I'm all wound up."

Bressen smiled. "All the better to do the lessons now then. You need to be able to practice in-"

"In less-than-ideal conditions," I finished for him. "Yes, I know. I'm going to embroider that here on your jacket so you don't need to say it anymore." I ran a finger across his chest.

He captured my hand to plant a kiss on my palm, and I felt the tingle from his lips all the way up my arm. Seeing the look in my eye, he started to bend down to kiss me.

"I thought we were supposed to be training?" I whispered before his lips got to mine.

He pulled back but then grinned wickedly. "This is your first lesson."

I cried out in surprise as Bressen turned me around and pressed me facedown over the top of the desk. I inhaled sharply as he began to pull up my skirt.

"Exactly what kind of lesson is this?" I asked breathlessly.

"I'm going to try to read your mind, and you're going to block me."

"What?" I asked, confused as to how this was supposed to work.

And then I knew. It was how he trained with Samhail, except instead of trying to keep a mind shield up while fighting, he expected me to keep one up while...Oh gods.

Bressen ran his hand over the swell of my backside before moving lower to caress the inside of my thigh.

"Are you working on your mind shield?" he purred to me.

"I don't know how," I breathed as his hand ran along the inside of my other thigh.

"You put up one in the Great Chamber before. Just do what you did that time."

"I thought you were going to kill me then. I was very motivated to keep you out of my mind."

Bressen paused to mull that over, and I thanked the gods for the slight reprieve it gave me as his hand stopped moving on my thigh.

"You thought I was going to kill you?" he asked as his hand resumed its slow caress.

I was starting to pant. "Yes."

"Hmmm. Well, let's find another way to motivate you instead."

Bressen pulled down my undergarment and lifted my ankles to free it. Then he nudged my feet to open my legs wider. I held my breath as he kissed a trail up the back of my thigh. I could move if I wanted to, but I had no willpower where he was concerned.

I jolted when Bressen's hands wrapped around my hips, and his tongue suddenly delved between my legs to lick languidly all the way up my center. I gasped and pressed my head into the desk as I tried to keep from bucking off it.

"So wet for me already," Bressen murmured. "I can still read your thoughts, though. You're supposed to be concentrating on a shield."

I moaned as his tongue began to lick again, playing with that sensitive spot at my apex. Nemesis take me, how was I supposed to concentrate on anything while he was doing that?

Bressen's tongue circled around my entrance, dipping inside me playfully, and I arched off the desk. Bressen stood up quickly and pressed me back down with a firm but gentle hand.

"Now, now, our lesson isn't over yet," he admonished.

He slipped a finger inside me, and I jerked as the sweet torment of longing spread through me. I wanted more. I needed more.

"You want me inside you. I can read that as clear as day in your thoughts," he said. "Block me out. You don't get what you want until you put up a shield."

He was pretending control, but I heard the need in his own voice.

"You want it too," I challenged him.

Bressen bent down to my ear and his voice was warm and sultry. "Oh, Cyra. I need to be inside you so badly right now that it's taking all my will not to bury my cock so deep within you that neither of us will know where one begins and the other one ends. I won't take you until you succeed in blocking me out, though, even if it leaves us both in agony." He slipped a second finger inside me and began to move them in a slow, sensual massage.

His words sent tremors through me, and I cried out as his fingers pledged a vow of future bliss between my legs. I tried to move my hips to enhance the sensation, but Bressen pushed his own against mine to keep them still. I felt the hard bulge of his length against my backside and tried to grind myself into him. Bressen groaned and pressed me down harder onto the desk to pin me there.

"None of that," he rasped, and I whimpered.

Protector save me, how I wanted this man.

Gods above, how I loved him.

My eyes flew open as I remembered Bressen was still reading my thoughts. Please, please don't let him have read *that* thought.

"You're trying to hide something from me," he said, his fingers moving in and out in exquisite torture. "I can't see what it is, but I can sense your attempts to conceal it."

Bressen pressed his fingers into me deeper, and I moaned loudly. My body tried to arch up again, but he held me firm.

"Please," I whispered.

"There are two ways to make this end," Bressen said, his voice as ragged as my own. "I can let you up now, and we both leave here unfulfilled, or you can put up a mind shield, and I can fuck you until your knees go weak."

I whimpered again. My knees were already weak.

"Block me out of your thoughts and the suffering ends for both of us, Cyra. You've already managed to hide something from me. Now put your shield up the rest of the way."

Bressen's fingers emphasized the point by pressing slowly into me again, and I writhed beneath him.

"Do you want me to let you up so you can leave?" he asked.

"No!" I cried and his fingers pushed deep into me again. I was ready to go over the edge, but he stopped, and a sob escaped me at being denied my release.

"Not yet. You know what you need to do, and to give you extra incentive, I'm going to try and break through the fog you have around that one thought to see what you're hiding. If you want to keep your secret, the only way to stop me is to put up a mind shield."

I shut my eyes tightly. Please, no. I couldn't let him see that secret.

I felt Bressen working at the fastenings of his pants, and then the head of his cock pressed lightly into me. I tried to push back against him, but he withdrew, refusing me.

Bressen tsked. "You know how to make this end." His voice was hoarse, and I knew he was just barely holding on, as I was.

I felt the tendrils of Bressen's mind creeping through my own then, probing at the dark cloud surrounding the one thought I didn't want him to know, *couldn't let* him know. Between my legs, the head of his cock probed at me as well, teasing me with its promise of pleasure.

I closed my eyes and forced myself to shut out everything but the feel of Bressen, our bodies and minds linked together, responding to each other. I was so fevered with desire I could barely think, but I concentrated every ounce of my strength into throwing up a wall between Bressen's mind and my own. Some part of me rebelled instinctively at the idea of erecting a barrier between us, but the need for self-preservation quashed it down.

Just do this one thing, I told myself. *Block his mind so he can fill your body.*

I felt the mental wall rise up out of my mind then, broad and impenetrable, and relief flooded through me.

The moment my shield rose, Bressen thrust into me, and I cried out as my body closed around him, welcoming him, enveloping him. Then he was moving inside me, hard and fast, and my fingers went white from my hold on the edge of the desk as I pushed back against his urgent thrusts. Both of us were stretched taut with our shared need, and my legs strained against the torrent of ecstasy that threatened to break me. My cheek felt deliciously cool against the desk as Bressen pounded into me again and again and again, each drive pushing me toward the edge of a bottomless abyss of pleasure.

Then, like a rope frayed too far, I snapped.

I screamed as an explosion rocked my body, sweet fulfillment spreading through every limb. As my body shattered, though, so did the mental wall I'd just built. It broke apart and crumbled under the violent surge of my climax. Both my mind and my body were now open, and I was aware of Bressen filling me fully, wholly, in every way possible.

Behind me, Bressen's body strained as he thrust deep into me one more time. He convulsed with his own release, and I felt him throb as he spilled himself inside me. He groaned as his forehead fell into the crook of my neck while he gasped for breath against me.

I was breathing hard as well, both from the force of my release, but also in fear that Bressen had read my mind in that moment when my mental shield broke down and the intensity of my love for him came pouring over it like a waterfall.

Neither of us moved for several long minutes as we let our breathing return to normal. Locks of my hair clung to my forehead against the fine sheen of sweat there. Finally, Bressen withdrew himself from inside me, but he didn't let go of me.

"Is that the secret you were trying to keep from me?" he asked quietly against my ear. "You're in love with me?"

I closed my eyes, and my body went rigid. He'd seen.

Bressen straightened up, pulling me with him off the desk. One of his hands tugged the skirt of my dress back down while the other held me to his chest, and I nodded against his shoulder. There was no point in denying it now.

He turned me to face him, one hand around my waist as the other cupped my face.

"Why would you try to hide that? Why wouldn't you tell me?"

I looked at him incredulously. "Because I'd be a fool to tell you something like that."

He flinched as if I'd slapped him. "I don't understand."

"Do I really need to explain this?" I asked, my voice breaking. It was difficult enough to live with the knowledge, let alone have to say it out loud and make it real.

"Yes!" he insisted. "If you're in love with me, why not tell me so?"

Just to hear him say it sent a crushing wave of grief over me.

"Because nothing can come of it. You're a lord of the Triumvirate. I'm a winemaker. You won't even admit we've been sharing a bed. Why would I admit to loving you?"

Pain marred every inch of Bressen's beautiful face, and his hand fell from my cheek. "I don't care about who you are or who I am. That means nothing. I thought you understood I didn't want anyone to know what was between us because it would only put you in danger."

"I know that's what you said, but I don't believe it."

"Why don't you believe it?"

"Because you're not the first man to keep me a secret. I know what it feels like to be hidden away. Besides, you don't love me. You want me, but you don't love me. Why does it matter if I'm in love with you?"

Tears welled in my eyes, but I wiped at them furiously.

Bressen's face darkened, and I thought I saw red anger flash in his eyes. He grabbed one of my hands and brought it to the side of his head to hold it there.

"Read my mind," he said quietly.

I looked into those eyes that never failed to make my knees weak, and our minds connected. I immediately jolted back as the strength of Bressen's feelings flooded over me. I could barely breathe as the riptide of his emotions pulled me under, and I struggled to keep from being buffeted by the force of what I felt pouring from him.

It was love, I realized with amazement. Not just love, but a deep, fervent, soul-binding love that almost drowned me with its strength. It was a love so bright and so pure that a burst of starlight flashed in my vision, blinding me for a moment. I gasped and tried to blink Bressen's face back into focus. Those turquoise eyes were the first thing I saw, and there was an intensity in them that held me captive.

"What did you see?" Bressen asked.

"I didn't see. I felt…love. Not love, something stronger." I shook my head in disbelief.

"Now do you believe me?"

I just looked at him for a moment before I balled my hands into fists and slammed them against his chest. I pushed away from him, and his expression changed to one of confusion.

"You bastard!" I said.

"Cyra?"

"You're upset I didn't tell you I'd fallen in love with you, when all the while you've been walking around with *that* hiding inside you?" I said, poking a finger into his chest.

He had the decency to look sheepish.

"Why didn't *you* tell *me* that you'd fallen in love with me?"

Bressen sighed deeply. "Lots of reasons, none of them good. To start, I was afraid of what I felt for you. I've shared my bed with plenty of women, but no one has ever captivated me as you do. No one has ever challenged or frustrated or driven me completely mad like you. I've led a fairly solitary life in many ways, and I've gotten used to that. The possibility of opening myself up to being with someone terrified me a bit. It still does."

The pain in his voice completely defeated me, and my anger dissipated. He'd spent his life holding everyone at arm's length, and now he needed to bend an elbow and let someone come closer. Gods above, he actually wore a dark halo to keep people away.

"Mostly, though," Bressen went on, "I didn't think I was worthy of you."

I blinked at him, inescapably reminded of the conversation I'd just had with Jerram.

"How could you possibly think you're not worthy? You're-"

"I'm a Triumvirate lord," he said, waving a hand. "Yes, but how does that make me worthy of you? Does it make Jerram or Ursan worthy of you?"

Jerram seemed to think so, but I said instead, "Fair enough, but what do you think could possibly make you so unworthy? Or me worthy, for that matter?"

"Being a Triumvirate lord has its pitfalls, and so do my powers," he said. "It isn't easy to avoid abusing such powers, and I haven't been perfect in that respect. I've taken advantage of the power I have over people on multiple occasions. I've invaded people's minds to learn their deepest, darkest secrets. I've taken lives, sometimes wrathfully, and not always out of necessity. I have a darkness in me I've worked hard to overcome, but it's always there and *will* always be there, waiting to come out. People call me the Nemesis Incarnate with good reason."

I shook my head. "You're not evil. You overestimate this darkness you think you have."

His expression turned rueful. "Do you know why I asked Samhail to deal with those men on the wharf?"

"I...just assumed you normally ask him to do things like that."

He looked at me sharply, and I realized what I'd implied, that as a lord he had others do his dirty work for him. "I'm sorry. I didn't mean it that way."

"No, you're right. I don't often take care of things like that myself. Even at Revenmyer there are others who help me keep the prisoners in line, those who take care of some of the less savory parts of the job. But I wanted to punish those men myself that night on the wharf. I wanted to hurt them…break them, for what they thought about doing to you."

"Why didn't you?" I asked.

He smiled sadly. "For one, I wanted to fly you back to the Citadel. I couldn't resist the chance to have you pressed against me again. I'd been craving it since our dance at the ball."

I bit my lip. I'd been longing for the same at the time.

"You can't imagine the thrill I felt at realizing you were nearby that night, and then the absolute terror I felt when your fear hit me a few minutes later."

I swallowed but didn't say anything.

"The other reason I asked Samhail to punish those men is that I wanted to kill them."

I let out a long breath. I'd expected as much, but it was still jarring to hear.

"Part of me wanted them dead too," I said, trying to soothe him. "That doesn't make you a bad person."

He shook his head. "You don't understand. I wanted to kill them in the slowest, most painful way possible. I would have started with their pricks and spent the entire night taking them apart, piece by piece. I would've held their minds captive so they couldn't move, but they would have felt every slice of my dagger, every piece of skin I peeled off their bodies before their eyes. I would've made them watch as I slowly turned each of them into a thousand tiny fragments of flesh, and I would've done it without feeling an ounce of remorse, because I saw what they wanted to do to you. I would've made their torture last for days, so I asked Samhail to take care of them instead. I knew he'd make it hurt, but as angry as he was as well, I knew he'd exercise at least a little more restraint than I would."

I closed my eyes and tried to banish the images, but he wasn't done.

"I almost killed Ursan and Jerram when I heard about the tigers at the Priory. They fear I'll kill them to take control of Thasia someday, but I never considered doing them harm until Samhail told me what they did. The only reason they still live is because Samhail convinced me you were fine and that killing two Triumvirate lords over an already-healed wound was inadvisable. But you have no idea how close the seer's vision came to being realized that second day you were here."

I was shocked at the depth of Bressen's anger and the need he'd felt for violent vengeance on my behalf. Everything I'd learned since I'd been here told me Bressen wasn't the monster people thought he was, but if what he said was true, there was indeed a kind of darkness in him, and one people were right to fear.

No, just the opposite, I realized a second later. A monster would have acted on his impulses. The men on the wharf suffered at Samhail's hands, but it was nevertheless a small mercy that Bressen had given them to Samhail. They were still alive because Bressen hadn't given in to the malevolence he insisted he possessed. Ursan and Jerram were still alive because Bressen wasn't the beast they – or he himself – feared he was.

Bressen lifted a hand hesitantly to my face. When I didn't pull away, he tucked a stray strand of hair behind my ear. "I'm capable of doing things you can't even imagine," he said. "It was true before you got here, and it's even truer now. I have no mercy where you're concerned."

My face fell. "I bring out your darkness."

He shook his head vigorously. "My impulses and my decisions are my own. My darkness is not your fault or your responsibility."

I took his face between my hands. "Jerram and Ursan are alive. Those men on the wharf are alive because you didn't give in to your urges. Why do you dwell on what you might have done rather than what you have or haven't actually done? We're defined by our actions, not by our desires." I leaned up to kiss him tenderly. "You're not a monster. You resisted."

He rested his forehead on mine. "At least until the next time someone threatens you."

"And you'll resist again then too."

He smiled. "Your faith in me is heartening, if a bit optimistic."

I smiled back. "I won't let the darkness have you, I promise. You belong to *me* now."

The knot at his throat bobbed as he swallowed, and I saw him fight back his emotions.

"Cyra, I don't want you to feel like I'm hiding you away," Bressen said finally. "You're the most remarkable woman I've ever met, and there's a part of me that wants to invade the mind of everyone in Callanus and let them know you're mine, but we're among enemies right now. Letting people know the depth of our feelings for each other makes us vulnerable."

I stiffened. I knew that. I really did, but part of me didn't care. Now that I knew Bressen loved me, that I wasn't just his whore, I wanted to shout it from the rooftops, regardless of how much danger it put us in. I opened my mouth to say something, but Bressen spoke again first.

"But," he said, "we can bring our relationship into the open if you want to. I only ask that you wait until tomorrow. There's someone you need to meet first. What he has to say may change your mind about what you want to do."

I frowned. "Who do you want me to meet?"

"It'll be better if you see for yourself, but taking you to him will be risky. We need to go to my home in Solandis. It's farther into Hiraeth than the vineyard, so we can't fly. We'll have to take a portal."

"A portal?"

"It's a gateway between two places, but we need to go to the Priory to have a priest there open one for us."

Gendris and Seatherny, the capital cities of the other two territories, were both close to Callanus, but Solandis in Hiraeth sat on the Aspan Ocean in the far northeast of the country. It was, I realized, about as far as I could get from Fernweh while still remaining in Thasia.

"When do we go?"

"Tonight. I'll come to your room after dinner to get you."

Bressen leaned down and gave me a long, lingering kiss. One of my hands threaded into his hair, and he groaned as I gripped his neck and pulled him down harder to me.

"You're asking to be fucked again," he growled against my lips, "but I don't have time now if we're going to Solandis tonight. I need to make preparations."

Bressen set me away from him and seemed to struggle with his composure. I pouted prettily but had mercy on him and walked to the door. I turned back with my hand on the knob, and he looked at me questioningly.

"I love you," I said. "I never actually said it before, so I wanted to say it now."

Bressen looked for a moment as though he might crumble into a million pieces, but then he crossed the room in several strides to pin me against the door with his body. His mouth came down on mine, and we kissed each other with all the passion of new love fully realized.

"I love you too," he whispered against my lips, "and now I need to spend the next hour proving it to you."

Chapter 36

I spent dinner that evening trying not to grin like a fool every time I thought of Bressen and our newly confessed love for each other. Twice during the meal, Bressen's voice floated into my head to light-heartedly tell me to stop smiling, and I'd quickly schooled my features.

Ever since our 'training' this afternoon, I'd been able to keep a mind shield up with little effort, even when I was no longer near Bressen. Like Samhail, though, I'd left a small sliver of the shield open to Bressen in case he needed to tell me something.

As always, Bressen did his best to pay as little attention to me as possible at dinner, but this time I didn't care. I knew without a doubt his indifference was an act. Moreover, it was one that worked. Jerram had confronted me this afternoon about spending time with Samhail, but he hadn't mentioned Bressen at all. The more I thought about it, the more it seemed like a good idea to keep our feelings a secret for now, at least until I heard what the unknown man Bressen wanted me to meet had to say.

I went straight to my room after dinner to get ready to leave. Raina helped me prepare for bed, but I dismissed her early to her chagrin. We usually talked or played cards after dinner to pass the time, and she was sullen when I told her I was tired and wanted to go to sleep early.

I wished I could tell Raina about Bressen, but while I was almost certain I could trust her, I also couldn't take any chances. Raina never brought up the obvious signs that I was now taking someone to my bed on most nights, and I didn't volunteer anything. I knew she thought Samhail was my lover, and after the Harmilan, that wasn't completely untrue.

My toes still curled a little remembering that night with Bressen and Samhail. I hadn't ruled out asking Bressen to send Samhail another invitation in the future, but I wasn't in a hurry to bring him back into our bed either. I was more than fulfilled by Bressen, and after today, I was deliriously happy to call him mine and let him call me his. At the moment, at least, there was no room in my heart or in my bed for anyone else.

I never told Raina any of this, although I very much wanted to. I'd never had a female friend in Fernweh. Not a close one anyway. It was too hard early on to keep a friend without risking that they'd learn about my powers. Then when I was old enough to take up work on the vineyard, I didn't have time to socialize anyway.

Now that I had the time, though, I found that Raina and I got along very well. More and more I wanted to confess things to her, but loyalty to Bressen's wishes and my own lingering fears about trusting others kept me silent.

Nevertheless, it was with some degree of guilt I shooed Raina out of my room a little before 10 o'clock that night so I could change back out of my night clothes and into something more suitable for traveling. Bressen touched down on the balcony a few minutes later, and I grabbed my cloak to go meet him.

Bressen folded me into his arms when I reached him, and our lips came together for a long, slow kiss. It was with great reluctance we both parted, but time was of the essence tonight, and we didn't have time to dally. Yet.

Bressen scooped me into his arms, and I felt the obfuscation glamour fall over us. Then we were off.

We landed again a few minutes later behind the Priory near what appeared to be a partially obscured back door, and I jumped when one of the shadows near the door moved.

"My lord," a man said as he emerged from the darkness and pulled back the hood of his cloak to reveal the smooth dark skin of a completely bald head and an attractive face that looked to be approaching forty or so.

"Phaedrus," Bressen said. "Thank you for coming. This is Cyra."

"A pleasure, my lady," Phaedrus said, inclining his head in a bow. "If you'll follow me?"

Bressen held out a hand to indicate Phaedrus should lead the way, and we followed the priest inside via the small door. He led us through a labyrinth of corridors and stairways in the Priory that I assumed were forbidden to the public.

"In addition to his power to call portals," Bressen told me as we walked, "Phaedrus is also our resident scholar extraordinaire at the Priory. He knows several dialects of ancient Arystrian, so he's able to study some of the oldest texts on the Trinity we have. He's also the one who taught me what I'm saying during the Ceremony of One on the Harmilan."

"Your lordship is too kind," Phaedrus said ahead of us. He turned around halfway to look at Bressen. "Which reminds me, I've been meaning to thank you for helping me secure access to the new text they found in the collapsed temple near Saltfell."

"My pleasure," Bressen said. "I'm happy to do whatever I can to assist your research. I look forward to hearing about anything intriguing you find."

"Of course, my lord," Phaedrus said. "You'll be the first to know."

Phaedrus finally led us into an empty room at the end of a lonely hallway. A bench stood against the wall at the far end, and there was a small table toward the middle, but for the most part, it looked like a room most inhabitants of the Priory had long ago forgotten.

Phaedrus turned to us, and I saw now that his eyes were a brilliant shade of ice blue that shined all the more against his dark skin the way my silvery eyes shined against my hair. I was momentarily mesmerized by them until he spoke.

"Once you're through the portal, I'll give you two hours before I open a return portal back to the Priory," Phaedrus said. "It'll appear in the house exactly where this one lets you out. If something happens and you can't return at that time, send me a message." He handed Bressen a couple message leaves.

"Wait a minute," I said as something dawned on me. "If you can make portals, why did I spend three days on a horse to get here?"

Bressen smiled. "Because Jerram and Ursan don't know Phaedrus can call portals. Had they waited for me to return to Callanus before they decided to send for you, I might have shared that option with them. They didn't see fit to wait, though, so Phaedrus gets to keep his secret a little longer."

"I would've advised against bringing you by portal in any case," Phaedrus said. "Portals work best when opened in places where magic is concentrated, and if I'm not mistaken, you live in the outer lands."

I nodded.

"There's very little magic out there," Phaedrus said. "Opening a portal would've been tricky. It was probably better you came by horse."

"What about the vineyard?" I asked Bressen, remembering we'd spent an hour flying there and back.

Bressen shrugged. "I try to only bother Phaedrus about portals if it's a distance I can't easily fly. He has other duties besides opening portals all day, and I already call on him frequently to get back and forth to Solandis and Revenmyer." Then he added into my mind, *Plus I wanted an excuse to feel you pressed against me.*

I gave him a look that said he was incorrigible, but he just winked.

"We should go," Bressen said, turning back to Phaedrus. "We don't have much time."

"Of course, my lord," Phaedrus said. He turned around to give us his back and extended an arm out before him. His hand made a slow circle in the air, and when it came all the way back around, the edge he'd traced glowed blue. Inside the glowing circle, I now saw the interior of a large house. Phaedrus spread his hands so the circle grew enough for someone to pass through, and he stepped aside to let us enter.

"Thank you," Bressen said. "We'll be back in two hours."

Bressen took my hand and led me toward the portal, but before we could step through, an urgent voice sounded behind us.

"Lord Bressen!"

We turned to see a woman coming toward us from the door, her long red hair making her easily recognizable.

"Jemma!" Phaedrus exclaimed as he moved to head her off. "What are you doing here?"

"I need to speak with Lord Bressen," Jemma said. She turned to Bressen. "Please, my lord. It's vital I speak with you."

"Lord Bressen is busy right now," Phaedrus said, turning her away.

"It's alright, Phaedrus," Bressen said. "Jemma, is it?"

She nodded, and I tried to tamp down the feeling of jealousy that prickled in my chest.

"I need to leave right now," Bressen said to Jemma, "but I'll be back in two hours. Can we speak then?"

Jemma hesitated but finally nodded, and I had to stop myself from grinding my teeth. Jemma wrung her hands as Phaedrus steered her to the door, and I couldn't help the satisfaction I felt at seeing her go.

"Two hours?" Jemma confirmed, looking back at Bressen.

He nodded, and she let Phaedrus usher her out the door and close it behind her.

"I'm so sorry, my lord," Phaedrus said, hurrying back to us. "I have no idea how she knew you were here or where to find us."

Bressen smiled. "She is a seer, is she not?"

Phaedrus looked dumfounded for a second but then nodded. "Of course, my lord."

"She seemed anxious to speak with me," Bressen said. "Just make sure she's here when we get back, and I'll see what's on her mind."

Phaedrus nodded. "Yes, my lord."

Bressen and I turned back to the portal again.

"Is it dangerous to touch the edges?" I asked, looking at the glow.

"No," Phaedrus said. "It may tickle you, but it's perfectly safe."

I nodded and stepped through the portal after Bressen. I couldn't resist extending a hand to let my fingers graze the edge. As Phaedrus said, a slight tickling sensation skittered through my whole body, but then we emerged on the other side.

Bressen and I stepped out of the portal, and it closed behind us.

We were in a huge room that looked to be some kind of living area. The furniture was covered in rich fabric like that in Bressen's bedroom, but it still looked plush and comfortable. It was arranged in several seating areas, including one by a huge marble hearth at the far end where a fire already crackled brightly. The vaulted ceiling was accented with gold, and tall windows lined one side of a long wall. Intricately woven rugs covered the polished wood floors in the seating areas.

"Welcome to Tide's End, my home in Solandis," Bressen said.

"It's beautiful," I said as my eyes roamed over the room, trying to take in everything at once.

I smelled the slight brine in the air now, and I remembered Solandis was on the coast of Hiraeth. I couldn't see out the windows because of the darkness, but I had a feeling we were close to the ocean, and the thought contented me. I loved being near the water.

There was also a familiarity about Tide's End I couldn't seem to shake. The place gave me a strange sense of…longing? I wondered if I was feeling Bressen's happiness at being back here. Of the three Triumvirate lords, I knew Bressen was the one who spent the least amount of time in Callanus. He preferred to be here in Solandis whenever possible, and now I understood why.

"Unfortunately, we don't have time for the full tour right now," Bressen said, "but when all this is over, maybe you'll come visit again." There was something in his voice that belied the casualness of the invitation.

I nodded. "I'm sure I will," I said, and meant it. There was something about the house that just made me want to be here.

"Come sit down by the fire, and I'll summon our guest," he said.

He led me to the seating area by the fireplace, and I sat down in one of the chairs.

"Wine?" he asked, holding up a bottle. "I serve only the best here." He grinned at me, and I saw the wine was one of ours. "Your wine gets shipped to Callanus, and from there my steward buys it from one of the merchants and has it shipped up here," he explained.

"You really go through all that trouble?" I asked.

"For several years now, in fact. Had I known the winemaker was so lovely, I would've arranged a private tour of your vineyard sooner," he said, winking at me.

Under other circumstances I might have kissed him, but our time was limited, and that was a distraction we couldn't afford right now.

"So who did you want me to meet?" I asked.

Bressen's expression grew serious. "The man I want you to meet," he said carefully, "has been a prisoner at Revenmyer for over two decades now."

I jolted in surprise. That was the last thing I'd expected him to say.

"Why would you want me to meet a prisoner?"

"I believe this man may be able to shed some light on your situation," Bressen said, "but meeting him may be...difficult for you."

"Why?"

"Let me bring him in. I think everything will make more sense when you meet him."

I nodded, and I felt that prickling sensation at the base of my neck.

"I debated whether or not I should tell you the specifics of who was here ahead of time," Bressen said, still looking uncertain, "but in the end, I thought seeing him would help you understand."

"You're not making any sense. Who exactly is this man?"

A figure appeared in the doorway at the other end of the room and walked toward us. He looked to be in his late thirties or early forties from what I could see, but he walked with a slight stoop and his head down, which made him seem older. He had golden brown hair and a neatly trimmed beard that was just starting to show flecks of gray.

I stood to greet the man as he approached, but when he looked up at me, I gasped and lurched backward in shock. Bressen reached for me as I fell back into the chair, and he was on a knee in front of me an instant later.

"Cyra, are you alright?"

I tore my gaze away from the stranger to look at Bressen. "Nemesis take me, what in the three hells is this?"

Bressen took one of my hands, and I felt him trying to send calming thoughts into me.

"Stop!" I said. "Don't try to calm me. Tell me what the fuck is going on."

Bressen looked a bit surprised. "Clearly I erred in not giving you more information ahead of time," he said reasonably, and I shot him a sarcastic look that said, *Do you think so?*

I looked back at the man and up into his eyes, those unnerving silver eyes that were a perfect reflection of my own, and I suddenly couldn't breathe.

"Cyra, this is Aramis," Bressen said, watching me closely. "As you may have already surmised, I believe he's your father."

Chapter 37

My father. Or at least, the man who'd sired me.

Yet none of those words had any meaning at the moment as I looked into the gaunt face of the man before me.

Aramis smiled down at me. "I'm pleased to meet you, Cyra. I know this is a shock for you, but I'm glad you agreed to meet me."

Remembering my wine, I reached for the glass with a trembling hand and drained it.

"More wine?" Bressen asked tentatively.

I nodded and held out the glass. Bressen refilled it, and I immediately took another sip, resisting the urge to down it again. Bressen seemed relieved that I didn't.

"Explain," was all I could say.

Aramis took a seat across from me. Bressen poured two more glasses of wine and handed one to Aramis before taking a chair next to me. I took another sip from my own glass, but not too much. I needed a clear head to wrap my mind around this.

"When I first met you in the Great Chamber," Bressen said to me, "your eyes startled me, but not for the reason they startle others."

I remembered that day. Bressen had indeed jolted back when he'd looked into my eyes, but I'd seen that reaction so many times before that I'd dismissed it.

"Your eyes caught my attention because I'd seen them before."

I looked at Aramis who smiled kindly at me. Seeing those eyes from the other side, I understood now why people found them so discomforting.

Up close, Aramis didn't look as old as I first thought. To be sure, he looked at least a decade older than Bressen, but it was the way he carried himself and the sunken look of his face that aged him. If he'd indeed been a prisoner at Revenmyer, that certainly explained the discrepancy. As far as his actual age, it was nearly impossible to tell with perimortals.

"I'd seen Aramis before at the prison," Bressen went on, "but I didn't know his situation. Of course, those eyes are very memorable, so the day after I met you, I took a portal back to Revenmyer to find Aramis and question him." Bressen looked at me apologetically. "That's why I wasn't at the Priory the day Jerram and Ursan tested you. Had I known what they intended to do, I would've put off my trip to Revenmyer."

I nodded, and he went on.

"When I looked into Aramis, I learned he was found guilty of kidnapping and killing his infant daughter."

I looked at Aramis in alarm, but his face was placid.

"You, Cyra," Bressen clarified. "He'd been convicted of kidnapping and killing you."

My head snapped back to Bressen. "Me? I don't understand."

"I brought Aramis before me and questioned him about his crime. He confessed to doing it, but he wouldn't say why. I asked him if he was sure he'd killed you, and he insisted he had. I entered his mind then to show him an image of you at the Citadel." Bressen paused and looked at Aramis. "He began to cry."

"You look exactly like your mother," Aramis said softly. He blinked back unshed tears. "Except for your eyes, of course."

"Why?" I asked him in a choked voice. "Why would you let people think that you'd kidnapped and killed me?"

Aramis smiled weakly. "To protect you."

I arched my brows at him. "Protect me? How?"

Aramis sighed heavily. "I knew what you were from the moment you were born. I'm a healer, so I can sense things about people most others can't, including their powers if they're perimortal. I knew you were a syphon, and I also knew that meant you'd be in danger your entire life if anyone found out. The idea that I wouldn't be able to keep you safe terrified me."

Tears trickled down Aramis's cheeks freely now.

"I knew it was only a matter of time before others learned what you were," he said. "If you grew up around other perimortals, you'd syphon their powers, and people would take notice. They'd be frightened of you. The only thing I could think to do was to bring you someplace there was very little magic, somewhere you were unlikely to encounter any other perimortals."

"You took me to Fernweh," I said.

Aramis nodded. "I met a winemaker and his wife there. They had a small son, and they wanted a daughter too. I asked them to take you."

My eyes filled with tears now too at the memory of the only parents I'd known until now.

"And they agreed to take me." I knew they had, but hearing the story from this side, it seemed so unlikely my parents would've agreed to this.

"Not at first," Aramis said, "but I told them I was dying and that you'd be alone in the world if I didn't find someone to take care of you. They were hesitant to take you, but they finally agreed. It was only after they'd promised to take you in that I also told them you were perimortal."

"What did they say?" I asked.

"They tried to go back on their promise. As you know, magic is feared in the outer lands, and they were afraid you'd hurt them or their son."

They weren't entirely wrong, I thought wryly, remembering the time I'd burned Jaylan.

"In the end, it was their son who convinced them to take you in. The boy wandered over to your basket while we were talking. You started to fuss, and he pulled you into his lap to calm you. He sang to you, and you fell asleep in his arms."

A sob escaped me. Jaylan had convinced them to take me in. He'd sung to calm me, and I knew without a doubt which song it was. I wondered if he even remembered. He'd been around five at the time, but I decided I owed him a big hug the next time I saw him.

"I trust they gave you a good home?" Aramis asked hopefully.

I nodded as I wiped away tears. "They died of the Great Flu when I was twelve, but they raised me as their own before that. After their deaths, Jaylan took care of me and my brother Brix."

"Jaylan, yes," Aramis said. "I remember the name now. I owe him and your parents a debt of gratitude I can never repay."

Something occurred to me. "Where was my mother in all this?"

Aramis heaved a heavy sigh and looked down. "Your mother died giving birth to you," he said, his voice breaking horribly. "You came early, and I was ministering to a very sick man several towns away at the time. Had I been there, I might've been able to save your mother. Not being there when you were born is my single greatest sorrow in life, the one thing for which I'll never forgive myself." His voice had become almost a whisper.

"Do you regret giving me away?"

Aramis looked at me sharply. "I didn't give you away. I gave you protection the only way I knew how. It was the hardest thing I've ever had to do, even harder than burying my beloved wife. I believed with all my heart at the time I was doing the right thing because I loved you more than my own need to have you with me. I only regret that my efforts to keep you as far from harm as possible appear to have been in vain."

There was a lump in my throat I couldn't seem to swallow down.

"Why did they accuse you of kidnapping and murdering me? You were my father. Surely you had a right to take me wherever you wanted."

"Your aunt, your mother's sister, was there when you were born," Aramis said. "Your mother's family had power and influence, and your aunt wanted to help raise you. Her family might've been able to help protect you better than me, but it wasn't a risk I was willing to take. I didn't even trust them to know what you really were, so I disappeared with you one night. Your aunt called the authorities, and because of who she was, they came after me."

"They found you."

"My plan was to raise you myself in the outer lands," Aramis said. "It's what I would've done if your aunt hadn't insisted that she wanted to help raise you. When she sent the authorities after me, my only option was to separate us."

Aramis paused as he seemed to remember making that decision, and I felt his grief in my own mind. The sheer force of the emotion was almost overwhelming, and I wondered if this was what Bressen regularly experienced when he encountered people who didn't use mind shields against him.

"I'd already given you to the winemaker and his family when the authorities found me a few weeks later in Derridan," Aramis continued. "I tried to get as far from you as possible so they wouldn't find you. When they saw I didn't have you, they assumed the worst, and I realized the safest thing for you was to let them think you were dead. I told them you'd gotten sick and died, but your aunt insisted I must have gone mad with grief at Lillian's death and murdered you. Given her family's influence, my trial was short and quick and an utter mockery of justice." There was definite bitterness in his voice.

I looked at Bressen. "He told you all this when you questioned him at Revenmyer?"

Bressen smiled in amusement and lounged back in his chair. "He told me to go fuck myself when I questioned him."

I looked at Aramis, who just shrugged.

"He didn't trust me," Bressen said. "He'd heard the stories about me, and he knew I was both his warden and his tormenter."

"His tormenter?"

"Have you never heard what happens at Revenmyer?" Bressen asked. "What the punishment for Thasia's worst criminals is?"

I did remember. "They're forced to relive their worst fears and experiences?"

Bressen nodded. "When prisoners arrive, either I or one of my seneschals overrun their minds and dig out their worst fears and memories, the ones they push deep down into their consciousness and never let anyone see. I drag those fears or memories to the surface and make sure they're at the forefront of the prisoners' minds at all times. A few never sleep again and eventually die of their madness."

I inhaled sharply as I looked at him in dismay.

"Before you judge me," Bressen said, "just know that some of the things I've seen in the minds of those prisoners…" His voice went hoarse as he remembered. "Well, let's just say I have nightmares of my own sometimes."

"Why do you do it?"

"That's how it's always been at Revenmyer. That was the burden and the responsibility I inherited as its overseer."

Bressen told me this morning he used people's darkest secrets against them, but I didn't realize he'd meant this. It was one of the things that made him feel unworthy, and I now understood why it affected him so much.

Yet I felt sympathy for him as well. Being able to see the worst deeds and depravities of everyone you met, being privy to the horrible things they'd done and wanted to do, must be a horrific and exhausting experience. It was no wonder Bressen felt a darkness in himself. Anyone would start to cultivate such darkness if they'd been subjected to the things he had.

I was surprised Bressen would have agreed to be a part of such treatment, but I saw how much this duty weighed on him. He felt an incredible sense of guilt over his role at the prison.

"I enjoyed being a punisher at first," Bressen said. "I took my duties as the 'Nemesis Incarnate' seriously for a long time, and I reveled in punishing people who'd committed terrible crimes. I was driven by a righteous sense of vengeance on behalf of their victims, and part of me fed off their fear and pain."

He paused to look at me, and I gave him the barest of nods.

"I told you before that my kind are defined by their capacity for both great light and great darkness," he went on, "but I was starting to feel as though the darkness was blocking out any light I had, at least until I met you."

His sincerity made my eyes well up again, and I trembled as I remembered the love I'd felt coming from him this morning.

"In any case, that's what Aramis knew of me," Bressen continued, "so he had no reason to tell me the truth."

"When he showed me your image," Aramis said, taking up the story, "I assumed he knew what you were and that I'd failed in my mission to protect you. It wasn't until Lord Bressen started questioning me that I realized he didn't know anything."

"You couldn't read his mind?" I asked Bressen.

He shook his head. "Aramis committed to keeping this secret about you for more than twenty years. He'd buried the truth deep in his mind under layers of protection. When someone commits that fully to protecting a secret for that long, the mind develops a kind of callous around it. He'd hidden the truth so deep I wasn't even aware there was something to discover. If I'd known there was more to his story, I could've broken through the defenses he'd built up, but I didn't know enough to try."

"Which is exactly what I was afraid of," Aramis said. "I told Lord Bressen to go fuck himself because I assumed he'd kill me on the spot and the secret of who you were would die with me."

"You didn't count on him not being the monster the legends claimed he was," I said.

Aramis nodded.

"I knew he must be hiding something," Bressen said, "but I didn't have time to explore his mind or dig it out of him that first day. I was wary of leaving you alone with Jerram and Ursan. Samhail was there to prevent anything catastrophic, but, as you saw, there's only so much he can do against two Triumvirate lords. I had to get back to Callanus, but as a show of good faith, I released Aramis's mind from his torture in the hopes he might come around."

"But you didn't come around," I said to Aramis, remembering that it was Samhail who'd figured out I was a syphon.

"No, I didn't," Aramis confirmed. "Lord Bressen came back several times to question me. I thought he'd try to search my mind to find the truth, but he never did. Instead, he came back to me just this afternoon and told me he'd discovered you were a syphon. I was terrified he'd expose you or even try to hurt you. As we spoke, though, I realized he was as committed to protecting you as I was."

"I've been trying to find the right time to bring you to meet Aramis," Bressen said. "When we discovered you were a syphon, everything suddenly made sense. I knew what secret Aramis was trying to hide. I thought you needed to understand what he went through to keep you safe, so I decided it was time to have you meet him."

I was still trying to wrap my head around everything I'd just been told. I knew on some level the man before me with the haunting eyes was my father, but what that meant to me and my life moving forward was still floating around in a void in my brain. The idea that the man who gave me life, the man whose blood I shared, was only a few feet away from me...Well, that was something I hadn't yet fully grasped.

Part of me was convinced I should be angry with him. On one hand, he'd taken me away from family who'd wanted to raise me and instead left me with strangers. On the other, Aramis truly believed I'd been in mortal danger, and he'd made the ultimate sacrifice to ensure I was safe. He'd taken a risk in leaving me with people he didn't know, rather than taking a chance on my aunt and the rest of my mother's family. We'd never really know which was the better choice.

Thankfully those strangers, my parents, were good people and had loved and cared for me. In truth, my heart hurt fiercely at the idea I might never have known Jaylan, Brix, and my parents if Aramis hadn't brought me to Fernweh.

"Are you alright, Cyra?" Bressen asked me quietly.

"It's a lot to take in. I'm not sure how I should feel right now."

Both Bressen and Aramis nodded at me.

"I understand why you felt I needed to hear this, and I'm grateful that you brought me to meet Aramis," I told Bressen. "I also agree with you regarding our...issue."

Confessions of love aside, I still wasn't sure how to define what we had, so perhaps it was best to keep it between us for now.

Bressen nodded, and Aramis looked between the two of us, obviously aware he was missing some context.

"So what happens to Ara-...to my father?" I asked, trying out the word. It felt strange on my tongue. This man was my blood, but he hadn't been my father for twenty-two years.

"For now, he's free," Bressen said. "He'll be staying in lodgings just outside my estate until everything is over. It's too apparent that you're connected, so he needs to keep his head down as well."

I looked at Aramis. I still had so many questions.

"Shall I leave the two of you alone for a bit to get acquainted?" Bressen asked.

I'd been holding my glass of wine the whole time but hadn't taken another sip. I took a healthy swig now and nodded to Bressen.

"You have another hour or so," Bressen said. "I'll come get you when it's time to leave."

Bressen left the room, and Aramis and I spent the next hour trying to catch up on twenty-two years. He'd spent most of that time in prison and wasn't particularly keen to relive it, nor was I eager to hear what he'd been through. Instead, he told me everything up to his capture. He talked about his life as a healer and about my mother, whose power was dream walking, which I made a note to ask him more about later. I told him all about my life on the vineyard and growing up with two brothers. We'd only scratched the surface when Bressen returned, but I knew we needed to get back.

I hugged Aramis awkwardly. He held me tightly for several seconds before releasing me, and I felt guilty for not being able to return the fervor of his embrace. He was seeing his child for the first time in decades. I was meeting a stranger who'd been in prison until now.

"My steward is waiting to take you back to your cottage," Bressen told Aramis. "He's right outside the door."

Aramis nodded and turned to go, but he stopped short and looked back at Bressen.

"Given your powers, Lord Bressen," he said, "I'm sure you already know how grateful I am for everything you've done for me and Cyra."

Bressen nodded.

"Will you grant me one more favor?" he asked, pausing to look between me and Bressen.

"If I can. What is it?"

"Speaking as a father, if Cyra will allow me," he said, hesitantly, "please don't give me any reason to wish you dead."

Bressen looked surprised for only a moment before he chuckled. "Now I know where you get your moxie from," he said to me. Then to Aramis he said, "Nemesis take me if I ever do."

Aramis nodded and turned to go. Despite my uncertainty about him, I felt the void of his presence before he'd even left the room. The man from Fernweh who'd raised me would always be my father. In truth, even Jaylan had more claim to the idea of "father" than Aramis did. Nevertheless, Aramis was the man who'd given me life, and he'd made a huge sacrifice to do what he thought was best for me. It would take a while for me to sort out my thoughts and feelings toward him, but it was an effort I was willing to make.

"Thank you," I said to Bressen. "I'm still not sure how to feel about all of this, but you've given me answers to a lot of questions about my past I never even knew I had, and for that alone I'm grateful."

Bressen bent down and kissed me tenderly. "You're welcome. Now we just need to figure out how Jerram and Ursan fit into all this."

We returned to the spot where the portal had opened and waited for it to appear again to take us back.

We waited for five minutes. Then ten minutes.

The portal never appeared.

Chapter 38

"Something's wrong," Bressen said. "The portal should have opened by now. Phaedrus is normally reliable to a fault."

"What do we do if we can't get back?"

Bressen exhaled deeply. "I'm not sure. It's too far for me to fly us. We'd never make it by morning, even if my wings could last that long."

"Can you send a message?" I asked, remembering the leaves.

"Nemesis take me!" Bressen said, digging into his pocket. "I forgot about that."

Bressen pulled out the paper and went looking for a pen in the drawers of the tables. He found one, wrote something on the message leaf, then held it up between two fingers. The paper vanished in a puff of smoke, and we were left waiting for a reply.

I reached a hand toward the place the portal had appeared before. My syphoning powers already felt stronger, and I wondered if I'd syphoned Phaedrus's ability to create the portals. I didn't remember touching Phaedrus himself, but I'd touched the portal on my way through it the first time and felt its energy. I wasn't sure if that would be enough to generate one myself, but it was worth a try.

I extended my arm out as I'd seen Phaedrus do and concentrated on the energy I sensed when I'd passed through the first time. I could almost feel the tickling sensation at my fingertips. That was promising.

"Cyra, what are you doing?" Bressen asked.

I didn't answer but instead started moving my hand in a circle as Phaedrus had done. I concentrated on picturing the room in the Priory that we'd left, but I wasn't sure if there was more to it than that. I paused when I reached the top of the circle, but nothing happened.

I tried again. I moved my hand slower this time and thought not just about the room in the Priory, but about where we were now. If the portal was a link between two places, maybe it was important to hold both places in my mind, not just the desired destination.

Again, nothing happened, and I looked at Bressen. He was watching me intently.

"Try it once more," he said as he came up behind me to rest his hands on my hips. I felt something pulse through me, but whether it was Bressen's power or just desire, I wasn't sure.

"I don't think I touched Phaedrus," I said, but I lifted my hand again and traced the ring once more. I was about to drop my hand in defeat when a circular blue glow shimmered to life. Through it, I saw into the room at the Priory as Phaedrus's shocked face peered back.

"Was that you or him?" Bressen asked, stepping around me to look through the portal.

"I don't know."

"Phaedrus," Bressen said through the portal. "Open it wider."

The portal was still only a few feet wide, and Phaedrus was jolted from his surprise by Bressen's order. Phaedrus extended his hands out as he had before, but nothing happened. He tried again, but it failed once more.

"It won't open further," he said, clearly confused.

"You try," Bressen said softly to me.

I stepped back and extended my arms in an imitation of Phaedrus. In my mind, I willed the portal to open wider, and it began to expand until it was wide enough for us to walk through.

Bressen grabbed my hand, and we hurried through the portal into the Priory.

"I don't understand," Phaedrus said. "I was about to open the portal, but I hadn't started yet. Where did it come from?" He looked from Bressen to me, and comprehension dawned on his face.

"It was you," Phaedrus said to me. "You were able to widen it. It was *your* portal."

I opened my mouth to say something – I wasn't sure what – but Bressen stepped in front of me before I could speak.

"It was your portal," Bressen said to Phaedrus. "You arrived just in time to create it."

My neck prickled, telling me Bressen had just used his powers, and I looked at Phaedrus. The priest seemed as if he'd been about to argue, but he stopped short. His eyes went glassy for a moment before he said, "Of course. I arrived just in time to create the portal."

"Why were you late?" Bressen asked Phaedrus, an authority in his voice I rarely heard him use except with Jerram and Ursan.

Phaedrus snapped back to himself. "My sincere apologies, Lord Bressen. You said you wanted to speak with Jemma when you returned, but we've been unable to find her. I'm ashamed to say I lost track of time while looking for her until I got your message."

"You haven't been able to locate her?" Bressen asked.

"No, my lord. I'm so sorry."

"Should we be worried she's missing?" Bressen asked.

Phaedrus shook his head. "I don't think so, my lord. The Priory is a big place. I'm sure she just found a hidden nook somewhere and is lost in her devotions."

"She seemed anxious to speak with me."

"I'm sure she is," Phaedrus hurried to assure him, "but it's not unusual for anyone here, especially the seers, to fall into a kind of trance and not be seen for days. They always turn up."

Bressen contemplated this for a moment. "Very well. I'll return tomorrow after breakfast to speak with Jemma. Ensure you don't misplace her again when she turns up."

"Of course," Phaedrus said, sounding relieved. "I'll make sure she's found tonight and is ready to meet you tomorrow."

Bressen nodded and took my hand to start toward the door. He stopped halfway there and looked back at the still-open portal.

"Do you need to close that?" Bressen asked Phaedrus.

"Oh yes!" Phaedrus said. He turned back to stand in front of the portal.

Follow what he does and close it, Bressen said into my mind.

I slipped over and positioned myself a little behind Phaedrus as he spread his hands and then brought them together until they were clasped. Nothing happened.

"Uh…" Phaedrus said, a bit embarrassed. "Let me try again."

Phaedrus opened his arms wide once more, and this time I mimicked him. We both brought our hands together, and the portal closed into nothingness.

I went back to where Bressen stood. He took my hand again and began walking toward the door. Phaedrus hurried ahead of us to open it and then led the way back down the maze of winding corridors and stairs.

We soon emerged from the small door behind the Priory, and Phaedrus closed it behind us, murmuring his continued apologies for the delay with the portal all the while. I felt Bressen's obfuscation glamour fall on us the moment Phaedrus was out of sight.

"You altered his memory," I said to Bressen.

Making Phaedrus forget what he'd seen was probably a good idea, but I still felt uneasy about it. Part of me thrilled at the possibilities Bressen's mind powers offered, but another part of me recoiled at them. Jerram had once tried to convince me Bressen was controlling my mind, and seeing how easily it could be done was truly terrifying. I didn't know if I could control minds now as Bressen did, but I was more nervous than excited to find out.

"We might've been able to convince Phaedrus that opening portals was a newly-discovered talent of yours," Bressen said, "but, knowing the man as I do, he would've eventually drawn the conclusion you're a syphon. Phaedrus has enough fear of me that he wouldn't willingly tell anyone about you, but the fewer people who know, the better. What Phaedrus doesn't know can't be tortured out of him."

I flinched but nodded.

"Did you have to break past his mind shield?"

"He didn't have one up. Phaedrus doesn't use one in my presence. He doesn't want me thinking he has something to hide."

I furrowed my brows. I'd stopped seeing Bressen as dangerous, since I knew he wouldn't hurt me, but I forgot other people still feared him, both for his power and his position as a Triumvirate lord.

Bressen lifted me into his arms, and then we were airborne and flying back toward the Citadel. We landed again a few minutes later on my balcony, and Bressen set me down. I didn't take my hands from around his neck, though.

He smiled down at me. "I assume I'm not allowed to leave yet?" he whispered huskily into my ear.

"Do you want to leave?"

His answer was to pick me up again and head to the bed. He set me down next to it and undid the fastening of my cloak before removing it from my shoulders and tossing it on the floor.

"Oh no," I said, pulling out of his arms and going to pick up the cloak. "Leaving things lying around almost got me in trouble with Raina once before."

I brought the cloak over to hang it on a hook near the balcony. Bressen was looking at me with amusement as I came back.

I poked a finger playfully into the hard muscle of his chest. "You can't just go tossing things where-"

I let out a squeal as Bressen scooped me up and tossed me on the bed as soon as I was within reach. Then he was on top of me, and his mouth was on mine, and any further admonishments were replaced by cries of pleasure.

Bressen left my bed just before dawn after making love to me three times throughout the night. Any thoughts I'd had of telling him we couldn't sleep together anymore had died with his declaration of love, but the downside was that I was once again kicking myself in the morning when the effects of a broken night of sleep reared their ugly head. I never napped at home, since there was too much work to be done on the vineyard during the day, but I found myself napping frequently since Bressen and I had begun our involvement. It was the only way I was able to make it through the day now since even coffee had started to fail me.

Almost everyone was at breakfast for a change when I went down to the dining room. Only Jerram was missing as I filled my plate at the sideboard, but he entered a few minutes after I sat down. He stopped short and looked a little surprised to see me before recovering himself.

"Troubling news from the Priory this morning," Jerram said as he stood next to the table. "One of the seers was found dead."

My head snapped up, and I couldn't help glancing at Bressen. He'd gone very still, and I quickly turned my head back to Jerram.

"Who?" Ursan asked.

I knew almost certainly who it was before Jerram answered.

"It was the seer who had the vision about Cyra," Jerram said. "Jemma was her name, I believe."

"Nemesis take me!" Ursan swore, banging his fist on the table. "We might still have needed her. What happened?"

I frowned at Ursan's lack of compassion. He wasn't upset that a woman was dead, but that Jemma was no longer a potential resource for them.

"They aren't sure yet," Jerram said, "but there were signs of torture."

My body went cold, and I chanced another quick glance at Bressen. He still hadn't moved, but a muscle twitched in his jaw.

"They found her body in the Priory garden this morning," Jerram continued. "There were burn marks all over it."

Jerram turned to look directly at me, and I blinked at him.

"Why are you looking at me like that?" I asked. "You can't possibly think I had anything to do with it."

"I can, and I do," Jerram said harshly, and I sat back in my chair as if he'd slapped me.

"Just because she was burned, and I have elemental powers?" I asked. "Is that your only evidence? You're an elemental as well. Maybe *you* did it."

I knew immediately I'd crossed a line. The entire room went silent, and even Bressen turned to look at me. His expression was one of urgent warning, as was Samhail's. Ursan and Glenora stared at me open-mouthed, and Jerram's face showed nothing but outrage.

"I'm sorry, my lord," I blurted out, lowering my head. "I didn't mean that. I'm just upset about Jemma."

There were several more seconds of silence before Jerram went on.

"To answer your question," Jerram said, his voice full of cold fury now, "being an elemental makes you suspect, but what I find more concerning is that when I sent guards to your room around half past ten last night to summon you, they found it empty."

My head snapped back up, and I was sure my face had drained of any color. Something dropped in the pit of my stomach, and I swallowed. I forced myself not to look toward Bressen with Jerram watching me, but I heard Bressen shift in his seat.

I was about to make some excuse about leaving my room last night to get some fresh air when I realized Glenora was with us. She'd be able to tell I was lying, so I had to handle this very carefully. The most immediate issue was Jerram's accusation that I had something to do with Jemma's death, but on that count Glenora's presence was a boon.

"I did not kill Jemma," I said, looking straight at Glenora. Then I added, "Nor did I torture her."

I held my breath as Glenora looked at me, seemingly unperturbed by the topic at hand. She considered me for a moment, and I wondered if she was surprised I knew what her power was. She'd never told me directly she was a truth seer, but she didn't seem troubled I knew.

"She speaks the truth," Glenora said finally.

I breathed a heavy sigh of relief.

Jerram looked a little annoyed to have been proven wrong, but he wasn't done with me yet. "Fine, but that doesn't answer the question of where you were so late last night."

"Why does it matter?" I asked. "And why did you need to speak to me so late anyway?"

Jerram narrowed his eyes at me, and Bressen shifted in his seat again. I realized I was treading on thin ice by speaking to Jerram like this. He was still a Triumvirate lord and had every right to question me about where I'd been, nor did he need to explain himself to me about why he'd wanted to see me last night. Having lived among the lords for several weeks now without any consequences, I'd gotten far too comfortable speaking to them as I might have spoken to my brothers, but I remembered now that I wasn't their equal. Still, Jerram's accusations and insinuations angered me, so I didn't lower my eyes as he glowered at me.

"Why I needed to speak to you is something you would have learned last night if you'd been in your room at half past ten where you were supposed to be," Jerram said coldly.

"I wasn't aware I had a curfew," I said, apparently unable to shut up for my own good.

Out of the corner of my eye, I thought I saw Samhail's head jerk, but I didn't look at him.

"Not a curfew," Jerram said, "but you're not supposed to leave the Citadel. The building was searched, and you were nowhere to be found."

"What?" Ursan asked, his head snapping to Jerram. "Why wasn't I told about this?"

"I was waiting to see if Cyra would turn up this morning on the chance my men had somehow missed her in their search," Jerram said.

Jerram and Ursan both turned to me, waiting for an explanation.

I opened my mouth, then shut it again. I had no idea how to explain my absence without lying. I wanted so badly to look at Bressen, but I didn't dare. I was waiting for him to send some advice or a suggestion into my mind about what I could say, but I heard nothing. He must be at a loss to explain my absence as well.

"Well, Cyra?" Jerram asked. "Where were you last night?"

My mind raced, but I couldn't think clearly. I waited desperately for Bressen to send me a message, but silence reigned in my mind.

"I...saw someone I haven't seen in a long time," I said finally.

Jerram looked taken aback. "Who? I wasn't aware you knew

anyone outside of Fernweh."

"Neither was I," I said under my breath.

"So who was it?" Jerram asked.

"With all due respect, my lord, I won't tell you," I said with as much courage as I could muster. "My status here at the Citadel is still in the air, and I won't bring down any trouble upon this person for simply knowing me. You're right. I left the Citadel last night, but I'm back now, and I have no plans to leave again in the future. That will need to be enough for you."

I looked directly at Glenora again.

"She speaks the truth," Glenora confirmed a moment later.

Jerram flashed her a look of annoyance, as if he expected her to say I was lying.

Ursan frowned. "How did you get out of the Citadel?" he asked.

"I...I recently discovered the servants' entrance," I said. It wasn't a direct answer to his question about last night, but also not really a lie. I glanced at Glenora, but she only sat silently.

"Fine," Jerram said. "Don't leave again under any circumstances."

I let out the breath I'd been holding, but Jerram wasn't done yet.

"And what about you?" he asked, turning to Bressen.

Everyone turned to look at Bressen, who raised a disdainful brow toward Jerram.

"What about me?" Bressen asked in a bored voice.

"When Cyra was missing, I went looking for you to help me find her. I figured your powers might be able to locate her, but you were gone as well. So where were you last night?"

My stomach dropped again, but Bressen's lips only curled into an arrogant grin.

"My dear Jerram," he drawled, "unlike the lady here, I'm not answerable to you. It's none of your fucking business where I was last night."

This time Glenora spoke up immediately. "He speaks the truth," she said as she tried unsuccessfully to suppress a smile.

Chapter 39

Hours later, I sat in my room where Jerram had confined me after breakfast and surveyed the cache of objects I'd managed to summon. Bressen's refusal to admit where he was last night had angered Jerram more than anything, and Jerram had taken his rage out on me. No longer willing to accept my promise that I wouldn't leave the Citadel again, Jerram had ordered his guards to escort me upstairs and lock me in before I'd even finished eating. Bressen, of course, had feigned indifference when Jerram ordered me to be confined, so as not to arouse suspicion.

With nothing else to do, then, I'd started practicing my powers.

On the floor around my feet sat a pillow, a large porcelain vase, a towel from the bathroom, and a smooth stone from the courtyard below my balcony. Each item had flown straight into my hand when I'd called it, although I'd been a little overzealous with the vase and had to grab it with both hands when it came hurtling toward me.

I'd also practiced my portals earlier by opening one to the vineyard in Hiraeth where Bressen had taken me. The grapes had been harvested since I was there almost two weeks ago, and I saw hints of gold and crimson on the leaves of the vines as they started to turn.

It was a mistake to see the vineyard. My heart ached as I looked through the portal at the rows of vines rolling in stripes over the hilly fields. The rustle of leaves in the wind, the tidiness of those perfect rows, and the lingering smell of grapes had called to me, and I'd been sorely tempted to walk through the portal to drink in the atmosphere, if only for a few seconds. I didn't know if there were any spells or other countermeasures in place that might let Jerram know if I tried to leave, though, so I remained in my room.

My powers were growing strong quickly. Yesterday I'd barely been able to syphon a power when touching its source, but my ability to call the portal in Solandis proved I was moving beyond that limitation. In the short time I'd been locked in my room, I'd mastered portals and summoning. I'd wanted to try forcefields, but that seemed like a potentially destructive power, and I didn't want to leave any evidence of what I could do.

Bressen and Samhail had been unable to tell me if my newfound powers were permanent or not. As they'd said, there hadn't been a known syphon in hundreds of years, so it was unclear whether I was only able to draw on certain powers for a limited time, or whether the ones I practiced were a permanent part of my repertoire. It was also uncertain whether or not I was drawing power away from my sources, or whether I was simply able to mirror what they were doing without affecting them in any way. Neither Samhail nor Bressen seemed to be negatively affected by my use of their powers, but I'd probably only drawn on a fraction of what they could do anyway.

I'd taken stock earlier of the perimortals I'd come in contact with besides the two of them, since each one was a potential source of a new power I should practice.

Aramis was actually the second healer I'd syphoned. Lorkin, the priest at the Priory, had healed me after the tiger slashed my leg, so it was very likely I had healing powers. I wasn't inclined to hurt myself just so I could try it out, but I remembered how quickly Bressen's wing seemed to heal the night I'd cleaned him up after he was shot with the arrow.

Then there was Jemma. She'd touched me to see if she could clarify her vision, and I'd seen what she had seen. She'd been surprised to find me in the vision with her, so it was possible I now had seeing abilities. Here again, though, I wasn't sure what limitations there were. Jemma was dead now, so perhaps her power had died with her.

This also brought up the question of my mother. I'd spent months in her womb, presumably syphoning her powers. Aramis told me she was a dream walker, but there'd been so much to discuss last night with him that I hadn't asked what that was, although I could guess.

Lorkin, Phaedrus, and Jemma weren't the only priests and

priestesses with powers, though. I'd spent the entire day at the Priory for the Harmilan, so who knew how many other perimortals I'd come in contact with. I was starting to see why Aramis took me to the outer lands, and also why people were afraid of syphons. The dizzying array of powers I might now have access to was simply overwhelming.

Then, of course, there was Jerram, Ursan, and Glenora, all three of whom I'd touched at some point.

I'd seen Ursan transform into a wolf and use his influence over animals, and those powers should be available to me. I remembered how one tiger had paused when I'd ordered it to stop in the Priory, but I didn't know for sure if that was due to me syphoning Ursan's influence over animals. As for his shapeshifting powers, I was too afraid to attempt a transformation without guidance. If something went wrong, I risked spending the rest of my life as an emu or some other creature.

Jerram was an elemental, but those were powers I already possessed. I didn't know what his dominant element was, but there was an opportunity to build some of my own elemental powers if I could find out. In particular, I'd been meaning to see just how much fire I could conjure, and I wanted to ascertain whether or not I could throw it, but now didn't seem like the time to test that out if I wanted to avoid the destruction of my room.

As for Glenora, I should be able to tell whether or not people were lying to me, but I wasn't exactly sure how her power worked. Glenora had put her hand over mine at one point when we'd had tea, and at the time I'd noticed a slight red glow to her skin that seem like a blush, but different. Perhaps Glenora had been lying to me then, and I just didn't realize it. I tried to remember what she was telling me when I saw the glow, but I couldn't recall. She'd been talking about how she and Ursan had met, but I couldn't remember anything specific. That conversation now seemed so long ago.

Now that I thought about it, Jerram had seemed to glow red when he told me Bressen was responsible for my blackout after the ball, and

I knew without a doubt that was a lie. Unfortunately, I didn't have anyone here on whom I could practice my truth seeing. Raina was forbidden to come in and attend me, so I was alone. Thus the powers I could practice while I waited here were limited.

I whirled around when I heard the click of my door opening.

"Bressen!"

He entered quickly and closed the door behind him. I ran across the room to throw myself into his arms, and he lifted me off the ground to swing me around once before he set me back down and claimed my lips for an insistent kiss.

"How did you get past the guards?" I asked when we stepped apart reluctantly.

He arched a brow at me. "I'm offended you'd even ask that."

I nodded. "As a lord, I suppose they had to let you in."

"Well, yes, but I don't want Jerram or Ursan to know I'm here, so your guards are currently asleep with their eyes open outside the door."

I smiled. That was a trick I needed him to teach me.

"So what's happening? When will I be allowed to leave my room?"

"Never, if Jerram gets his way," Bressen said, running a hand through his dark hair. "He wants you confined here indefinitely."

I flinched. "He can't really do that, can he?"

"Not if I have anything to say about it, but I have to be careful how I approach this."

"Jerram's angry with me. He's trying to punish me."

"You probably did push him a little farther this morning than I might have advised."

"Jerram also thinks I'm sharing a bed with Samhail," I said. "Regularly," I added when Bressen cocked an eyebrow at me.

"He said that? When?" Bressen asked.

"Yesterday when we walked in his garden. I forgot to tell you because I was distracted by the bear and the arrows in his parlor."

"You do spend a lot of time with Samhail, but I didn't realize Jerram was paying such close attention."

"He dislikes Samhail. He calls him a brute."

Bressen nodded. "I'm well aware how Jerram feels about Samhail. So you think Jerram wants you confined to keep you away from him?"

"I don't know. I only know that Jerram and I didn't really part on good terms after that conversation. He probably thought I was with Samhail last night, and that's why he was so angry at breakfast."

Bressen inclined his head. "Possibly. In some ways, it's better if he thinks you were with Samhail."

"I was hoping you'd tell me what to say this morning when Jerram questioned me, but I never heard anything from you."

Bressen shook his head and his brows furrowed. "I was trying to prompt you, but it was apparent you didn't hear me. I'm not sure why. My powers seem to be spotty all of a sudden, and I felt...unwell at breakfast this morning. I would have flown up to your balcony just now, but I was afraid of being seen if my obfuscation glamour failed."

I felt the color drain from my face, and Bressen's expression turned to one of concern. "What's wrong?"

"You're having trouble with your powers. What if...I'm syphoning them away from you?" I asked in horror.

Bressen's look of surprise said he hadn't considered that. "I'm sure that's not it," he said, but his denial sounded perfunctory.

"What if it is? You and Samhail said yourselves that no one knows enough about how syphoning powers work. It's possible that, in using your powers, I'm taking them from you."

My voice was shaking by the time I finished, and Bressen drew me into his arms to calm me. The implications of what all this might mean sent waves of panic through me.

"Don't do that," Bressen said quietly as he bent down to plant a kiss on the top of my head. "Don't work yourself up about this. Right now, I'm the only person who seems to be having problems. Samhail's powers are fine, so it's unlikely you're the cause of my issues."

I nodded against his chest, but I wasn't sure I believed him.

"Is there any news about what happened to Jemma?" I asked.

432

Bressen pulled back and nodded gravely. "We saw her body. She was tortured rather brutally and likely raped. There were burn marks all over her body. She was found naked and strangled to death in the maze at the Priory."

I inhaled sharply. "Oh gods, no."

Bressen pulled me against him again, and I laid my head on his chest. My feelings toward Jemma had never been very charitable, both because she was the seer who'd turned my life upside down, and because she seemed to have an interest in Bressen I didn't particularly appreciate. I never would've wished harm like this upon her, though, and I now felt guilty for any ill-will I might have borne her.

"Do you think her death had anything to do with what she wanted to tell you last night?"

"I'm almost certain it did," Bressen said. He loosened his hold on me and ran a hand roughly through his hair again. "Nemesis take me, if only I'd given her five minutes before we left for Solandis. She was so anxious to talk to me. She might still be alive if I'd taken the time to meet with her."

"It wasn't your fault," I said taking his face between my hands.

Bressen pressed his forehead to mine, and I ran my thumb along his cheek, savoring the scratch of his ever-present stubble.

"I remember now that she approached me at the Harmilan as well," he said. "I assumed she wanted to spend the night with me, but I realize now she just wanted to tell me something important."

I remembered as well. I was jealous he might choose her over me. Between Bressen and I, we had plenty of guilt to go around where Jemma was concerned.

"How are you faring up here?" Bressen asked.

"I've been practicing my summoning," I said, pulling away from him to gesture to the pile of objects. "Watch."

I reached out toward a clock on the mantel over the fireplace, and it flew into my hand. Bressen looked impressed.

"Cyra, this is incredible. What else can you do?"

I told him about all the other powers I thought I might have but was afraid to test out given my current circumstances.

"You do need to be careful," he said. "If you were caught using a power you're not supposed to have, it could put you in a lot of danger."

"That reminds me," I said carefully, "I need to ask you something."

"Of course. Anything."

I hesitated. "I was just wondering how many of your powers I've actually syphoned. What powers can I use besides mind reading? Can I compel people to do things or alter their memories?"

"I'm not sure. Probably. We'll have to test it out sometime."

"What about…other things?" I asked. I looked at him cautiously, and I saw the moment he knew where I was going with this.

"You want to know if you can kill people with your mind," he said.

"I…I don't *want* to do it. I just need to know if it's something I could do…if I had to. At the very least, I should probably know if it's possible so that I don't do it accidentally."

He looked at me for a long time, and I began to flush under his steady gaze.

"I don't think you'll be able to," he said finally. "Not at this stage of your development, in any case. And even if you could, I don't want you to."

I frowned. "Why not?"

Bressen exhaled deeply. "Killing someone is a very different power from reading minds. Whether you take a life with a blade or with your thoughts, you have to let in a certain amount of darkness. I've done it before, more times than I care to count, and it's not an experience I want for you. For that matter, I'm not convinced you have the capacity for darkness you'd need to even try."

"Why do you say that? You don't think I have darkness in me?"

The question came out sounding almost petulant. I myself had doubts I could kill another human being, but something about hearing him say that I wasn't capable of doing it prodded a stubbornness in me that suddenly, inexplicably, wanted to prove him wrong.

He put a hand on my cheek and gave me a slightly exasperated look. "Fortunately, we don't have a way for you to practice that particular power, so let's just assume for now that you don't have it."

"You didn't answer my question," I pressed him, not about to let him off that easily.

"Do I think you have darkness in you?" he clarified.

I nodded.

He smiled and pulled me gently against him. Then he leaned down, but instead of kissing me, he just brushed his lips against mine in a playful tease.

"I'm not the best person to ask about this," he said against my lips. "All I see when I look at you is light. You're the beacon on the shore that's kept me from drifting out to sea these last few weeks."

Elation walked its way up my spine.

"And what if I told you," I said, bringing a finger up to brush it lightly over his chin, "that I can't stop wanting to bite this little dimple? Isn't that dark?"

He grinned down at me. "I think you're confusing darkness with wickedness, and I know all too well that you have plenty of the latter in you." His lips brushed my forehead.

"Bressen?" I didn't really want to stop him, but now that I had someone here, I needed help with one more thing.

"Hmm?" he murmured at my temple.

"Since you're here, I need you to help me test one more power."

He leaned back and looked down at me with a wary expression.

"It's nothing bad," I assured him quickly.

"What do you need me to do?"

"Lie to me," I said.

He blinked. "What?"

"Glenora's power. I think I syphoned her truth seer abilities, but I need to test it. I need you to tell me a lie to see if I know it's a lie."

He nodded and thought for a moment. "I'm definitely *not* thinking about throwing you down on that bed right now and spending the night fucking you."

My stomach did a somersault at the thought, and I smiled back at him. "I don't need Glenora's power to know that's a lie," I said running a hand down his chest. "I need you to tell me a real lie, something I wouldn't otherwise know was true or false."

He looked at me for a long time, and I thought he might be on the verge of refusing me.

"Alright," he said finally, his face serious. "The first time I ever saw you was in the Great Chamber the day you arrived in Callanus."

I narrowed my eyes at him. That *had* been the first time we'd seen each other. What was he doing?

As I looked at Bressen, though, a red glow bloomed on his skin, much like the glow I'd seen on Glenora and Jerram.

"That's a lie," I whispered.

Bressen smiled softly and nodded.

"I don't understand. When could we possibly have seen each other before?"

"The first time I ever saw you," he said, "was in my dreams."

Chapter 40

I stared at Bressen. What he'd just said was impossible, but the red glow had vanished from his skin at the words. He spoke the truth.

"Your dreams? When? How is that possible?"

Bressen exhaled deeply. "About a week before you arrived, I woke from a dream a few hours before dawn. I was searching for something in the dream, and I'd just found it when I was suddenly ripped awake. I couldn't remember what I'd found when I woke up, but I felt such an acute sense of loss I couldn't fall back to sleep that night."

My breath caught in my throat as his words sparked something in my own memory.

"It all came back to me when I saw you in the Great Chamber," Bressen went on. "I suddenly remembered there'd been a woman in my dream. I only caught a glimpse of her, but I knew then without a doubt it was you. I don't know how it happened, but I know with every fiber of my being it's the truth. You walked into my dream several days before you walked into that chamber."

"I had a dream too," I said quietly. "The day the bear attacked me, Brix woke me a few hours before dawn to harvest the grapes, and he interrupted the dream. I was looking for something as well, and when he woke me, it was like I'd been cast out of some kind of paradise."

"Yes," Bressen said, his voice eager with understanding. "Can I show you?"

I nodded, and he brought my hand to his temple.

As soon as my fingers touched his head, I was doused in the same longing I'd felt a month ago that fateful morning. I gasped as the ache of it dripped down me like a bucket of cold water, but the feeling lasted only a couple seconds before it was replaced by the sense of being somewhere familiar. It was the same thing I'd felt when I'd first stepped out of the portal into Bressen's home in Solandis, that gnawing sensation that I'd been there before.

A scene materialized in my mind, and I realized I was in fact in Bressen's house. It was dark, but I followed a moonbeam that slid along the floor. With each step, I had the growing sense I was getting closer to what I was looking for, closer to something I hadn't known I wanted, but something I couldn't live without now that I knew it existed.

Then I turned down a hall and saw it. No, not an *it*, a *who*.

The figure of a woman stood silhouetted against the large window at the end of the hall. Watery blue moonlight streamed in from the floor-to-ceiling panes, and I had the overwhelming sense of having found something that was lost. I moved down the hall toward the figure, stepping quickly so that each stride brought me urgently, blissfully closer to the woman. Her back was to me, but she turned as I approached, and I saw...

I jolted in shock as I realized the woman was me, and I remembered then that I was in Bressen's dream and not my own. Seeing the encounter from this perspective prodded my memory, though, and I recalled my own dream.

I'd found myself in this same corridor then, and I remembered looking out the window at the ocean bathed in moonlight. I'd felt a presence behind me and turned, but I'd caught only the barest glimpse of the man who stood behind me before Brix had torn me from sleep. In that brief moment, though, I'd felt the utter joy of being...whole.

I didn't know how Bressen had stolen into my dream, or how I'd stolen into his, but I knew we'd come together in the realm of dreams just over a week before coming face-to-face in the Great Chamber. I hadn't recognized him at the time, but he'd recognized me.

The fog of the dream cleared as Bressen and my room materialized once again in front of my eyes.

"So now you know how to truth see," he said.

"How did we appear in each other's dreams?"

He shook his head. "I don't know. Some perimortals can dream walk, but I don't think that's a power I've ever had."

Something finally clicked into place for me, and my eyes widened. "Aramis said my mother was a dream walker."

Bressen raised his brows. "That would certainly explain it."

My mind was suddenly a maelstrom of thoughts and questions. "When you grabbed my face in the Great Chamber, that's when you recognized me?" I asked.

"It was a two-fold recognition. I recognized you from my dream, but I also saw your eyes and remembered Aramis. You have no idea what a shock you gave me, and it's very hard to shock me."

I smiled. "I'll have to do it more often."

"You already surprise me on a daily basis without even trying. I might drop dead from astonishment if you actually put some effort into it," he said as he brushed his lips over mine, and I couldn't help wondering how the last several weeks might have gone differently if I'd realized sooner that it was him I'd seen in my dream.

Bressen's mouth claimed mine more urgently, and then he lifted me up to walk me toward the bed. He tossed me onto it, and my giggle was cut off when he came down on top of me a second later, his mouth and body pressing into mine. I wrapped one leg around him and tugged at his jacket while his own hand pulled up my skirt.

"I can't seem to get enough of you," Bressen breathed against my ear. "I love being inside you, of feeling you tighten around me, of spilling myself into you…"

I'd begun writhing beneath Bressen as he spoke, but Bressen's last words made me go still.

He noticed the change in me and lifted his head. "What's wrong?"

"Every morning, Raina brings me turrow berry tea. It prevents pregnancy." I paused to see if he'd glean where I was going with this, but he just cocked his head in question.

"It does. Why?"

"The Creator knows I don't want to bear you any bastards," I said, and I couldn't keep the bitterness from my voice, "but I'd appreciate being warned before having things slipped into my drink. As you can imagine, I'm a little wary of that nowadays."

Bressen's eyes narrowed, and he sat up so he was looking down at me. "Cyra, what are you talking about?"

"I'm talking about how a couple weeks ago my morning tea was suddenly being steeped with turrow berries," I said, sitting up on the bed as well.

Bressen's frown deepened. "But you obviously know what the tea is for. Why are you upset?"

I raised my brows. "I'm upset because someone apparently knows you're sharing my bed and took it upon themselves to make sure I don't get pregnant. Not that I want to be, but that's not someone else's decision."

Bressen stared at me. "Cyra, I have no idea what you're talking about. No one knows I share your bed."

"Someone must know because my tea wasn't steeped with turrow berries for the first couple weeks I was here. The morning after we were first together, though, my tea was suddenly pink."

Bressen thought for a moment. "That would have been the morning after we went to the vineyard. A week before the Harmilan."

"Yes, why does that matter?"

"Cyra." Bressen reached up to put a hand on my cheek, but I pushed it away.

"Don't."

"Cyra, the week before the Harmilan, turrow berries were added to everyone's tea, not just yours," he said.

I frowned at him. "What?"

"As you saw, the Harmilan brings out people's carnal sides. In preparation, most of the city drinks turrow tea for the week before and after the celebration. We'd have a huge surge in births months from now if they didn't. In fact, the Citadel's treasury pays for the tea so it's available without cost to everyone in Callanus who wants it. It's been common practice for a long time now to serve it to everyone at the Citadel in the two weeks surrounding the Harmilan."

"So…" I said, trying to wrap my mind around his words.

"So no one knows what's between us," he assured me. "The berries were added to your tea in preparation for the Harmilan. I'm sorry no one told you that."

"Are women required to drink the tea?" I asked, still not sure I believed this was as innocent as he made it sound.

"Not at all. No one is. If a couple wants to conceive a child on the Harmilan, they're more than welcome to forego the tea."

"They?"

"Yes. The tea is a contraceptive for men as well. Were you not aware of that?"

I shook my head. "No. Do you drink it?"

"Of course," he said and then smiled. "I don't want to get you pregnant."

I flushed red. "I'm sorry. I misunderstood."

Bressen raised a hand to my cheek, and this time I didn't shake it off. "You don't have to drink it if you don't want to. I started drinking it a few days before our first time together since…I didn't trust myself around you."

I almost laughed to see the sheepish expression on his face, but I managed to stop myself.

"Feel better?" Bressen asked, and I nodded. "Good, then can I make love to you now?"

"Please do," I said.

Bressen pressed me back down onto the bed and kissed me, but a second later he flipped us over so I was on top of him instead. I lifted myself up to straddle his hips, and I felt the bulge of his erection pressing between my legs. I undulated my own hips to grind against him, and he groaned as his hands ran up my thighs.

"I love it when you ride me," he said, moving his hands up to my hips to help me move against him. "It drives me absolutely mad."

He gathered the skirt of my dress and sat up so he could pull it over my head, but he stopped suddenly.

"What is it?"

Bressen was looking toward the balcony, and I twisted around to see what had caught his eye. A single pigeon sat on the railing watching us. I was about to ask him again what was wrong when I saw the u-shaped white spot on the bird's breast and gasped.

Bressen urged me off him carefully before sliding from the bed. He took a few steps toward the balcony, and the pigeon suddenly flew toward us. A few feet inside the room, the bird inflated and transformed until Ursan appeared before us, fury etched across his face. I shot off the bed and stood behind Bressen as Ursan's feet hit the floor, and he stalked toward us. Bressen reached a hand back to keep me behind him and threw the other out toward Ursan.

"Ursan, stop," Bressen said to the Lord of Polaris, and fear rose in me at the alarm I heard in his voice. "It's not what you're thinking."

"Really?" Ursan said, his anger preceding him. "Because it looks like you and our guest have gotten rather close. How long have you been taking the girl to bed, Bressen?"

"It just-" Bressen started to answer, but Ursan cut him off.

"I realized something wasn't right that day you and Samhail showed up in the woods," Ursan went on. "I wondered how you knew so quickly something was wrong."

"Ursan, let me explain," Bressen said.

"Are you controlling her mind?" Ursan asked, completely ignoring me as his eyes remained on Bressen.

"No!" Bressen said, his temper rising to meet Ursan's.

"You expect me to believe that?" Ursan yelled. "You've been her champion since she arrived, always trying to convince Jerram and I to send her back to Fernweh. You've been manipulating her to be sure you're the one she doesn't destroy when this vision comes to pass."

"No!" I yelled, taking my turn to object this time. I stepped out from behind Bressen. "That's not what he's been doing."

"Stay out of this, girl!" Ursan snapped, turning cold eyes on me.

Bressen moved to put himself between us again. "Ursan, you're

442

being ridiculous. Just listen to me."

"Have the two of you been in on this the whole time? You and your little whore?"

A surge of Bressen's power reverberated through the room, and my hand flew to my chest at the sudden pressure there. His power made the paintings tremble on the walls, and a pair of crystal candlesticks on the mantel went crashing to the floor. I knew without seeing Bressen's eyes that there was fire in them, and I gasped and stepped back in shock as dark smoke suddenly curled at his feet.

In front of us, Ursan went very still, and his eyes fixed on the smoke coiling around Bressen's legs as if he expected to see something emerge from it. He took a step back.

"You know as well as anyone," Bressen said to Ursan, his voice deadly quiet, "that if I wanted to destroy you and Jerram, I wouldn't need Cyra to do it."

It was the wrong thing to say. Ursan's eyes flew back up to Bressen's, and he took another step back.

"Ursan," Bressen said, his tone warning.

Ursan only spun and ran for the balcony as his stout body shrunk back into the pigeon in a second. The bird flew out the open doorway and immediately dove for the ground.

"Nemesis damn me," Bressen swore as the smoke dissipated from around him. He turned to me. "I have to go after Ursan. I can't let him get to Jerram."

I nodded urgently. "Go!"

Bressen's wings unfurled at his back, and he ran for the balcony. The wings spread wide as he cleared the threshold, and a second later he was soaring out into the open space and diving toward the ground after Ursan. I ran after him and looked over the balcony into the courtyard, but I saw neither him nor Ursan.

My heart hammered as I recalled how often there were pigeons on my balcony. Protector save me. Had Ursan always been among them?

A hot flush hit my face as I remembered some of the inane things

443

I'd said to the pigeons in those early days when I'd been bored out of my mind. I heated even more at the thought of other things Ursan might have seen me do in my room. Thankfully it seemed like this was the first time he'd caught Bressen and I together, but the thought was far from comforting.

"My lady?"

I swung around when I heard Raina's voice. She was carrying a tray with my dinner, and I hurried toward her. I looked at the door, remembering that Bressen had put my guards to sleep.

"The guards?" I asked her.

"They let me in," Raina said, smiling. "They have to let you eat."

Under other circumstances, I would've been thrilled to see Raina, but my heart was in my throat right now as I wondered if Bressen had gotten to Ursan yet. Then it occurred to me how close Raina had come to walking in on Bressen and I in bed, and I blushed furiously.

"Are you well, my lady?" Raina asked, setting the tray of food down on a nearby table.

"I'm fine, I-"

The flapping of small wings drew my attention toward the balcony again, and I stepped back as the pigeon with the white mark on its chest flew across the room at us. A second later, the bird had once again transformed into Ursan and was stalking toward me and Raina.

"Lord Ursan, let me explain," I said, pressing Raina behind me.

"Get away from her!" Ursan shouted, and it took me a moment to realize he wanted me to get away from Raina.

I turned to Raina. "Go. Get out of here."

She shook her head. "I'm not leaving you."

"Raina, please, I don't want you to get hurt. It's me he's angry at."

"He won't hurt me," she said, and I wasn't sure where Raina – who seemed to be afraid of everything – had suddenly gotten such courage.

"Raina, leave!" Ursan ordered, and I was surprised to hear him call her by her name.

Raina just raised her chin and stared Ursan down.

"Don't worry about her," I said to Ursan, trying to pull his attention back to me. "I'm the one you're angry with. Let me explain."

"There's nothing to explain," Ursan thundered. "It's clear what's been going on, but I'll do now what I should've done weeks ago."

I was about to argue back when Ursan transformed again, but not into the pigeon. This time it was the giant black bear with the white heart on its chest that stood before me, and I screamed as I tried to shove Raina further behind me.

The door to my bedroom flew open as the guards from the hall rushed in, but they stopped when they saw the bear. The bear roared at them, and they quickly retreated to the hallway and closed the door, apparently recognizing Ursan. I'd get no help from them.

The bear advanced on us again, and I yelled for Raina to stand back, but my arms met only empty air as they swiped behind me for her. I glanced over my shoulder, but Raina was gone.

The cry of a raptor sounded somewhere above me, and I looked up to see a beautiful peregrine falcon soaring near the ceiling. It made a circle of the room and then suddenly dove for Ursan with a shrieking cry. I watched in horror, waiting for Ursan to swat at the bird, but he only ducked his large head as the falcon screamed by. Then the falcon was at his face with its talons outstretched. Ursan swung his head from side-to-side trying to shoo the bird off, but it cried again, and Ursan took a couple steps back. He refused to attack the falcon, I realized.

I watched wide-eyed as the bear shrank back down and Ursan once again stood before me. More incredibly, Raina now stood in the place where the falcon had been.

"Leave her alone," Raina said to Ursan.

"You don't understand what you're doing, girl," Ursan said to her.

"No, *you* don't understand," she shot back. "Cyra hasn't done anything wrong."

"She's been conspiring to destroy the Triumvirate, to destroy *me*!"

"No!" I said, shaking my head vigorously. "No, I haven't. I swear!"

"She's my friend," Raina said. "I know her. She wouldn't do that."

"Don't be naïve, girl," Ursan said with disgust. "She's only out for herself. What makes you think you know her?"

"She saved my life," Raina said, surprising both me and Ursan.

"What are you talking about?" he asked.

"I snuck Cyra out of the Citadel one night," Raina said, and I stiffened next to her. This story might get me into more trouble, not less.

"I wanted to go out for a drink before the Harmilan, and I had no one to go with, so I made Cyra come," Raina went on, and I saw the red glow bloom on her skin. I only hoped Ursan couldn't see it as well.

"We wandered too close to the wharf," she continued, "and we were attacked by four men. Cyra fought them off and wouldn't let them hurt me."

The red glow disappeared from Raina's skin. I waited to see if she'd include Bressen and Samhail in the story, but she appeared to be done.

Ursan turned to me. "You saved my daughter's life?"

"Daughter!" I exclaimed, looking at Raina. "*Ursan* is your father?"

Raina looked at me apologetically and nodded. My eyes dipped then to the V of Raina's collar where I remembered seeing a small birthmark on her chest when the man at the wharf ripped her shirt. There between her breasts, just barely visible above the fabric, was the u-shaped spot that marked her as Ursan's.

"Is it true you saved Raina's life?" Ursan asked me again when I continued to look between father and daughter.

"Yes, my lord," I said, still somewhat dazed. "Raina remembers the details of that night a little differently than I do, but I did try to protect her when the men attacked us."

"And what about you and Bressen?" Ursan asked me. "What's your involvement with him?"

"In all honesty, my lord, I'm not sure. It's true he's been sharing my bed for a couple weeks, but beyond that, I'm not sure what we are to each other."

Raina gasped softly, and I sent her my own apologetic look. It seemed we'd both been keeping big secrets from each other.

"Please," I said to Ursan. "I didn't come here to hurt anyone, and whatever is between me and Lord Bressen has nothing to do with Jemma's vision. It was just something that happened."

Ursan looked at me for a long time before he heaved a deep sigh. "I believe you. Maybe Bressen was right, and we should have left you in Fernweh."

I swallowed, not daring to think I'd somehow finally convinced him I wasn't a threat.

"I'll talk to Jerram tomorrow," Ursan said. "Between Bressen and I, we can probably convince him to let you go back."

Exhilaration welled in my chest at the idea of finally going home and seeing my brothers again, but it was followed quickly by a leaden weight that settled in my stomach. Going back to Fernweh meant leaving Samhail and Raina. Even more devastatingly, it meant leaving the man I now loved so deeply that life before seemed like merely a prelude to meeting him. A painful knot stuck in my throat, and I tried unsuccessfully to swallow it down.

Somehow I managed to smile. "Thank you, my lord."

"I'll go find Bressen and let him know," Ursan said as he turned toward the door.

"My lord," I said, stopping him before he got there. "Can I ask you one question?"

Ursan nodded.

"Did you send that bear after me in Fernweh? Did you know something about me?"

Ursan grimaced and sighed. "No, I didn't send the bear after you. Not directly. I do send bears all over to be my eyes and ears. The outer lands especially have never appreciated the idea of being ruled over. You're very independent out in Fernweh, but that doesn't mean I don't check in to see what's going on there from time to time. It was an unfortunate coincidence that my bear wandered onto your vineyard looking for breakfast."

"Did you...feel it die?"

Ursan was quiet a moment. "I did," he said, and I regretted asking as something clenched in my stomach at the pain in his look.

"I'm sorry," I said.

Ursan just nodded and exited through the door after knocking loudly to signal the guards. The guards glanced quickly inside the room before the door closed behind Ursan, and I wondered if they were surprised to see me alive.

I turned to Raina, and we both looked at each other.

"Ursan is your father?" I asked her, incredulously.

"You've been fucking Lord Bressen?" Raina asked, even more incredulously. "I was certain it was Samhail."

"How did you know I was sleeping with someone at all?" I asked.

Raina gave me an exasperated look. "My lady, you can only wake up naked and exhausted so many days in a row before someone will get suspicious. Feigning ignorance is part of my job, but I'm not oblivious."

I chuckled. "Fair enough, but how could you not tell me Lord Ursan was your father? You said your mother was Glenora's lady's maid, right?"

Raina nodded. "That's how Ursan met my mother. They started an affair together right under Glenora's nose, but you can only keep a secret like that from a truth seer for so long. Ursan didn't know my mother was pregnant when Glenora sent her away. That's the real reason my mother didn't want me to work at the Citadel. Ursan didn't know he had a child, and she wanted to keep it that way, but I wanted to meet him."

"You told me your father didn't want anything to do with you."

"I worked in the Citadel for six months before I confronted him about who I was," she said. "He didn't believe me at first, but he saw the resemblance to my mother and eventually to himself." Raina parted the collar of her shirt to bare the heart-shaped birthmark on her chest. "Then, of course, there were my shapeshifting abilities."

"You're perimortal."

"I'm half perimortal," Raina corrected, "and not very powerful. The only animal I can transform into is the falcon, and only for short periods of time."

"So Ursan knows you're his daughter, but you're still just a servant here?"

"Ursan cares for me in his own limited way, but he has no intention of acknowledging me as his own. He can't. It would only shame Lady Glenora."

"Does she know about you?" I asked.

"I don't know, but she must suspect. As Ursan found, it's hard to keep secrets from her."

Raina sat with me for the next few hours as we both filled each other in on what we'd been keeping secret. I hoped Bressen would return with news that he'd spoken to Ursan, but he hadn't returned by eleven o'clock when Raina finally told me she needed to go to bed.

I'd walked Raina to my door when the loud clanging of a nearby bell made us jump, and Raina suddenly froze. The bell was too close to be from the Priory, so it must be coming from the Citadel itself.

"What is it?" I asked, noticing Raina's sudden alertness.

"Nothing good. That bell is only ever rung to deliver a warning or bad news."

"Which is it this time?"

"I don't know. I'll see if I can find out."

Raina hurried from my room, and the guards closed the door behind her.

I went out onto the balcony to see if I could hear what was happening. There was some kind of nervous activity below, but I couldn't hear anything from up here.

I tried to stay awake, waiting for either Bressen or Raina to return, but hours came and went and neither of them did. When no one returned by two in the morning, I gave up and went to bed. Or I tried to, anyway. Sleep eluded me for most of the night as I continued to wonder where everyone was and what had happened. Every flutter of the curtains near my balcony drew my eye, just as every stray noise, both inside and outside my room, had me searching the darkness for Bressen, but he never came.

I finally fell into a fitful sleep just before dawn but popped fully awake and shot out of bed when I heard the lock of my door click. Raina entered carrying a tray of food and my morning tea as I rushed toward her.

"Raina!"

I pulled up short when I saw her eyes were red and puffy from crying. Raina was normally cheerful and bright in the morning, sometimes excessively so, but today her limbs seemed heavy, and her body dragged as she carried the tray with my breakfast into the room.

"Raina, what is it? What's happened?"

Raina's expression was pained, and my dread grew as she looked at me as though she was barely seeing me. The tray of food rattled in her hands, and I took it from her to put it on a nearby table before placing a hand on her arm. "Raina, what is it?"

She looked at me then, and I knew instantly something terrible had happened.

"Lord Ursan," she said, "...my father, is dead."

Chapter 41

I stared at Raina. "What did you say?"

Raina's expression begged me not to make her repeat it, and I took a step toward her. She let out a sob and launched herself into my arms. I pulled her against me and let her cry softly into my shoulder.

"How?" I asked when Raina's sobs finally subsided.

Raina pulled back and dabbed at her eyes with a handkerchief she pulled from her pocket. "Lady Glenora found him last night in his study. He…It looks like he hit the back of his head on the corner of his desk."

"It was an accident?" I asked.

"Possibly, but lady Glenora doesn't think so. She thinks he was murdered."

The last word hung in the air between us.

"Murdered? By who?"

Raina looked at me miserably. "She thinks it was…Lord Bressen."

"What? That's impossible!" He wouldn't. Would he?

The last time I'd seen Bressen, he'd been furious at Ursan. Had Bressen confronted Ursan before Ursan could explain his change of heart? Had something gone wrong in their conversation? Bressen admitted he'd almost killed Ursan once, but I didn't think he had any cause this time.

Raina wrung the handkerchief in her hands. "It's just one of the rumors being whispered among the servants. Lord Ursan's body was sent to the Priory to lie in state. One of the seers will examine it later to try and determine what happened."

I looked at Raina as she spoke about the body of the man who'd once been her father. I noted she was back to calling him Lord Ursan rather than just Ursan.

"How are you, Raina? Are you alright?"

"I don't know what to feel," she said after a moment. "It upsets

451

me that he's dead, but not as much as I feel like it should. I can't stop crying, but I'm not sure if I'm actually…sad."

I hugged her again. "Don't feel guilty for not being more upset. Your relationship with him was complicated."

Raina nodded and sniffled into her handkerchief.

"Can you take some time off from your work?" I asked. I was surprised she'd brought my breakfast.

She shook her head. "No one knows Lord Ursan is…was my father. We couldn't risk Lady Glenora finding out. I still can't."

"You should go back to your room and rest. I don't need anything from you I can't do myself."

"They'll just find something else for me to do," she said.

"Do you want to hide out here then?"

"No, I'll be fine." Raina straightened herself and steeled her expression. "Staying busy will keep me from thinking about it."

My heart broke for Raina. She'd come to the Citadel to meet the man who'd fathered her, and he was now gone. She told me Ursan wanted nothing to do with her, but his protectiveness last night said otherwise. Given enough time, the two might have been able to form a relationship, but that time had run out.

"Let me know if you need anything from me," I told her.

Raina turned toward the door to leave, but I called her back. "Raina, do you know where Lord Bressen is right now?"

"No, my lady."

"I need to go find him right away."

"The guards are still outside your door."

That was a hurdle, but not an insurmountable one. I needed to speak to Bressen. He wasn't a murderer, and I chastised myself for having even considered the possibility.

I wasn't as certain about Jerram, however. Jerram was angry the other day when he realized the bear that attacked me was Ursan's. Ursan assured me the animal's presence on the vineyard was only a coincidence, but maybe Jerram had suspected something about

Ursan's motives and confronted him.

Aside from wanting to discuss all this with Bressen, I needed to be sure he was alright. He hadn't come back to my room last night, nor had he sent me any messages, and I was starting to worry. For my own peace of mind, I needed to talk to him immediately.

I thanked Raina for bringing my breakfast and then headed to my closet as she left. I put on the pants and shirt I normally wore to train with Samhail, then went to the tray of food Raina brought and drained my morning tea. It was still pink with the turrow berries, but I didn't mind them anymore now. I shoved a slice of bacon in my mouth and devoured a piece of toast before going to the door to begin my escape.

It occurred to me then that I could call Bressen mentally and it might not be necessary to go looking for him at all.

Where are you? I need to see you right away, I said, aiming the message at Bressen.

I made sure my mind shield was down as I waited for an answer, but I didn't get one. Even if Bressen's own shield was up, I was sure he'd leave a crack open for me. My mind remained silent, though.

It was possible he'd returned to Solandis for some reason. Bressen had told me once that his mind powers didn't reach from Solandis to Callanus, but I knew he would've sent me a message if he'd left the fortress. I waited another minute, but my resolve hardened when I received no word from him.

I wasn't sure if I needed to see the guards for this to work, but I figured I would try it through the door first. I leaned close to it and closed my eyes, letting my mind reach out to the two guards on the other side. I felt my consciousness connect with theirs, and I sent my command.

Sleep.

I heard two thuds in the hall and opened my eyes.

"Hello?" I called. No answer.

I tried the handle of the door, but it was still locked. I put my hand over the locking mechanism and tried to send a small forcefield into it.

Small was apparently a relative term, though, because the door blew off its hinges to fall on top of the prone bodies outside in the hall.

I grimaced at the two guards slumped in a heap. I'd meant to put them to sleep standing up with their eyes open as Bressen had yesterday, but apparently that required more finesse than I currently had. Hopefully I'd have more success with my obfuscation glamour.

I should've asked Bressen how the glamour worked when I had the chance, but it was too late now. I knew what the glamour felt like, so I concentrated on that and the idea of concealing myself. A moment later, I felt the heaviness of the glamour fall over me and set off toward Bressen's wing of the Citadel.

I went first to Bressen's study before searching his suite. Both were empty. I lifted the glamour so I could speak to his guards, but none of them had seen him since last night, and his bed looked unslept-in.

The guards seemed unconvinced when I tried to tell them Bressen was missing. They were apparently used to their lord keeping odd hours and disappearing for long periods at a time. I found Damian at one point and tried to convince him something was wrong, but even he dismissed my concerns. The guards simply believed Bressen was too powerful to ever be in trouble.

I did a room-by-room search of Bressen's entire wing starting from the top floor and working my way down, but I found neither him nor Samhail. I had to break down a few doors in the process, but I was beyond caring at this point. I needed to find Bressen.

When it was clear he wasn't in his own wing, I began to search the rest of the Citadel. I started with Samhail's rooms, but neither he nor Bressen were there. Nor were they in the training yard, so I tried the main dining room next.

I saw a figure seated at the table as I entered, but the size and build told me it was likely Glenora, and my heart sank.

I froze as I tried to decide if I should make my presence known. I wasn't sure what to say to a woman who'd just found her husband dead, but I felt I owed her more than to creep quietly out of the room

454

and pretend I'd never been there. She knew I was supposed to be confined to my room, but some pull of human connection told me that showing compassion was more important than whatever trouble I might get into for being out.

I dropped the obfuscation glamour and approached her.

"Lady Glenora?"

She turned toward me the slightest bit but didn't say anything.

Glenora sat at the head of the table with her back to the door in the spot where Ursan usually sat at breakfast and lunch. Ursan was the only one who sat in a different seat depending on the meal. For the first two meals of the day, he always sat in the seat at the head of the table. It was only during dinner that he took one of the side seats so that he was equal with everyone else, eschewing that normal 'place of honor' at the head of the table. I'd never asked him why.

I came around to face Glenora.

"May I sit?" I asked.

Her hand moved an inch or two toward the seat next to her, and I took that as her invitation to sit. There was a pot of tea in front of her, and Glenora sipped some from her cup.

"Lady Glenora, I'm so sorry about Lord Ursan. Please accept my deepest condolences for your loss."

The words sounded hollow to my ears, but I didn't know what else to say. I'd always been bad at things like this, never quite able to express my regret or sympathy in a way that sounded genuine.

Glenora smiled weakly and gestured to the pot of tea. "Help yourself. It's the only thing that settles my stomach lately."

I got up from the table and took a clean teacup, saucer, and spoon from the sideboard before sitting back down. I looked around for tea leaves and a strainer, but there wasn't anything on the table.

"It's already steeped," Glenora said, noticing my search.

I poured myself a cup of tea and took a sip. I wasn't sure how long Glenora had been here, but the tea was still steaming hot.

"Do you know what happened?" I dared to ask. I was finding the silence unbearable, and I took another sip of tea, if only to give my mouth something else to do.

Glenora locked eyes with me, and I remembered the last time we'd had a conversation over tea. She'd asked me to consider what it might be like for her to be a widow if Jemma's vision ever came to pass, and I felt a stab of guilt that what Glenora feared most those weeks ago was now a reality. I selfishly wondered if she blamed me for it, but I refused to ask.

"I'm sorry. Forget I asked," I said, taking another sip of tea.

Glenora was dressed for mourning in a deep blue dress and a veil tucked into her hair at the top of her head that could be pulled over to cover her face. I wondered if she'd been crying. Her amber eyes didn't appear red or puffy, and her face seemed devoid of emotion. Everyone grieved in their own way, though, and it didn't surprise me that Glenora might approach Ursan's death with quiet reserve. I imagined part of her had been expecting his death on one level or another since Jemma's vision, so perhaps she'd already worked past her shock and sorrow.

"You're not supposed to be out of your room," she said, sipping from her own teacup.

I went still. I didn't know what to say, so I remained quiet.

"Looking for your lover, I assume?"

My head snapped to her, and I saw a smile play on Glenora's lips. It was on the tip of my tongue to deny it, but she'd be able to see the lie for what it was. I also wasn't sure who she was talking about. It was possible that, like Jerram, she assumed I was sleeping with Samhail.

I nodded instead and took a sip of tea. "Have you seen him?"

Glenora met my vagueness with some of her own. "Yes, but he's not here now."

I'd figured that much out for myself.

"Where is he? Do you know when he'll be back? I really need to speak with him."

"About Ursan?" Her expression was unreadable, neither angry nor sad, just placid.

"About a lot of things," I said, hoping that was true enough.

"I'm sure you've realized by now that half of the seer's vision is fulfilled," she said.

I gave her a sympathetic look and nodded.

"The only question is whether the second lord to die will be Jerram or your lover."

I stiffened. Glenora looked at me knowingly and a chill ran down my spine. I took another sip of tea to buy me a few seconds. "You think my lover is Lord Bressen."

"I know he is," Glenora said as a smile curled her lips, the effect strangely unnerving.

"Jerram thinks you've been warming Samhail's bed," Glenora went on, "but you and I both know you've been fucking the 'Nemesis Incarnate.'"

Her voice had a sharp edge, and warning bells went off in my head.

"How did you know?" I asked.

Glenora waved a dismissive hand. "Men are hopeless. They never look below the surface. Jerram saw you spending all that time with Samhail during the day, and his simple little male mind assumed you'd also been spending your nights with him."

She gave me a wry grin. "Us women see deeper, don't we. We read the subtler signs. For instance, you're a beautiful woman, yet Bressen barely looks at you when you're in public together. It's overcompensation. He makes such an effort to ignore you at meals or pretend he's not interested in you that he might as well be marking his territory like a dog. It's a wonder he hasn't whipped his prick out to piss all over your leg by now."

Her voice turned sour, and I frowned at the crudeness of her words.

"That's your evidence? That he doesn't pay attention to me?"

"That's what made me suspicious," Glenora said, "but I know other things as well, like how Bressen took you to his home in Solandis

457

the other night."

My eyes widened, but I tried not to give any other sign that would confirm what she'd said. My head was starting to hurt.

"Our dear Lord Bressen has been doing a lot of sneaking around lately, as have you."

"Me?"

"Jerram mentioned yesterday that you'd seen the stuffed bear in his parlor and made the connection with the bear that attacked you," she went on.

I didn't realize she and Jerram spoke that often. Perhaps she'd just been in the room when Jerram confronted Ursan.

"Jerram rightly assumed you'd go running to Bressen to tell him what you'd found. Well, Jerram assumed you'd go to Samhail. *I* knew you'd go to Bressen," she corrected herself.

"What are you saying?" I asked her.

"Bressen would, of course, assume Ursan was behind your attack and start looking into him. Ursan was becoming a liability, even before his change of heart last night."

I canted my head in question. "His change of heart?"

I knew what she was talking about, but I couldn't yet see how all this fit together.

"I found Ursan in his study last night," she went on. "He'd just come from your room. He was agitated and almost jumped out of his skin when I came in. When I asked him what was wrong, he rambled on about finding you and Bressen together, confirming what I already knew. He told me how he'd thought the two of you were plotting against him, and I thought he'd finally come around to my way of thinking."

I frowned at her.

Glenora shook her head. "I thought Ursan finally saw the wisdom of getting rid of Bressen, as I'd been urging him to do for years."

My mouth fell open, and my heart beat faster as my inability to find or contact Bressen now seemed more ominous. My hand began to shake, rattling the teacup in its saucer, as my mind went to the worst possible scenario. Bressen couldn't be dead. He couldn't be.

"As it turns out," Glenora continued, "you'd actually convinced Ursan nothing nefarious was going on and that he should let you go back to Fernweh."

A familiar wave of dizziness hit me, and my stomach went leaden. I looked at the cup of tea in my hand, and it clattered even louder on the saucer. My eyes snapped to Glenora, but I was having trouble bringing her face into focus now.

"The tea. You drugged me."

Glenora just nodded.

"You don't think Bressen killed Ursan, do you? He didn't! Is he still alive?" I asked, my rising panic only making my head spin more.

Glenora just smiled at me.

"Why are you doing this?" I asked. The room started to spin, and I gripped the table to keep myself steady. "Bressen didn't kill Ursan!"

I had to make her believe me. I had no idea what I might wake to if I lost consciousness now with Glenora believing that Bressen – or perhaps Bressen and I both – had done her husband harm. That's if I woke at all.

Then something clicked into place, and I looked back at Glenora again. Her face swam in and out of focus as I tried to stay conscious.

"You're a truth seer. You know Bressen didn't kill Ursan."

"Oh, I don't need my truth seeing abilities to know that," Glenora said. "I know Bressen didn't kill Ursan because *I* did."

I wasn't sure I'd heard her correctly, but the cruel grin that split Glenora's face told me everything I needed to know. She'd always seemed so kind, and I felt bad for the way Ursan dismissed her, always keeping her in the dark about Triumvirate business. I'd seen her as a balancing force among the three lords, someone who could check their antagonistic impulses, but the expression that twisted Glenora's face now made me shudder under the hatred I saw there.

"You killed Ursan?" I asked, struggling to stay conscious. "Why?"

"Ursan never believed I was capable of much. He ignored every piece of advice I ever gave him. He was an idiot, and he underestimated what I was capable of. It's a mistake he won't make again."

My eyes fluttered, and I fought to keep Glenora in focus.

"We fought about you last night. He told me he'd promised you could go home, and he wanted to find Bressen to tell him so. I tried to convince him it was a mistake to let you leave before we'd figured out how you were related to the seer's vision, but as usual, he wouldn't listen to me. He told me he didn't need or want my opinion on the matter, and I finally snapped. When he turned away, I hit him in the back of the head with a stone bookend. It was a foolish impulse on my part. I'd already decided to kill him, and I'd brought some belladonna with me, intending to lace the wine he kept in his study. I put the belladonna in the wine anyway then poured some down his throat just to be sure."

I pushed my chair back. I should've tried to run the second I'd felt the effects of the drug, but I'd been too stunned by Glenora's confession.

"What's in this?" I asked Glenora, holding up the teacup. The cup shook in my hand, and I lost my grasp on it so that it fell and shattered on the floor.

"Just a strong sedative," she said. "We still have a use for you."

I tried to stand, but my legs wouldn't work, and I slid off the chair onto the floor. I felt shards of the teacup digging into my thigh through the leather pants.

"We?" I asked, looking up at Glenora. She hadn't bothered to move from her chair at all.

"Jerram can answer the rest of your questions when you wake up," she said, and my body went cold just as my mind went black.

Chapter 42

Cold gritty stone pressed against my cheek when my eyes flickered open again. A crowd roared somewhere in the distance while a voice projected loudly as if giving a speech. I blinked but saw only brightness. I tried to lift my head, but it felt heavy, and the effort sent shooting pain down my neck. Something throbbed between my eyes, and the memory that Glenora had dosed my tea surfaced in my mind.

Panic cleared the last of the fog from my head, and I pushed at the stone, trying to rise. My limbs were stiff and wouldn't obey me, though. The crowd sounded closer, and I could tell now that the voice I heard belonged to Glenora. I listened but couldn't discern her words.

I pushed myself up with difficulty, and Glenora's voice went silent for a moment.

"Ah, our second guest of honor is awake. Now we can begin."

Feet scuffed near my head, and I was grabbed roughly under each arm and hauled upward. I cried out as pain shot through my limbs, and I was set unsteadily on my feet. I strained to lift my head, and what I saw sent enough fear careening through me that both my mind and body came alive again.

I stood on the stone landing in front of a huge building I didn't know. Thousands of people stretched out before me in a wide-open courtyard at the bottom of a stone staircase. The first half of the crowd closest to the stairs wore uniforms like soldiers. Behind them was a sea of people that looked to be citizens of...wherever I was.

Glenora stood in front of me.

"What have you done?" I asked her.

She raised her brows. "I did what Ursan never had the ambition to do. I dissolved the Triumvirate and took Thasia for Polaris."

"What? How?" I asked. My stomach roiled as her words sunk in. "Where's Bressen?"

"See for yourself." Glenora gestured to my left, and my blood went

461

cold. I lurched forward, struggling against the two guards holding me.

"No!" I screamed.

Bressen was strapped to a large T-shaped wooden frame, his arms outstretched and secured to it with leather straps at his wrists and elbows. His chest and feet were both bare, and burn marks seared the skin on his torso alongside angry red lashes, a few of which were trickling blood. His head hung down, but he raised it to look at me when Glenora motioned toward him. He barely had the strength to stand, but there was fury in his eyes.

"What have you done to him?" I yelled as I renewed my struggle to pull loose from the guards. I felt a surge of power and used one of Samhail's forcefields to send the guards flying backward before I ran toward Bressen.

The crack of a whip rent the air before I reached him, and white-hot pain lashed across my stomach as I cried out and fell to my knees.

"No! Cyra!" Bressen's shout reached me through a haze of pain. He strained at the straps that held him to the frame, but only barely. His face was pale and sweat beaded on his forehead.

Another crack sounded, and I screamed as pain scorched my back this time. I slumped to the ground and willed down the nausea that gripped me as I tried to breathe against the burning.

"Stop!" Bressen growled, but his voice was weak, and dread slithered through my limbs.

I tried to rise and move toward Bressen again, but the sound of the whip split the air once more, and I felt a pain so blinding across my back that stars clouded my vision. I struggled to stay conscious as I heard the crowd in the square roar its approval of my torment.

"That's far enough," came Jerram's voice from somewhere close by. I looked up and saw him standing a few feet from where Bressen was strapped to the frame. I'd been so focused on Bressen that I hadn't seen Jerram next to him with the whip in his hand.

"If you hit her again, Jerram," Bressen rasped, "I'll-"

"You'll do nothing but die, Bressen," Jerram spat out, and he

462

cracked the whip savagely across Bressen's chest.

Bressen's body jerked under the lash, and he grunted before his head sagged again.

"No!" I cried.

I eyed Jerram and struggled to pick myself up off the ground, but he didn't lash me again.

"What have you done to him?" I asked again, but this time there was fury in my voice.

"What we've done is conquer the 'Nemesis Incarnate,'" Glenora supplied, practically spitting the last two words. "Everyone is so afraid of the great Lord Bressen, the Punisher of Thasia, but if you take away all his powers, there doesn't seem to be much left."

"You took away his powers? How?"

Glenora shrugged. "A little poison in his morning drink weakened him enough to make him docile."

"Poison!" I gasped.

"Jerram helpfully lets me grow the belladonna in his gardens along with the rest of my special plants, like the ones we used to sedate you."

Bressen didn't look well at all. I'd thought it was because he'd been whipped, but I saw now his eyes were bloodshot, and his body was covered in sweat, even in the cold air.

"It wasn't enough poison to kill him. Just enough to weaken him so Jerram could do what he needed to do," Glenora went on.

"What did you do?" I asked Jerram between clenched teeth.

Jerram smiled cruelly. "I was just another elemental in Bressen's eyes, and not a powerful enough one by his standards. He tried to read my mind a few times lately, but he failed to do so, of course. I'm sure he thought I finally strengthened my mental shield enough to block him out, but really I've been strengthening another power I didn't realize I had until about a year ago. It's been extremely handy since I learned about it."

I glared at him, but Jerram was enjoying the reveal.

"You see," Jerram said with an ugly grin, "I have the ability to

463

nullify the power of other perimortals."

I gasped and looked at Bressen. He turned to me, and I saw something in his face akin to…regret? Apology? I wasn't sure.

"We could have used a caronium cuff on him," Glenora went on, "but it's so much more satisfying for Jerram to negate Bressen's powers this way instead."

I knew that caronium was one of a few things that could weaken perimortals, but I didn't know exactly how it worked. I also wasn't exactly sure what a caronium cuff was, but I guessed it wasn't good.

"He's completely helpless right now," Jerram said, moving closer to Bressen to give him two hard pats on the cheek. A small flame erupted in his hand, and he pressed it to the middle of Bressen's chest.

Bressen tried to stay quiet, but after a couple seconds he screamed and jerked as the fire seared his skin. I launched myself toward him, but guards grabbed my arms to pull me back.

"Stop! Stop hurting him!"

Jerram just smiled and pressed the flames to Bressen's side. Bressen screamed again and tried to lurch away, but there was only so far he could go while strapped to the frame. The smell of burning skin wafted to me, and I swallowed down the bile that rose in my throat. I tried to call another forcefield, but terror for Bressen overwhelmed me, and I couldn't focus enough energy to make it happen.

"Where's Samhail?" I asked Glenora, suddenly realizing he was missing. "What have you done to him?"

"He's back at the Priory watching over the body of my dear late husband as it lies in state, and he'll be there for some time. He's unaware of anything happening here now, and by the time he finds out, it'll be too late."

"He'll kill you if you hurt Bressen."

"Samhail is a skilled warrior, but he's only one warrior. As you can see, I have thousands," Glenora said, sweeping her hand out toward the soldiers.

I looked out over the sea of people, most of whom were in

uniform. I didn't think Samhail could fight that many soldiers by himself, but I wondered if the beast I'd seen in his mind might be able to. I recalled that Glenora and Jerram likely didn't know what Samhail really was. If they did, they would've taken steps to better contain him. As it was, they'd only stowed him out of the way for the moment.

"When we return to Callanus," Glenora went on, "Samhail will see the wisdom of falling in line and serving me and Jerram."

"You and Jerram?" I asked in surprise.

Glenora smiled and gave Jerram a fond look. "Jerram and I have been in love for some time now. Luckily, your arrival at Callanus and this whole vision business gave us the perfect distraction to start setting our plans in motion."

A blush bloomed on Glenora's skin, making me question how she and Jerram really felt about each other.

"What exactly are your plans? Where are we?" I asked.

I didn't understand what my role in all this was. Why was I still alive? Why was Bressen still alive, for that matter? They needed to kill him to fully dissolve the Triumvirate. Perhaps even more importantly, he'd kill them both instantly if he ever got his powers back, so they couldn't take that chance and let him live.

The realization that Bressen wouldn't live past today threatened to buckle my legs, but I forced myself to stand up straight. I wasn't dead yet, and neither was Bressen. Moreover, I still had my powers. Either Glenora and Jerram didn't know what I was, or they didn't believe I was a threat regardless, and that gave me an advantage. I had to come up with a plan.

Glenora raised her voice to magically project the answer to my question for the crowd's benefit. "You're in Gendris, and you're here to witness the start of our revolution," she announced, and the crowd roared its approval in response.

"How did we get all the way to Gendris?"

"We had a little help with that." Glenora gestured to the other side of the stone landing, and Phaedrus shrunk back in shame. I gasped. I hadn't seen him standing there.

"It seems Bressen was keeping a few secrets from us," Glenora said. "Like Phaedrus's ability to create portals. Luckily, when Jerram spoke to Jemma the night she died, she was very forthcoming with this information. She volunteered that you and Bressen had left for Solandis using a portal a little before we arrived, and that Phaedrus was the one who created it for you."

I stared hard at Phaedrus. He looked miserable and wouldn't meet my eyes. My intuition told me he was here under duress, and a plan started to form in my mind. If I could get him to help me, we might have a chance.

"Now we know how Bressen has been getting back and forth from Hiraeth so quickly all this time," Glenora mused, but I was only half-listening to her now.

Phaedrus, I said into his mind, *if you can hear me, look at me.*

Phaedrus looked up in surprise, and relief flooded over me.

"The priestess also finally shared the rest of her vision with us," Glenora was saying. "It turns out Jemma was holding back some crucial information she'd been trying to tell Bressen for weeks."

My eyes snapped back to Glenora. "What?"

"Our dear Jemma wasn't completely forthcoming with everything she'd seen in her vision," Glenora said, "but Jerram was able to torture it out of her before he killed her."

I looked back at Jerram again, and I made no effort to hide the loathing I felt for him. He just grinned back at me.

"Jemma also told us your little secret," Glenora said to me.

"And what secret might that be?"

"That you're a syphon," Glenora said. "The first known syphon in almost four hundred years."

My eyes widened and my heart dropped into my stomach. How had Jemma known that? Was it part of her vision?

Regardless of how Jemma knew I was a syphon, Jerram and Glenora now knew as well, and my mind started to race. I needed a plan immediately.

"It makes sense, of course," Glenora said. "The rumor among the Citadel guards was that you threw Samhail into the wall in the training yard. Being a syphon explains how you were able to do so."

I remained silent. I couldn't deny it because she'd know I was lying.

"Given this new information, Jerram and I decided we needed to take a few precautions to make sure you didn't do anything drastic."

Glenora held up a hand and snapped her fingers. Figures emerged from a doorway to the side where Phaedrus was standing, and he hung his head again.

No. Gods above, no.

My knees did buckle then, and the guards holding me had to pull me up to keep me on my feet. Across the courtyard, another set of guards led Jaylan, Brix, and Aramis out of the building. All three had their hands tied behind their backs, and the guards forced them down onto their knees. Once on their knees, a guard behind each of them put a sword to their throats. Jaylan and Brix both looked terrified, but Aramis only watched me closely.

I couldn't speak as I stared at the three members of my family now in mortal danger, and I remembered what Bressen had said about how if anyone ever got to my brothers, they could make me do whatever they wanted. He'd been right. I would do anything Glenora asked of me now to keep her from hurting them.

"Phaedrus was very resistant to opening a portal to the outer lands," Glenora said. "He seemed to think it was too dangerous, but when we made it clear his life was forfeit if he didn't do it, he found a way to make it happen. It's amazing what people can do when properly motivated."

I'm so sorry, Phaedrus whispered into my mind.

I spun to Glenora. "Leave them alone. They have nothing to do with this."

"They'll be perfectly fine if you do exactly what we say. They're just here to make sure you behave."

I knew it for the lie it was, even before I saw the red glow flare around Glenora.

We have to stop them, I said to Phaedrus. *Will you help me?*

He nodded the barest amount, and I heard his *Yes* echo back into my mind. I sent him another message telling him what I needed him to do, and he nodded again.

The next part was harder. I needed to let Samhail know what was going on, but there were several huge barriers. First, he was all the way back in Callanus. I had no idea if my powers were strong enough to send a message that far. Even if they were, Samhail kept formidable mental shields up at all times. He left a crack in his shields for Bressen, and I only prayed he also thought to leave a crack open for me. I forced myself to tamp down my terror and send a message to Samhail. I tried to show him an image of where I was and what he'd be facing, but I had no idea if it reached him.

"I suspect Bressen has known you're a syphon for a while now, and he's been trying to hide it for his own gain," Glenora continued. "It was a clever plan to seduce you so you'd be on his side. He always could be charming enough when he wanted to be."

I didn't say anything. I didn't believe for a minute that Bressen only wanted me for my powers, but it was better if Glenora assumed he was just using me. I'd almost let Jerram convince me once that Bressen was controlling me, but this time I was certain of what he felt. He'd saved me from harm more than once since I'd come to Callanus. Now it was my turn to repay the favor.

Bressen has been poisoned, I said into Aramis's mind. *How do I help him? Is there a way to heal him?*

The answer came back immediately, as if Aramis was waiting for me to ask.

You can draw out the poison, but you need to be touching him. Imagine yourself pulling it from his body.

Having to touch Bressen would complicate things, but I'd figure out something. I already had an idea about how to give Bressen back his powers. It seemed almost too simple, but if I couldn't get the poison out of him, getting his powers back might not help much.

"What part of the vision was Jemma holding back?" I asked. I had to keep Glenora talking while I put my plan in place. I needed to buy time. I sent my message to Samhail again with the hope that, if he hadn't gotten the first one, he might get the second.

"The seer lied when she said she didn't know which of the Triumvirate lords lived," Glenora said.

I blinked as I recalled the face that swam into view when I'd seen Jemma's vision in the Priory and she'd cut the vision short. Realization dawned on me.

"Bressen," I said, understanding now why Jemma kept trying to talk to him. "Jemma saw that Bressen was the only lord still standing."

Glenora nodded. "I would've known the girl was lying about not seeing who was left if I'd been there the day she reported her vision to Jerram and Ursan, but of course, I was only Ursan's wife. There was no reason for me to be present."

Not for the first time, I heard the resentment in Glenora's voice about how Ursan kept her removed from Triumvirate business.

"One would think that after two hundred years, my husband might see the value of my gift and let me take a more prominent role in the ruling of the country or even the territory, but Ursan never did know how to use the resources at his disposal."

I was barely listening to Glenora now. That Jemma had seen Bressen alive at the end of this made my spirits soar. Bressen's claim that visions were often self-fulfilling came back to me, and I had a surge of confidence that my plan was going to work.

"So Jemma was trying to tell Bressen what she saw?" I prompted Glenora. I had to keep her talking while I figured out how I was going to get to Bressen to remove the poison from his body. Running toward him would only earn me more lashes from Jerram's whip.

"She wanted to tell him when they brought you to the Priory, but of course the great Lord Bressen had more important things to do than

469

go with Jerram and Ursan."

I looked at Bressen. Guilt marred his face as he listened to Glenora. Bressen hadn't come to the Priory that day because he'd gone back to Revenmyer to find Aramis and question him.

"Jemma tried again to get him alone the night of the Harmilan, but I imagine she failed to entice him because he spent it with you."

Both me and Samhail, I remembered with a slight flush. I looked at Jerram, and there was anger in his eyes. He'd tried to take me to his own bed that night, and the fact that I'd gone to Bressen's bed instead added fuel to the fire of his hatred. I felt it coming off him in waves.

"She finally got Bressen to agree to meet with her the night he took you to Solandis, but luckily for Jerram and I, our spies at the Priory found out about the meeting and Jerram was able to get to her first. He tortured the information out of her and then killed her before Bressen returned."

I looked at Bressen again. His eyes were closed now, but I could still see him breathing shallowly.

Hold on, I tried to tell him. *I have a plan. Just hold on.* But he gave no indication he heard me.

"How does killing Jemma stop her vision from coming true?" I asked.

As I waited for her answer, I threw an idea into the head of one of the guards near Jaylan.

Your nose is itchy, I told him, and the guard wrinkled his nose as if trying to get rid of an itch. He didn't dare try to scratch it, but his nose wiggle was all I needed to confirm I could access his mind.

"It doesn't," Glenora said. "But killing Bressen does."

I went still and turned my full attention back to her.

"This is insurrection. You've already killed two people. Do you think the citizens of Thasia will really stand for this?" I tried to speak loudly, but the crowd gathered in the courtyard couldn't hear me. My voice didn't magically project the way Glenora's did when she spoke.

Glenora smiled. "As I'm sure you know, the citizens of Polaris are a proud people. It's never been hard to convince them we should rule all of Thasia, but Ursan was always too afraid of Bressen to act against him. Ursan refused to listen to me whenever I brought up the idea, but Jerram was willing to hear me out."

I looked at Jerram and bristled at the smug smile on his lips.

"The people of the Derridan territory will, of course, get behind Jerram. Then when he and I marry, the whole country will fall under our rule."

"You seem to have worked this out rather neatly. These people don't know you killed Ursan, do they."

Glenora looked at me innocently. "My dear, Bressen killed their beloved Ursan, and you killed Jemma in a fit of jealousy over her attentions toward Bressen."

I looked out over the sea of people gathered at the foot of the stone steps. They clearly couldn't hear what we were saying up here. The soldiers stood at attention in lines awaiting orders, and the people behind them murmured to themselves as they watched the scene raptly. I didn't want to believe these people – my people – would go along with this, but here we were.

"The only thing holding the people of Polaris back has been their wariness of Bressen," Glenora went on. "He does have a fearsome reputation, so convincing them to rise up before now was difficult. When they see him die up here today – when they see you kill him, in fact – their fears, and that vision, will die with him."

I blinked. "You want me to kill Bressen?"

Glenora held up a hand, and my brothers gasped as the swords were pressed closer to their throats. "Yes, because your choice is between the lives of your brothers and father, or the life of your lover. Either you kill Bressen, or I'll kill them."

Jerram cracked his whip across Bressen's chest again. Bressen jolted forward and groaned as a new red welt appeared where the whip hit him, and the crowd roared its approval.

"Stop it!" I yelled at Jerram.

"I wanted to kill Bressen myself," Jerram sneered, "but Glenora convinced me that making you do it would be much more satisfying. If you won't, though, she'll let me whip him to death." He grinned, and the smile contorted his face into something terrible.

"At least at your hand, Bressen will have a quick death," Glenora said. "If Jerram gets his way, Bressen's death will be long and painful."

Bressen met my eyes and nodded, and I realized he was giving me permission to kill him. It wasn't going to happen.

Glenora's order to kill Bressen would get me near him, though, I realized with elation. All that remained to be seen was whether or not I was strong enough to do everything I needed to do at the same time. The powers I'd need to pull this off were far beyond anything I'd practiced to this point, and I would need to do about four different things all at once for it to work.

"Don't do this," I begged Glenora. "You don't need to do this." I didn't think there was any chance she'd relent, but I had to try.

"We're well past that point, my dear. Now kill Bressen."

I looked at Jaylan, Brix, and Aramis, and I was silent for a long moment as I pretended to contemplate my options. I needed Glenora to believe this wasn't an easy decision for me. I just hoped her powers could only sense direct lies and not the hidden meaning of my words.

"I need a sword," I said finally, putting as much anguish into the request as I could.

Glenora shook her head. "Kill him with your mind."

I just stared at her. "I can't."

"You're a syphon," she said. "If Bressen can do it, so can you."

"Don't you think I would've killed you already if I had that ability?" I spat back at her.

Glenora flinched but nodded toward my brothers and Aramis. "You know they'd be dead before my body hit the stone if you tried," she said menacingly. "Now do it."

"I can't," I insisted. "I asked Bressen just yesterday about this, and he didn't think I'd be able to do it. I've never killed anyone before. Not

472

a person anyway. The power to kill with my mind is beyond me."

When Glenora just looked at me, I added, "I know you can see I'm telling the truth."

The whole truth was that I couldn't kill Bressen at all. My mind wouldn't allow me to hurt him, especially not in the way Glenora was asking me to.

Glenora nodded finally. "Fine, but you can have a dagger, not a sword. Having you spill his blood makes for a better show anyway. I suggest slitting his throat. It's the quickest way."

She motioned to a guard who pulled a dagger from a sheath at his waist and handed it to me. My heart hammered in my chest as I took it. I had everything I needed now. In a few minutes my plan would either work, or we'd all be dead.

Bressen's eyes locked with mine as I approached him, and I tried desperately to reach him again, to reassure him I had everything in hand, but all I saw was sadness in his face.

"I don't know why you chose *him*," Jerram said under his breath when I stood before Bressen, "but I suppose he's at least better than Samhail. I should have known you'd never take that filthy brute to your bed." There was disgust in his voice.

I let every ounce of hatred I had for Jerram show in my eyes as I stared him down. "You know nothing about me," I spat at him. "You've always underestimated Samhail, and it will be your downfall."

"I'm about to celebrate my victory," Jerram said. He dropped his voice before he added, "You and I could have ruled Thasia together, but instead you'll follow Bressen to the Nemesis."

I spat in his face. "I'd rather die with Bressen than rule with you."

Thanks to Samhail's training, I saw the blow coming and ducked just in time so that Jerram almost spun around when his fist didn't connect with my cheek. Without thinking, I threw an elbow into his ribs, then sprang back and lifted the dagger toward him. The movements were so automatic I didn't even realize what I'd done until I finished. I'd almost stabbed Jerram as well, but I remembered my brothers and Aramis just in time before swinging the dagger.

Jerram hunched over to clutch his ribs, and Bressen shifted next to me, straining at the straps that held him.

"Enough!" Glenora yelled. "Get on with it already!"

"I need a minute!" I said to her. "Just give me one more minute with Bressen. Please."

"You have thirty seconds," she said. "Say your goodbyes quickly."

I turned to Bressen and brought my hand up to lay it on his face.

"Cyra, I'm-" Bressen rasped, but I shook my head and shushed him softly.

"You're not dying today," I whispered to him.

His eyes met mine, and I saw fear in them. "Cyra, no," he whispered. He shook his head, but I drew his forehead down to rest it on mine.

"Be still and be ready."

I held his gaze as I moved my hand to his chest and concentrated as hard as I could on drawing the poison from his body. I only prayed that I'd syphoned enough of Lorkin and Aramis's healing abilities to do so. It was a moment before anything happened, but then Bressen's eyes widened as he realized what I was doing.

I focused hard to make sure only the poison was affected. Jerram or Glenora would suspect something if they saw the wounds on Bressen's chest start to heal, so I left them for now, although it pained me to do so. There'd be time enough later to heal those.

Seconds passed before I finally felt the last of the poison leave Bressen's body. His breathing became stronger as his chest rose and fell more deeply, and I sighed with relief.

It was time. I sent a message to Phaedrus.

Now.

Chapter 43

Bressen's gaze never left mine as I finished drawing the poison from his body, scattering it as mist on the wind. My heart soared to see the gleam return to his eyes, and I looked him over for other signs he was recovering. The burn and whip marks were still on his chest, as I'd intended, but he'd stopped sweating, and some color had returned to his skin.

"Cyra," Bressen said, and I heard the strength back in his voice.

"Do it now!" Glenora snapped. "Kill him or your brothers and father die!"

"I love you," I said to Bressen, then turned back to Glenora.

Behind her, Phaedrus was opening a portal, and next to him, all the guards stood frozen and glassy eyed under my mind control. I sent another mental command to the three guards holding swords to Jaylan, Brix, and Aramis's throats, and they all dropped their blades.

Glenora turned at the sound of the swords clattering to the ground. "What are you doing?" she yelled at the guards.

Jerram looked around in bewilderment as well, and I lunged to grab his hand now that he was distracted. He jolted in surprise at my touch, and in that moment, I saw the truth in his mind. Jerram hadn't moved from Bressen's side because he only had a tenuous hold on Bressen's powers at best. Jerram couldn't negate my powers because it was taking everything he had to keep Bressen under control. He could only hold one of us at a time, and he'd determined, rightfully so, that Bressen was the greater threat. But he'd still underestimated me.

I stared Jerram straight in the eyes and concentrated all my energy into syphoning his negation powers to turn them back on him. My greatest fear was that I'd accidentally negate my own powers, but the gods were with me today it seemed.

Jerram's eyes widened as he felt his hold on Bressen slip. He tried to pull his hand away from me, but it was too late.

"No!" Jerram cried, and I felt his terror rise.

I knew the moment my attempt to negate Jerram's powers worked because his face went white, and Bressen let out a roar of fury.

Then several things happened at once.

I let go of Jerram and moved to cut the straps that held Bressen to the frame, but I needn't have bothered. Bressen growled and yanked at them, his muscles bulging and straining to free himself. The straps snapped a moment later, and Bressen's eyes flared bright red as he turned to Jerram. The Lord of Derridan's body went rigid, the look of terror frozen on his face, as Bressen captured his mind.

"Kill them!" Glenora shrieked behind me.

On the other side of her, a roar came from the large portal Phaedrus had made, and the priest threw himself out of the way as something enormous hurtled through it. What came through was not Samhail, though, or at least, not the Samhail I knew. What came through was the giant stone-like creature I'd seen in Samhail's head the time I'd read his mind. Samhail in his gargoyle form.

His huge body, twice as big as normal, looked like dark gray stone, and I could only barely see the black markings at his forearms that confirmed it was him. Even the creature's wings appeared to be made of stone, although they didn't move with the rigidity of it. None of Samhail did for that matter. The gargoyle moved swiftly and smoothly on animal-like legs, and his tail lashed out behind him, cracking into a stone column next to him and sending crumbles of it pattering across the terrace. The fingers on his huge hands ended in razor-sharp claws, and the unnatural blue glow of his eyes scanned the area as the beast threw back its head and roared, displaying the sharp fangs that extended from both his top and bottom jaws. Even knowing who the beast was, I took an unconscious step backward at the sight of the monstrous creature.

I remembered my brothers and father all of a sudden, and I sent an order to run and hide into their minds. They'd been stunned by the sight of Samhail's arrival, but my mental warning broke them from their shock, and they threw themselves out of the way only a moment before Samhail's tail knocked the guards that had been holding them off their feet. I heard the crack of bones even from across the terrace, and I was certain if any of those guards survived, their bodies would be shattered.

The gargoyle beat its giant wings, and the massive stone body was suddenly airborne in a feat of aerodynamics that I was sure couldn't be possible without some kind of magic.

Out in the courtyard, people at the back of the crowd screamed and ran for the exits while the soldiers at the front surged forward.

They didn't get far. Before they'd climbed more than a step or two, the first several rows of soldiers collapsed into heaps like the men on the docks in Callanus.

I turned to Bressen and saw his eyes were still blazing red. They flashed again and several more rows of soldiers crumpled to the ground out in the courtyard.

Samhail landed in the middle of the phalanx and began knocking soldiers over with great sweeps of his tail, wings, and arms. A few perimortal soldiers shot jets of flames or other magical weapons at him, but nothing seemed to hurt him in the slightest. He simply grabbed each offender and sent them hurtling through the air. When one larger group of soldiers attempted to rush him, he sent a forcefield through their ranks that blew back anyone within fifty feet of him.

A jet of fire shot toward me from one of the soldiers who'd stepped over his comrades, but I threw out my hands to block it. A powerful wind swelled up in front of me to disperse the flames, and I continued to stir the winds into a whipping, swirling funnel before sending them out toward the next line of soldiers. The force of my winds knocked them backwards and sent men flying into the air.

More rows of soldiers dropped to the ground, either dead or unconscious – I wasn't sure which – and I turned back to Bressen. His eyes continued to blaze red as he moved toward Glenora. He wasn't walking, I realized, but floating toward her, his feet hovering a few inches above the ground. His huge black wings had emerged and were flared out behind him, but they didn't beat. He seemed to be held up by some kind of power.

A dark cloud formed behind him as waves of black smoke undulated and crawled around him. This wasn't the dark halo I'd seen him wear on several occasions, but I remembered seeing similar smoke around his feet when Ursan confronted us in my room. I recalled Ursan's terror at seeing the smoke and felt a sudden sense of unease.

A cold chill crept off the dark cloud, and a strange clambering rose from its depths as I sensed something menacing and dangerous within it. Indeed, the entire sky had gone dark, as if night had fallen early.

Glenora was backing away from Bressen. She turned to run, but I sent one of Samhail's forcefields at her and knocked her to the ground. Dark curls of smoke reached toward Glenora, and she shrieked as one of them brushed her ankle.

"Please!" Glenora begged, but Bressen continued to close the distance between them.

Then Glenora started to scream in earnest, and when I turned to Bressen again, I understood why.

Hundreds of small, gray monstrous-looking creatures began to emerge from the dark cloud around Bressen, as if the smoke itself was taking shape and becoming solid. The creatures were around a foot tall, and each one had glowing red eyes that matched Bressen's. Their long fingers ended in sharp claws, and pointed teeth gleamed out from their open mouths. Their skin was stone-gray like Samhail's, but where his seemed rough, theirs had a smooth, scaley quality to it.

I gaped in disbelief as the creatures spilled out of the dark cloud around Bressen like foam spilling from an overboiling pot. Glenora shrieked as the monsters engulfed her, piling over her and reaching for her with their sharp little claws. I flinched as I waited to see blood and flesh spurt into the air beneath the roiling mass, but all I saw were the bodies of the creatures crawling over one another in their eagerness to reach Glenora. I wanted to look away, but I couldn't seem to pull my eyes from the undulating mass that had completely overrun her, and within seconds her screams were muffled under the horde.

Time slowed as my mind struggled to take in the chaos around me. In front of me, Bressen still hovered a foot or so above the stone terrace while smoke, blackness, and the creatures churned around him. His burning red eyes gleamed all the brighter in the unnatural night that had fallen over the entire city, while the matching eyes of the creatures flickered in and out like candle flames around him as they dove and struggled over each other in a tangled pile where Glenora had once been.

Off to the side of the terrace, the guards I'd immobilized lay scattered around like broken dolls. They'd been unable to run when Samhail emerged from the portal, and the blows from his arms, wings, and tail had sent them flying into walls and across the terrace. Many had cracked skulls and broken bones protruding from under their skin, and I almost hoped they were dead, because the thought of the pain they'd be in if they woke made me shudder. I tried to remember they'd been willing to slit the throats of my brothers and father, but I just didn't have the stomach for such violence. Luckily, Bressen and Samhail did, or we might all be dead.

Glenora and Jerram had assembled a force of thousands to enact their plan, but Bressen and Samhail alone had all but decimated their army. Bressen had taken out hundreds of the soldiers simply with the power of his mind, and those that remained were now fighting a losing battle against Samhail. Whatever powers the perimortals in their ranks had were useless against the gargoyle. Jets of fire, bolts of ice, and even regular spears just bounced off his stone-like skin while sword blades scraped across his body leaving nothing but superficial scratches. A few soldiers continued to charge him, but the waves of attackers became fewer and fewer as soldiers realized the futility of their efforts and began to flee.

Glenora and Jerram's plans had hinged on neutralizing Bressen and keeping Samhail out of the way, but they'd made a mistake in underestimating how quickly I'd learned to use my powers. I couldn't defeat them myself, but their miscalculation allowed me to unleash the two people who could.

I looked to where Jerram stood frozen in place, the whip still clutched in his hand. His mouth was partially open as if getting ready to scream. He'd started to lift the whip, but that's when Bressen's mind had locked onto his and stripped him of any ability to move. Only Jerram's eyes still darted around in their sockets as he watched Bressen and Samhail tear apart both his carefully laid plans and his lover.

I turned my back on the carnage out in the courtyard and walked over to Jerram. His eyes clearly conveyed the hatred he felt for me, and that was fine. I hated him too.

The servants and guards of the Citadel often had an uncanny knowledge of what went on in every corner of Callanus, and Raina had filled me in with chilling detail the night I'd been confined to my room on the ways Jemma had been brutalized. Her body showed signs that she'd been beaten, burned, raped, and then strangled to death, likely over the course of an hour or more, and I knew Jerram was responsible for it all. I'd seen that much in his mind when I'd connected with it a few minutes ago.

I wanted to hurt Jerram, not just for Jemma, but also for Bressen, and for every slight and insult he'd ever directed at Samhail. And for me as well. I wasn't sure what he'd intended to do to me the night he drugged me, but the fact he'd even tried was enough. If I ever found the capacity within me to inflict physical pain or even death, Jerram might be the one person who would drive me to it, but that wasn't yet a step I was ready to take.

"You didn't know Samhail was a gargoyle, did you," I said to Jerram. "I told you that you underestimated him."

Anger and hatred flashed in his eyes, but it only fed my satisfaction at seeing him helpless right now, as I had been the night of the ball.

"You and Glenora underestimated me too. You should have just killed us quickly rather than going for the spectacle."

A noise I took to be a combination of disgust and fury bubbled up from Jerram's throat.

"You were right about one thing, though," I continued, smiling wryly at him. "Let me show you."

I reached a hand up to lay it on Jerram's temple, and I felt my mind connect with his, or what was left of it. I felt Bressen's mind there as well, and his power merged with my own to amplify the images I now flooded into Jerram's head.

Jerram's anger and repulsion surged as I poured the events of the night of the Harmilan into his mind. I showed him everything, every kiss and caress, every lick and every thrust of my night with Bressen and Samhail. I let him feel what I'd felt as Samhail's tongue teased and tantalized me while I'd taken Bressen into my own mouth. I showed him how I'd ridden Bressen while I turned my tongue's ministrations to Samhail, and how Bressen pulled me down onto him again and again until we'd both exploded with our pleasure. I showed Jerram how Samhail had pushed me down on the bed, and how my body bowed up to meet him as he entered me. I hoped every thrust from Samhail buried itself in Jerram's mind as deeply as Samhail had buried himself in me, and I took satisfaction in feeling Jerram's loathing as he saw Samhail pull cry after cry of pleasure from me.

I showed Jerram what had happened later that night when the two men had pulled me onto my knees to take turns slamming into me. Finally, I showed him the end of the night when they'd filled me completely, both in front and behind, until we'd all collapsed together on the bed, spent and unable to move.

Jerram was nearly trembling with rage when I removed my hand from his temple and looked back into his eyes. "Was that how you imagined it?" I asked him, my voice icy with contempt.

He couldn't answer, but I could see all I needed to in his eyes. I smiled at him then and turned away to walk back toward where Bressen still floated in mid-air in the midst of the dark cloud of ravenous, roiling creatures. The temperature dropped as I got closer, and the cold bit at my skin. Bressen's eyes still glowed red, and he seemed to almost be in a trance, but it was time for him to stop.

"Bressen!" I called out to him, but my voice was swallowed by the din around him as the creatures continued to hiss and growl and click their claws. A wind not of my making swirled around Bressen, and fear rattled up my spine as it carried an unnatural chill that set my teeth on edge. The wind sucked in dirt and leaves and other debris from around the terrace, but the dark cloud at its center continued to billow and crawl of its own accord, seemingly unaffected by anything around it.

Tendrils of dark smoke crept up Bressen's legs like vines, becoming more solid as they went. I had no idea what the dark tendrils would do to him, but I knew I needed to pull Bressen back from whatever this was. I'd thought the darkness he spoke of was figurative, emblematic of how he viewed himself, but what surrounded him now was a very real manifestation of that darkness. In his rage at Jerram and Glenora, he'd unleashed it, given it free rein, and I knew instinctively it was now trying to claim him.

I wouldn't let it.

I pressed forward toward Bressen, but I was met with an invisible force that pushed me back. I summoned my strength and moved closer, fighting the force with all my might. I was within a few feet of Bressen when the dark cloud sensed my presence, and tendrils of its smoke slithered toward me.

I screamed as the first one touched my leg. It was so cold it almost burned, and I had to force myself to take another step, even as more tendrils licked at my legs. They felt much like the whip lashes Jerram had doled out, and I flinched as each one coiled around me.

I tried to reach out to Bressen with my mind, thinking I might be able to touch him mentally if not physically, but I was met with a dark wall of resistance there too. I knew Bressen was still in there, though. I'd connected with his consciousness in Jerram's mind, but here the darkness was blocking me out.

I pressed forward another step and pushed through some kind of invisible barrier. The resistance disappeared, and I was suddenly lifted into the air to float toward Bressen. My feet hovered inches off the ground as his own did, and I could feel a pull in my chest, as if some force had reached inside me and was now tugging me toward him. The coldness that spread through my body was like nothing I'd ever felt before. It ripped through me like teeth tearing through flesh, and my mouth opened wide in a scream that was instantly swallowed by the dark smoke swirling around me.

My body continued to drift toward Bressen, but he didn't seem to notice. His red eyes stared out into nothingness as he floated just above the ground, his arms outstretched on either side of him as if he was welcoming me into an embrace. Seconds later my body stopped in front of his, and I felt his power tug at me as something painful tightened in my chest. He was drawing my power, I realized, and my eyes flew open in panic as I felt myself weaken.

"No!" I cried, but the sound was absorbed into the unnatural night.

Fighting the heaviness now overtaking my limbs, I reached my hands up toward Bressen and laid them on either side of his face. Bressen was normally so warm, but he was deathly cold now, and it was an effort not to pull my hands back as the chill bit at my skin.

Our minds connected, but only just barely. The Bressen I knew seemed so far away, as if he was at the end of a long corridor that went for miles and miles, but at least he was there. I reached out down that corridor and sent a light, a beacon, into the darkness.

"Bressen, come back to me," I said. The words on my lips were mere breaths of air, but they sounded loudly and clearly down the corridor between our minds. "Come back."

I felt a pulse, like a heartbeat, answer back, and I redoubled my efforts to send that flare of light toward the end of the corridor.

My eyes fluttered as more of my power drained away, and I struggled to reach out to Bressen. I was so tired, but I had to hold on a little longer. He was coming. He had to be.

Then I saw him. Or I saw what I thought was him. It was just a shape moving in the dark, but I marshalled all my strength and reached out as far as I could. My light was fading, and my vision was growing faint, but I had to hold on. The figure came closer by the second, but I only had seconds left myself before I lost all consciousness, before I could no longer reach out or light the way back. Even now I couldn't tell how far away the figure was, or if it was Bressen at all. I only hoped it was him and not some shadowy monster emerging from the recesses of his mind.

Hurry, I said into Bressen's mind. *I can't hold on much longer.*

My strength waned even further as the images in my own mind started to dissipate. I stretched my hand out farther to the figure moving toward me and tried to call out, but I couldn't make a sound. I could barely see my outstretched hand in front of me, and terror overtook me as the hand suddenly seemed to turn to ash and drift apart, my body starting to scatter to the wind. The figure before me reached out its own hand, but it was too late…too late…

Strong hands folded firmly over mine, and my eyes flew open. My vision cleared as if a fog had lifted, and I looked into the bright turquoise of Bressen's gaze. The tightening in my chest released, and a moment later, my feet touched back down on the ground. I still held Bressen's face, and his own hands lay gently over mine.

Behind Bressen, the dark cloud was breaking up, and the sky was returning to normal. Bressen's feet also touched back down onto the stone landing, and his black wings folded in, disappearing back into his body. He stood barefoot and bare-chested on the terrace, the burn and whip marks on his torso somehow gone.

I looked behind me, but the demon-like creatures were dissolving back into tendrils of smoke that dissipated into the air. There was nothing on the ground where Glenora had been huddled, no trace that she'd ever been there. I thought for sure the creatures had torn her apart, but there was no blood, no shreds of flesh, nothing whatsoever.

I turned back to Bressen. My hands were still on his face, and his own had curled more tightly over mine.

I collapsed against him then, and he caught me as we both sank to our knees. His arms anchored around me as my head fell against his chest. His skin was once again warm under my cheek.

"Don't ever do that again," I whispered.

"Do what?" he asked softly.

"Almost die."

He chuckled and stroked a hand down my hair. Somehow I managed to raise my head, and then his lips were crushed against mine in a kiss that released every ounce of fear and anxiety we'd felt at the thought of losing each other. I threaded my fingers into his hair and gripped it in a way I was sure must have hurt, but he didn't so much as flinch. He just pulled me tighter against him as our mouths ground together, and I relished the feel of his body against me.

"You brought me back," Bressen said, as our mouths parted just enough to draw breath.

"You came back," I said softly.

He smiled. "You're my tether. I'll always come back to you."

He kissed me again and helped me to stand before nodding toward Jerram. "That was evil of you, by the way. I take back what I said about your capacity for darkness."

"He deserved it," I said.

"I'm not talking about what it did to Jerram," he amended. "I'm talking about what it did to *me*. It was evil of you to remind me of that night when I can't tear your clothes off and bury myself inside you."

My face flushed, but Bressen and I were jolted from our carnal thoughts when Samhail landed so hard next to us that the stones of the terrace cracked. He was still in gargoyle form, and I had to crane my head upward to see his face, monstrous and terrifying with its razor-sharp teeth and glowing blue eyes. I looked out over the courtyard, but the crowd of thousands that had been there only minutes before was almost completely dispersed. The people near the back had all fled early, but the bodies of the soldiers who'd been at the front lay everywhere, and those that remained who could still move were retreating as fast as they could.

Without a word, Samhail turned and walked toward Jerram who was still frozen in place next to the frame where Bressen had been strapped. Jerram's eyes followed Samhail as he approached and then widened in fear as Samhail reached out toward him with giant hands.

Samhail put one hand on Jerram's shoulder and grabbed Jerram's head with his other. He paused just long enough for Jerram to realize what he was going to do, then, with a quick twist, he popped Jerram's head off his body and tossed it to the side.

I realized a moment too late what Samhail intended. I shut my eyes so I didn't see Jerram's body fall, but the snap of his spine as it was severed reached me across the terrace, and my stomach lurched. Bressen put a hand on my cheek and turned my face away.

"Are you alright?" he asked me as he scanned my body for injuries. He growled when he saw the whip lash across my stomach, but I just threw myself against his chest again, and he pulled me tightly into his body. The lashes across my back burned where his hands touched them, but I didn't care.

"I was sure I was going to lose you," he breathed into my ear. "Thank the Protector you're alive. I wouldn't have been able to bear it if anything happened to you."

I brought my hands up to grasp his face, and our mouths melded together again as if we could consume one another, body and soul.

When we finally parted, Samhail stood next to us once more.

I watched in fascination as his body shrank into its human form. His wings retracted into his back, and the gray stone-like skin seemed to draw into the markings at his wrists. Fangs, claws, and tail all retreated into nothing, and the eerie blue glow faded from his eyes the way the red did from Bressen's. Samhail was bare-chested, but a pair of black pants materialized on him as he returned to normal.

I arched an eyebrow at him. "Magical clothing?"

Samhail inclined his head toward Bressen by way of explanation. "It's a glamour. I'm going to need some pants soon."

"That's a little dramatic for you, no?" Bressen asked Samhail as he gestured to where Jerram's body lay on the ground, its head tossed several feet away.

"I've been wanting to do that since I met him," Samhail grumbled.

"You got my message," I said to him.

He grinned. "Both of them."

"You left an opening in your mental shields for me?"

His smile softened. "Always."

I started to respond but heard my name called across the terrace, and I turned in Bressen's arms. Jaylan, Brix, and Aramis were running toward us from where they'd been hiding, followed a little ways behind by Phaedrus.

Bressen let me go reluctantly as I slipped out of his arms and ran to meet my brothers. The three of us threw our arms around each other and hugged tightly.

"Thank the Protector you're not hurt," I said as we broke apart.

"Cyra, what in the three hells was all that?" Jaylan asked. "Aramis said you were responsible for freeing us."

I looked at Aramis, who was smiling proudly.

"I got reacquainted with Jaylan and met Brix during the battle," Aramis said.

Phaedrus approached us, and he threw himself down on his knees in front of Bressen.

"My lord, please forgive me," he begged. "I had no choice. I was forced to help them."

"Stand up, Phaedrus," Bressen said, but there was no threat in his voice, and the priest got unsteadily to his feet.

"I know you'd never willingly betray me," Bressen said to him.

Phaedrus flinched at the word "betray" but didn't otherwise move.

"Cyra, Phaedrus helped you by opening the portal for Samhail?" Bressen asked.

"Yes. I was trying to do several things at once, and I'm not sure I would have been able to open the portal as well. Phaedrus agreed to open it without hesitation. His help was invaluable. As was Aramis's," I added. "He told me how to pull the poison from you."

Bressen looked at Phaedrus and Aramis. "Then you both have my eternal gratitude. I owe you for both my life and Cyra's."

Phaedrus bowed low and stepped back.

Aramis just smiled. "I think you and I are even now, Lord Bressen."

"Lord Bressen?" Brix said in surprise. "Wait, he's the Nemesis Incarnate?"

Jaylan couldn't find Brix's foot fast enough to stomp on it.

"Lord Bressen," Jaylan said quickly, bobbing a little bow, "please forgive my brother. He doesn't always think before he speaks. We meant no offense."

"And you must be Cyra's brothers," Bressen said stepping toward them. His tone was serious, but he wore a slight smile.

"Yes, my lord. I'm Jaylan, and this is Brix."

"Then I owe you my thanks as well, both for taking care of Cyra when Aramis left her with you…and for the wonderful wine you make. In that order," Bressen said with a smile.

Jaylan just blinked, and it was a few seconds before he spoke. "You…you're welcome, my lord."

"Cyra, are you…with him?" Brix asked me, inclining his head toward Bressen.

"Brix!" Jaylan hissed under his breath. "Stop talking."

I looked at Bressen. So much had happened in the last two days that I had no idea how to answer Brix. Bressen saved me from having to respond as he slipped an arm possessively around my waist.

"Yes, she's with me," Bressen said to Brix. He paused before adding, "That is, as long as she still wants to be."

I let out the breath I'd been holding and leaned back against Bressen, ignoring the pain in my back. His other arm wrapped around my shoulders, and I melted into him.

Yes, I said into his mind. *She still very much wants to be.*

Chapter 44

The rest of the day was a blur of activity as Bressen moved quickly to head off further chaos. He was now the only remaining Triumvirate lord left with three territories to manage, two of which had just tried to mount an insurrection.

The first thing Bressen did, after having Aramis heal my wounds, was enlist me and Phaedrus to open several portals so he could move people he trusted into Derridan and Polaris. After sending Samhail back briefly to the Citadel for some clothing – he hadn't been kidding about the pants – Phaedrus opened a portal into Seatherny so Samhail could assess the situation in Derridan. Meanwhile, I opened a portal to Solandis so that Bressen could bring his own advisors and soldiers into Gendris to take control of the city until he could determine the best way to proceed. Ursan and Glenora didn't have any children, so there was no succession in place.

Jaylan and Brix would come back to Callanus for at least one night while we sorted everything out. I hadn't seen them in so long, and I wasn't ready to let them go back to the outer lands just yet, especially since Phaedrus had taken such a risk to get them here. I opened a portal to the Citadel and brought them through to get them settled before taking another portal back to Gendris. Jaylan had been speechless at how my powers had grown since he'd seen me last, but Brix – never at a loss for words – peppered me with questions the entire time we were together until I finally told him that further answers would have to wait until later so I could get back to help Bressen.

Aramis had declined a portal back to either Solandis or the Citadel and insisted instead on being put to use in Gendris. He helped me search Ursan and Glenora's palace for any lingering threats, but we found none. On the contrary, when we searched the dungeons, we found several of Ursan's advisors and generals who'd been imprisoned there when they refused to support Glenora's rebellion. After reading their minds to be sure of their allegiance, Bressen assigned the advisors and generals to work with his own people to hash out a temporary plan for governing Polaris.

Aramis was then reassigned to work with Gendris's own healers to begin attending to the wounded guards and soldiers. Bressen hadn't killed any of the soldiers who'd fallen, just rendered them unconscious. They were revived and detained by Bressen's own forces to be dealt with later.

The soldiers who'd engaged Samhail weren't as lucky. Broken bones, torn limbs, and plenty of other gruesome injuries abounded. At least a hundred were either already dead or beyond Aramis's healing abilities, so the work of letting Polaris's people claim and bury their dead also began.

It was late in the evening when Aramis and I finally took a portal back to the Citadel. I showed him to another guest room, and then we found Jaylan and Brix and went down to dinner. None of us had eaten all day, and we dug into our meals with abandon. Even Brix was overwhelmed by the array of seemingly unlimited and exceptionally delicious food, and Jaylan had to help him back to their rooms when Brix stuffed himself to the point of bursting. Nearly dying today hadn't dulled my brother's appetite one bit.

Samhail entered the dining room as we were leaving, and I sent my brothers and Aramis on without me so I could speak to him. My brothers regarded Samhail with awe and skirted around him, even more wary of him now than they'd been upon meeting him in Fernweh.

Samhail and I took a moment to look each other over as if checking for injuries that we hadn't seen earlier in the day. In addition to the whip welts, Aramis had also healed frost burns on my legs where Bressen's dark smoke had curled around them.

I broke the silence between us first. "You look unharmed," I said running my fingers down his arm. I took his large hand in mine to turn it back and forth as if examining it. "No chips or cracks."

490

Samhail grinned. "None but the one still in the training yard wall," he said, and I blushed.

"Now I know why you have so few scars," I observed.

Samhail nodded. "It's hard to hurt me when I transform. Are you alright? You looked a little queasy when I popped Jerram's head off."

His words brought back the sound Jerram's spine made when his head was severed, and I closed my eyes for a second. Jerram deserved his death, but that sound would haunt my dreams for some time.

I opened my eyes. "I'll be fine." I gestured to his lower body. "I see you found a real pair of pants."

Samhail tsked and grinned at me. "Always so concerned with my pants. You're going to make Bressen jealous."

I sobered at the mention of Bressen. There was a time I'd imagined being with Samhail, and the night of the Harmilan hadn't necessarily quelled my persistent attraction to him. I'd known for a while that Bressen was the man I loved, though. Bressen had completely redefined my understanding of not only physical attraction, but of love and the depths to which I was capable of feeling it. I couldn't live without him now any more than I could live without air, food, or water.

Samhail sensed the direction of my thoughts.

"I'm happy for you and Bressen," he assured me sincerely. "I'll admit I'm a little jealous he gets to have you whenever he wants, but it seems only fair since he can give you something I can't."

I looked at him questioningly.

"Gargoyles don't really fall in love," he answered, "but Bressen is deeply in love with you, and I won't come between that." He shook his head. "I've never seen him like this. You...bewitched him."

Samhail winked at me, and I smiled back, knowing we were both remembering Eddin's accusations that I was a witch.

I knew Bressen loved me, and if even Samhail recognized that love, contrary to his nature as he suggested it was, it must be strong indeed.

"Gargoyles also don't learn to care for others very easily," Samhail continued a bit hesitantly, "but I'll admit I've come to care for you greatly, Cyra. I count you as one of the few people for whom I'd lay down my life without hesitation."

I blinked in surprise at his admission. I had no idea what I'd done to deserve that kind of devotion from him, but I vowed never to take it for granted. It couldn't have been easy for him to admit, and tears welled in my eyes.

Samhail stepped forward and pulled me into the closest thing resembling a real hug I'd ever gotten from him.

"You're getting better at this," I sniffled into his chest as tears ran freely down my cheeks.

He chuckled. "I've been practicing."

I laughed and pulled back from him. "I hope you'll always keep that sliver in your mental shield open for me."

"Of course. I never know when I might get an invitation I can't refuse."

"Maybe next Harmilan. I hear three is a divine number."

He chuckled again. "I'll await my invitation. In the meantime, keep Bressen out of trouble while I'm gone. It finds him all too often."

"Gone?" I said, my face falling. "You're leaving?"

"Not immediately, but Bressen needs help getting the territories in line. He asked me to stay in Derridan for a while as a deterrent to any further uprisings. I told him I'd go."

I nodded, but there was a lump in my throat now. Samhail had been with me from the beginning of all this, and I already felt the gargoyle-sized hole in my life at the thought of not having him around.

I stood up on my tiptoes to kiss him on the cheek. He still had to bend down for me to reach it.

"You better get something to eat," I told him.

He nodded, and I turned to go find my brothers and father.

"Get your rest tonight," Samhail called after me. "I don't want you using the insurrection as an excuse to miss training tomorrow."

"I wouldn't dream of it!" I called back over my shoulder, and Samhail's laugh followed me down the hall.

Jaylan, Brix, Aramis, and I stayed up late into the night talking. I had so much to tell my brothers, and they were eager to hear about my time in Callanus. I glossed over a few parts here and there, but otherwise I told them everything. Jaylan and Brix were particularly interested to hear about my training with Samhail, and even more fascinated to hear how I'd sent him flying across the training yard into the wall, although I left out the details of how he'd goaded me into it.

In return, Jaylan and Brix brought me up to speed on the vineyard and how our newest vintage was coming along. It was shaping up to be a great one, thanks to the help Ursan had sent, and I felt a pang of sadness as I thought of the late lord. My dealings with Ursan had been complicated, and my feelings toward him were equally so, but he'd ultimately been a decent if highly imperfect man.

It was after midnight when we all finally retired to our own rooms. Bressen hadn't returned to the Citadel yet, so I climbed into my bed and tried to fall asleep. I almost sent him a mental message to be sure he was okay, but he was extremely busy right now, and I didn't want to bother him. Nevertheless, lingering concern for Bressen kept me awake for more than an hour after I'd put out the lights. I didn't know how long I'd been asleep when I finally felt the bed dip as Bressen climbed in behind me.

"You're back," I said, instant relief sweeping over me. "Is everything alright?"

"It is now," he whispered as he pressed his body up against mine and snaked an arm around my waist to pull me closer. "Go back to sleep. We'll talk tomorrow."

His breathing became steady a couple minutes later, and I fell back into a much sounder sleep than before.

When I awoke the next morning, I was still in the same position with Bressen pressed up against me. It was a testament to our exhaustion that neither of us had moved in the night. I wondered if he was still asleep, but I got my answer seconds later as his thumb brushed against my breast. I moaned softly, and he nuzzled into my hair.

"How is everything in Gendris?" I asked as my nipples perked to attention under the thin fabric of my nightgown.

He sighed. "As well as expected given everything that happened yesterday. Things are still precarious, but we have control of all three territories for now."

"We? You're the only Triumvirate lord left. All of Thasia is yours."

Bressen sighed again. "For now. Working with Ursan and Jerram wasn't always easy, but it was less complicated than keeping three separate territories in line. I never had any ambition to rule the whole country by myself."

I nodded against the pillow. "Can I ask you something?"

"Of course," he said as he ran his hand down my thigh.

"Not *that*," I said softly, laying my hand on his to stop it from running any further. I paused. "What happened to Glenora? Those creatures…what did they do to her?"

Bressen turned me over so I was on my back and our eyes met.

"The creatures are nightmare demoni," he said. "As a group, they're called a wrath, and they help me guard Revenmyer. That's where Glenora was taken."

I took a moment to digest that. I wanted to ask Bressen more about the demoni, but his other news grabbed me first.

"Glenora's not dead then?" I asked. I wasn't sure if I was relieved or disappointed by that. Despite all she'd done, I still had a difficult time wishing her dead.

"No, just imprisoned," Bressen said. "Glenora's crimes are serious, and she needs to be held accountable for them, but…there's a complication."

"A complication?"

"Glenora is pregnant. We're not yet sure if it's Ursan's or Jerram's."

I gasped and sat up. "Pregnant? And she's in Revenmyer?"

494

Bressen propped his head on his hand. "There's nowhere else to put her given what she's done. I'll do what I can to ensure the child survives her imprisonment, but Glenora is also older than most women who normally bear children. That will make things even more difficult."

I was looking at Bressen without really seeing him. My mind was too preoccupied with this new information and my conflicting feelings about Glenora.

"Cyra," Bressen said, drawing my focus back to him. "She would have killed you and your whole family for her ambition."

"She would have killed *you*," I said, my voice breaking a little.

"But you saved me." He sat up and ran a hand down my arm. "You learned about your powers only a little while ago, and yesterday you used them to save us all. I owe you my life."

Bressen leaned in and kissed me, but I was still preoccupied, and he pulled back a moment later. "What is it?" he asked.

"So it's really over?" I asked. It had just occurred to me that Jemma's vision, the reason I was here, had come to pass.

"Yes."

"But what does that mean for-"

"For what?" he prompted.

"For…us. I suppose I need to go back to Fernweh now."

Bressen's face went serious. He didn't answer but swung his legs out of bed and walked to where he'd thrown his clothes onto a chair last night. He was naked, and I bit my lip at the sight of his perfect ass as I watched him pad across the floor and pull something out of his jacket pocket. I forced myself to look up at his face when he turned around and got back into bed.

Bressen held up something in his hand, and I looked down to see a ring set with a large tear-drop emerald between his fingers. The stone had a slight bluish tint to it, making it almost more teal than green, and it sparkled in the morning sun coming through the windows.

My eyes flew back up to Bressen's.

"The ring is a family heirloom, my great grandmother's," he said. "I took it out of my vault while I was in Solandis yesterday."

"Are you…?" I started to ask, but I couldn't finish the sentence.

"I want you to stay with me…to marry me."

I gasped.

"I know I'm asking you to give up your family and your vineyard, so I'll understand if you refuse, but if you accept, I can offer two things," he went on.

I just looked at him.

"I promise you'll be my partner in everything. I don't know what will happen with the rest of Thasia just yet, but you'll rule Hiraeth with me as my equal."

I just gaped at him. I had no words.

"The second thing I can offer you is a replacement vineyard," he went on.

I furrowed my brows. "What?"

"There's a vineyard near my estate in Solandis. The man who owns it, a mortal, is getting older and wants to retire. He has no children to give it to, so I could buy the vineyard for you."

"You'd buy me a vineyard?" I asked incredulously.

"I'd expect to have first choice of anything you produce, but yes." He winked at me.

"So let me get this straight," I said, looking him squarely in the eyes. "You want me to help you rule your territory, and possibly the country, while also running a vineyard?"

He winced a little to hear it put that way but shrugged. "I was told you like to be busy." His mouth quirked into a hopeful smile.

"I did say that, didn't I."

"You did."

"Very well, then I accept your proposal."

He blinked at me. "You do?"

I smiled widely. "Yes, I do."

Bressen tackled me back down onto the bed and rolled on top of me as his mouth came down on mine in an ardent kiss. I could barely feel my limbs from the joy coursing through me as Bressen slipped the ring on my finger and his mouth claimed mine again. Heat flooded my body as he cupped my breast, and desire hammered in my ears so loudly that I didn't even hear the bedroom door open.

I heard Raina's shriek, though. She'd stopped dead in the middle of the room as she looked at Bressen, still naked, lying on top of me.

"My lady," Raina stammered, "I mean, my lord. My apologies, I didn't realize..." She set her tray down and started to back away while looking anywhere but at the bed.

Bressen propped his head back up on an arm as he looked at Raina.

"Raina, is it?" Bressen asked in the voice he used when he wanted to charm someone.

"Yes, my lord," Raina said, still trying desperately not to look at us.

"Your lady and I are going to need another hour or so alone."

"Yes, my lord," Raina said and turned quickly toward the door.

"After that," Bressen said, halting her retreat, "please dress Lady Cyra in her finest gown. I need to address the people of Callanus, and that's also a good time to introduce them to my bride-to-be."

Raina gasped, and both my head and hers snapped to Bressen. He looked at me with an innocent expression.

I thought you wanted to make our relationship public, he said into my mind.

I narrowed my eyes at him, but a smile tugged at my lips as I answered back. *It's one extreme or the other with you, isn't it.*

Raina was inching toward the door again.

"One more thing," Bressen said, and Raina froze once more. "Please move all of Lady Cyra's things into my room. She'll be staying there from now on when we're in Callanus."

"Yes, my lord." She paused. "Is...that all, my lord?"

"Yes, thank you," Bressen said.

Raina turned and practically ran for the door, but she met my eyes as she closed it behind her. Her expression told me I had a lot of explaining to do.

"Now where were we?" Bressen asked.

"I believe you were about to thank me for saving your life and accepting your proposal."

He smiled wickedly. "Indeed," he said as his head disappeared below the covers.

❦

Two hours later, I stood with Bressen, Samhail, Aramis, Jaylan, and Brix just inside an upper balcony that overlooked the main square. Bressen would address the people of Callanus there shortly.

Instead of choosing one of the new gowns made for me when I came to the Citadel, I'd had Raina pull out the emerald green off-the-shoulder gown I'd brought with me from Fernweh. It was a simple but elegant dress, and wearing it today felt right. Raina had also attempted to recreate the whole look she'd put together for me that first night when I'd had dinner with the three lords and Glenora.

The marks of the bear's claws still showed faintly on my shoulder and collarbone and would probably always be just visible there, but I no longer worried about people seeing them. They were a reminder of how far I'd come. They were also a reminder that, had it not been for Ursan's bear, I never would've met Bressen, Samhail, and Raina. I still didn't know exactly how the bear found its way to our vineyard that morning, but I was now eternally grateful it had.

The one difference in my ensemble today was the addition of Bressen's ring, which Samhail had noticed as soon as I entered the waiting room off the balcony before Bressen arrived. To my utter shock, Samhail came over and knelt down on one knee in front of me in a deep bow. I immediately grabbed his arm to pull him back up.

"Don't ever do that again," I hissed at him under my breath.

He just smiled. "Yes, my lady."

I would have chastised him further, but Jaylan, Brix, and Aramis had come over by that time and noticed the ring, and then there was hugging and congratulations and celebration. Bressen had entered a moment later, and the handshakes and congratulations started anew.

Bressen smiled approvingly at me when he saw the dress I'd chosen. The shirt he wore with his usual black jacket and pants was the same shade of emerald as my dress.

"Something told me to wear this shirt today," Bressen chuckled as he leaned down to kiss me.

A minute later, his herald went out onto the balcony to get the crowd's attention, and Bressen prepared to make his entrance. He would address the crowd alone first and explain what happened yesterday, then give an overview of how he intended to move forward. While he would rule the country alone in the short term, he had every intention of replacing Ursan and Jerram and restoring the Triumvirate. After that, Bressen would introduce me and announce our engagement in the hope of ending the address on a positive note.

The herald announced Bressen, and he kissed me before heading onto the balcony.

"Don't forget your halo glamour," I told him jokingly. I actually couldn't remember the last time I'd seen him wear that dark, undulating aura.

"I was thinking I might break out a different accessory for a change," he said with a wink as he stepped onto the balcony.

As soon as he cleared the doorway, his wings sprang open from his back, and I gasped. Far from the raven-black wings I knew, those that unfurled now were bright white, so pure and perfect they almost glowed in the morning sunlight. The effect was stunning against his night-black hair and clothes, and all the more impressive given the absolute beauty of the wings themselves.

"Did you know he could do that?" Brix asked in awe next to me. I just shook my head.

Samhail appeared quietly at my other side.

"Did you know he could do that?" I whispered to him.

Samhail shook his head. "That's a first for me."

I looked at Samhail. "I've been meaning to thank you. I wouldn't have made it through my time here in Callanus without your support and advice. The training came in handy as well."

"Oh?" Samhail said.

"Jerram tried to hit me, but I ducked and elbowed him in the ribs."

Samhail grunted in appreciation. "Good for you."

I shrugged. "I was going to rip his head off, but I wanted to save something for you."

Samhail clamped a hand over his mouth to hold in his bark of laughter, and he stepped away to compose himself.

I turned back to listen to Bressen's speech for a few more minutes. He began talking about the importance of unity and how it was needed more now than ever in light of yesterday's attempted coup.

"And in that spirit of unity," Bressen said to the crowd, "I hope my final news to you will offer some hope for the future of Thasia as we begin to heal together as a people."

It was time. I smoothed my dress and squared my shoulders.

"Many of you know Cyra of Fernweh came to Callanus several weeks ago at the request of the Triumvirate after a warning of imminent danger from the Priory," he said. "Some feared she might be the cause of that danger. In fact, she proved yesterday to be our savior from it."

I arched my brows.

"Cyra of Fernweh not only saved this city and our country," Bressen continued, "but she saved me as well, both body…and soul."

My mouth dropped open.

"It's with the greatest pride and joy I present to you Cyra of Fernweh, my future wife and the new Lady of Hiraeth," he finished.

A deafening cheer went up from the crowd, and tears welled in my eyes. Bressen turned toward the balcony doors and waited for me to join him. I wanted to run to him and wrap him in my arms, but my legs had gone weak, and I was having trouble getting my feet to move.

My life as a winemaker in Fernweh had been a good one. I'd loved working with my brothers, but I knew now I'd always wanted more.

The vineyard ultimately belonged to Jaylan as the oldest, and it was only a matter of time before my role there would end. Had I stayed in Fernweh, my life as a winemaker likely wouldn't have continued. Bressen had offered me the opportunity to manage my own vineyard, but more than that, he'd offered me a place at his side as his partner, his lover, and his wife. Glenora resented Ursan because he didn't value her abilities or her input, but I knew that Bressen would never take mine for granted. I'd seen that in his mind when he'd asked me to marry him. He'd shown it to me willingly, proudly.

I smiled as I looked at the man who'd given me so much and promised me even more, the man who'd just told an entire city that I'd saved not only his life, but his soul.

I walked forward out of the shadows then, toward Bressen, toward my future, and into the light.

Epilogue

The man growled low in his throat as he spilled himself into the whore beneath him with one last brutal thrust. The girl issued a soft cry, not from pleasure, but from relief that he was finally done with her. He liked his sex rough, and this body was especially good for that. It was about the only thing the body was good for.

Well, that and fighting. Fucking and fighting, which wasn't bad in the short term. It was the long-term use of the body that was a problem. It was mortal, and he could feel it dying all around him every day that he bothered to drag it out of bed in the morning.

The man withdrew from the girl and lifted himself off the bed to find his clothes. The girl, no older than her late teens, rolled onto her side and curled into herself.

Twenty-five years ago when he'd first acquired this body, he'd still looked about the age that a girl like this might have been interested in him. Now he looked old enough to be her father. Not that he wanted her for anything but a quick fuck. He'd never wanted any woman for more, and he'd used this body plenty of times to satisfy his urges.

Once the body had healed, that is. The healing had taken time, though. A long, long time. The body had been just barely alive when he'd entered it, bleeding from multiple slashes across its chest and arms and a stab wound in its side. One leg was broken along with at least three ribs, and its helmet was crushed in a little so that its skull was pressed tightly between the metal.

The pain had been excruciating when he'd entered the body, like nothing he'd ever felt before. He'd entered it to escape death, but once inside, he almost wished death had taken him instead.

Those had been his only options at the time, this form or death. In a sea of mangled and broken bodies, it was the closest one in which he'd sensed a faint consciousness, and he'd thrown himself toward it out of sheer self-preservation. There hadn't been any time to think, to search, to find something better. He hadn't had time to move, let alone make a conscious decision when that spear had come hurtling toward him, straight for his head. The realization he was going to die was secondary to the idea that he needed to get away, to abandon ship, so to speak. Thus his mind had leapt, immediately and unthinkingly, into the first consciousness it found.

He'd taken this body over certain death, but he'd regretted it instantly as he was inundated with the agony of every slash and stab and broken bone. He'd gone from whole and alive one second, to shattered and nearly dead the next, and the memory still woke him in a cold sweat on some nights.

His biggest mistake had been turning his head while he waited, unable to stop himself from looking. He'd wanted to see, *needed* to see, one last time. And by the gods, he'd seen.

He'd seen his old body lying on the ground with the wooden shaft of the spear sticking out of the middle of his face, the spear's tip dripping crimson blood from the back of his skull. He'd tried to turn this head back again, unable to bear the image of his own dead body crumpled in a heap, but pain had taken over, and he hadn't been able to move again. He could only close the body's eyes and pretend his own corpse wasn't lying there among the others being picked at by crows.

He didn't know how long he'd lain there praying to the Nemesis to take him before someone finally found him. It was only a small mercy when they'd loaded him onto a wagon with the few others who were still alive. He didn't even know which side this soldier had fought for until he saw the Thasian flags flying in the camp they brought him to. His enemy's camp.

His recovery was long and painful, but it was the realization that his consciousness had fled into a mortal body that was the most difficult to handle. He'd killed the other consciousness he found here with his last bit of strength and claimed the body for his own, but this was as far as he could go. This body wasn't perimortal. It had no capacity for magic, and thus *he* had no magic. He had no way out and no power to jump minds again.

It was telling that, even after twenty-five years, the man still didn't think of this body as his. As far as he was concerned, he was only renting it. He fed it, clothed it, and sheltered it only because it was in his best interests to keep it healthy and alive, but it was never his body, and it never would be. He spent years searching for some way to get back into a perimortal body, but so far, he'd found nothing.

The man looked down at the girl on the bed as he buckled his belt. Welts already formed on her skin from that same belt, and her breasts would bear the marks of his teeth for a couple days.

In his old body he'd been able to hold the minds of the women he fucked so they'd serve his will. He couldn't do that now, but the tradeoff was that this body was strong enough to make women do anything he wanted. Not that he'd had to make this one do anything. This girl was bought and paid for, his to do with as he pleased.

The man pulled on his shirt then grabbed his coat and left the room. Out in the main lounge of the brothel, scantily clad women lounged on chairs and couches, waiting for customers. The madam watched him go as he strode through, and he knew she'd head straight for the room he'd just left as soon as he was out the door. She'd been able to hear the whore's cries from outside – everyone likely had – but no one had dared to come see what was going on.

Pain was a fascination of his. This body had already been covered in scars from various brawls and battles when he first entered it, and he'd added to the number since then. He liked to cut the body, marring it with slashes whenever he could stand it, as if he was punishing it for being weak and mortal. He was careful to clean the wounds afterward to avoid infection, but it gave him a strange pleasure to cut its flesh, even though he felt the white-hot pain of every slice.

Years ago when he'd felt the body start to age around him, he began to take his frustrations out on young women instead. He'd select a girl he liked and take her to an abandoned building or some other out-of-the-way place close to where he lived. Sometimes he took whores, but just as often he seized a barmaid or seamstress who lived and worked in the area. He kept the girl for days, fucking her, beating her, and cutting her flesh before finally strangling her to death when there was barely anything left of her. He punished these girls for his own body's traitorousness.

He'd killed close to twenty women before he realized someone was hunting him. He'd moved around to avoid leaving too many missing women in one place, but at some point, someone had noticed what was going on and begun tracking him. Luckily, the person hadn't known who they were looking for, so he'd offered up a sacrifice.

One night, he'd left a trail that led to another man. That man was found days later, disemboweled with his cock cut off and shoved down his own throat. After that close call, he'd gone back to merely whoring and cutting himself, letting his would-be assassin think they'd taken care of him.

The cold night air licked at the man's skin as he headed toward home. He still had to go to work tomorrow so he could afford to feed and clothe this worthless hunk of flesh.

He felt the presence before he saw the figure following him about thirty feet back. This body wasn't usually good at sensing when things were off, but it did now, and the hair on its arms stood on end.

He walked a little farther, not altering his pace, and he turned down a side street to see if the figure tailing him would follow. It did, and he continued down the side street until a narrow alley opened up to his right. He turned down it, drew the knife from the sheath at his waist, and pressed himself against the wall in the shadow of some crates stacked near the corner.

He wasn't afraid as he waited. This body was strong enough to handle most mundane threats. Perhaps the brothel had sent someone to collect more money for what he'd done to the whore. If so, the person would regret it if they tried to make trouble for him.

Footsteps approached, and the figure's shadow stretched out down the alley. The person paused at the entrance, cautious now that its quarry was no longer in sight. Boots crunched against stone as it moved forward.

The man struck as soon as he saw the tip of the figure's hood appear at the edge of the crates. He lunged out and grabbed the figure, pushing it across the alley and pinning it up against the far wall with his knife at its throat.

"Who the fuck are you, and why are you following me?"

Lightning flashed in the alley, and the man jolted back as a shock of electricity zapped through his body. He leapt back away from the figure he'd pinned against the wall as he tried to clear his head and calm his vibrating nerves. He still held the knife out in front of him, ready to strike if necessary, but he was unsteady on his feet.

"I have to say," the hooded figure said as it stepped away from the wall, "I thought you'd be happier to see your old friend."

The man froze. He knew that voice.

"Sandrian?" he asked incredulously.

The figure pulled back his hood to reveal a gaunt-looking face that appeared to be in its mid-thirties with dirty blond hair and pale skin. In another lifetime, the hooded man might have been considered handsome, but there was a hollowness to his features and a flat look in his eyes that suggested he'd seen a thousand horrors. He was thinner now, his features sharper, but Morland still recognized Sandrian, the former king of Rowe.

"How?" Morland breathed.

"I might ask you the same thing," Sandrian said, smiling wryly. "You look a bit different than the last time I saw you."

"So do you," Morland grumbled, although there was clearly no comparison. Sandrian still looked like himself, albeit a much thinner, wearier version.

"Twenty-five years in Revenmyer aren't usually kind to a person," Sandrian said, bitterness tinging his normally melodious voice.

"How did you get out? Release or escape?"

"Escape, with a little bit of help. There'll be time to tell you the whole tale later when we have some wine to wash it down with."

"How did you find me? How did you even know I was alive?"

"That too is a story that deserves to be told somewhere besides a back alley. We should find a quiet place to talk. We have much to plan."

"Plan?" Morland said. "What do we need to plan?"

"Have you not heard the news from Thasia?"

Morland frowned. He'd overheard two men mention Thasia a few nights ago at a tavern, but he immediately blocked out their conversation as he always did when he heard the name of that accursed place, the place that had doomed him to a pitifully short life in this wretched body.

"Thasia is in chaos right now," Sandrian explained, seeing Morland's confusion. "The lords Ursan and Jerram are dead. Only Bressen of Hiraeth remains of the Triumvirate."

Morland hissed at the third name. "He killed the other two lords?"

Sandrian shook his head. "Much of the information from Thasia is only rumor and the other half is pure nonsense, but I've secured a few reliable sources. Ursan's wife and Lord Jerram killed Ursan and attempted a coup. Bressen himself was taken prisoner and almost killed, but he managed to escape and regain control."

Morland growled. "So we were almost rid of the arrogant prick? How did he escape?"

Sandrian's lips curled into a smile. "That's the most interesting part. Word around the ports says he was saved by a woman, but not just any woman. A syphon."

Morland's eyes went wide. "Impossible."

"I'm still sorting the truth from rumor, but the story of the syphon is persistent. Whoever the woman is, Bressen announced his engagement to her the day after the failed coup."

Morland snorted. "Of course he did. Anything to make himself more powerful."

"Samhail was also in residence at the Citadel until just recently. My sources say Bressen has since dispatched him to Derridan to keep order."

Morland's face darkened. "Whatever plans we make, they better include the slow, excruciating death of that fucking gargoyle."

"Oh, they do, my friend, but before that, we need to get you back into a perimortal body."

Morland let out a mirthless laugh. "Don't you think I've tried? I spent twenty-five years looking for a way. Do you have any idea what it's like to feel this carcass withering around me?"

"I assure you," Sandrian said coldly, "I know what it's like to be trapped in hell for the last twenty-five years."

Morland nodded apologetically. "Of course. I'm sorry, my king."

"I'm hardly a king right now," Sandrian said in disgust. "Bressen and Samhail saw to that, but now is the time to strike while Thasia is putting itself back together, and the first step is getting you out of that...carcass, as you call it."

"How? I told you, I spent the last quarter century trying to find a way to do it. I've scoured every library I could get into on the continent looking for some spell, potion, or magical object to use. There's nothing."

"No, there's likely no one spell, potion, or object that would do the trick, but what if you had a combination of those things as well as a syphon to help bind them?"

Morland went very still. He never would've thought of that, mainly because the lack of a syphon made the effort moot, but if this syphon really did exist, there might be a chance. Whatever individual powers the woman had were incidental compared to who she was as a whole. Syphons were a nexus of power unto themselves. It gravitated toward them. If they could harness that power and put Morland himself at the center of it, this could almost work.

"Are you ready to get out of this alley and go raise a glass to our reunion?" Sandrian asked him.

"To our reunion, to my return to a perimortal body, and to the forthcoming destruction of Bressen and Samhail. We may need more than one drink to celebrate all that. I thought my night was over, but it looks like it's just getting started."

"*We're* just getting started," Sandrian corrected him. "Soon we'll have our revenge, my friend."

Morland smiled and followed his king out of the alley. Twenty-five years ago, he'd entered this body to keep from dying. Now, for the first time since then, he actually felt alive.

Acknowledgments

I'd like to acknowledge and profusely thank the following people:

Joshua Hamel for allowing me the use of Sammhael (aka Samhail). He may not be who you envisioned Friday nights at Eckerd, but he's one of my favorite characters, and you're one of my favorite people.

Karen Pasquale (aka KP1) for volunteering to read the book when I first asked for readers. Who knew that we'd have so much fun sitting at the winery for hours workshopping this series. I can't even begin to express how invaluable your feedback and ideas have been throughout this process. I look forward to our next "Aha!" moment over a bottle of Sauvignon Blanc. (Thanks to Gouveia for supplying the wine.)

Mindy Petruck, Liza Boritz, Karen Milanese, Jennifer McDermott, and Emily Rice. Thanks so much for your honesty and feedback on various drafts. You each helped make this book better.

Janice Eidus, my editor, for boosting my confidence with encouraging comments and very helpful feedback. Thanks for letting me use your CUPPA workshops to develop my characters and scenes.

My husband Pat McDermott, who wasn't eager to be pulled away from online gaming to read a romantasy, but who did it anyway. Thank you for letting me 'cheat' on you with Bressen and Samhail. You'll forgive me when my "Penthouse forum with dragons" helps pad our retirement. (There are no actual dragons in the book, to Pat's dismay.)

Mick Estabrook, for designing my cover art. Thanks for your patience every time I said, "But what if you try…" And Erin Estabrook, for reading the book and giving Mick ideas for designs.

My Facebook friends, who let me crowdsource ideas from them.

Christy Meisler, for her valuable information about libraries.

And finally, the state of Florida, whose extensive list of banned books prompted me to pick up *A Court of Mist and Fury* and discover the genre I was meant to write. (Thank you to Sarah J. Maas for writing the book that changed my life!) PS - Can someone in Florida make sure that this book gets onto one of those banned books lists? Thanks!